The Third Generation Series

Book 3

Wanda: Risking Life to Live

By

MARGARET GREGORY

TAT Publishing

Also by Margaret Gregory

TYMOREAN TRUST SERIES:

Book 1 - Power Rising
Book 2 - Great Ones
Book 3 - The Return to Earth
Book 4 – Earth Mission
Book 5 – Alien Contact
Book 6 - Invasion

ATAPI SORCERESS SERIES:

Prequel – Korvu: The Beginning
Book 1- The Wild One
Book 2 – Atapi Sorceress

THE THIRD GENERATION SERIES:

Wanda – Early Days (anthology)

Cover designed by msgdragon
Cover image: © Can Stock Photo Inc. / CBoswell
Cover image: © Can Stock Photo Inc. /Meinzahn

For permission requests, address the request to the author c/o
Permissions,
C/o TAT Publishing
PO Box 150
Glen Waverley, Victoria, 3150

www.tatpublishing.com

Chapter 1

The two completely black clad figures slid into the Scars Salon through the slightly opened rear door, then closed and locked the door behind them. They stopped just inside the door and the taller stockier figure went to a metal cabinet where an array of red, green and orange LEDs glowed. Within minutes, he had opened the cover and clamped bypasses to specific terminals. He gave his a companion a slight shove. The shorter, slender figure, wearing a backpack, ran lightly up the stairs to the office of the manager, seeming to have no trouble seeing in the dim security lighting.

The taller figure entered the ground floor showroom and wandered around the display cases, forcing open the ones with the most expensive displays of jewellery and sweeping the contents into soft fabric bags. These disappeared into pockets of his outfit - ones designed for the purpose. When all his special pockets were full, he followed his companion upstairs.

The smaller figure now knelt in front of an opened safe. She was carefully emptying the contents into the vinyl backpack. If she saw or heard his approach, she made no sign. Even when he lightly touched her shoulder, she didn't jump. She glanced at him quickly and saw him tap his watch. She nodded, finished emptying the safe, re-closed it and followed her companion.

They both trotted soundlessly downstairs to the rear entrance. The tall man uncovered the luminous face of his watch and went to the alarm system cabinet to remove his work. Once the by passes were off, they would have ten seconds to leave the building or the alarms would sound. He reached in to begin, but the woman grabbed his arm. She was staring at the door, not at the man.

The man dropped his arm and in the faint light coming from a dim security light, saw his companion glance at him and mime smoking a cigarette. He glanced at his watch again.

Two minutes later, although it seemed like twenty minutes, the smoker outside moved on. The smaller figure inside nodded, allowing her companion to reset the alarm system he'd disabled fifteen minutes earlier and unlock the door.

Once outside, they paused in the doorway, smelling the trace of cigarette smoke as they looked around for watchers. Then they ran quietly, keeping to the deepest shadows, until they reached the street where their car was parked. By then, they had removed the black mask hoods they had adopted in the store. No one paid any attention to the dark green ford as they drove off.

The woman, now crouched in the back seat, was pulling off the black clothes and putting on the spare clothing she had ready. The shimmering disco dress would confuse anyone who stopped them. It was so very inappropriate attire for a sneak thief.

After four years of practice, the rapid change was mere routine. Only when she finished did the woman realise that they were not headed back to her small apartment. Instead, they were on the freeway, headed for Beverly Hills. She gave the change of route some thought as she wrapped her tool kit in the black jumpsuit and pushed the bundle under the back seat.

Harry, as she had long since christened her companion, did not encourage questions. She still did not know his real name, but she had stopped wondering about it. He only knew her as Wanda Dean, and that was not her real name either.

He answered to Harry, on the odd occasions when talking was safer than silence. Besides, he was a wizard with alarm systems, something she knew nothing about. Her job was opening safes and the two of them now worked seamlessly together. Only twice in their partnership had unexpected guards surprised them; each time, Harry had dealt silently and efficiently with them.

A sudden thought brought a smile to the woman's face. Beverly Hills. Maybe Harry was taking her to the Boss's place.

Wanda knew her boss only as Harrison – he was a middle-aged man, still in rigorous good health and fitness, who dressed expensively. Once or twice, she had seen him in pictures of parties at homes in Beverly Hills, always in the background and never identified by name.

Ever since he had convinced her of the advantages of working for him, she had been trying to impress him. Now, her technique was to be efficient in her work and minimise her femininity. She had seen Harrison with a succession of seductive types; none had ever stayed with him for long.

He was a widower. She had deduced that when he had first approached her, but that was all that mattered about his personal life. She intended to impress him enough for him to move her out of her small apartment – and then – who knew. It was irrelevant that he already had two sons that were older than her.

"Have you got your belt on?" Harry asked unexpectedly.

She had, this time.

Wanda sat up straighter and looked around. A police car, with lights flashing, cut in front of them and slowed. Harry pulled the car to a stop behind them. He had donned a cap and was reaching unobtrusively for the gun he had in the pocket beside him.

The police officer approached and spoke to Harry through the driver's window. Wanda slid into a graceless sprawl and pretended to be asleep. She made no sign of being aware that a second officer had a torch shining on her.

This possibility was the reason for her quick change act, and twice before, it had deflected interest in them.

"What is the trouble, Officer?" Harry asked politely. He was relaxed, knowing he had broken no driving rules.

"Are you aware that your tail lights are not working?" the first officer asked.

Harry did not need to act surprised. He kept his car in top condition, he was too careful to invite police attention to it.

"No. No I didn't."

"Can we see your licence and registration papers, Sir?"

Harry complied at once, reaching up to the sun-visor to get them. He also pulled down his chauffeur's licence. He handed the lot to the officer who took them back to his patrol car.

Harry took the opportunity to get out and walk around to the back of his car. He swore expressively when he saw the smashed taillights.

"The Boss is not going to be impressed!" he said to himself.

"Do you have much further to go?" the second officer asked.

"Several miles," Harry estimated. "I have to deliver a rich, spoilt brat home before two thirty. I do have spare globes in the back, but not the covers."

Harry glanced at his watch.

"If I put new globes in, would I be able to continue? Once I have delivered her, I can get someone from the company to help me, even if I have to wait an hour or two."

"Where do you have to go?" the first officer asked, returning.

"Sunset Drive," Harry improvised.

"Okay, put the globes in. We'll follow you there. I'll hang onto your licence until then."

"Thanks Officer, I owe you one," Harry said amiably. He promptly went to the back of his car to get the globes.

Harry hid his anger well, but Wanda, still feigning sleep but peeping through narrowed eyes, sensed his tension as soon as he was back in the driver's seat. She'd figured out, long ago, that if Harry loved anything, it was his car. The lights would have been intact when he left to pick her up. She had not noticed the damage when they had returned from the job, but at that time, getting away was the priority.

Harry pulled up in front of a house in Sunset Drive. He had used his cell phone on wi-fi as he drove to call the Boss and arrange to get support for his story.

As Harry walked up to the door of the house, it opened.

"Cutting it fine, Karl," the man in the doorway commented. Then he saw the police car.

"Had some trouble with vandals," Harry/Karl explained. "The police were kind enough to follow me here so I could get your daughter home. I have someone from the company coming out to help me. I'll just help your daughter out."

The woman in the back of the car stirred when the door opened. She needed help to get out and more to get herself to the door. It seemed obvious she was too drunk to walk straight.

"You're a disgrace Cherie-Ann," the man from the house said audibly as he took over from Karl.

"Thanks for seeing me here safely," Harry/Karl told the officers once he was back at his car. "Do you need to write me a ticket?"

"We'll waive it this time," the officer told Harry. "Just don't drive the car until you have it fixed."

Harry forced a grin and took his papers and licence back. Then he leant against the car, reached for his cell phone and pretended to dial a number as the police car drove off.

A dark sedan arrived within five minutes. Harry took the black wrapped bundle from under the back seat and the backpack from the floor and tossed them into the sedan. As he locked his car, Wanda and the man from the house were hurrying out and within a minute everyone was in the car and it was being driven off.

The car turned into the driveway of a large estate only a few miles away, and stopped at the metal gates. A guard came out to examine the driver. At his nod, the electronic gates swung open and the car moved quietly along the drive to the house. As the car approached close to the building, a garage door opened so that the car could drive straight in.

Wanda took her cue from Harry. He did not seem worried by the events of the drive here, so she relaxed. The driver and the man from the house did not seem hostile, but neither spoke further to her.

Harry passed Wanda's backpack and wrapped tools to her, then led the way out of the garage, into the house.

Wanda expected the house to be grand, but her amazement was unfeigned when she saw the reality of it. It was even more opulent than the place Harrison had owned when she had first visited him. One day, she promised herself, she would own a house just like it.

"Miss Dean," a soft voice spoke beside her.

Wanda turned around and saw a servant beside her. She had been so impressed by the house that she had not sensed his approach. "The Master wishes to see you in the front parlour. This way please."

Wanda glanced at Harry who was walking into a passage on the far side of the hall. She followed the servant into a room at the front of the house.

"The Master will be here shortly," Wanda was advised. "Would you care for a drink?"

"Do you have diet coke?"

The man nodded and fetched a small can from a bar fridge hidden in a panelled section of wall in one corner of the room.

"What should I do with this stuff?" Wanda asked when the man had handed her the can.

"The Master will tell you." He bowed slightly and left the room.

Wanda decided not to remain standing. She walked to a two-seater couch and curled up on it. She was tired, having worked a twelve-hour shift at the restaurant before going with Harry. She want to sleep but it had been hard enough staying awake in the car.

She did doze off, but the slightest sense of not being alone, made her suddenly alert.

Harrison was striding into the room. Wanda sprang to her feet and watched him.

"What did you bring me?" he asked her.

Wanda reached for the pack and put it onto a low table. Harrison examined the papers and the special jewel cases as she unloaded each item.

"Good work. Any trouble?" Harrison repacked the bag.

"Not inside. We had to wait for a guard or someone to finish a cigarette before we came out. That was all. Then we had that trouble with Harry's tail lights."

"Harry?" Harrison asked sharply.

"You know. The guy I work with. I call him Harry. He's never told me his real name."

"Why Harry?"

"He works for you!" Wanda blushed faintly.

"Harry then. Yes, he told me about the car lights. Mistakes like that can cause all sorts of trouble," Harrison commented mildly.

"The damage had to be done while we were on the job," Wanda told him immediately. "They were fine when we left the car and we don't hang around after a job."

"Do you think the police noticed you particularly?" Harrison asked, still mildly.

Wanda shook her head.

"One of them shone a torch on me, but I had my hair mussed over my face. And I never look like me on a job."

"What about on jobs I haven't sanctioned?"

Harrison suddenly reached out and gripped Wanda's wrist.

"What do you mean?" Wanda asked, meeting his gaze. She guessed he had learnt about her little excursion of two nights ago.

Harrison drew a folded piece of paper from the pocket of his evening jacket. He unfolded it one-handed and showed it to Wanda. It was an artist's sketch of a woman that could have been her.

"Is that meant to be me?" Wanda asked, studying it.

"Is it?" was the sharp question.

"Where did it come from?" Wanda asked.

Harrison's expression stopped being genial. "A woman, whose description could be yours, broke into the apartment of the wife of a prominent business man and threatened to harm her two year old son if she did not hand over a valuable leather coat. Was it you?"

Wanda stared defiantly at her employer.

"Was it?"

"Yes. So what?" Wanda finally admitted. "I got away clean."

Harrison slapped her face hard, twice. Tears sprang into her eyes from the stinging pain, but she made no sound.

"You have no need to steal such things," Harrison said coldly. "I pay you enough to buy several coats or whatever else you want. Why did you go to the woman's place and steal it?"

"I was going to buy it," Wanda said carefully. "I had it in my hands and she grabbed it off me. I wasn't going to make a scene in the shop."

"You could have got a different one."

"I wanted … that one!" Wanda stared at Harrison.

She was ready for the reaction to her defiance. She moved her head away from the next slap.

"You and I have a deal. You do not do any jobs except what I tell you to do. You do remember that I trust?"

Wanda met his angry gaze and nodded. She let the defiance slip away.

"The police don't like people who harm or threaten to harm, children. Even if the woman gets her coat back, they will still be looking for you. You will have to be very, very careful."

Wanda finally dropped her eyes.

"I have the coat," Harrison told her. "I will see that it is returned. I will not be paying you for this night's work. If you try such a stupid stunt again, I will not be so forgiving. You have a very poor record of staying free on your own."

"I won't do it again, Mr Harrison," Wanda promised, keeping her eyes down, but not acting cowed.

"See that you don't!" Harrison finished. He paused to be sure the message had sunk in. Then he demanded, "Who is the boy camped outside your apartment?"

Wanda looked up in surprise. "Outside mine?"

Harrison nodded. "Sylvester saw him there and told him to move away."

"I have no idea who it could be," Wanda said honestly. "I don't date anyone and if I did it would be a man, not a boy."

"If he is there when you go back, tell him to stay away or I will make the removal permanent."

Wanda knew Harrison meant exactly that.

"It will be best if you stay here until morning. I'll have my man show you where you are to sleep."

Harrison made a definite exit with the bag full of stolen items.

Wanda slumped into one of the chairs near the table and rested her head on her arms. With her face hidden, she allowed it to relax into a grin of exultation as she savoured the adrenalin rush of surviving her encounter with Harrison.

She had guessed right, played her part exactly right. He had a chance to remind her of his control of her and she had not behaved like a weak woman. He could have had one of his men beat her for her disobedience, but he hadn't. Yes, she was warned; she could not afford to disobey him again, but she didn't want to. She had his attention – that was what she wanted.

"Miss Dean," the same soft voiced servant roused her. "I am to show you where you will sleep."

Wanda controlled her face before she looked up. "Thank you. I can barely stay awake."

She realised, belatedly that her face must look red. The man stared at her a moment longer than courteous. Well, who cared what he thought anyway?

She followed him along a long corridor and up a flight of stairs. He showed her into a room, so opulent that she was sure it had to be a mistake. The bed was king sized and had curtains that could be drawn around it. There was a corner with chairs and a coffee table, and another with a TV and stereo system that looked state of the art, but she was too tired to investigate it. The man withdrew.

The bed drew her attention. On it was a satin nightgown in a beautiful lavender shade. Wanda ran her hand on it and delighted in the feel of it. In moments, she was out of the evening dress and into the nightdress. She carefully folded her discarded clothes and put them on a chair.

As she climbed onto the bed, she realised something about the nightdress. What she had thought was the front seam of the calf length sheath, was actually comprised of delicate press-studs, from the crotch down. Did this mean what she thought it meant?

A wave of heat coursed through her body and she lay on the bed without getting between the satin sheets. She tried to stay awake, but dozed off anyway.

Firm but gentle hands were exploring her body. Wanda tensed for a moment, and then relaxed. She could smell a trace of the expensive body scent Harrison used. He was on the bed next to her, doing the things she dreamed of him doing and she was not about to ruin it by talking. His hands were rousing her body, making her moan with pleasure.

"Do I excite you?" Harrison whispered in her ear.

"Yes, please don't stop," Wanda begged.

"Do you want me to keep going?"

"Yes, oh yes."

"You have to earn that privilege," Harrison whispered. "You have to prove yourself worthy of me. I have to forgive you first."

"Anything. I'll do anything – whatever you ask," Wanda promised rashly.

"See that you do," Harrison murmured, doing something that brought her to a crescendo of sensation.

While her body was helpless, she was aware of him undressing and then felt him slipping into the bed. She dared to crawl under the covers next to him, and then felt him pull her next to him. His arms went around her and she fell asleep, feeling triumphant.

When one of the servants woke her at five o'clock next morning, Wanda was alone in the king-size bed. For a moment she thought that she had dreamt Harrison had been with her, but the second pillow had the impression of a head on it and smelt of body scent. She smiled to herself before rising to dress in the clothes she had removed the previous night.

Chapter 2

Wanda woke from an uneasy sleep. It was only seven-thirty but someone was pounding on the door of her apartment.

She rose, rubbed her eyes and reached for her ankle length dressing gown to hide the fact that she was still almost fully dressed. When she had arrived back at six o'clock, she had only had enough energy to remove her shoes before collapsing on the bed.

"Who is it?" she called through the door leading to the passage outside.

"Sandy!" the voice sounded young and male.

"Sandy who?"

"Your brother! Come on Sis, I know it's you. Open up!"

Wanda fumbled with the catch and opened the door slowly. She hadn't even put the safety chain on when she had arrived.

An older, but still recognizable, version of her younger brother sidled in through the part opened door.

Wanda quickly closed the door again. "How did you find me?" was her curt greeting as she held the gown tightly closed.

"Elisabeth told me where you were," Sandy Willard informed his oldest sister. "She wanted to know you were alright. Aren't you glad to see me?"

"No!" Wanda snapped. "You'd be better off forgetting you found me."

"If you feel that way, why do you write to Elisabeth?"

Sandy looked like their father, too much for Wanda's peace of mind, but he had blond hair like his mother's had been. She looked nothing like him. She took after her own mother, who had died when she was four. Her light brown hair was all she had inherited from her father. Few who saw them together would guess they were related. And that was fortunate for Sandy Willard.

"That's my business. I never gave her my address. So how did you know where I was?"

"Alright, I asked a private enquiry agent to trace you. I didn't have much to go on. Elisabeth knew what part of town you posted your letters in and an idea of what this place looked like. I had on old photo of you and gave him that. It took him a few weeks to find you. Why did you change your name?"

"Look, Sandy, I'm doing you all a big favour. I'm keeping out of your lives. Now do me one. Get out of here and don't come back!"

Sandy's eyes flashed with suppressed anger and he kept his mouth shut. This was not going the way he hoped. Time to play his trump card.

"Elisabeth is very sick! She needs you to come home. The doctors think you can help her."

Wanda's face didn't change.

"I can't help her!" Wanda said, knowing it sounded callous. "Sandy, get out of here! I have a boyfriend who doesn't know I have a brother and who won't stop to ask questions if he finds you here. He told me he'd terminate you if he saw you here again."

"Who? That jerk that told me off last night?"

Wanda said nothing.

"Is he your boyfriend or your pimp?" Sandy challenged. "I heard you worked nights."

Wanda felt herself blushing, thinking of the previous night.

"Your precious detective obviously didn't find out much. I waitress from noon until midnight. If I choose to be out after that – what I do and with whom – is my business. I don't intend to live all my life in this shoebox!"

"You haven't changed!" Sandy snapped. "I thought you at least cared for Elisabeth. If you change your mind, I'm working at Taggerty's Sports Store for the next three weeks, and then I'll be at the Police Academy."

Sandy turned on his heel and let himself out. He was half way down the stairs when he saw the tailor's dummy from the previous night, walking up them.

"I told you to stay away from here," the man spoke in a soft menacing voice.

"Mate, you are welcome to the bitch," Sandy shook off the man's grip. "She can rot in hell!"

As he continued to stomp down the stairs, he didn't see Sylvester Franklin smile.

Sandy went and sat in his car, which was parked opposite the block of apartments. He berated himself for losing his calm and probably blowing the only chance Elisabeth had to live. How could two people who had the same mother and father be so different?

"Damn it! It's been six years – she can't still be holding a grudge!"

Sandy recalled the night Wanda left home. The memory was still vivid enough to make him angry. He remembered Wanda screaming obscenities at their father, calling her stepmother horrible things and refusing to stop seeing the young louts she had teamed up with. It was the only time he had ever heard his father lose his temper – over anything.

He had predicted she would end up in jail and he wouldn't help her if she did. He had not actually disowned her, but he never mentioned her. Yet his father had not stopped him from going to look for her. If Senator Charles Willard could forgive his daughter, why couldn't Wanda, as she now called herself, try to forgive him?

When Sandy saw the man from the stairway walking across the road towards his car, he decided it was time to leave. The man was dangerous. Couldn't his sister see that?

Sandy drove around until he came to Landler Park and stopped in the parking area there. It was too early for him to be at work. He took out his cell phone and dialled Elisabeth's mobile.

The phone rang for a long time. Sandy pictured Elisabeth walking slowly and painfully to answer it. He had got her the mobile so she wouldn't have to walk – but she wouldn't keep it with her. She was stubborn. In that way she was like Wanda, but in all other ways she was the opposite. Elisabeth was the sweetest, most decent person he knew.

"Elisabeth Willard."

"Hi, Liz, it's Sandy."

"Did you find her?" was Elisabeth's breathless question.

"Yeah, I found her."

"And…"

"It's hopeless. She says she can't help you."

Elisabeth was silent for a moment.

"She will, Sandy. You have to keep at her."

"She told me to get out and not come back. She has her own personal bouncer. He's warned me off twice!"

"Find somewhere else to see her."

Sandy counted to ten slowly.

"Sandy?"

"I'm here."

"She's in trouble. I know it, but I don't know if she knows it."

"If she's in trouble, it's where she wants to be. She hasn't changed. She is still the bitch she was six years ago."

"No, she's not!" Elisabeth insisted. "I know she's not!"

"Okay, I'll keep trying. I'll do it for you! But there is only so much I will put up with from her."

"Don't do anything rash, Sandy, please," Elisabeth begged. "If she had a phone I'd call her myself. See if you can give her my number. Maybe she will call me if she isn't afraid of Mum or Dad answering it."

"I'll see what I can do," Sandy sighed. "Bye, Liz."

Wanda was waiting on tables when she saw her brother walk into the restaurant. It was obvious that he was trying to get her attention, so she ignored him and let her young colleague, Kylie, tend to him. Well, she didn't want anyone to think he knew her. There was no doubt in Wanda's mind that Harrison's warning was to be taken seriously. She may not want to have anything to do with her family, but she didn't hate them enough to want them hurt. Why didn't he just do as she said, and keep away?

He would ruin what she had achieved. She had just got Harrison to notice her as a woman. She had to keep her nose clean with him or the consequences wouldn't be pleasant. She knew that instinctively, but it didn't matter. He was her ticket to a life of riches and he made her feel alive, totally, scintillatingly, every nerve extra sensitive – alive.

"Sis!" Sandy whispered as Wanda had to pass him with a pile of dirty dishes. She ignored him again and disappeared into the kitchen.

Though he waited, she didn't reappear. He guessed she wouldn't until he left.

He raised his hand to get the attention of the cute little waitress that had served him.

"Can I have my bill, please?"

Kylie went to the front desk and began to add it up for him.

Sandy was watching her, so he saw the man he'd seen near Wanda's place enter with an older man. The other man had steel grey hair and if the younger was dangerous, the elder was evil itself.

The little waitress smiled at the pair and showed them to a table that had, until then, a reserved sign on it.

They must be regulars, Sandy thought, turning his head away so they wouldn't see him.

He risked a peek at the table where the men were seated, but only the older man was there and his sister was hurrying out of the kitchen, hastily fixing her frilly little apron.

He was too far away to hear the conversation, but his sister was writing something on her order pad. Kylie returned with his bill.

"Wait a minute will you?" Sandy requested as he drew out his wallet. His bill came to under ten dollars but he drew out a ten and a twenty and a small photograph with a number on the back.

"Keep the change," Sandy smiled at her.

"It's too much," Kylie protested, sure it was a mistake.

Sandy covered hers with his and spoke softly.

"If you give the photo to Wanda, without the two gents over at that table knowing it, I'd be grateful."

Kylie nodded, catching on quickly.

"Ah, thanks," she said, glancing quickly over his shoulder and hurrying away.

Sandy had only that much warning of the man's approach. He stood up to leave.

"Hello, Friend!" the voice sounded genial but the owner of the voice clapped him on the back so hard that he almost staggered into a nearby table of diners. "The old man suggested that you join us."

"I've already eaten, thanks," Sandy backed away, sensing the menace in the words.

"No problems. We'll buy you a drink."

Sandy backed into another diner and turned to apologise only to feel his arm being held in a painful grip. Wedged between two tall, powerful men, Sandy had no option but to go where they wanted.

Wanda hadn't left the table yet, nor could she see him coming. The old man had his hand on her wrist, but she didn't seem to be objecting. As he was pushed around in front of her, he saw a smile on his sister's face that seemed genuine. It vanished the moment she saw him. Was it a trick of the light or for an instant did she look panicked before a look of distaste replaced it?

"Bring an extra drink for your friend here, Miss Dean," Harrison ordered. "A strong whisky."

"He's not my friend!" Wanda said coldly, and then moved off to fill the man's order.

"Have a seat," Harrison invited Sandy. He had no choice – his two escorts pushed him down before seating themselves. They looked ready to spring at him if he moved.

"I believe you have been told to keep away from Miss Dean," Harrison said with quiet menace. "Twice!"

Sandy shrugged. "I told your friend here that he was welcome to her."

"So why are you here?" Harrison persisted.

"That's my business," Sandy snapped.

"If you want to leave here in one piece, I suggest you make it my business," Harrison suggested quietly.

Sandy looked around for inspiration. He licked lips that were suddenly dry. Like an answer to his prayer, he saw Wanda returning with a tray of drinks. She placed one in front of each person, keeping her eyes away from each of them.

Harrison held her wrist again. He was rubbing the back of it with his thumb, but this time, Sandy saw her rigid posture. His guts went into knots. He took the whisky and swigged half of it before the man on his right deliberately knocked his arm so he spilled the rest of it down his front.

Wanda laughed softly, looking at the mess her brother was in. It was a calculated move and she felt Harrison's grip loosen.

"You know him then?" Harrison asked Wanda.

"Yeah, I do. Took me a while to place him. I last saw him six years ago when he was an obnoxious spotty faced brat. I knew his sister."

"What did he want?"

"He's just a messenger. His sister wants me to go back to Hicksville and be her bridesmaid. I told him I wasn't interested. I have better things to do here. He just doesn't have the message yet. Excuse me, Sir, your entrée's are ready."

"I'm feeling generous tonight," Harrison said mildly, but Sandy sensed the menace. "I'll give you one final warning. Go home! If you are seen near Miss Dean again – it might be fatal."

Harrison waved his hand and Sandy felt his arms, released.

"Go!" he was told.

Sandy decided it was a good order to follow and stood up and left the table. He was so intent on getting away from the men that he didn't see that one of the younger men was following him, five paces behind.

Wanda noticed as she delivered the plates to the table, but didn't obviously look in that direction.

"Where's the men's room?" the other younger man asked.

"Down the passage next to the kitchen," Wanda told him.

"Show me!"

Harrison nodded. Wanda walked back towards the kitchen, but instead of entering the passage, she was pushed into the kitchen. Her boss watched without comment as she was forced to walk through to the restaurant's rear door.

Wanda was released and nudged in the direction of the service alley. She felt a moment of panic until she heard noises from further ahead. The noises sounded like fists on flesh and her fear took a new turn. Fortunately, it was dark, she did not have to hide her expression and by the time she stopped, she had it under control.

Her brother was lying on the alley stones. Harrison's goon was leaning over him, feeling his clothing.

"He's a bit too old for you, Syl," the man behind Wanda said.

Syl growled. "He's carrying no wallet!"

"He had one a little while ago," Wanda said clearly. "He had to. He paid Kylie for his meal. He must have dropped it inside."

Syl stood up and brushed his clothes back into position.

"Clean up your mess!" Syl told her before he and the other walked off.

"Hands off me, Bitch," Sandy snarled, refusing help to get to his feet.

"I warned you, bro," Wanda said very quietly.

"Yeah and if I ever see you again it will be too soon," Sandy continued in a loud voice.

"I'm sorry, Sandy, I really am, but I can't help Elisabeth." Wanda insisted quietly. "Please stay away from me."

"What have they got on you?" Sandy asked quietly as he stumbled along the alley towards the car park.

"I'll help you to a taxi," Wanda said loudly, avoiding the question.

"Hands off! I don't want your help!"

"Please yourself!"

In a low voice, Sandy said, "I hope you know what you're doing, Sis. It seems to me you are on a one-way trip to hell. And I don't think you are wasting time getting there."

Sandy increased his pace towards his car, stumbling on the rough surface. Wanda watched him until he sat in his car. It was obvious to her that he was in pain and trying to ignore it.

Why didn't you just leave me alone, Wanda thought, watching him drive off. She began to walk back to the rear of the restaurant.

"Back to work, Dean!" the manager, Green, pounced on her the moment she re-entered the kitchen. "You can get back to the dishes."

"Yes, Mr Green," she agreed willingly.

Wanda was relieved. At the moment, she wasn't sure she could hide her inner thoughts from that trio of customers. Doing dishes would give her time to regain her control.

Damn Sandy anyway! He pranced back into her life, confusing her priorities. She couldn't go home. Wouldn't.

If she were to ask for time off from Harrison, he'd want to know why. If she just went – well she couldn't – he'd find her and have her beaten. He'd never trust her enough to make love to her.

Kylie brought more dishes to stack on her pile.

"Your friend gave me something to give to you," she said to the stiff back of her colleague.

Wanda stopped scrubbing and turned. "What friend?"

"The cute one at table 11."

"He's not a friend," Wanda corrected.

"Well, he gave me this and a twenty dollar tip."

Kylie handed over the photograph. Wanda wiped one hand roughly on a towel to take it.

The blond girl in the photo looked haggard and frail. The sight of Elisabeth, looking like that sent shivers of dread up and down Wanda's spine. She turned the photograph over, saw the telephone number, and memorised it in moments. Then she shrugged and threw the photo in the bin near the sink.

"He must have the wrong girl. I don't know who the hell that was."

Kylie did not really care. She had done as she had been asked.

Wanda went back to doing dishes until the manager called her away.

"Take coffee to table 20," he told her.

Wanda again replaced her frilly apron and took the tray over to Harrison. Only one cup. Yes, the other two men had gone.

"I have a special job for you," Harrison told her quietly. "Harry will meet you as usual. Twelve thirty – don't be late."

Harrison had a faint smile on his face as he called his other operative 'Harry'.

"Will that be all, Mr Harrison?" Wanda asked.

Harrison nodded, and Wanda went off to fix his bill. When Harrison left, there was a $50 dollar tip. Wanda relaxed slightly. Harrison, it seemed, was pleased with her.

Chapter 3

Harry was waiting for her, as usual, outside the rear door of the restaurant. He was there so often that the police officer on the beat no longer queried his intentions.

Wanda followed him in silence, and did not try to prompt Harry into giving her details of the night's job. He would tell her when he was ready.

They were in Harry's car when he said, "We're going to do a snatch job."

"Who?"

"Who doesn't matter."

"Okay, what? Man, woman or child?"

"Male."

"And I'm to do what?"

"Your usual, open locks. But, you'll need to wear nothing under your suit!"

There was almost a sneer in the way Harry said it. Wanda took the suggestion as an order.

"The Boss had better pay triple for this. I'm no whore!"

"He'll make it worth your while," Harry promised.

Harry waited in his car whilst Wanda went up to her apartment to prepare. She took her make-up case out and considered each of her favourite disguises. It was no good looking Hispanic on this outing, the skin under her suit would give her away. Instead, she darkened her hair and gave her face, hands and feet a fake tan. She let her hair loose and she blow waved it so it fell over her face.

When she was ready, she walked down to Harry's car. He drove to one of the most expensive hotels in downtown LA and parked in the street nearby. On the way, he had explained what they had to do, and what she was to do.

Using stealth, they entered the hotel's basement garage and used the fire stairs to by-pass the lobby. They both had a backpack carried on one shoulder. At the third floor, they entered the main part of the hotel and took the patron's lift to the tenth floor. This was the level below the pent house, which was their destination.

The penthouse had a private lift from the garage and lobby. It was next to the main lift, but went express to the top floor.

Harry strode along to room 10-11 and indicated that Wanda was to open it. She complied immediately, and then moved aside to let Harry precede her into the suite. She followed and closed the door after hanging a do not disturb sign on the handle in the corridor.

Wanda's keen ears heard slight sounds of a struggle and then nothing. Harry re-emerged from one of the bedrooms in the suite and entered the other.

A faint odour of ether clung to Harry as he pointed to a window. It overlooked the side of the hotel and the narrow way between it and the next building. Wanda unlocked the window, but this time, she climbed out first and using cracks in the brickwork, found a way up onto the roof where the penthouse garden hid their arrival. Harry was only moments behind her.

Using hand signals, Harry indicated that they would be leaving via the roof of the adjacent building.

"You go in first. There should only be one person in there, unless he invited a whore into his bed. Pretend to be stealing his jewellery, but we don't want to take it – just him."

Wanda had a very good idea what was going to happen, and wondered how he intended the man to wake up. She did not intend to do it.

However, she obeyed Harry's instructions. This sort of activity put her mind into high gear and a zest into life.

Wanda forced the door lock on the French windows leading from the garden and crept stealthily through the suite to the bedroom. Harry had not been wrong. A gold watch, rings and a platinum pin set with a diamond lay carelessly on the side table.

The man, a foreigner, to judge by his looks in the faint light of her torch, lay asleep on his back. Wanda was aware of Harry approaching – it was like a sixth sense – probably the result of working together for so long.

Suddenly the phone gave two rings. The man on the bed woke suddenly, saw Wanda beside him and grabbed.

He was strong, and rolled off the bed, holding her and pushing her to the floor. He was on her before she could get up. Faster than a snake could strike, he had her arms pinned behind her.

Only then did the man seem to realise that his prisoner was a woman. He reached for something under his pillow.

"I have a gun," he said in accented English. Wanda guessed him to be Spanish or South American.

"Roll over," he ordered.

Wanda obeyed slowly, seeing he was indeed armed.

The man pushed the hair off her face and began to unzip the front of her body suit.

He began to chuckle when he realised the woman was naked under it.

Unlike Harrison's touch, this man's hands on her made her skin crawl, but even as his attention was on her, Harry caught his head between his side and his arm and held an ether soaked pad to his face.

While the man struggled, Harry ogled his companion. When he fell limp, enabling Wanda to use her hands, she quickly zipped herself up and took a loop of elastic from her wrist and tied her hair off her face. She glared at Harry until he began to bind the man's wrists, ankles and mouth. He continued his task, using a sheet from the bed to wrap the unconscious man in. Together, they carried him outside and placed him next to the wall nearest the adjacent building.

Harry took his pack off and pulled out a small air gun, a coil of strong rope and a padded grappling hook. He assembled his equipment efficiently and shot the line across the gap between buildings. He tied off the nearest end once the hook had gripped.

Then he improvised a carry harness for the unconscious man and Wanda helped him sling the limp bundle across his shoulders. With an agility that Wanda envied, Harry used the rope to cross to the other building.

It was Wanda's turn. She took from her pack a second coil of line, and clipped one end to a certain part of the knot securing the near end of the other rope. She played out the slack on that line, because she didn't want to pull it too soon. It was to release the first line, once she was across. Skilfully, but with less finesse than Harry, Wanda swung from the rope and crossed to the other building. As soon as her feet were on a solid base again, she yanked the second rope and released the first. Then she pulled both ropes up as fast as possible.

Even with the weight of the man on his back, Harry helped her to re-coil the ropes and stow them neatly back in the packs. Only then did they make their way to the fire stairs of the building.

"Meet me at the car," Harry told her, and indicated that she should precede him.

This building, Wanda knew, was mainly offices with shops on the bottom two floors. So without wasting time, Wanda opened the door and began running quietly down the concrete stairs, all senses alert for guards.

There were signs on all doors warning that the doors were alarmed. Wanda wondered what Harry expected her to do. He was the alarm expert, but then no alarm had gone off on the top floor.

On the ground floor, Wanda crouched under the stairs to catch her breath. She hoped to hear Harry following her but after five minutes there was still no sign of him. It meant she had to use her own initiative. Her only thought right now, was escape.

Wanda unlocked the outer door and pushed it open. The alarm clamoured noisily in the night time hush, but Wanda was well away before the first police car screeched to a halt.

Wanda slowed to a walk once she was a block away from the building. She kept to shadows as much as possible so it was less likely she'd draw attention to herself. It took her only a few moments to orientate herself and quickly realised that she was in the wrong street to reach Harry's car. It was parked a block away in the next street across and police cars were converging from all directions.

Wanda kept walking, trudging rather, with her pack slung over one shoulder. She looked neither left nor right, only at the footpath ahead of her. At the next corner she turned left and continued walking to the next main street and then she turned left again. She was now heading back towards the focus of the police activity. Harry's car was not far ahead.

The patrolman appeared in front of her like a phantom. Wanda walked into him then immediately apologised.

"Sorry, I'm not quite awake yet."

"Where are you going," the patrolman asked her.

"To work, at the hotel. I start at four," Wanda lied glibly.

"What do you do?"

"I'm a cleaner. I start in the bars and restaurants and later in the day I do rooms if I'm needed or windows."

"What's in the bag?"

"Some ropes and tackle," Wanda admitted at once. "I usually keep it at work, but I had to get some bits repaired."

"Mind if I look?"

Wanda shrugged, glad that she had not kept any of the foreigner's jewellery and that they had taken the time to tidy the ropes and disassemble the gear.

She watched the patrol officer as he examined her bag. He was a bit suspicious of her, but not ready to take her in.

He never had a chance to do more than that. Harry came quietly up behind him and coshed him. Wanda grabbed her bag and raced the short way to Harry's car.

Wanda wondered where Harry had stashed the man they had abducted. However, she knew better than to ask. Perhaps he was in the boot of Harry's car. But then, maybe not. It probably would not be smart of Harrison to have the man at his own house.

Harry drove them again to Beverly Hills, this time without trouble. Wanda had put a skirt and blouse over the body suit this time and pushed her pack under the seat. The few tools Harry had brought for her to use had gone back into Harry's pockets.

At the house, Wanda followed Harry to Harrison's office. Even though it was early in the morning, Harrison was awake.

"Any trouble?" Harrison asked.

Harry shook his head. "Worked just as you expected. The guy thinks with his balls. We split up to come down. I got the package to Syl and the kid distracted the guards. We had to quiet a patrolman, he'd cornered the kid."

Harrison turned his attention to Wanda. "Tell me about it."

Wanda complied and related the incident in detail. She finished by saying that the man was about to let her go when he went down. She made a point of saying that she thought coshing him was unnecessary, because now he would suspect her for sure.

Harrison considered the reports thoughtfully; Harry glared at Wanda.

"You may be correct," Harrison agreed. "But he's in charge."

Wanda shrugged. Harry smirked and left the room when Harrison dismissed him.

"Good work," he praised her. "Go and get a few hours sleep. You can use the same room as before."

Wanda let a smile appear on her face. Harrison smiled back.

Yes, Wanda thought to herself.

Chapter 4

Wanda almost jumped a foot from the ground when her brother tapped her on the shoulder in the bank queue.

"What's made you so jumpy today?" Sandy Willard hissed as Wanda spun to see who had touched her.

Her brother's face was badly bruised and several deep scratches had scabbed over.

"Nothing," Wanda lied. "I wasn't expecting to meet anyone."

"Are you pleased with the result of your handiwork, sister?" Sandy challenged with quiet anger. Wanda controlled her expression with difficulty.

"Did you find your wallet? I pinched it so they couldn't identify you."

"Yes, damn you."

"Good. Now nick off." Wanda turned her back on her brother.

"Why? Are your pimps watching you still?"

"I don't think so. I think they are busy this morning."

Wanda felt sure that she had not been followed from her apartment.

"Don't worry, Sis. I am going home! I just wanted to tell you that they had to rush Elisabeth to hospital last night. She's in the ICU at Oxnard Special Hospital. If she dies – it will be your fault!"

Sandy strode off after delivering his message.

Wanda watched him go and suddenly felt as if her life had lost its focus. She moved forward in the queue automatically, but when she reached the teller, she had decided not to put all of Harrison's three thousand dollar bonus for her last job into the bank. She kept out a thousand dollars, just in case she needed some ready cash. For what – she wasn't sure.

After returning from the bank, Wanda spent an hour cleaning her tiny apartment and tidying her few belongings. Most of what she owned was clothes and some cheap paperbacks that she kept exchanging at the local book exchange. No ornaments or photos, no handcrafts, nothing she would miss if she had to leave.

Wanda caught herself. "Had to leave?"

Why would she want to leave? It was cheap rent, big enough for her needs. If she moved out, she intended it to be into Harrison's mansion.

"Had to leave," suggested running away. She wasn't going to run away. She wasn't planning on going anywhere.

The newspaper fell from the arm of the couch. Wanda leant down to retrieve it and remembered the impulse to buy it. She did not have a TV so the paper and her little radio were the only ways she had to find out the results of her nights' work. Many times, though, no one even knew that she and Harry had been somewhere. They did not always rob the places they visited. Sometimes they copied documents, or planted false evidence or simply 'looked'. Last night was her first snatch.

The main headlines were of some national crisis. Wanda did not care for politics. What she wanted was on page two. There was the article she sought about the abduction of the Spanish-Italian businessman Tony Vanetti from his penthouse suite.

Reading about the snatch was as exciting as doing it, Wanda decided. For a few moments she savoured the remembered thrill of the deed, the escape and later. Particularly later.

She felt invincible.

Wanda stopped reading, prepared an early lunch, and thought about getting ready for work at the restaurant.

She returned to the paper with her sandwich, intending to read the comics but the stop press caught her eye.

"Elisabeth Willard, daughter of Californian Senator Charles Willard, was rushed to hospital last night with an unidentified illness. Her condition is given as critical."

Wanda had tried to ignore her brother's news; tried to keep the hard shell around herself. At that moment, her protections vanished and her world went flip flop and upside down.

In the space of a heartbeat, Wanda felt four years old again. She remembered all too well her mother dying, slowly, painfully. She remembered the fear that the same fate would be hers.

"No!" Wanda said aloud, denying the truth. "It's not right! It shouldn't be her! She was all right. It should be me in that hospital, not her!"

"Elisabeth is my one friend. The one person who knows what I am and yet doesn't judge me. My conscience."

The other side of reality intruded. Her life – now.

"If she dies – it will be your fault!" Sandy had told her.

"If you disobey me again – I won't be so forgiving," Harrison had warned her.

The choice had seemed easy, a week ago.

Harrison might be pleased with her work now, but he would not have forgotten her disobedience, not yet.

She had never let herself dwell on the truth of Harrison's nature. He was dangerous. That was part of the thrill he held for her. And he was a killer. If she failed him now he would kill her. If she were lucky – he would do it himself. He would rouse her first, then ….

"Stop it!" Wanda told herself firmly.

She took twelve long, deep breaths to clear her mind.

It was then that she realised that she would go to Elisabeth, without telling Harrison.

Elisabeth was more important than anything.

Wanda had a bag of clothes and necessities packed within a few minutes. The money she had not banked was shoved into a corner of it. She tossed the bag onto the top of her wardrobe. From amongst the books on her shelf, she took a map of California and stared at it for a while. Then she gathered her work clothes and apartment keys and left her apartment. She stopped at a phone booth on her way, called the bus company, and asked about buses to Oxnard. The woman rattled off a list of times and routes. Wanda memorised them all. The one that stood out in her mind departed downtown at midnight and stopped about twenty minutes later two blocks from her apartment.

Wanda did not intend to tell her boss she was taking time off. After the other night when he had just stood by and let Harrison's goon walk her outside, she suspected he would blab to Harrison if she told him. If Green fired her, she would worry about a new job later.

Every minute that passed without seeing Harrison was a minute of hope. He did not come in every evening, but his appearances had been increasing of late. This was one night she did not want to work for him.

She was jumpy and nervous and snapped at Kylie and the other waitress. Both of them decided to keep their distance from her.

The manager had words with her when she dropped two plates.

"Dean! Take ten minutes outside," he told her bluntly.

Wanda walked out without comment. He would dock her pay for those 10 minutes too. She did not care. Outside, she concentrated on clearing her mind and breathing deeply. Tricks she had mastered and used to survive that year she had spent in the training centre. They still worked. Push away the memories, concentrate on now.

A few minutes longer than ten, Wanda went back in to work, noticeably calmer.

"Get out on the tables," Green told her. "He's asking for you."

Wanda nodded and put a smile on her face.

"How are you, Miss Dean?" Harrison asked as she reached his table.

"Fine, Sir. What can I get for you today?"

"Just coffee and cake of some kind," Harrison ordered. He was early today; it was only mid-afternoon. The café was almost deserted, so she would not be in trouble for chatting.

"Green told me you were feeling off colour," Harrison said, confirming her suspicion that her boss would tattle on her. "I took a couple of Paracetamol and some fresh air. I feel much better now. A touch of PMT I think."

"Can you work tonight?" Harrison asked.

"I can always work for you, Sir," Wanda smiled to hide her dismay.

"Usual time and place," he told her.

Banner Allied Insurance was their target. The company occupied the whole of the fifth floor of the new Allard Tower. Wanda knew it. The tallest of the older buildings around it was twelve stories tall. That was where they would enter. The security in that building was scant as most of the levels were empty. It was scheduled for renovation. That part of the job was no challenge to the skilled team of Harry and Wanda. They made it to the roof of that building and locked the fire door behind them to ensure no unexpected surprises. So far, so good.

Wanda crossed to the edge of the roof nearest their target. The gap was only six feet. She looked down. All the offices on this side of the Allard Tower were dark. Good!

Using a similar method to that of their successful raid the previous night, Harry shot a long rope up to the top of the taller building. This one had knots at intervals along it to help with the upward climb. The thud of the compressed air gun and the muffled thunk of the grappling hook seemed loud to them but it would not carry to ground level.

"You first," Harry instructed.

Like always, Wanda obeyed immediately. She was already feeling the adrenalin rush of the need for a dangerous climb – three storeys up over a drop of twelve. The moral issue of what she was doing had long since ceased to bother her. This was her real job. It paid well, that was what mattered.

Before she started, Wanda checked that she had securely fastened her tool belt around her waist and the backpack was comfortable. Harry had constantly drilled her with the need to check everything and pay attention to details. It was instinctive now.

Wanda climbed onto the edge of the parapet, took hold of the knotted rope, and lowered herself so that she dangled from it. Quickly then, she swung herself up the rope. She reached the roof of her destination and paused only for a moment before swinging herself over the low wall there. Her senses gave her no warning of danger. In that alone, Harry listened to her. If she said stop, wait, he did.

Harry was waiting for her by the stairwell when she finished her circuit of the roof. He had already tied the rope to a stanchion on this end so they could now recover it from the other side. The folding hook was in his pack.

Wanda pulled a pair of flexible gloves from her pocket and put them on. The door to the fire stairs was not locked so she did not need to apply the talent that had impressed Harrison enough to recruit her. Damn, it was not time to think of him now.

The two intruders walked quietly down the fire steps, jamming each fire door leading to the upper floors. At the door on the fifth floor, Wanda signalled Harry to be quiet.

Her sense of danger was warning her. Five minutes later, she signalled to proceed. Harry opened the fire escape door slowly. He had put the waiting time to good use by applying oil to the hinges.

The corridor in front of them was empty, as was the one going off to their right. Harry indicated straight ahead. Wanda moved forward as Harry closed the door behind them. No guard occupied the guard station that was right in front of the main entrance to Banner Allied Insurance.

Harry had warned her that this night's work was not going to be easy. It seemed to Wanda that he was relying heavily on her sense of danger on this job.

They were working on the assumption that the guard had just left on his rounds. Wanda waited by the door, whilst Harry examined the guard's desk and moved a few switches. He nodded to Wanda, and when she opened the door, no alarm sounded. They relocked the door after them. Harry indicated for her to hide down behind some furniture in the outer office. That was so when the guard returned, he would see no movement through the floor to ceiling glass wall.

Harry had told her that the guard left his desk for five minutes every half hour. They had to wait twenty-five minutes for their next step.

"The next door is wired," Harry breathed quietly in her ear. "It can't be controlled from out here. An alarm sounds if you open the door with anything but a special electronic key. I have the key."

Wanda could see the guard from her position. While she waited for him to leave again, she pondered the ease of their task so far. Harry was brilliant when it came to alarms, but so far this night, he had not had to use his skills. She did not count turning switches off at the guard's desk as skill. It was as if he knew exactly what to do there – and how had he got that key?

During the guard's next five-minute absence, Harry let them into the company director's office and closed the door again. Now they could work without fear of interruption. The office had a movement sensor, but it was dark, disabled. Harry put a dark cloth over it – just in case. Then he scanned the director's safe with a small device while Wanda checked all the drawers in the director's desk. She slipped the man's daily diary into her backpack them moved to open the safe.

Papers, letters, folders, discs and money were distributed between her pack and Harry's. Wanda relocked the empty safe and checked the time on her watch. Still five minutes before the guard was due to leave again. Harry crossed to the door and reached for the handle. Wanda grabbed his arm before he could touch it. Not a moment too soon. In the silence of the office, the sound of the handle being turned was clearly audible. This was not a normal part of the guard's round. Harry gestured her to flatten herself next to the wall on the other side of the door from him. The handle returned to its normal position and the door did not open. Wanda waited for her heartbeat to return to normal then tried to listen through the door. She could hear no sound, but she still did not feel it was safe to emerge, even though the guard should be on his round. Harry glanced up at where the movement sensor was placed. A green light was shining dully through the dark cloth. He swore quietly.

They waited until well past the time that the guard should have gone on his round before Wanda let Harry open the door. He swiped the electronic key along the inside slot and the office door opened a crack. The fact that he did not open it any further told Wanda that the guard was at his desk. Wanda checked her watch. That was where he should be.

"He's on the phone," Harry breathed. "Be ready to run when I say. Don't bother to be neat."

It was still too early for the guard's next round when Harry gave her the order to run. Wanda still looked before she ran. The guard was indeed away from his desk. She went to the door of the outer office. No one was visible in the passage in either direction. The way to the fire escape was clear. Harry switched the door alarm off at the board inside the office door.

"I think they are onto us," Wanda warned before they left the office. She had a sense of imminent disaster.

They edged up to the right angled corridor, it was empty. They ran to the fire escape door

Harry heaved on the bar but the door did not budge. Wanda felt a moment of panic. She could not be caught this time – she had to get to help her sister.

"Open it," he hissed.

Wanda tried the lock. "It's jammed, not locked!" She spun around then and saw the armed guard behind them. "Harry!" she warned softly, even as she raised her hands away from her sides to show she was unarmed.

Harry turned slowly, almost contemptuously, and sized up the situation.

"Don't move," the guard, tall, broad and powerful warned. He spoke in a tone intended to be obeyed. His gun was aimed at them and his eyes never left them even as his free hand reached down for the radio hooked on his belt.

Wanda stared intently at him, thinking only of his eyes dropping for a moment and ready to act when they did. She saw the eyes move and dived for the man's stomach. She was under his gun arm before he had time to realise his danger and by then he was fighting for breath.

Wanda snatched his gun as Harry punched him in the face and sent him sprawling unconscious on the floor.

"Another one," Wanda warned, soon enough for Harry to flatten himself against the wall next to an ornamental tree in a pot. He caught the gun Wanda threw at him.

Wanda remained in plain sight, searching the guard for keys and seeming to be oblivious to the approach of the second guard.

That one never saw Harry and had no chance to challenge Wanda. He slumped unconscious beside his mate.

Before Wanda could rise, the first guard suddenly grabbed her and swung his leg around to trip her. He had the chance to grab her knitted black mask.

"Let her go, bastard!" Harry growled, holding the guard's own gun on him.

The guard maintained his grip even though Wanda was struggling. He managed to pull off her mask but only had an instant to glimpse her face before Harry's boot kicked him in the side of the head.

"Go and get the lift up here!" Harry hissed.

Wanda scrambled to obey, stopping only to grab her mask. She knew by the pain in her scalp that he had pulled out hair when he had pulled off the mask.

She remembered seeing a lift in the other corridor, not far down. She brought the car up, she heard the hiss of the near silent motors, and held the door open. Harry strode in a few moments later. Wanda had already pressed the button for the top floor and judging by the lighted ground floor button, someone was trying to recall it.

The roof was quiet but from the street below, sirens could be heard approaching.

"Go!" Harry ordered, sending Wanda down the rope first to the lower building.

He crossed as soon as she was safely across and did not even bother to recover his rope. He simply untied the nearer end and let the rest dangle down the side of the other building. They wasted no more time getting back through the fire door on the roof and down the stairs of the lower building. Wanda made no comment. She had heard the sounds of someone trying to bash open the fire door of the Allard Building.

Wanda decided that the ambush by the guards had spooked Harry. It was unlike him to leave anything behind. He was normally too careful to give the police any clues.

If anyone should be worried, it was her. She was the one who had lost her mask and been seen, not him. But then, this whole job was odd. Maybe Harry had bribed one of the guards to look the other way and he had reneged. Perhaps that was how Harry got the electronic key?

Wanda stopped worrying about what was past and concentrated on the present and trying to stay ahead of the police cordon.

They reached Harry's car unchallenged and slipped inside. Harry did not start the motor right away. Wanda, busy changing in the back seat, caught flashes of blue and red light and realised why. She changed into a skirt, skivvy and sandals and shoved her body suit under the seat. Harry was pulling a green jumper over his suit. Wanda then pulled forward the back of the passenger-side rear seat and shoved the two backpacks through to the luggage compartment and out of sight. The two facemasks followed before she put the seat back to normal.

Harry watched for a time when the street was clear of police traffic before driving off in a leisurely manner. He was not heading for Beverly Hills this time, but for Wanda's apartment. He dropped her off a block from there and continued on.

Wanda was glad of the peaceful night sounds – the absence of police sirens in particular.

It was not until she tried to open her door that she realised her hands were shaking. Reaction to the narrow escape, no doubt. She took several deep breaths and tried to open her door again. This time she succeeded.

Wanda went first to her tiny kitchen and put the kettle on to boil. A soothing cup of herbal tea was what she needed after such an eventful evening and it would keep her alert. She still intended to catch a bus before morning. She fetched her bag from on top of the wardrobe while she waited.

As her trembling eased, Wanda felt the return of the adrenalin high. It was more intense than normal and she revelled in it, enjoyed every minute of its effect, even as the tea grew cooler in her cup. She wanted it to last longer but other demands intruded.

The sudden drop from the adrenalin rush brought her to instant wariness. It was her danger sense that had just kicked in. Her first instinct was to glance out the window. She was just in time to see the last flash from the lights on the police car.

They might have come for any number of reasons, but she was not about to wait around and find out. She left at once, walking down the back stairs and jumping over the fence with her pack. There was a warren of laneways between her apartment block and the ones around it and she knew them well. A street away, she saw a cruising taxi and hailed it and asked the driver to take her to the train station. It was near enough to the bus stop she would need to catch the four-seventeen bus from downtown. She had time to get there without having to wait very long for the next bus.

Chapter 5

The bus drew into Oxnard at seven-thirty in the morning and stopped at the rail terminal. Wanda collected her bag and went in search of strong black coffee and a washroom in the Amtrak station across a driveway. The latter was the more urgent priority. When she discovered that the facility had several showers, she availed herself of the chance to wash the dark colour from her hair.

Thanks to the brief sleep on the bus, Wanda felt refreshed and more awake. She bought some coffee, a muffin and an early edition newspaper. It was much too early to try to visit Elisabeth at the hospital.

After a few sips of the hot coffee, Wanda opened the newspaper.

"Guards killed in break-in."

The headline sent a knife-thrust of shock through her, even though she knew she wouldn't have been the only thief active last night. She read further, the paper shaking slightly when her eyes scanned the words "Banner Allied Insurance".

She felt all the blood run from her face, but forced herself to read on, to betray nothing. A deep-rooted fear gripped her and churned her stomach. She felt real terror for the first time since she had started working with Harry.

The guards had been alive when she left them, and in no condition to raise an immediate alarm. Harry had kept back when he sent her to get the lift and it seemed he had shot them at point blank range. She had heard nothing.

Why had he done it? Why had he been carrying a silenced weapon? He never carried a weapon. He'd told her often enough of the fine difference between robbery and armed robbery. Why last night?

The guards had seen her face, but that should not have worried Harry. Unless, one or both of the guards had recognised him too – somehow?

Why he had done it did not matter – he had done it. It made her an accessory to murder.

Murder!

Wanda felt a shudder run through her and desperately began her calming routine. She had no qualms about burglary and theft or what she guessed was industrial espionage. The few remaining scruples she'd had at the end of her 12 month stint in the training centre had been beaten out of her by Harry and Harrison in the first few months of their association.

But murder! No – she could not tolerate murder.

Wanda did not want to think the thoughts crowding into her head. The foremost being that she was not invincible. Five and a half years of unsuspected criminal success did not guarantee forever. What she had been doing for Harrison was fun, exhilarating, and totally wrong! She had to face the fact that one day she would go to jail.

There had been a moment in time when she could have stopped – could have chosen to be honest.

"It's not the end of the world," Elisabeth had told her.

Elisabeth, her friend, her conscience, her sister.

"You've made a mistake. Pay the penalty; start anew when you come out. I'll be here for you."

Elisabeth – the only person to whom she had ever confided the humiliating details of that year in the training centre.

"Start afresh, come home, go back to school, find a job" Elisabeth had advised.

Wanda remembered her answer.

"No, I won't come home. I won't burden my family with what I am. I will learn to support myself; make something of myself."

"I'll be there for you," was all Elisabeth had said.

It was too late now. Wanda had been targeted by Harrison from the moment that she had been out on the streets again. Now, if Harry had killed once, he would do it again and she was in too deep with Harrison to get cold feet. Any sign of wavering loyalty, especially now, would be constituted as treason.

Wanda stopped looking at Harrison through a rosy romantic glow and forced her mind from the way he made her body feel. He might act like a nice old man, but she had seen and heard enough to know he was not. He was part of an organisation, a highly organised one. He had to be because Harry knew so much about each of the places they entered. And she knew what would happen if she disobeyed Harrison. He would think she was running away.

Think!

"Okay," Wanda said to herself. Hearing her own voice steadied her.

I had to leave my apartment. The police were there. I had no way to call him. I wasn't going to lead the police to his place. She was letting the heat die down before coming back to suss out the situation.

"Okay," Wanda repeated, putting the paper down and picking up her cooling coffee. She idly glanced around and almost spluttered.

No more than six feet away stood two men in spotless suits, expensive ties and diamond tie clips and rings. One was Syl, the other was the second man that had been with Harrison and who taken her out to witness what would happen to any male friends she had.

She carefully raised her paper again. Had they been looking for her? Why hadn't her danger sense warned her?

"I can't see him," Wanda heard Syl say.

"He can't be far away," the other said. "You keep checking in here, I'll look outside."

Wanda let out the breath she was unconsciously holding. First mistake – she knew that Harrison had her apartment watched, but she had never even considered that she might have been followed. But if those two weren't after her – who were they after?

Hearing the tone of a cell phone, Wanda risked a glance above the paper. Syl stared at the terminal door and spoke monosyllables into his phone. When he closed the flap and ended the call, he strode outside.

Wanda gulped the rest of her coffee, wrapped the muffin in a serviette, pushed it in her bag, grabbed it and her paper, and headed towards the side entrance to the terminal. From memory, she knew that the local bus that went past her father's house left from there. Somehow, the thought of going home suddenly held less fears than staying in the open with Harrison's goons wandering around.

"Oh no!" Wanda saw Syl getting into a car outside the door and the other talking to him. Wanda backed into the terminal further and prepared to seek shelter in the ladies room.

Suddenly Syl pointed and the other took off across the road towards a park. Wanda had a momentary glimpse of a running figure in jeans and a baggy jumper. Syl revved the car engine and dived into a gap in the traffic then pulled out and raced down the wrong side of the road.

Wanda felt a sudden sympathy for the young man being chased and hoped he would elude them, mainly because she wanted some minor vicarious revenge on them for bashing her brother for no good reason. Maybe they would then get the rough edge of Harrison's tongue for messing up.

That idea made Wanda smile, and she decided it was safe enough to venture out and check the bus timetable at the stop outside. However, she pulled a beret from her bag and pushed her hair up under it. Not much of a disguise, but it was all she could do.

She had just missed a bus. The next was not due for another fifteen minutes. Wanda decided not to wait where she was and to start walking towards the next stop and skirt the park.

She heard a police siren, coming closer, and turned to see where it was headed. Someone running from the park flattened her. As she picked herself off the footpath, she recognised the fawn suit of Harrison's goon and the dark blue sedan Syl was driving.

"Come on, Rocky. Hurry!"

Wanda laughed as the police car kept going after Syl.

"Are you alright?" a young male voice asked with concern.

Wanda turned, brushing her hands on her clothes.

"Yeah," she told him, recognising him as the person Syl and his mate had been chasing.

"You got away from them then?"

"Yeah!" the young man agreed with a grin. "I climbed a tree. I couldn't see them getting their suits dirty."

"Hands, yes, suits, no," Wanda agreed.

"Do you know them?" the other asked cautiously.

"I've seen them in action," Wanda said obliquely.

"They weren't after you too, were they?"

"It seems not!" Wanda considered.

"But they might have been?"

"Yeah – they might have been," Wanda said softly, then louder. "I've got a bus to catch in ten minutes. I need to cut through the park."

Wanda began to walk off; she sensed the other following.

"You don't want to be involved with them!"

Wanda didn't turn.

"I don't need you to be my conscience. I already have one."

"Do you know who they are?" the other persisted.

"Harrison's bully boys," Wanda muttered, pausing to look at the speaker.

"Harrison Franklin?"

Wanda shrugged. She had assumed that Harrison was his surname.

"Those two in the suits were Sylvester and Rocky Franklin!"

Wanda felt herself go pale again. She had heard those names before as being members of a powerful crime syndicate. And if Harrison was Harrison Franklin, the patriarch of the Franklin organization - he was definitely not a nice old man.

"Oh God! I'm in trouble!" Wanda groaned. "Are there any more of their goons after you?"

"Possibly. I must have been followed from the casino. That's probably how they found out where I was. Why would they want you?"

Wanda shook her head. "Why do you care?"

"Why do you?" was the retort. "My name's Mike."

"Wanda," she responded automatically. "Mike, I'd like to stay and talk to you, but I am a dangerous person to know. If they are already after you for whatever reason. They'll be doubly after you if you're seen with me."

"You're not that bad a person?" Mike insisted.

"You don't know me!" Wanda snapped. "I'm not a nice person."

"I don't believe you. What is Harrison Franklin to you?"

"What does that matter?"

"I want to know."

Wanda wanted to know why she wanted to confide in a perfect stranger.

"What are you to them?" she countered.

Mike sensed the wariness in the woman.

"I work for Sylvester Franklin, up in 'Frisco," Mike admitted cautiously. "I hate his guts, but he's got me tied up – I can't walk out on him. But I found some information about him and passed it to a friend. I didn't want them to suspect me so I disappeared to the casino for a few days – but now they are looking for me."

"What do you think they'll do to you?" Wanda asked in a small voice.

"I've given them no reason to doubt me for the past five years, so they'll probably beat me up and send me back to work."

Mike seemed to be calm outwardly, but Wanda sensed he was worried.

"I work for Harrison," Wanda admitted in return for Mike's confidence. "I have some personal business to attend to. A very sick friend needs me. It's none of his business, so I didn't tell him I was going. I don't want him to know about my friend and anyway I need to lie low and no one will look for me in a hospital up here."

"He won't like that," Mike told her seriously.

"I know! Mike, you're a nice guy, but please go away. If Harrison's men see you talking to me, he'll have you killed."

Mike nodded sagely.

"So that's it!"

"What?"

"He's put his claim on you. Are you fucking him too?"

"Sort of, and that's what I want. I told you, I'm not a nice person. He's my ticket to a better style of living."

"You are nice, but he's poison. Once he claims you – you'll only be free of him if you are dead. And I know for a fact that some of his past women are dead – or insane. Are you absolutely sure you want to stay loyal to him for life?"

"You're trying to scare me," Wanda accused.

"Too right! Stop it going any further."

"No!"

"He's not worth dying for," Mike told her. "Believe me – he expects loyalty, he doesn't give it."

Wanda tried to shock Mike into leaving her alone and described in graphic detail how Harrison made her feel."

Mike did not even blink.

"I know he's good. I've seen him at it. He once gave Sylvester a lesson in how to deal with a woman. I was allowed to watch too. She wasn't much older than you, and believed his nice old man act. That was until she realised that he was going to make love to her with an audience. Naturally, she didn't want that and fought him. But in a short time, he had her helpless in his control. She allowed him to do as he pleased. Actually begged for him to rape her again –

and it was rape. He wasn't gentle. Then he made Sylvester take her while he watched."

"And you?" Wanda asked, horrified.

"I was not to be so privileged. I was reminded, very clearly, of certain 'facts' of my employment and warned to keep my mouth shut."

"I'd even do that for him," Wanda said, horrified at herself.

Mike took her face in his hands and very deliberately kissed her. He meant it to distract her, but he was unprepared for the electricity that passed between them as their lips met. Wanda sensed it too.

"No." It was almost a yell. She pulled away and ran off along the path.

Mike let her go and cursed his fate. He was not as hopeful about his future as he pretended. If the Franklins had found out about the tape he had arranged to get to the police, they would be after him first, in spite of his misdirection. If they were convinced of his guilt, his life was measurable in days or hours. Best to let her go – keep her ignorant of … damn it. Love at first sight was an overrated myth. But if he survived his little ruse of misdirection, and he could make use of the information he had learnt at the casino … Sylvester Franklin would go down!

Wanda ran; her mind totally confused. That kiss had been something important. Harrison had never kissed her like that – in such an intimate gesture. He played with her – like she was a toy, a possession – not a reasoning, thinking human being. He gave her pleasure, but he did not let her pleasure him. She was not his equal.

A sense of shame overwhelmed her. I'm no better than a pet dog, whining to be petted or kicked by its master, she thought in disgust.

"Forget about that!" Wanda told herself, aloud.

It was not easy. Having an eidetic memory was useful, but it had drawbacks. However, she had learnt to control and ignore unpleasant memories.

Like she had learnt to ignore the consequences of being a criminal, an insidious little mind voice interrupted. She ignored the voice.

"I have to get my head straight," Wanda said. "First – I have to help Elisabeth."

That's it. Nothing else matters right now. The police are looking for me. Harrison will be and I can't let my family be connected with him. So I have to get home; without being noticed, and lie low until I have done all I can for Elisabeth. Then I will have to deal with the rest of my life as it comes. If I die – it won't matter – not if Elisabeth survives. I don't care what happens, if only Elisabeth gets better.

Wanda kept repeating that rationalisation as a mantra, all the way to the bus stop. By then she had forced all her other worries into a state of limbo. The notion of taking a taxi crossed her mind, but the need to be inconspicuous was still foremost in her mind. Taxi drivers often had inconveniently good memories. She would be noticed less on a bus.

When the bus arrived, Wanda flashed her prepaid ticket at the driver. She was right; he didn't even look at her.

A new mantra replaced the other in Wanda's mind.

"I'm here to help Elisabeth."

Chapter 6

Wanda took two deep breaths and rang the doorbell of the house she hadn't been in for over six years. She heard childish voices behind the door, then it opened.

Sandy Willard glared at her.

"I'll tell Dad you are here," he said without inviting her in.

Wanda felt particularly exposed on the doorstep and took the initiative of entering and closing the door behind her.

Two toddlers stared at her, both with thumbs in their mouth. Two older boys, about four or five, eyed her from the doorway leading to the dining room.

Funny, she felt like an intruder in her old home, but never did in strange buildings.

How many stepbrothers and sisters did she have now?

Charles Willard hastened to the hallway, when Sandy had told him that his eldest daughter had come home. He was closely followed by his second oldest son, Paul who was even taller than his brother and much taller than Wanda.

"Gwen?" Paul exclaimed in delighted surprise.

Wanda forced a smile. "Yeah, it's me."

"Wow! This is great. How long are you staying?"

Wanda shrugged, avoiding looking at her father.

"Paul, you can talk to her later. Gwen has come a long way and we need to talk."

"Sure, Dad," Paul agreed readily and turned to the four younger children. "That guys, is your oldest sister."

Wanda followed her father along a vividly familiar passage and into his home office. The memories of her last days at home were equally fresh. It wasn't the time to revive those arguments. She was here to help Elisabeth.

Charles Willard moved two chairs into a corner away from his desk. It was a deliberate ploy to distance them both from their last 'talk'.

Wanda appreciated the gesture and sat in the chair that was usually reserved for her father's important guests.

"Hello, Dad," Wanda hoped she did not sound as tense as she felt.

"Hello, Gwen," Charles Willard greeted gently in reply. "Are you well?"

"Well enough," Wanda answered, trying not to step back into the manners of her fifteen-year-old self. "How ... how is Elisabeth, really?"

"Failing fast," Charles admitted with a catch in his voice. "She's hooked up to so many machines – they are all that's keeping her with us."

"What do they think I can do?" Wanda was keeping control of herself by the narrowest margin.

"You are her full sister. You are not sick. They want to run tests."

"Damn, it's Mum – all over again." Wanda stood abruptly, and turned her face away from her father so he could not see she was crying. "The people I let myself care most for, get sick and die."

"It wasn't your fault!" Charles told his daughter. "The illness is genetic."

"I know. But they said Elisabeth had no sign of it. Why did she get sick?"

"She had an odd fever, about twelve months ago. She seemed to get over it, but the doctor's think it weakened her immune system."

"I thought it was safe to keep in touch with her. I need her. I need her to be well," Wanda said with anguish in her voice.

"They told me you did have signs of the illness," Charles reminded her. "But you are well."

"I learnt to fight," Wanda said.

"We need you to teach Elisabeth to fight."

"Not like I do!"

Charles Willard had a sudden revelation. The answer to why his eldest daughter had become a stranger. He stood up and walked over to her and placed his arm lightly around her shoulders.

"So that is what brought it on. You were afraid you would get sick. Afraid to die like your Mother."

"Not afraid. I was sick." Wanda told him. "I was feeling exactly like Mum was feeling when she was sick."

"How could you know? You were only four then," Charles asked gently.

"You don't understand, Dad. I shared her pain."

"We all shared her pain," Charles told her.

"No, not like that. I felt her pain, all of it. I used to think I was helping her, but I began to hate her. I wanted her to die so it would end. I hated myself for wishing that."

"Don't blame yourself for that. I often wished to be able to ease her pain. She was a wonder; so sick, but thinking only of us. She said, often, that it was only because of you that she kept going."

"Then I rejected her, and she died."

"She would have died, sooner or later. She lasted longer than I dared hope, because of you. Now Elisabeth needs you. However you did it before, you had the strength to overcome the illness. Elisabeth needs that strength."

The office door opened and Sandy brought in the morning paper – carefully folded to show the major headline. He glanced at the tableau of his father seeming to hug his oldest sister, scowled and left. "Just brought the paper in."

"Stuart didn't think you'd come," Charles broke the silence.

"I wasn't sure I could," Wanda admitted. "It isn't the most convenient time to have time off from work."

Charles didn't make the mistake of asking questions.

"I'm glad you came. I don't want to lose both of Katya's children."

"You haven't lost me exactly," Wanda told him. "I just don't want … you to be associated with me."

"I'm not going to ask you to tell me anything you don't want to," Charles promised, though it was a difficult decision.

"I appreciate that," Wanda said honestly.

"Stuart told me you changed your name," Charles commented.

"Yes."

"Wanda Dean."

"Yes, but for now, I'll be Gwen Willard. What else did Sandy tell you? Did he say he thought I was a prostitute?"

Charles sidestepped the question.

"He told me you worked long hours in a restaurant."

"Well, you can assure him that I don't earn my money in bed!"

Charles managed a chuckle.

"What else do you know about me?" Wanda asked abruptly.

Her father weighed up the risks of being too candid, but Wanda seemed to be demanding honesty.

"I know you were sent to a training centre for twelve months. Elisabeth told me you had a rough time of it."

Wanda nodded.

"Just so you have things straight," Wanda said carefully. "I'm not a nice person to know. I intend to leave as soon as I've done all I can for Elisabeth. You would be advised to forget my new name and not try to find me again. I have done everything possible to disassociate myself from you. Please respect that. Whatever my future holds – I'll deal with it on my own."

Charles carefully lowered his arm. The moment of rapport was over.

There was a knock at the door.

"Come in."

Sandy stood in the doorway.

"Vera just called from the hospital. Elisabeth is worse. If she is going to do anything useful – you need to get there right away."

"I'm ready," Wanda said, her face under control again. Her feelings and emotions were now hidden behind a mask of indifference.

Charles Willard grabbed his jacket and newspaper, indicating for Wanda to precede him.

Sandy held the car keys.

"I'll drive," he told them. "That way I can bring the car back, if you decide to stay."

"Fine." Charles Willard agreed.

As he waited for the car to be backed out of the garage, Charles Willard used his mobile phone to call ahead to the hospital and spoke to Elisabeth's specialist and told him who he was bringing to the hospital. They would be ready for Wanda when she arrived.

Chapter 7

Wanda was introduced to her father's third wife, who met them outside the intensive care unit. This must be the mother of the four youngest children at the house and the fifth slung in a sling in front of her.

Wanda turned her head away after a brief, "Hello" and stared at the activity inside the unit. The woman might be her stepmother, but she was a stranger and she meant to keep it that way.

"They had to resuscitate her," Vera Willard was telling her husband and eldest stepson.

Wanda made no sign that she had heard.

Sandy glanced at his sister's impassive face and wondered if she really cared.

The specialist came out of the ICU a few moments later, and introduced himself to Wanda.

"I'm Doctor Rickard. I am glad you are here. We need to take various samples from you and run all sorts of tests…"

"Do whatever you need to, Doctor. That's why I'm here," Wanda interrupted. "I'm ready when you are."

"Great, this way then. We will get you admitted and all your details."

"Let's go," Wanda directed.

"Do you want me to come with you?" Vera Willard offered generously.

"No thank you," Wanda refused, turning to follow the doctor.

Sandy gave a snort of derision. "Rude bitch."

"Stuart!" Charles Willard rebuked his son. "She came. Let her be."

"Read your paper, Father," Sandy suggested. "Then you'll see why she came. She's hiding."

"That's enough!" Charles glared at his son. "Take Vera home, will you. I'll stay a while."

Charles walked down the passage to the visitors lounge and settled himself in one of the armchairs. The staff would find him if they needed him. He opened his paper.

The headline on the front page concerned the murder of two security guards at the new Allard Tower in downtown LA. He read that one suspect had been arrested and police were seeking another, a woman. A sketch taken from a security film was reproduced in the paper. Even without reading the name and other details of the woman suspect, Charles knew why his son had made comments about Wanda, as she chose to call herself now, being in hiding.

The woman in the sketch had black hair and oriental eyes, but the artist had captured the bone structure in the face and there was no mistaking the likeness of this person, to his dead first wife. The make-up might fool people who did not know Wanda…

"Wanda."

The name came out involuntarily. It was the pet name his first wife had given her first child. Elisabeth was Lishka. He had not thought of that in years.

"Senator Willard," a nurse approached him. "Your daughter seems to have stabilised. If you wish to sit with her you may."

"Thank you," he answered and he made his way into the now distressingly familiar maze of equipment and monitors.

He moved a chair back to the side of the bed so he could hold his daughter's hand. She was still in a coma, still as pale as death.

"Wanda has come," he said softly to the unresponsive form on the bed. "Wanda has come to help you. She is here, at the hospital. Can you feel her near you?"

The monitors continued their monotonous pinging and the respirator continued its set rhythm. He wanted to think that Elisabeth could hear him and gain strength from his words, but he could discern no changes.

He continued to repeat his message.

Wanda was installed in a private ward, just down the hall from the ICU. The staff wasted no time starting the 'tests' and when her father and step-mother entered the room, the third round of the doctor's invasion had just concluded.

Wanda had a foul headache, mainly from lack of sleep, and was sore in more places than she cared to count. Her mood was even less cordial than usual.

"How are you?" Charles asked.

"I've got a fucking headache and this pack of vampires and ghouls won't give me anything and I really just want to sleep," Wanda did not bother toning down her comments. "Don't feel obliged to visit me. I would rather you didn't."

"If you want anything, have the nurses ask me," Charles offered, ignoring the tone of her answer.

"Fine. Whatever. Shut the door after you."

Vera Willard was not used to anyone speaking to her important husband in that way.

"Has she always been like that?"

"She's … not as tough as she is making out," Charles told is wife. "And that was mild, compared to six years ago. I'll ask you to respect her wish to be left alone, and not to visit her."

Vera held her tongue, rather than say that she would not give her husband's oldest child a civil time of day.

The hospital staff called her Gwen and tried to jolly her into a better frame of mind. They assumed her taciturn manner was due to worry about her sister. It was in part, but it was also because she had too much time to think about what Harrison must be making of her disappearance. The police were a minor worry by comparison.

Her peace of mind was further eroded by reading in the paper about the death of a prisoner in custody. The man's name was Jack something, but he was a suspect in the murder of the security guards. There was mention of an organised crime link. Now the police had redoubled their efforts to find the dead man's accomplice - her.

After catching up on her sleep, Wanda convinced the doctors to let her walk around between the sessions of tests. Some of the time, she spent sitting with Elisabeth, and if her stepmother or brother were with Elisabeth when she arrived, they would get up and walk out. It suited her fine.

Her father would usually stay, but he said nothing unless she asked him questions.

Elisabeth was holding her own, but not improving.

Other times Wanda simply walked around the hospital. She had promised to stay within the building containing the ICU and to respond to any summons aimed at her.

She had returned from one such walk and was staring out the window of her room at some activity on the lawn below when a tentative voice spoke her name.

Wanda spun around, her body ready to run.

"Mike?"

"Sorry to startle you."

"Why are you here? How did you find me?"

"It was a guess and I spotted you downstairs earlier."

"Why are you still around? Aren't you afraid they'll find you?"

"Nuh! This is the last place they'd expect me to be, and I don't intend to stay much longer. I'll head back to work tomorrow, and act innocent. I prepared my alibi by going to their casino, losing a wad, and leaving a trail an idiot could follow. I have always played dumb, so they don't consider me particularly clever. They will easily believe that I decided on a gambling spree. At worst, they'll catch up to me, bash me a bit, feel superior and not be surprised if I act meek and scared. They have no evidence to suggest that I knew anything of the tape."

"It's an awful risk," Wanda told him, her guts were in knots.

"I know, but now isn't the time to explain why I hate Sylvester and what I had to do for him. But it was where I wanted to be. I am just about ready to pull the plug on him. When I am ready, I'll go to the FBI and they will put me into witness protection."

"I'm scared for you," Wanda admitted. "But I would like to see Sylvester Franklin put away."

"And Harrison?" Mike probed.

"If he goes, I'll be with him," she said flatly. "I'm gone anyway."

"The murder of the guards?"

Wanda nodded.

"Go to the police, offer to testify against them," Mike urged.

"No, I can't. I can't prove anything against them."

Mike put his face into his hands for a moment.

"Okay, listen. Do something for me?" Mike looked earnestly at her.

"I have copies of the stuff that I intend to get to the police in a small flat I own at Stimson's Beach - 23A Worths Lane. I also have a deposit box key there, it's for a box at the local bank where I have papers for a new identity I have as David Martin. If you need to escape, go there. Get the stuff and offer it to the police in exchange for protection. Just leave the key, okay."

Wanda nodded.

Mike leant forward and gave her a long lingering kiss.

"I wish … things were different," he murmured. "I have to go. I need to be back in Frisco before Sylvester gets back."

"I have money with me," Wanda offered. "Take what you need to get there fast."

She went to the cupboard and dragged out her bag. From it she pulled about five hundred dollars.

"Here, take it."

"I owe you one," Mike said, moved by her generosity. He was reluctant to leave.

"Code Blue, ICU. Code Blue, ICU."

Mike saw the horrified expression on Wanda's face.

"Oh, NO! Elisabeth."

Wanda ran out of the room, Mike's presence forgotten.

He decided it was a good time to leave.

Elisabeth had stabilised again, but it had been a near thing. She was getting worse. Wanda didn't think she was helping at all. She had been sent back to her room like a naughty child and had paced the room until the nurse came and told her the crisis had passed. She was waiting now for the doctor to come and see her.

When he entered, Wanda rounded on him.

"Why aren't you doing anything to help her?" she yelled at him. "I'm here. Why isn't there anything I can do?"

"You are helping her and us. It's just that your sister has a number of competing problems." Rickard began, calmly. He gently propelled Wanda towards a chair.

"The main one is that her body is producing a protein that is causing her organs to fail. Dialysis is helping, but the levels are still increasing. We've identified the structure of the protein and found the same substance in your blood but at very low levels. We have also discovered that your body has created anti bodies to negate the protein. We are trying to synthesise an anti-body to match it."

"You're running out of time," Wanda told him.

"I have a proposition, a last ditch attempt to stop the levels rising further," Rickard started.

"What is it?" Wanda demanded.

"The procedure will be dangerous for you."

"I don't care!"

Rickard studied the woman before him and nodded. She had not complained about all the intrusive tests he had ordered. He had not expected her to pull back from this.

"I want to hook you up to your sister, and use you to filter the protein out of her blood."

"So my anti bodies will catch the protein in her."

"Exactly. The risk is that the levels in her might overwhelm your system too. Before you can create enough anti bodies."

"Can you start slowly and work up?"

"That's the plan."

"Ok, do it! What other problem does she have?"

"Her immune system is seriously depressed."

"AIDS?"

"No, we've eliminated that possibility. When we have her stabilised and she is stronger, we want to try a bone marrow transplant. You are a perfect match. We hope that will help her and give her the anti-bodies so that she can start producing her own."

"Let's start now," Wanda insisted.

Wanda lay awake in the dimness, staring at the roof of the ICU. Sleep eluded her and they could not give her any drugs because they could harm the subtle balances in her sister. She had a headache and felt nauseous; symptoms she had dutifully reported to the nursing staff. Every hour, the nurses changed her position slightly, propped her with pillows and being careful not to disrupt the critical connection to her sister. Wanda had those tubes in her right arm and a fluid drip in her left. Even with the regular movements, Wanda felt she urgently wanted to move. The inactivity was painful. Nor could she read, or watch TV. The patients in ICU were normally not well enough for either.

She felt as helpless now as she had at sixteen, except the doctors and machines were not the cruel sadistic warder or the older, longer serving inmates. She was too tired to fight off the memories she evoked.

At sixteen, veteran of the streets for almost a year, she had been cocky and self-confident and proud of her new skill of lock picking. Then she had been caught, charged, sentenced. Even then, it had seemed a joke. Free lodging for a year with a bed, no matter how rough. The reality had been an emotional trauma.

Most of the warders had been strict, no nonsense and fair. Several had seen her as a naïve child, ripe to abuse and torment for their pleasure. And she been naïve. In there, she had nowhere to run from trouble. Nor would she tamely submit to being everybody's slave — the lowest scum in the supposedly non-existent pecking order. So they beat her, kicked her, hurt her in any way they could. After a time, when that treatment only roused stoic indifference, they progressed to worse humiliations. Such as stealing her clothes and making her stay naked all day. And being held down and raped by two of the oldest girls. This had happened over and over again for perhaps a month. She had learnt by then to bear the pain, show no signs of it and she had finally made friends and had the support to stand up to the others who had begun to be bluffed by her lack of fear.

Valuable lessons for dealing with the Franklins. Something she'd have to do all too soon.

The pain she felt now was different, but familiar. It was a bone deep muscle ache, the pain of merely breathing, in and out. It was the pain that surged when they moved her.

She wouldn't give in to it. Wouldn't.

She fell into and out of a doze, aware at times of the jab of a needle as blood was taken from her and machines being connected to her and the doctors discussing her in worried tones.

She was hot, thirsty. She called out for a drink and got no answer.

Chapter 8

Someone was putting coolness on her head. It felt like heaven. And there was something like ice on her lips. Her tongue moved towards the moisture. She wanted to protest when it was removed, but a straw was placed there instead.

"Drink, Gwen," a familiar but implacable voice urged.

It was an effort to drink, but it was worth it.

"She's coming around."

Wanda opened her eyes but it took a while for her to focus enough to identify which brother was staring at her.

"Glad you are awake," Sandy said mildly. "I hope you don't mind me saying that you look awful. If I might judge, you look worse than I did after your friends finished with me."

"Is that all the thanks I get?" Wanda said in a weak drawl. "I'm sick. Go away!"

"No you're not. You never get sick. You're faking."

Wanda refused to comment. She felt like a steam roller had run over her.

"Don't you even want to know how Elisabeth is doing?"

"She's better," Wanda said, knowing it was true, though she couldn't say how she knew.

"She's probably aching in every muscle in her body – like I am."

"The doctor unhooked you two days ago. You were running a dangerously high temperature. It's been slowly coming down. I'll give you this, Sis. I couldn't have done what you did, even if I had been suitable."

Sandy began to massage her arm with a firm practised skill. He worked his way to the other arm and then to each leg in turn.

"You need to get up and walk around. Get some gentle exercise to get the blood flowing more quickly."

"You're probably right," Wanda agreed. "I can't stay here for ever. When do you start at the Academy?"

"Just under a week," Sandy told her."

"I'll be gone by then."

Sandy stopped massaging. "You won't be better by then."

"I'm only faking, remember," Wanda gave his words back to him.

"Why by then?"

"When I leave here, I'll go back to being Wanda Dean and no relation to you. So you, the trainee cop, will have no conflicts of conscience. You will be able, if the topic comes up, to say you don't know where I am. And when I leave here, I'll be the unpleasant bitch you met in LA and arresting me will be a public service."

"When you leave here, everyone will be looking for you," Sandy decided to warn her.

"Not just the police," Wanda agreed.

"Did you know that they arrested the man that killed the guards?"

Wanda nodded.

"They have your picture in the paper. Not just your made up face, but your real one and your name."

"I know."

"Do you know that they have linked that robbery to the abduction of the European trade consul the night before," Sandy went on relentlessly. "He was found floating near the docks. He was a rival of one of the large crime syndicates."

Sandy was watching his sister's face and saw the flash of fear.

"Scared? I'm glad, because your partner, the one who killed the guards, was found dead in his cell. Your boss obviously feared he knew too much. Now, even if you didn't pull the trigger, you are being hunted. They want a conviction. They want to send someone to the electric chair. They will want to milk you dry first about your boss. No doubt your boss will be hunting you just as assiduously to make sure you don't."

"Tell the doctor I want to talk to him," Wanda said, her face impassive again.

"He'll be in this evening."

Sandy walked out

Wanda wanted to get up. Sandy's massage had been effective in reducing the muscle ache. His summation of the situation of Wanda Dean had reminded her of secondary priorities.

Now was not the time to stay wallowing helplessly in bed. She picked up the wet face cloth and washed her face. The drip in her left arm was a nuisance, and the two remaining monitors, more so. The latter she ripped off and she had just taken out the drip when two nurses burst into the area.

"What are you doing?" the older one demanded.

"I don't need the monitors and I don't need the drip!"

"You've just woken up after being unconscious for five days," the other nurse protested. "It is not up to you to decide what you need."

"I don't need them," Wanda repeated defiantly. "I need to be able to walk around. I won't get better by lying here."

"Nurse, bring a new kit for the drip," the senior woman instructed.

"I'll take that out too!" Wanda threatened.

The nurse chose not to comment and busied herself taking Wanda's pulse, blood pressure and temperature."

The younger nurse returned with the kit and Doctor Rickard.

The doctor looked at her chart, made an examination of his own and offered a compromise.

"The monitors can stay off," he told the nurse who glared back at Wanda's smirk.

"But, young woman, the drip will remain! Your temperature is still elevated and you have not had proper nourishment for a week. In addition, the levels of substances in your blood are a long way from normal. You will be able to walk around with the drip. The catheter will also remain in, at least until I see you in the morning."

Rickard watched as the drip was re-inserted. Wanda had massive bruises around the site of the previous drip insertion and the blood transfer site. They had to find a vein in her wrist.

"How are you feeling?" Rickard asked once Wanda had subsided. She told him what he wanted to know – as she guessed that Elisabeth, who couldn't tell him, would be feeling the same.

"Was it your idea to send Sandy in to annoy me?"

"He obviously got you raring to go," Rickard commented. "I was very concerned about your condition the last day or two. That is why I had to disconnect you from the transfusion process. Your vital signs were alarming."

"What about Elisabeth?" Wanda asked him "Did I help her?"

"She is showing signs of coming around," Rickard sounded pleased. "The physio treating her and massaging her has noticed an improvement. It is still too early to say if the crisis is past, but since the transfusion procedure, there haven't been any more alarms. Her blood levels are normalising. The level of the invading protein has dropped, though yours rose as the substance was shared between you. The important thing is that her levels are still slowly dropping. We think she might be starting to produce the antibody. We need to watch you carefully too. You have a lot of the protein in your system still and we need to make sure your body is coping with it. Especially after that raging fever you had. So rest for tonight, I'll prescribe a mild sedative to help you sleep and I will let you up in the morning."

The sedative wasn't working. Wanda lay awake, more relaxed in body but not in mind. The aches, at least, had subsided since having the sedative. She wondered if they were due in part to tension.

Wanda needed to stop lying around. She sat up and waited for a bout of dizziness to pass. Then she swung her legs over the side of the bed nearest the drip and felt the catheter against her leg.

"Damn, drips at both ends," she murmured to herself.

It didn't stop her sliding to her feet. She wanted to see her sister with her own eyes. To do that, she had to walk around the bank of machines. Her first walk in almost a week and she felt as weak as an ancient crone. All she'd been doing was lying in bed. She refused to admit the relief when she sat herself on the chair next to Elisabeth's bed. Her left hand still held the lower drip bag, but her right went from the drip stand to her sister's hand.

In the subdued lighting, Elisabeth's face looked grey and she had dark shadows around her eyes. She had lost weight. The lines of her face were sharply defined and the bones in her hand felt like a delicate filigree.

"Damn it, Lishka, you gave me a fright. I thought I had lost you, and I need you. I need you alive. You are my anchor, the only thing keeping me from being totally out of control. You are my one true friend. The only person who knows the worst of me and doesn't despise me. And I can't stay here much longer."

"Wanda?"

The voice was like a wisp of thought.

Wanda watched the eyelids flutter, and she very gently increased the pressure on her sister's hand.

"I'm here," Wanda assured her sister. "I came for you."

"I felt … you here."

Wanda felt the tears in her eyes as her sister focussed on her face. She didn't care.

"I knew… you would."

The night Nurse came into the room.

"Why are you out of bed?"

"She's awake," was all Wanda said.

The nurse checked all the monitors and made notes on Elisabeth's chart.

"Glad you are back with us, Elisabeth. Gwen, you mustn't tire her."

"I won't, I promise. I just want to see her, talk to her. When she is tired, she can sleep. I couldn't."

"I could increase the dose of sedative," the nurse offered.

"No," Wanda refused. "I don't like the fuzzy minded feel. I'll sleep when I get sleepy."

"I like … her here"

"No more than ten minutes."

Wanda nodded.

When the ward was quiet again, Wanda spoke.

"I can't stay any longer, Lishka."

"Trouble?"

"Yeah."

"I wish…another way."

"I have to do things my way. I can't fight the illness by lying in bed. I need the risk, of death, of failure … but I need you too. I need to have you in my mind, to talk to, to imagine you talking to me, to be my conscience."

"Don't stop...talking … to me. I need you… alive … too. That man … grey hair … puts …darkness on you."

Wanda thought of Mike and made a decision.

"I will, if I can, distance myself from him." She wondered how Elisabeth had known about Harrison.

After a while, "They want to do a bone marrow transplant - when you're stronger. I can't stay that long."

"I … understand. Are… you well?"

"No, but I've beaten this before. I'll do it again, but it's got to be my way."

"Go … tonight."

Wanda stood and leant over her sister and gave her a brief kiss.

The night staff never saw her go. They returned for their next check and found the drip and catheter disconnected, an empty bed and all Wanda's things missing. The police were notified, but there was no trace of Gwenda Willard.

Chapter 9

Wanda found a truck driver willing to take her back to L.A. and when he stopped on the outskirts for fuel, she left him. She was on her home territory now and knew how to get to her intended destination.

Even though it was early morning, and the restaurant where she worked would be closed, it was one place that Wanda knew how to get into and to neutralise the alarm. In there, she would be able to find a place to curl up in for a few undisturbed hours of sleep.

A rough hand shook her awake and rolled her over.

"You've some nerve coming here!" Green shouted at her.

"I didn't have anywhere else to go!" Wanda said sullenly. "I even lost my keys."

"You look like you've been mugged!"

"A really brilliant observation," Wanda commented sarcastically.

"Police were here – asking for you!"

"What for?"

"Don't care! Don't want you here!"

"You owe me two days wages," Wanda countered, crawling to her knees.

She was hoping that if he got near a phone, he would call Harrison. She was sure that he knew she worked for him, was almost sure he would know how to call him. It was her main reason for being there.

It was a calculated risk too. He might just call the police – but Harrison was more likely to reward him for finding his missing employee.

While Green was out of the room, Wanda walked around to get her muscles less stiff.

"He had your stuff brought here," Green said when he returned, money in hand. "Police have your place staked."

Wanda shrugged. "I'll have my stuff too, then."

Green shoved the money in her hand. "I'll get it and then you can go!"

After waiting five minutes, Wanda decided the man was dawdling on purpose. In another five minutes she was sure. The man who walked in the back door was one of Harrison's goons – well, sons.

It had to be Rocky Franklin himself. It was salutary to see the look of distaste on his face. Wanda did not smile, but she knew she looked almost as bad as her sister had and all the bruises on her arms were visible. However, he could not see all the bruises from the doctors' procedures.

"So, you decided to return," Rocky sneered. "The Old Man wasn't happy about you running off."

"Would he have been happier if I had stayed in my place and been caught by the heat?" Wanda stared at Rocky as if she had no guilt in her mind. At the same time, her appearance would make him feel she was no threat.

"What was I supposed to do?"

Rocky shrugged, and Wanda took that as a victory and turned her back on him to pick up her "stuff".

"What does he want me to do?"

"You're to come with me," Rocky said flatly.

"Where?" Wanda pulled a large pack onto her back to hide her shudder. The interview with Harrison was going to be difficult.

Rocky didn't answer. Wanda shrugged acceptance and waited expectantly. She followed when he turned and walked out the back door to the alley.

Wanda had the distinct impression that Rocky did not want to touch her. He was watching her out of the corner of his eye and his nose was twitching as if he smelt something rotten. It amused her and she hoped it had the same effect on Harrison. Wanda was immune to her smell. The truck driver had smelt of sweat, stale beer and the foul cigars that he smoked. Her clothes had absorbed the odour - and she had not had a decent shower for a week. It should certainly help distance her from the boss.

The car that Rocky led her to was a black Mercedes limousine and the driver was on hand to open the doors. Wanda noticed his nostrils twitch too but his face remained blank. Wanda went in first to the far corner of the seat. Rocky took that nearest the open door. The driver closed it and went to his seat. He turned on the air-conditioner and that spread a deodorising fragrance.

The car moved off silently and although the windows were darkened, Wanda felt sure of their destination – Harrison's mansion in Beverly Hills.

Her hunch was correct and on arrival, she followed Rocky to Harrison's office.

He was facing the window that overlooked the front garden. He would have seen them arrive.

"So you decided to come back?" he said without turning.

Wanda knew he was preparing to remind her of her place and his power. She said nothing. She stood quietly looking neither defiant nor grovelling. She concentrated on thinking that she had overcome diversity to get there.

He turned, and gave her a penetrating stare. "What happened? Why did you run off?"

"I'd just got home after the last job with Harry," Wanda said. Her voice was unsteady and she was feeling weak. "I happened to see the police car pull up outside my place. I didn't know if it was after me, but I wasn't about to wait and find out. I grabbed a bag, threw a few things into it and left out the back way."

"Where did you go?"

"I just walked around, keeping out of sight." Wanda lied. "I suppose I was going generally north. I got to a bus stop just as a bus drew in so I hopped on it. I didn't even notice where it was going. I got off at the last stop and looked for a place to flop."

Wanda had thought her story out carefully. She claimed to have woken when she was hit by sticks and a pipe; then again in hospital with a drip in her arm and concussion.

"As soon as I could get out of the hospital I did and hitched a ride back."

"A pretty story," Rocky sneered. "You reckon you're streetwise."

"I was tired, and I'd had a fright. I was more interested in keeping out of sight of police."

"Didn't they talk to you about your accident?" Rocky accused.

"It sounded like I was the latest of many and I told them I knew nothing."

"Did you give them your name?" Harrison asked. He was still watching her closely.

"No, I made one up."

"What was it?"

That wasn't a question she wanted to answer.

"I saw a newspaper with an article about Senator Willard. I said I was Gwen Willard."

Wanda forced a mirthless laugh.

Harrison began to prowl closer, his nose noted the stink of her clothes.

"You should have contacted me," Harrison accused.

The option was ludicrous.

"You have never given me a way to contact you," Wanda tried to sound matter of fact. "I didn't want to come here if the police were watching me. Where were your people when I needed them? Or do they only protect me from baby boys?"

"What makes you think you are that important?" Harrison's tone was dangerous.

"I thought…" Wanda began to lose her train of thought. "I thought I was at least useful to you if nothing else."

Wanda turned away from Harrison, as if trying not to cry in front of him. In fact, she was trying not to show how much her muscles were aching. They were painful enough to bring tears to her eyes.

Harrison turned her head around, saw the pain in her expression and mistook it for something like rejected devotion to him.

"We will finish this conversation after you have cleaned up and slept."

Wanda nodded and felt her legs collapse under her. Harrison was close enough and fast enough to catch her. He felt her lightness and the lack of flesh on her bones.

Someone had stripped her of her stinking clothes and put her in a bed in a small room. There were clean clothes folded on a chair, along with towels and soap.

Neither Harrison nor Rocky would have touched her in her filthy state. So, it must have been some woman servant and Wanda hoped that she had reported all the other bruises to Harrison.

A small clock by the bed told her it was evening. Wanda hoped it was still the same day. She felt stronger now that she had slept well.

Wanda rose from the bed and realised she was fully undressed. She did not let that worry her as she investigated the two doors on the side wall. One was an en-suite and the other a wardrobe.

Wanda spent a long time in the shower washing herself and her hair. Then, as she was dressing, she made use of the expensive toiletries in the room.

Harrison still had not asked her about the last job with Harry. She knew what she intended to say and how. It might make Harrison angry – but she was not going to pretend to be too stupid.

The door of the room was not locked and that made Wanda feel more comfortable. There was, however a servant sitting on a chair outside her door who jumped up as soon as the door opened. The magazine she had been reading fell to the floor.

"You're awake then. The Master was worried."

Wanda doubted it but did not disagree.

"I have a pounding headache," Wanda did admit. "Can you get me anything for it?"

"Certainly, madam."

"And I'm hungry but I don't want anything heavy to eat."

"The Master is at dinner, Mam. You are permitted to join him."

Another good sign.

Wanda followed the woman to the dining room. It was large and expensively furnished. The table, made of polished wood, could seat twenty and had exquisitely carved legs. The carpet underfoot was thick and there was expensive artwork on the walls. The room surpassed anything she had seen before in the homes she had visited with Harry.

What struck Wanda most though, was that for all his reputed wealth, Harrison was the only diner. She almost felt sorry for him, but she remembered Elisabeth's words.

The maid stopped six feet away from Harrison and waited for his attention.

"I've brought Miss Dean, Sir."

"Join me Miss Dean," Harrison instructed.

The maid pulled out the chair nearest where they stood and Wanda slipped onto it. It suited her to be away from Harrison.

She was also glad that she did not have to make polite conversation. Harrison continued to eat, watching her but saying nothing. His regard was unsettling.

A waiter set a place for her then brought in a glass of water and tablets for her headache. He returned in a short time with some soup for her.

It had been a long time since Wanda had worried about table manners but she did recall what she had learnt before she left home. No doubt, compared to Harrison, she was uncouth and uncultured.

Concentrating on her food gave her a reason to ignore Harrison, and the soup was delicious. It was about all her stomach could handle after having no solid food for a week. She hoped she would not be sick. Part of her feeling of weakness was, no doubt, due to lack of food.

"You have created a problem for me," Harrison said, unexpectedly. He had studied her for a long time after he had finished eating and the table had been cleared.

Wanda looked up from contemplating her fingers.

"I can't let you wander around. It seems the police want you and are treating it as a priority to find you."

"I know!" Wanda interrupted him, sounding sour. "They say I'm to be charged with murder, and I didn't kill anyone – it isn't fair."

"They would do it to frighten you," Harrison told her. "Then they'd offer to reduce the charge if you tell them all you know."

"I wouldn't…" Wanda began to protest.

"Do you want to die by electrocution?"

Wanda shuddered.

"If you can't earn your keep, because it is too dangerous on the streets, how can I justify keeping you?"

"Aren't I entitled to some sick leave?" Wanda dared to ask, without looking at Harrison.

She heard him chuckle.

"Tell me about the last job?"

Wanda began when Harry picked her up and gave her opinion of what Harry had done wrong, making no secret of her opinion that the killing had been unnecessary.

"They saw you," Harrison pointed out.

"Yes, but when I'm working for you, I'm always made up to look foreign. Just seeing my face wouldn't have risked Harry or me. Unless one of the guards knew him anyway. He had an electronic key, I thought you had arranged it but he might have bribed a guard."

Harrison continued to quiz her without mercy. All of the stuff they had taken in that robbery had been left in Harry's car and the police had recovered it.

Finally, Wanda said, "I don't question Harry. It is dangerous on the job, and he would belt me one of I did. And you told me very firmly that he was in charge. I do remember some things we saw in the safe."

Harrison was keen to hear all she recalled and seemed to be less intimidating.

"What am I to do with you?" It was a rhetorical question. "If you were me – what would you do?"

"I'm not you! I don't know half of what you know. I just want to keep working for you."

"And if you can't?"

"I don't know. I'm not really smart. Working for you is all I'm good at."

Harrison seemed satisfied with her answer.

Chapter 10

A servant brought in a cordless phone and presented it to Harrison.

"Mr Richard, Sir."

That something of major importance had happened was obvious from the undisguised look of anger on Harrison's face.

"We must get that film at all costs," Harrison said in a tone that allowed no disagreement. "Get Sylvester's PA. I am long overdue for a talk with that creature. Find out where the film is and have our agent ready to meet us at the airport. Bring in any of our people that will be needed."

Harrison stared right through Wanda as if she did not exist. After a while, he rang for a servant and stood up.

"You're coming with me," Harrison told Wanda.

The servant arrived.

"Have the car ready in five minutes and call the airport. The jet must be ready to fly to San Francisco when we get there."

Wanda followed Harrison like a shadow as he went via his office to take a briefcase from under his desk and a paper wrapped object from his safe. He also grabbed a roll of cloth from in his desk. The wrapped objects went into his case. He went directly from there to the car. The driver was settling his jacket as they arrived in the garage but he was ready to open the doors for them.

The drive to the airport seemed short, but the walk through the terminal with so many people about seemed like miles. Wanda kept close to Harrison and hoped her gaunt appearance would make her unrecognisable.

Harrison's executive jet was waiting on the tarmac, its engines warming up. They crossed to it from a ground level door. Wanda had never flown before and the noise of the engines surprised her but the thought of actually flying, excited her.

Harrison entered first up the steps and seated himself in a seat facing forward. He indicated for Wanda to take the seat facing him.

The steward came by and showed Wanda how to buckle up then returned to the rear of the plane.

Wanda was torn between looking out the window and examining the cabin which looked like a lounge room.

Harrison said nothing until the jet had taken off.

"How are your hands?" he asked and Wanda glanced down at them.

"They are okay, Mr Harrison."

"Good. Are you fit to work?"

"I don't think I can climb ropes, but I can work."

Harrison was amused by Wanda's eagerness.

"The job will be too urgent for ropes and fancy methods. You would have to use your wits and you would be constantly at risk of being identified."

Wanda's eyes lit up with the thought of the challenge. This was the sort of thing she needed to recover, the thrill of danger and the chance to prove to Harrison that she could work independently.

"What do I have to do?"

"If I need you – I will tell you," Harrison promised.

The flight was shorter than Wanda expected. It was almost ten o'clock when they arrived at San Francisco airport. Richard Franklin met Harrison and the two spoke urgently as they walked to the waiting limousine. Wanda could not follow their conversation as they were using many unfamiliar references, but it was definitely Sylvester in trouble.

Wanda tried to keep a small profile as she joined a group of strangers in the stretched limo.

"They've moved Syl to the holding cells down town," a gruff voiced man reported. "The tape is in the evidence safe in the prosecutor's office. They'll question Syl tomorrow."

"What's the layout of the prosecutor's office?" Harrison asked.

A different man spoke up and gave the required information, including the security in the building this late at night. Wanda already had a good mental picture of what was needed.

"Who do we have to handle the security?"

"Peters," Richard pointed to a nerdy looking young man.

"Who can handle the safe?"

"Janovik. He can blow it."

"Too noisy, too obvious, no finesse. We don't want them to know we've taken the film."

Richard shrugged. "It's a top of the line model."

Harrison looked at Wanda.

"I've got someone for that. What's the plan, Richard?"

Wanda listened, occasionally shaking her head. It was not how she would handle it.

The decision was that the man who had spoken first would take Wanda up to the prosecutor's office – she would be some important witness. The prosecutor's assistant would follow, that was the second man who had spoken. Wanda would open the safe, take the incriminating tape and replace it with one that would be embarrassing to some other person, close the safe and leave with the others. Overall, the plan seemed rushed and poorly conceived.

"We'll do it," Harrison decided.

All the passengers except Richard and herself left the car to travel in their own vehicles.

"You are going to let her do it?" Richard looked at Wanda as if she were something unpleasant.

"She can do it," Harrison said firmly. "If she fails, she knows that it will be her last failure. But I expect her to succeed, and you need someone good up here."

He didn't have to mention LA was too hot for her.

"You'll need tools and gloves," Harrison said to Wanda and he drew the cloth parcel from his case.

Wanda unwrapped the tool kit and checked what was in it. Richard simply glared at her as she slipped the belt around her waist and hid the toolkit under the loose jumper she was wearing.

"Has Vaughn got the other tape?" Harrison asked.

Richard nodded.

"Then we are set."

The group of four rode up to the twelfth floor in the elevator from the garage. Two of her escorts had badges proving their authority to be in the building at any hour of the day or night. The security guard waved them through because Vaughn, an assistant prosecutor, had called ahead to let them know he was coming in with two witnesses.

The security nerd had no need to do anything until they needed to by-pass the security on the evidence safe. Wanda watched him work and could appreciate his skill. He made Harry look like an amateur.

As soon as the alarm was neutralised, Wanda went to work, displaying her own skill to the amazed audience. She let Vaughn take out the relevant video of the three in the safe. He confirmed his choice with the detective and replaced it with another video that they had with them. The detective had marked it identically to the one they had removed. The safe was closed quickly and the security reset.

Wanda had a premonition of danger as they returned to the outer office. She was closest to the big desk and quickly dived behind it, taking the video with her.

The door opened unexpectedly. Vaughn, the assistant prosecutor, glanced around and saw both Wanda and the film were missing. His relief was tempered by concern about where they were. Then he found it necessary to explain to his superior why he was in the office that late. He had prepared for that, and his boss went into the inner office to prepare for the interrogation of Sylvester Franklin.

Vaughn had to go through the process of interrogating his witness and taking notes, but he was inwardly panicking in case the girl was caught. He had not seen her leave.

Before he left, he asked his boss if he was needed and was relieved when he was waved off.

Wanda had scooted for the door when the tall prosecutor was concentrating on the explanation of his subordinate. She dared to use the lift to return to the basement, crouching down near the floor as the door slid open so that the lift appeared empty to the guard at the security station. Keeping in the shadows, she inched around to where the car she wanted was parked. It was by no means the only car in the garage, so she had cover to hide her movements.

She checked the number plate and the warmth of the muffler, then forced open the luggage compartment. The car had been backed into the space, so the movement was concealed and she only opened the cover far enough for her slight frame to enter, then locked it behind her.

The space was cramped due to the equipment racked there and she used that to hide the video, then she inched around to find a more comfortable position and waited. She still had her gloves on and did not intend to remove them yet.

Finally, she heard the car doors opening and closing and the engine start. There were voices coming from inside the car but they were not clear enough to understand.

When the car engine finally died and the car stopped, Wanda forced the luggage door open. As she slowly lifted the cover, it was yanked from her hand and three guns were aimed at her. The detective holstered his gun and dragged her out.

"Where's the video," he demanded, shaking her.

"In amongst your junk!" Wanda told him in a neutral voice. She watched him hunt for it, aware that Rocky Franklin was giving her a calculating stare.

The entire group followed Rocky to the room where Harrison Franklin waited.

He received a report on the raid along with the assistant prosecutor's estimation that Sylvester would have to be released in the absence of the videotape. All Syl had to do was protest his innocence and let his lawyer handle the rest.

Rocky raised the subject of Wanda arriving in the luggage compartment, but she only smiled as the detective described her disappearing trick. The man had not been amused. Wanda took that to mean he had been on the verge of panic.

"Sure I ran off, but I heard that man coming and acted. You'd left the tape on the desk in plain view. Besides, you probably handled him better without me in the room and there was no chance he'd find the evidence on you. Not to mention the fact that I've got a particular reason not to want to be seen at the moment."

That led to the question of why the report had not mentioned the appearance of the prosecutor.

Wanda let the others deal with that and went to curl up in a chair. She was tired and hungry but she listened to the talk and began to have a hunch about Sylvester's taste in very young bed mates of either sex. The notion sickened her, and it seemed that his family did not want him to continue to pursue it.

Finally, Harrison dismissed them all. Each person left with a bundle of untraceable cash. A similar bundle landed in Wanda's lap. She looked up.

"You did well and kept your wits about you," Rocky Franklin admitted grudgingly.

"Thank you, Sir," she answered in her most respectful tone.

Harrison came and sat in a chair near hers. He reached out and held her wrist.

"I told you if you did well, you could work for Richard. Will you work as well for him as you did for me?"

Wanda nodded. It suited her to be away from Harrison, even if Rocky was as bad as, or worse than, his father.

"You still need to keep a low profile, but we will find you a job and a place to stay. Richard is taking over control of the business up here, and Sylvester will be returning to LA with me."

Wanda nodded, and her stomach growled.

"Richard will show you where to sleep and I'll have some soup sent up. We may need you again in the morning."

Chapter 11

Wanda entered the room that the Franklins used as an office at their mansion. Rocky had summoned her and she had arrived in time to overhear the end of a conversation.

From the sullen look on Sylvester's face – Wanda decided that he had already received a tongue- lashing from his father. Harrison looked angry. His lips were thin and his face reddened.

"I questioned him last time, Father," Sylvester was protesting. "He'd been gambling at the casino. Anyway, he doesn't know where I keep my tapes. He just sends them off for me."

"Maybe, he kept one back," Harrison suggested.

"No, I check the orders against the outgoing parcels, and no one complained they didn't get their order."

"That may be," Harrison allowed, "But he does know what you are doing and few people like it."

"More than you think, Father. I make a fortune selling the tapes."

"You sell tapes of yourself?"

"Of course not! I make tapes of others and I can blackmail them later. There are lots of people who like the pictures."

"You and I can discuss this later," Harrison told him, ending the discussion. "I intend to be sure of your assistant's loyalty. Bring him in."

Wanda managed to look disinterested as two heavy looking men dragged Mike Johnson into the room.

Bashers, Wanda thought immediately and she was right.

Harrison asked the questions and if he did not like the answer, a slight head movement caused one of the men to hit the smaller man.

Sylvester said nothing and did not seem to care about the treatment his personal assistant was getting.

Mike had not noticed her sitting curled up in the deep armchair, trying not to watch and to act bored. It was a difficult pretence because every time Mike was hit, she seemed to feel it too. To distract herself she listened to his answers.

"Of course I know about his porno business," Mike was saying, in spite of a bleeding lip. "I'm his personal assistant. My job, as you keep reminding me, is to do as he tells me. As for telling anyone about it – no way – I don't want to be connected to it."

"But if Sylvester was in jail, you'd be free of him," Rocky suggested.

"I doubt it. If he went, I'd be the next one the cops went for. And I've heard how the other prisoners treat paedophiles."

The word was out, the one the Franklins were skirting around.

Mike was bashed four times for his directness.

"Were you obeying him when you went off to play games at the casino," Harrison asked directly.

"I was due some days off," Mike claimed.

"You were due nothing!" Rocky snapped. "We own you – you have no rights, you don't shit without our permission."

Wanda recognised the tactic she herself had used. If you give them a chance to exert their dominance over you, they would have no doubts about your later docility.

Nothing Mike said gave them any proof of his working against Sylvester. In spite of the bashing, he did not admit to what Wanda knew he had done.

"You work for me now, Scum," Rocky told Mike Johnson, warning him. "If I even imagine you to be working against me, this will be a mere fraction of what will happen to you. You are not to leave this house unless I tell you to."

Mike Johnson looked cowed and frightened. He hunched his shoulders and stared at his feet. As he left the room, when none of the others could see, he winked at Wanda and she was relieved.

Rocky wandered over to Wanda.

"Let this little demonstration be a lesson to you. A lesson in the art of obedience. Keep doing as well as you did today and I will treat you well. Cross me and you will be hurt. I expect your obedience, respect and total commitment."

"I'll give you no less than my best, Sir. Mr Harrison expects that. I'll do what you ask, unless it's suicidal. As for respect – I'll give you what you deserve. You have to earn it."

Wanda expected the slap that made her head ring. She expected more but, surprisingly, Harrison stopped him.

"If she doesn't live up to my reference, I'll deal with her."

Rocky nodded. "Very well!"

Harrison gestured to Sylvester and they left the room.

"My father wants us to search this house and find where my brother hides his tapes and where he takes his young friends."

Wanda was in no hurry to succeed in the search. Looking, gave her the excuse to prowl through the mansion and around the gardens. Rocky was not always around, but the servants made it obvious they were watching her.

Rocky described his brother as being in a sulk because their father was treating him as a child. He refused to tell where his room was – it seemed that he had added the room himself or Rocky would have known of it. Rocky dropped muttered curses when he was helping to search that implied this job was beneath him. And why, if Harrison wasn't averse to making money from child pornography, did he need to find and seal the room.

It seemed that Harrison objected to Sylvester being on film himself, i.e. being involved personally, not just using other people. He insisted that his sons, like himself, had impeccable public images. Sylvester had seriously damaged that façade.

"Do you have plans of this house?" Wanda dared to ask Richard Franklin on his next visit, three days after starting to search.

"What do you need them for?" Richard asked coldly.

"I think there is one more window on the rear face of the building than I can account for inside." Wanda scratched her head and tried to look perplexed.

"Show me!" Richard insisted.

Wanda nodded to her new boss and walked outside.

"I count fifteen windows on the second storey," Wanda said.

"Fifteen indeed," Richard mocked after doing a quick count.

"Now come inside," Wanda began to walk quickly to the house. She caught a quick glimpse of Richard's scowl as he had to stride to catch her up. He moved ahead of her to climb the nearest stairs. He did as Wanda had done two days earlier, looked in every room and counted windows.

"There is one more in that room that opens off the other passage," Richard drawled without checking his statement.

Wanda went and poked her nose in that room, there was, as she had already discovered, no window in that wall in that room. Richard followed, prepared with a demeaning statement on his lips.

"This room is shorter than it should be," he managed to say calmly enough. "By about six feet, I would say."

While he was examining the wall, looking for a hidden door, Wanda went back into the last room on the other passage. She was on hands and knees feeling along the angle between wall and floor when Richard came in. She timed finding the door latch under a flap of carpet with his arrival. He used his foot to push her away.

"I'll handle this now," he said. It was an obvious dismissal.

Wanda shrugged. "I'll be in the pool room if you want me."

She showed no interest in what was behind the door, because she had already seen everything!

Half an hour later, Richard summoned her back. A third of the wall area had moved sideways revealing the little room that contained films, videos, DVDs and boxes. There was also a computer, scanner, printer, a TV as well as a video and DVD player.

"There's another room somewhere," Richard told her. "I'll let you look over the plans."

"Are you sure it's here?" Wanda asked.

"Keep looking," Richard told her. "I'll enquire about other places."

Wanda went off, hiding a smile of malice. Some random tapes where hidden elsewhere in the house, hoping for a chance to give them to Mike. Giving Mike more evidence against Sylvester gave her no sense of being disloyal to Richard or Harrison.

Wanda decided that if Sylvester were bringing young guests here, his special room would not be far from the garage. However, she examined all the rooms on the lower floor and found nothing. Eventually, Richard allowed her to view the plans of the mansion. Perhaps he would have been more wary if he had realised that Wanda had a photographic memory because in a very short time she had memorised the layout of his whole mansion.

Already, she knew that the plans were incorrect. There were rooms in the attic with steel doors and electronic locks; probably had alarms on them too. Wanda had found them on an illicit night sortie from the window of her room. Later she had looked for the door of these rooms with tiny windows under the eaves. No doubt, Richard knew of those rooms and had looked there already. Wanda was also sure that Mike Johnson was in one of them.

The only other option was cellars – the plans showed a wine cellar and food store, but there could be more.

Wanda went to the garage and poked around. There was a private stair from the garage to the assistant's little office (which was next to the business office). Mike had admitted to operating the hidden cameras from there.

Richard found her just as she accidentally triggered the door release, the wall section opened by swinging inward. Wanda froze as Richard's hand touched her neck, but she did not jump. Her nose had detected a trace of the body scent he used.

"I don't think you are as mentally lacking as you try to convince my father," Richard said with a trace of warning. He propelled her forward into a room that might resemble a king's private chamber. There was a huge bed with red velvet curtains drawn back, gold lame and velvet soft furnishings and a mirror above the bed.

Wanda looked for the cameras, and found four, each planted in the posts around the bed. There were two more in the mirror and at least three in the walls.

One wall had a curtain across it. When Richard drew it back, they saw there was a virtual reality set up. Wanda glanced at the control panel. The possible scenarios would have any teenager or pre-teen drooling to try them.

Wanda moved on. The room was making her nervous and when she opened a cupboard, again hidden behind a curtain, she saw a shelf of drugs, a range of restraining devices and other things for which she could not comprehend a use.

"Quite a comprehensive range of options," she said in a voice devoid of emotion. "Your brother seems to have a grasp of what his clients want."

"My brother may be good at business, but he's a fool to get too involved in it," Richard said with mild distaste. "You will not tell anyone about this room."

Wanda waited until the house was quiet and rose from lying on her bed. She took several deep breaths and began a series of stretching exercises. She was feeling almost as good as new. She was intending another foray over the roof of the mansion and the anticipation was exciting.

The raid on the court building and sneaking around the mansion, eluding the servants meant to watch her, had given her a boost of energy. She felt that she was fit enough to go back to work and if Richard did not bring up the subject soon, she would. So tonight might be the last night she was there and she really wanted a word with Mike Johnson.

Thanks to the plans of the mansion, she knew that the roof over the hidden rooms was alarmed and exactly where to disable the system.

Dressed casually in dark clothes, Wanda opened her window and looked down over the now familiar part of the back garden. She also knew the timing of the guards' round and she waited until her watch said 8:39 before pulling herself out the window. With the help of a drainpipe and the gaps in the brickwork, she pulled herself onto the roof and lay flat on the tiles.

After five minutes of quiet, she risked a peek. Two guards conversed below, casually, oblivious. A few minutes later, they both moved away and Wanda began to inch her way along the roof to the window of the room where she had deduced Mike Johnson to be. Before she lowered her head to whistle in the window, she again checked the activities of the guards.

Wanda was familiar with the sensation of blood rushing to her head and ignored it. Through the window, fifteen inches by six and opening only half an inch – Wanda saw Mike pacing the room. He was startled by her whistle but quickly moved the chair so he could stand on it to talk to her.

"Idiot, what are you doing?" Mike hissed.

"Listen!" Wanda ordered. She quickly told him about the tapes she had hidden, the secret rooms and some gossip about Sylvester and Richard Franklin.

Mike grinned and Wanda began to make her way back to her room.

Richard was waiting for her. He sat in the darkened room, watching her shadow climb in through the window. Wanda had sensed his presence, too late to change her plan, and decided to continue. She was not surprised when the light suddenly went on.

She had her reasons ready - would he accept them? Adrenalin surged through her body.

"Your guards are not very alert, Mr Richard," she said calmly, with no trace of guilt.

"It seems not," Richard said coldly. "Why were you climbing in and out of windows in the middle of the night?"

"I was testing myself," Wanda said bluntly. "I haven't been in top form for the last week or so. I wanted to know what I was capable of."

"And?"

"And, I should be able to do whatever I need to do for you."

Richard saw her looking directly at him, making no attempt to look away. He was impressed. Few people managed that, even if they were quite innocent.

He stood up and approached Wanda, who stood her ground. He reached out with one hand and gently squeezed her neck.

"I don't trust you," he said as his other hand frisked her for hidden items. "You are going to have to earn my trust – do you understand me?"

"Yes, Sir," Wanda said at once. "Was there something else you wanted me for?"

"Why would there be?" Richard drawled.

"You were in my room waiting for me."

"So I was," Richard released her abruptly.

"I've arranged an interview for you with our Human Resources Director for 10am tomorrow. It will be up to you to convince him you are worth hiring. The details you need are on the paper by your bed."

Wanda looked and went to read it.

"Ted Carey, H. R. Director, Level Ten, Franklin Building, Elmhurst Bvd. S.F," Wanda read. "I have no idea where that is."

"I'm sure you can find it. Consider it a test of your resourcefulness."

"Can't I hitch a ride to work with you, Sir?"

"I don't intend anyone to think you are associated with me," he said coldly. "I will advise you that the company has a strict dress code. You will need to find some decent clothing. You can take what you need from the wardrobe here."

"Thank you, Sir," Wanda said most deferentially.

Richard strode from the room and left her alone.

"Decent clothes – that I can live with."

As she opened the cupboard door, she allowed herself to laugh. She had won that round against Richard Franklin.

Chapter 12

Wanda used a taxi to get to the interview, but decided to buy a street directory on her way home. She would need to memorise it if she had to find her way around San Francisco. A public transport map would also be useful.

The idea of a job interview in a place like the Franklin Building was completely new to Wanda. When she had started in the restaurant in LA, she had seen a sign in the window and simply walked in off the street. Here, she had to go first to the desk on the ground floor, state her name and business and whom she was here to see and wait while the receptionist rang upstairs. When her appointment was confirmed, the man gave her directions and turned back to his work.

Wanda felt she had already passed the first test. The man had not looked at her as if she should not be there. The clothes and the care she had taken with her appearance were worth the effort. It helped too that she had not needed more than a light layer of make up to hide the fading shadows under her eyes. The other bruises were also fading, but they were demurely hidden under the business suit she was wearing.

Wanda found Ted Carey's office without trouble and introduced herself to the assistant.

"You are right on time," the woman commented with a smile that Wanda returned. "I'll tell Mr Carey you are here."

"Thank you," Wanda replied, well able to be polite when she wanted to.

The assistant showed Wanda into a room with a large desk that incorporated a computer workstation and half a dozen chairs, wood frame with padded leather seats. The window dominated the far side of the room and pastel prints decorated the walls.

Wanda quickly deduced that Carey thought she had asked for this interview. It meant that she had to think quickly.

"Why do you want to work here?" Carey asked her as he seated himself behind the cleared section of his desk.

"Franklin Industries is a big company. It has a reputation for considering the small people – like me. I've just come up from L.A. I'm looking for work – something with more prospects than waitressing. I'm good with people and finding my way around and I'm willing to start in any low position available. I work hard and learn fast. I want to be able to work up to a position where I can help other people. I hope that a company as big as FCI can find a place for me."

Wanda had started slowly but imbued her answer with as much enthusiasm as she could - always meeting Carey's gaze.

Carey studied her, thinking that she only looked eighteen or nineteen, but impressed by her initiative in coming to him.

"What schooling have you had?"

"I had to leave school at sixteen," Wanda claimed and that was true enough. "I would have liked to have continued. I have a good memory."

"How strong are you?"

Carey saw Wanda as a slender woman, with little spare flesh on her face at least.

Wanda shrugged. "Reasonable, I guess. I used to have to lug heavy trays around without dropping anything."

"We have an opening in our mail department," Carey finally revealed. "The position involves collecting and delivering our internal mail and collecting the out going mail from the various departments. Some days the bag can get very heavy and often you will be running up and down stairs rather than using the lifts."

"Sounds like one wouldn't need to go to a gym to lift weights and keep fit," Wanda grinned. "Would you give me a try?"

Carey smiled. "I'll give you a month's trial. If you measure up, I will recommend you for the position. He went on to give her details of the pay and conditions, as well as when and where to report to work."

"Thank you, Mr Carey. I will work hard."

When a smiling Wanda left the building, Carey had a visit from Richard Franklin.

"Mr Franklin, Sir. How can I help you?" Carey stood up as he recognised the company's new director.

"I require the personnel files on all of my brother's top advisors and those of that group of disadvantaged workers he took on. The re-training and development program. Have them sent up today."

"Certainly, Mr. Franklin," Carey agreed immediately. Then he looked thoughtful and added, "I have just taken on a young woman, to fill a vacancy we had in the mail department. She came here to ask for work, has not much in the way of work skills, but seemed eager for a chance to make a start. I think she would fit into that re-training program."

Richard nodded, "Get her details and have her fill in the usual assessment forms. Add your own impressions. I'll make a decision then."

"Yes, Sir."

"That's all for now," Richard nodded at the Human Resources director and strode from the room.

Richard hid his smile. The girl had passed this first test.

It was ironic that Carey had suggested her for the Company's special program. He was more right than he knew.

Carey had no connection to the illegal aspects of FCI and no idea that the retraining program was the cover devised for the group of Sylvester's agents who did some less than legal tasks for the company. Those same agents would shortly learn that they now had a new controller.

Wanda felt extremely pleased with herself as she sought a place to get a celebratory cup of coffee. It was also good to feel that she could wander around in relative freedom, without feeling that every police officer was about to arrest her. It was good to be away from LA.

Her wanderings took her past a newsagency, and she retraced her steps when she recalled her intention to buy a street directory. Then she decided that she should do something about finding her own place. Richard had not mentioned the subject, but it was unlikely that he would let her stay at his mansion much longer. Therefore, the day's newspaper was her second purchase. Was Richard going to be impressed by her initiative? Or was he going to feel the need to exert his dominance?

Wanda shrugged, whatever he did, she did not care. He had told her that he did not want their association well known and he was going to have to get used to her using her own initiative and like it!

With the knowledge of what she would be paid, which was a lot more than she'd got waitressing, Wanda was able to find an apartment she liked. It had three rooms, was accessible from the roof, close to the fire escape and faced over the back of the building. It also had the advantage of being within walking distance of her new job.

Her hunch that Richard was having her watched, seemed confirmed by his lack of surprise at her announcement. He simply told her to, "Move out, then." and dismissed her.

Wanda was more than pleased with her new job. In spite of being everyone's gofer, she kept a friendly smile on her face and was determined to fit in. The shorter hours than her last job gave her the feeling that she was not working as hard. Within a week, she had settled in to the job and had earned the approval of her immediate boss. She was allowed to collect the mail on her own, and due to the myriad offices in the twenty storey building, and being new, she had the perfect excuse to get lost on a regular basis. This way, she quickly learnt her way around the building whilst amusing her colleagues with her amusing and self-depreciative anecdotes.

She never let on how much she was learning about the FCI building. Everywhere she went on legitimate errands and when she was 'lost', she observed everything. Her keen eyes, honed to detecting security sensors, automatically noted them as she scanned each office. The information her eyes saw, was stored in her retentive memory. If she wanted to, she could enter any of the offices she had visited, undetected.

None of her colleagues in the mailroom would have thought her smart enough to do any of that. They thought her dumb, because she knew nothing of computers and had trouble comprehending e-mail.

After work, aware of the watchers set by Richard, Wanda went directly home, except when she had to get groceries or went to get clothes. Her evenings were spent watching TV, studying the street directory or studying something she needed to learn for work. She chose to keep to herself outside of work and did not encourage casual acquaintances either. The only exception to this was the girl in the apartment opposite her own, and that was for her own, less than legal reasons.

After two weeks, Wanda was beginning to wonder when Richard was going to put her work. She had not even seen him since starting work at FCI and she had no authority to go up to the top two floors which were the precinct of the Director and the senior managers. Brad, one of the older couriers, did those floors.

Therefore, it was a surprise when the Chief Sorter, told her to go to an office she knew to be vacant. Wanda still went, as she was not expected to know it was empty and she was curious. At the door, she knocked as if she expected an answer. She did. The voice was muffled, but it told her to "Come in."

"Sir, I've come to collect your mail," Wanda said before she recognised Richard sitting behind the empty desk.

"Close the door!"

Wanda obeyed, before moving closer to the desk. She was not invited to sit down, so stood warily in front of the desk. To her, Richard was like a snake that could strike in any direction without warning.

"I hear you keep getting lost," Richard watched for a reaction as he challenged her.

Wanda grinned faintly.

"I get to see more of the place that way."

"Do you indeed," Richard considered her thoughtfully. Her pert answer forced him to re- evaluate the report he had received on her.

"A clever tactic," he agreed at last. "So you've been here two weeks and you've been lost just about everywhere."

"Except the top two floors, sir." Wanda corrected, sensing that Richard was leading up to something. She hoped so. Sneaking around in the guise of being lost was less than thrilling.

"Let's see how clever you are," Richard said carefully, staring at his employee. "There are five numbered blue marbles in five of the offices on that list you got this morning. For everyone that you find, and bring to me on Saturday evening at the Director's Dinner, I will give you one thousand dollars. For everyone that you fail to find – you will owe me one favour."

"What kind of favour, Sir?" Wanda felt the thrill of a dangerous challenge. Her eyes shone. The favour was sure to be something he did not expect her to like.

Richard Franklin considered what he knew of the woman before him.

"You will help me to entertain one of my guests."

Wanda took a moment to realise what he meant and her unguarded reaction was met with a malicious smile.

"I'm no whore!"

"It didn't stop you trying to crawl into the Old Man's bed!" Richard snapped.

"That's different. I like him!"

"You like dangerous things and you like his money!" Richard accused. "Well, all my guests will be rich, important men. Please them and they pay well."

"I'm no whore!" Wanda repeated.

"Find all the marbles then or be prepared to give first class service."

When she had controlled the impulse to swear at Richard Franklin, the thrill of the challenged surfaced.

"Very well," was all she said.

Richard nodded, amused. "Off you go!"

Wanda left to finish visiting the ten remaining offices of the sixteen on her list. She was already considering how to approach the job.

Chapter 13

Wanda was dressed in a simple but elegant, long sleeved evening dress of pale blue satin. Over it was a wraparound coat of dark blue wool.

The taxi dropped her at the door of Richard Franklin's mansion just on eight o'clock and the door attendant recognised her and allowed her to enter.

As she waited for the precisely dressed butler to take her coat and escort her to Richard, Wanda felt her heart pounding and her hands growing moist. She wiped her hands unobtrusively on her coat.

In her small shoulder bag, were four blue marbles. She would swear there were no more to be found. It would be like Richard to want to see her humiliated. He did not like the fact that his father favoured her and he would want to show his own power over her. Well, she had agreed to his proposal and could not back out now if she wanted to live.

The front lounge was full of the smoke from expensive cigars and the men within were drinking from Richard's supply of potent spirits. Wanda recognised six of the men as senior managers of the company – their pictures were in the foyer of the FCI building. The women with them were, presumably their wives or escorts.

Wanda saw Harrison and walked over to where he was talking to three other men. She chose to be nearer him than the others.

"Well?" drawled the voice of Richard Franklin from behind her.

Wanda turned and reached into her bag. "I found four, sir," she shrugged and passed the marbles over.

One of the men talking to Harrison stared rudely at her. "This your daughter, Harrison?" he asked in a drunken drawl.

Harrison shook his head and Wanda realised that he would not protect her. She had a sudden vision of the video equipment in the room beyond the garage. It would be next to this room.

The drunk grabbed her crudely and Wanda saw Harrison staring at her, saying nothing, but his meaning was clear. Then he glanced at Richard, who turned away.

"Patrick, let's move out of the crowd and discuss your proposal further," Harrison suggested. He took the man's free arm and urged him from the room. Wanda, still held to the man's other side, by a hand on her almost bared breast, was forced to follow.

The side room was smaller, with several armchairs and a couch set around a low coffee table. Patrick dragged Wanda to the couch and fondled her more openly.

Harrison poured more drink from the carafe on the table, into a low glass. He ignored Patrick's actions and continued the conversation they had started in the other room.

Wanda felt her face growing warm, but she had survived worse than this man's rough handling.

Harrison acted as if Wanda was not there. He was concentrating on convincing Patrick to agree to some proposal. He did not even react when the top half of Wanda's dress was lowered and the man's hand went exploring further.

As a means to distract her mind, Wanda noticed that the more Patrick mauled her, the less he seemed to know what he was saying. He was coming to be repeating what Harrison was saying.

"Ah, ye little tart! Ye have panties on!" Patrick said in disgust.

Harrison responded smoothly. "Just sign here, Patrick, and I am sure she'll let you take them."

The man obeyed, mindlessly. He signed where the pen was placed. His eyes never left Wanda's breasts.

"Another drink, Patrick," Harrison invited then. The man held out his glass with his right hand, the left was too involved to get free.

Wanda saw him swig the drink in one swallow, the hand in her pants was pressing more forcefully. Suddenly he fell heavily, pinning her underneath him.

Harrison walked over and pushed Patrick partly off her, then he began touching her in the way he was so good at, rousing her from revulsion to lust. He brought her to a crescendo and in that instant he withdrew and Wanda was barely aware of a flash.

When she next took notice of her surroundings, Richard was roughly dragging the drunk, Patrick, off her. He took as much notice of her state as he did of the couch. Wanda stood up and adjusted her clothes, then simply watched as Richard sat Patrick straighter on the couch and undid the man's belt and fly and poured a small amount of some liquid onto him.

What exactly he intended, Wanda did not want to know, but it seemed the man was meant to think he had performed with her and mistimed. Richard left the man there and shepherded Wanda from the room.

Harrison kept Wanda close to him until all the guests had departed, though Patrick had not reappeared.

"Are you convinced?" Harrison asked Richard, who did not turn to face his father.

Harrison was stroking Wanda's arm as if he was patting a cat.

"Very well, Father, I trust her!" Richard said finally. "I didn't think she'd do so well and I didn't think she'd come if she didn't find all the crystals. I certainly didn't expect to her to let that moron do what he did with you watching! Are you satisfied?"

Wanda relaxed a fraction, breathing easier. It seemed she had passed some sort of test. And it was amusing to consider that Harrison expected obedience from his sons as he did from her.

"I think you need to talk to her about how she evaded your security," Harrison spoke to Richard as if she was not there.

"Yes, Father," Richard agreed in a carefully neutral voice.

"Then you should make use of her skills," Harrison directed.

"Very well, father, but you said she knows nothing about alarm systems."

"Rectify the problem! I have concluded that she is not as stupid as she tries to pretend."

Richard turned to Wanda.

"Get out of here. Come up to my office at 10am tomorrow."

Wanda was glad to leave. She collected her coat and when the butler appeared, she asked him to call her a taxi. He did not oblige her.

"You there!" he spoke to someone standing in an alcove. "Drive the lady home!"

Wanda saw the young man approaching and recognised Mike Johnson. He did not smile at her and although Wanda felt her heart beating faster just at the sight of him, she kept her face impassive too.

"This way, Mam," Mike instructed, leading her along the passage to the garage.

"They trust you again?" Wanda asked softly, once the car was moving down the drive.

"Where to, Mam," Mike said in reply.

Wanda gave her address and the trip continued in silence. She wondered if Mike was disgusted with her.

Near her apartment, Mike stopped the car, got out and opened her door. He took her arm and walked away from the car.

"They've still got you trained like a pet dog," Mike said in a low angry voice. "Thanks for the tapes though!"

"Mike…"

Mike turned and put a finger to her lips. "Don't say anything. I'll try to ruin the negative of that photo I took tonight."

"Photo?"

"Of you and that drunken sot!" Mike's disgust was evident.

"Don't risk yourself," Wanda insisted. "I wasn't hurt. You don't want to be beaten again."

Mike turned to walk back to the car, and then changed his mind. He returned to where Wanda stood and kissed her like he had before, turning Wanda's mind into a turmoil. Then he returned to the car and drove off.

"What's the big boss doing here?" Brad Longford muttered to Wanda as they sorted the mail just delivered by the post office truck. She looked up and saw Richard Franklin walking into the room, and heading in the direction of the Chief Sorter.

Wanda shrugged and kept working. Brad watched covertly.

"What have you done to make you so edgy?" Wanda asked him.

"Nothing!" Brad protested, distracted.

"Well stop acting as if you expect him to jump on you!" Wanda advised. "Don't you see him everyday when you get the mail?"

"No, just his PA, that twit Joseph," Brad told her. "I never know if he's in his office or not."

"Have you heard anything back about your interview for that IT job?"

"Not yet, but I doubt that I will get it."

"It was a trainee position wasn't it?" Wanda reminded him.

"Yeah, but heaps of people want it," Brad sighed. "How are you going with your computer lessons?"

"Slow, but the light is beginning to penetrate."

"I can't get over how you've never used a computer before now," Brad said, shaking his head.

"I told you – I was too busy working my butt off just to survive."

Wanda straightened suddenly. Brad turned and straightened too.

"Mr Franklin, Sir!"

"Congratulations, Mr Longford. Your name topped the list for the trainee position. Report to Mr Anderson on Monday."

"Wow! I mean, uh, thank you, Sir, for letting me know."

Richard turned his attention to Wanda.

"Miss Dean, isn't it?"

"Yes, Sir."

"I have heard you are now on permanent status. You will have to take over Mr Longford's duties in addition to your own until we get another staff member in here."

"I'll do my best, Sir," Wanda said earnestly.

"Make sure you wear your ID badge," Richard reminded her, noticing that she was not wearing one. "Or security won't let you on the top floors."

"Oh, yes, Sir." Wanda said, shuffling her feet a little and looking down at her hands.

Richard strode off.

The other sorters came up to congratulate Brad and Wanda overheard comments directed at her about 'The Boss's new pet'. Wanda asked Brad about it later.

"Ignore them," was Brad's advice. "They think that doing the mail run up there will get them noticed and the boss will want to date them. They have no hope! They started that with me, but when I started collecting from the top, Sylvester Franklin was here. He was creepy, sneaking up on you. Richard might as well be the Ice King. I've never seen him with a woman, even when his picture is in the paper."

It was obvious to Wanda, once she reached the top floor, why her photo ID card was necessary. There were so many security personnel present, that you almost had to ask permission to sneeze. They scrutinised her and the mailbag before they let her anywhere near the Director's office.

In fact, Wanda began to wonder what exactly they were guarding. It could not be the Director, because Richard Franklin did not have any guards when he wandered around the lower levels.

Wanda took notice of everything she could see; trying to determine what was so valuable up here. Her scrutiny instinctively took in all the non-living security devices as well as the guard positions. She was there just in time to see the guards changing positions in a coordinated action that put her in mind of a game of chess.

The guards checked her bag again when she was ready to leave, laden with letters and parcels.

Wanda had a hunch what the security was for, but short of going in to have a look, there was no way to be sure. She knew that FCI was a cover for some criminal enterprises, but all the businesses on the first eighteen floors were completely legitimate, as her investigations had so far proved. But if the records of the criminal activities were kept here…

Well, she was not about to go poking around in Richard's office without a good reason. It was one thing to go checking safes looking for the damned marbles and seeing what she could see at the same time, but even to attempt such an action in the director's office would require a lot more reconnaissance.

A week after her promotion to Brad's job, Wanda went up to the top floor at her usual time to collect the outward mail.

Richard's Personal Assistant, or 'secretary' as Wanda thought of him, told her she would have to wait as the Director was in a meeting and he had not signed the letters yet.

"No problems, Joseph," she said with a malicious grin. "You can have the pleasure of my company for as long as it takes!"

Joseph scowled. He did not like to be reminded of the previous week when he had made the mistake of making a pass at the new courier. She had not been the little mouse she had seemed to be. Awed by neither his exalted position nor manly charms, the attempt to – well, chat her up - had backfired. He still blushed at the language she had used.

Wanda did not mind the wait. The view from the twentieth floor was amazing. She could see the bay from there and part of the bridge and it gave her the opportunity to test her memory and learn to identify the other tall buildings nearby.

Even though the wait would mean she would be late leaving, it was amusing to know that her presence was causing Joseph to fume quietly at his desk.

When Richard's door opened, Wanda heard his voice and that of another. She turned around.

"That's my evaluation, Mr. Franklin, though I've heard that the share prices have risen recently. That may indicate that the new directors have managed to turn things around. Those figures are six months old."

"Leave it with me, John," Richard advised. "I'll have someone look into it and we can discuss it at the next board meeting."

The tall, stoop-shouldered man with glasses, carried a case and a bundle of papers. He nodded at Richard and began to cross to the door.

"Afternoon, Joseph," the man said in passing to the PA.

"Hurley," was Joseph's brusque reply. Then he spoke to his boss.

"Miss Dean is here for the mail, Sir. You need to sign these."

Richard paid no attention to Wanda, simply took the letters into his office with him.

Wanda was aware that Hurley had not left the room. She turned, idly, and watched him. He was trying to stop his pile of papers from sliding apart in four directions.

Joseph saw the object of her gaze.

"Don't just stand there like an Ice Statue. Go and help him."

Wanda shrugged, but by the time she had wandered over to the door, gravity had won and the papers were all over the floor. She glanced at the papers as she helped collect them, but it was not obvious because she was making no effort to sort them or orientate them in the right direction. Hurley thanked her for the help and struggled again to carry everything.

Joseph sighed.

"The letters won't be ready for another five minutes. Perhaps, Miss Ice Queen, you'd be good enough to help carry things for Mr Hurley?"

Wanda decided to comply, not because Joseph thought he had the right to order her around, but because she was curious, about what position Hurley had. She tried to take the pile of papers, but he handed her the case.

"Thank you," Hurley said again.

Wanda shrugged. "No trouble."

She followed him down the passage around corners and into a warren of offices. He went into a section signed Accounting and they eventually arrived at a large, ledger lined office.

"Why Ice Queen?" Hurley asked as he took the case back from Wanda.

"What?"

"Joseph called you that."

"Oh, him!" Wanda belittled his importance by not naming him. "Sour grapes. The second time I came up, he made a pass at me. I told him to shove off. He calls me that when the boss isn't around – it's because I work in the basement."

"What has that got to do with it?" Hurley seemed curious to know.

"Some old company joke about the basement being cold," Wanda shrugged. "The guy's a twit."

"Well, thanks for the help," Hurley dismissed her.

Wanda nodded and sauntered off. Hurley watched her go; she seemed to be looking everywhere and had no trouble finding her way out.

"Ice Queen!" Hurley said to himself. "Maybe that's what the IQ stands for in the books. She doesn't look much."

Chapter 14

"I don't know what he wants," the Chief Mail Officer told Wanda. "He said he wants to see you and he sounded annoyed. Just get up there and sort it out!"

Wanda had a scowl on her face as she stalked out of the mailroom in the direction of the elevator. As she walked, she remembered to take her ID out of her pocket and put the ribbon part around her neck.

"What does flea brain Joseph want?" Wanda muttered to herself. She wished that she had the time to take the stairs, just to make him wait, but she only had half an hour before her scheduled computer lesson.

She did not want to miss that. It was not because her tutor was male – he was the nerd who had been with the group sent to steal the tape of Sylvester Franklin from the Prosecutor's office – but because she was learning about security systems as well as computers.

The nerd, Peters, had not been too keen at first because he had thought she would become competition for the covert tasks he did for Richard Franklin.

Wanda had eventually asked him what he was afraid of. Knowing that she was also a covert operative for Franklin, he told her.

"I get 2.5% of the value of whatever we steal – me and Brad," Peters the nerd admitted. "If you're going to be doing it too, that's less jobs for us."

Wanda nodded understanding his concern.

"Well, I don't know exactly what he has in mind for me to do," Wanda admitted in turn. "But in the past, I did more sneak and look raids than actual theft. Looking in people's safes and photographing stuff. Nothing taken so no one suspects that I've been there. It's possible you might be the ones to go in later – after I've scouted the places."

When Peters thought about that he had decided she was a possible ally, not a rival and the more she knew about and could recognise, the safer he might be one day. In fact, he was pleased with her increasing grasp of his subject of expertise.

When the elevator door opened at the top floor, Wanda returned her mind to the subject of her intended argument with Joseph. If he was going to blame her for something …

Wanda surprised the guards by coming up in the elevator, not the stairs, and without her mailbag.

"Joseph sent for me," she told them, pulling a face as she spoke.

They let her pass.

Franklin's outer office was empty when Wanda strode in.

"Useless bastard! Where is he? He wanted me here in such a hurry," Wanda said aloud, thinking she was alone. She turned and surveyed the room.

"I sent Joseph off to get some reports," Richard Franklin said, causing Wanda to turn back quickly. "He was upset about some letters that did not go off on time. I told him I would deal with the matter. My office will do."

Wanda did not know what to expect. She followed Richard into his office. It was opulently furnished with three ultra-modern armchairs around a small table in one corner, a state of the art computer set up in another table and his desk, a large affair made from mahogany in the third. The door was effectively the other corner. She stepped onto a thick rug as she crossed to a fourth armchair placed in front of the desk.

Richard went around his desk to his deep, leather swivelled chair and invited Wanda to sit.

"Sir, about those letters…"

Richard waved her concern aside. "The fault wasn't yours. It just suited my purpose to let him think I believed him."

Wanda allowed herself a faint smile.

"I've had good reports on your lessons," Richard commented. He did not need to specify which lessons. "Something has come up that I think will be a suitable test for you."

Wanda sat up straight and stared intently at her boss.

"I have been advised of a shipment of diamonds, due to arrive at Patterson's this afternoon."

Wanda recognised the name. They were jewellers that did a lot of business with the Import division of FCI.

"They will have to be kept on the premises tonight. Now these diamonds have been imported, without coming through us. I want them confiscated."

Richard went on to tell Wanda the address of Patterson's, the layout of the building, plus the details of the security alarms and patrols. Someone had done an excellent job of scouting the building. He suggested how she should proceed.

"When you have the diamonds, get them to John Brady in Sales."

Wanda smiled. "As good as done!"

"I expect you will need some equipment."

Richard tossed a small paper wrapped parcel at her and smiled with approval as she caught it neatly.

"You won't want to let anyone find those things on you – or in your apartment," Richard warned.

Wanda slipped the parcel in her pocket.

"Now, take this package and these letters. The letters need to go off express post today. It seems you didn't collect them two days ago."

Wanda knew that was not true and said in a mild voice.

"My apologies, Sir. I'll see they go off at once. It won't happen again."

There was a faint smile on Richard's face as he dismissed her. Wanda wiped the smile off hers and deliberately frowned. She did not look at the now returned Joseph. Let him think that she had been chewed out if it amused him.

Wanda ate a high-energy snack when she got back to her apartment, then began to change her appearance. She did not shower first to remove the perspiration odour. That was a disguise in itself. She took her make up case out and began to take out what she needed. It had been a long time since she had last done this. The night Harry had killed the guards, in fact. Enough time had passed so that she did not treat that thought as a bad omen. The memory did serve to remind her that the 'look' she had used then – should never be used again.

As she blended colour for her face and hands – she intended to look part Negroid this night – she went over all the details she knew about the job ahead. Richard had suggested a way in but while she remembered it, she knew there would be other options. The final details would be decided when she was on scene.

Her dark clinging clothes were decorated with glittering, fake jewellery: belt, necklace, and bangles. Anyone seeing her would think disco, not thief. Over it all, she donned a coat of light satin cloth.

Part of Wanda's plan was to go to a dance club close to Patterson's and stay there until nearer the time she planned to the job. Then she would remove the gaudy ornaments and the coat and hide them until later. With the glitter removed, she would be able to sneak out, using the dark alleys to get to Patterson's – timing her arrival for the interval between the police and security patrols.

Franklin had suggested that she enter through the rear door or the ground floor window. The door was alarmed, and she now knew how to deal with that. The window had steel bars, but no alarm. She had been provided with an acid paste to enable her to remove the bars. One weakness of that plan was the time needed for the paste to work. A more obvious problem was how to prevent the security patrols from noticing the state of the window, once she got in.

When Wanda arrived at the back of Patterson's she quickly sized up the scene and changed the plan. There was a second storey window, easily accessible by means of a well-secured downpipe. At that height, she would be above the security lighting and able to crouch on a narrow ornamental ledge while she worked.

After scaling the pipe as quietly as a shadow, it turned out that the higher window only had wire reinforcing in the glass, no bars. The acid paste would work as well on the sealing compound around the window, as it would on steel.

Wanda drew plastic gloves on over her leather ones before handling the paste and worked quickly to apply it. She stood, holding the drainpipe whilst the acid worked and the police and security patrolled unsuspecting below her.

The next stage was tricky. Even with the putty now soft, she had to ease the window out of the frame and lower it inside the room without making a noise. Using a small hooked tool from the belt around her waist, she pushed through the soft putty and turned it so it hooked onto the glass and pulled until the glass was leaning outwards by two inches. Wanda felt around the inner frame for wires and found none. With infinite caution, Wanda eased the window into the building. It was scarcely wider than she was and much shorter. During the process, she braced herself on the bricks around the window and trusted her instinctive balance. Once she had had to hold the window whilst a police car stopped below her. If they had looked up at that time, she would have been clearly visible in the red and blue strobe lights. It was a relief to slip into the building after the glass. Once inside, Wanda removed the plastic gloves by inverting them so any acid on them would be inside. She still had on her pair of very flexible leather gloves.

The window led to an office and Wanda quickly checked the contents. There was nothing of interest. Whoever used it seemed unconnected with Patterson's. Not surprising, the office purported to contain the diamonds was up another floor with a safe set into a concrete wall.

Wanda left the second floor office and closed the door behind her. It was her primary escape route. She sensed no guards as she moved to the staircase to go up to the next floor, but she felt a need to be extra careful. Something did not seem right about the set up.

From Richard's information, she quickly found the office she wanted. As her hand moved to turn the knob, she felt her danger sense kick in and saw a dull moving gleam through the glass in the office door. Moving back, Wanda felt for the door of the office almost behind her. She turned long enough to force the lock and slip inside. As she eased it shut, her ears caught the faint snap of the door opposite opening. She risked using her small torch to scan the room. It had a narrow beam and she kept it down. There was a faint sound at the door behind her and she dived for cover behind the desk and chair. It was not the best place to hide but they were the only items big enough to shield her.

From a subtle difference in the air, Wanda knew the door had opened and someone had come in. She risked a glance, but could only make out a tall, solid man, black clad like she was, so she drew back and curled into a small ball.

The figure was not expecting trouble. He flashed his torch quickly around the room, until he found a particular picture and went over to it. Wanda heard the sound of a combination lock turning and the rustle clink of jewels in a bag. It seemed that someone who knew the way to open the safe had moved the diamonds. But why?

Wanda waited until the sound of man's breathing had gone from the room. She heard the door close again. She stood and walked to the picture and revealed the safe. She had not consciously noted the clicks as the man had manipulated the lock but as she began to turn the knob, the numbers seemed to come to her and the door came open at her touch. Wanda let the door swing open, sure that no alarm would sound and felt inside for the soft bag and took it out. She risked using her torch for a quick check. Yes, these were diamonds.

A new compulsion urged her to seek a clue as to who occupied this office. She drew out papers and folders from the safe and examined them briefly. They all related to Patterson's business. A sheet of paper caught between two folders told her more than she cared to know. It was a copy of an agreement between Patrick Patterson and Harrison Franklin in which the company was handed over to Franklin Consolidated Industries.

A more imperative compulsion to leave – too strong to ignore – overtook Wanda. She did not know who was trying to double cross who here this night, but she was right in the middle. It was definitely time to 'get the hell out!'

It did not mean that Wanda neglected caution; the opposite was true. Instead of going downstairs to her primary escape route, as most people would, her instinct was to go up.

Using every bit of caution learnt during five years of illegal activities, Wanda left the office, proceeded to the stairwell and climbed up to the roof. She carefully felt around the doorframe to see if the door to the roof was alarmed. It was not. Nor was it locked. The roof area outside was small, with air-conditioning vents and cooling machinery taking up most of the space. Wanda eased between them, using the light filtering up from the street to look at the rooves of the adjoining buildings. Neither roof was flat, but her shoes would grip on the slope. She chose the roof with the steeper slope and the two-foot high façade. It was a simple matter to step over the low obstructions to reach it.

Barely ten seconds later, the eerie sound of an alarm began to disturb the quiet of the night. It was coming from Patterson's and Wanda knew she had not activated it. She ignored the noise and continued to walk across the roof to the next one. She could already hear the police sirens converging, but she still had time to get out of sight. The next roof was sloped less, but had no façade. Wanda skipped quickly across it to the one further on. It had a partly opened skylight and Wanda grinned. The sirens were very loud now, so she did not bother with caution and opened the skylight wider. The hinges were corroded, and the noise seemed loud, but the police sirens would mask it unless there was someone in the space below. Wanda lay on the roof and looked into the building. Some light from the neon signs opposite was getting into the storeroom below. Wanda shone her torch straight down. There was nothing immediately below to hurt her when she dropped, but it looked like the floor was seven foot down. That was not too bad.

The sirens stopped. That meant the police were in the street below – no time to waste. Wanda lowered her feet into the skylight and continued until she hung from her hands before dropping the remaining two feet. With legs relaxed, she sprang up on landing and looked around.

Her memory told her that this building housed a bookshop. She had made a casual appraisal earlier in the evening on her way to the club. She doubted that there would be a guard and any alarms would probably only be on the doors and windows.

A vague sense of warning tingled along her spine as she moved silently down stairs. One level down, she heard a weirdly arrhythmic noise. It took her some moments to realise it was the sound of someone snoring. As she crept past an open door, the noise increased. The owner, she assumed, was asleep in bed.

That complicated her plans. She had intended to stay downstairs until the police dispersed, neutralise any alarms, then leave. That still might still be possible – if she could find a secluded corner. Wanda scouted the lower floor. The shop area was too open. The closet sized bathroom was not a good idea in case the owner needed to use it. The office was risky, but still a better option that trying to fit in amongst the cleaning equipment in a broom closet.

Wanda sat on the floor behind a desk for yet another time that night, and prepared to wait. A digital clock on the desk enabled her to keep track of the time. She needed to be back at the dance club before it closed at three am.

Twice in the two hours that she waited, she heard the lumbering footsteps of Abe the owner coming down the stairs, followed by the sounds of the toilet in the bathroom being flushed. Abe did not come into the office, though he did check the saleroom with a quick flash of his torch. A careful thief could easily outwit him. A violent one would find him an easy victim.

Wanda did not sit still the whole time she was waiting. She had made several forays out to study the alarm system and to keep from stiffening up. When she was ready to leave, it was childishly simple. The police had gone from the rear alley, the security patrol was not due yet so Wanda relocked the door of Abe's shop behind her and took to the deep shadows. There would be just enough time to return to the club, recover the stuff she had hidden in the ladies toilet and redress in it to go home.

Wanda reached her apartment, still on a high from her success. She undressed and removed her makeup before going to bed. Her mind was too active to sleep yet, so she considered what she had seen and learnt at Patterson's.

Was the figure she saw Patrick Patterson, trying to outwit Franklin? Or was it another of Franklin's operatives trying to beat her to the prize as a way of testing her?

Richard would want a report – she would tell him exactly what she had done and why. And what she had seen. He could make what he chose of it. He could not deny that she had the goods he sent her for.

John Brady notified Richard Franklin the moment the proceeds of Wanda's raid reached him. The latter was more than satisfied with the outcome. Patterson had agreed to buy all his stock through Franklins Import Division. The boss would make him pay to get them back and to teach him a lesson for trying to abrogate the agreement.

Joseph, however, was not pleased to see Wanda that same morning. She was entirely too bright and cheerful, and even smiled at his veiled insults.

He did not know how she had done it, but he had watched her enter the building the night before, beaten her to the diamonds, re-hidden them in a different safe, and when he was sure she was trapped inside, set off the alarms. Yet here she was, unscathed and disgustingly smug.

Well, he had done what he had been told, no more and no less and reported to the boss. Maybe later he would hear how she had done it.

"Go in," he snarled at Wanda. "Mr Franklin wants to see you."

Wanda refused to be defensive about not following Franklin's methods the night before.

"Sir, you weren't the one on the spot. I prefer to take the path of lesser risk."

"Really?" Richard interrupted.

"Comparatively less risk," she amended. "My aim is to succeed and not to be caught."

Franklin gave her the ghost of a smile.

"You did well," he finally admitted. "There will be a bonus delivered to you this evening. Off you go! Don't forget the letters."

Wanda walked jauntily past Joseph, grabbing the pile of letters as she went. She smiled at his annoyance. At the door, she calmed herself to her usual behaviour and returned to work.

Chapter 15

Wanda became very busy at night, doing special jobs for Richard Franklin. At first they seemed trivial, because he never explained why she was to visit certain places, only what she was to do there. However, a pattern began to emerge and Wanda realised that the jobs were getting to be more "sensitive".

The pay was good too. When she went after valuable items, such as the diamonds, she received as a bonus, five per cent of their value. For the more numerous snoop and photograph raids, she received a flat fee. These bonuses went into a special account, opened in her name on Richard's instructions. She withdrew amounts from that account on a regular basis and paid them into another account that she hoped Franklin's people could not access. They were different accounts from those she used in LA.

This was like the work she had done for Harrison, but now she revelled in the freedom of working alone.

One early morning, about three months after her test at Patterson's Wanda returned to her apartment and sensed that someone was inside. The awareness was mild, not like when her danger sense kicked in. She debated whether to hide the stuff in her pockets before she went in, but felt there was no need. All the same, she unlocked her door and sidled in around the frame.

"Close the door," a voice urged in a whisper. The tone sounded familiar.

When the door was closed and locked, a light went on in her bedroom. Wanda moved swiftly and arrived as Mike Johnson turned.

"Oh!" she exclaimed softly in shock and pity. Mike's face was blackened and bloodied.

"What happened?"

Wanda moved towards him, but he flinched away.

"Sorry, but there isn't much of me that isn't sore," he whispered.

"Mike…"

"I'll be okay. I just came to say goodbye. I'm going to the Feds tomorrow. I won't be able to see you again."

Wanda felt tears forming in her eyes. An unexpected sensation. "I … understand."

"I wish it were different," Mike said, emotion almost choking him. "Come with me?"

Wanda felt tempted.

"What happened?"

"Rocky figured out what I did. I don't know how. I think – one of my friends used the information to save himself." Mike shuddered. "He set his bashers on me."

"How did you get away?"

"They left me for dead, locked in a room downstairs. I waited until dark, and then got out. They hadn't found the tool I use to open locks, but they will be after me. I can't stay and endanger you."

Wanda laughed, but it sounded like she was choking.

"Richard is civil to me, now. I keep forgetting that 'Rocky' isn't a respectable member of the business community."

"Don't forget it. One slip – and Richard will become Rocky towards you."

Wanda turned away from Mike to consider what to do. She came to a difficult decision.

"Mike," she said turning back to him. "You're something special and I hope you make it out of this business, but I can't come. Not now."

"You'll be pulled down with them," Mike protested. A whisper was all the voice he had.

"I'll have to risk that," Wanda told him and he could see the battle in her eyes.

"Even knowing what they are like?"

Wanda nodded.

"I don't understand you," Mike shook his head. "I thought … there was something between us. This could be your chance to break free."

"Mike, I can't explain. It's just – I need the danger – the risk of capture. It is like a drug. It keeps me alive."

"You're right, I still don't understand," Mike said in disgust.

"I'm not a nice person. I told you that," Wanda reminded him. "But I won't mention you to Richard – Rocky – and I won't warn him that you are going to talk. If he and his family fall, I'll take my chances. It's what I deserve."

"What if he tells you to kill someone," Mike tried. "What if he makes you watch while they kill me?"

"Get Out! Damn you!" Wanda said, her voice breaking. She didn't want to think of such things, or the murder charge she would face if the police caught her. He was confusing her mind again. She liked what she did. She chose her life. He was …

Damn it! She couldn't fall for him – it wasn't fair – she couldn't.

Mike knew he'd lost. He stood up and moved closer to where she stood and took her face gently in his damaged hands. He saw her tears and kissed her. She seemed to melt into him, just for a moment.

"I love you, Wanda Dean. But I let you go. Take care. When you are ready, I will be waiting for you, somewhere. Maybe, one day we will have a chance."

"No!" Wanda denied. "Go!"

Wanda did not hear him leave. She stood for a long time with tears streaming down her face. She wanted to call him back, to try to explain. How could she? What she was doing was wrong. She knew it was wrong. She still did it. She still wanted to do it, still wanted the approval of dangerous and deadly men. She was letting them use her and manipulate her. She was a bitch. A trained bitch.

"I can't stop," Wanda said aloud. "I've got to forget him."

Slowly, Wanda got herself under control. She took from her pocket the spare memory card for the little digital camera. In her handbag were the camera and a second card. The pictures stored on the cards were from the office of the governor and she had no way to copy them.

"Copy them?" Wanda said aloud. "Why would I want to? I have to package them and take them to work."

Wanda tried to remember how to package them.

"Damn him! I'm all confused."

She took three deep breaths. "Ok, I need the special carrier…"

Wanda put the cards in the holder and wrapped it in brown paper. The address label was already prepared and the 'from' label was showing the name of an advertising firm. The little parcel went into her workbag.

After that, she carefully removed all the makeup from her hands and face then changed from her work clothes.

She thought of the night's success, eluding the guards, breaking into the Governor's office and the escape.

The feeling of euphoria did not come. Instead, she felt sick. Mike's bruised face haunted her.

"Damn you!" Wanda said weakly, throwing herself on the bed.

Sleep eluded her, though she tried every calming exercise she knew.

The face in the mirror had dark circles under the eyes from lack of sleep. Wanda rinsed her face and began to dress for work. She normally wore no make up to work, but today she needed to use skin-toned cream to hide the shadows. Her hands were shaking as she tried to open the tube.

When she had finished, she closed her eyes, took twelve long slow breaths, and looked in the mirror. She looked normal. However, the thought of food nauseated her, so she decided against breakfast.

With a deliberate effort, she took up her bag and her keys and left her apartment.

The walk down the two flights of stairs left her legs trembling. She had to stop and rest in the little foyer where the mailboxes were. A voice hailed her from behind.

"Wan, you okay, hon?"

Wanda turned, "Hi, Janet. I'm okay, just a touch of flu, I think."

The girl from the apartment opposite hers was just coming home from work.

"You don' look okay. You go back to bed, hon, and I'll bring you a hot brandy."

Wanda had to force a smile. "I can't miss work today. Got a chance at a promotion."

"Well, you take it easy, hon. Come home early."

"Good idea," Wanda agreed, and forced herself to cross to the door with her normal stride.

The cool morning air outside revived her, and she began to walk to work but at a slower pace than normal. At the lights where she crossed the main road, she had to wait for the walk sign. A limousine drew up in front of her. While she waited for the light sequence to cycle, she stared at it without really noticing it. A window at the back rolled down and a face was staring back at her.

Just before the light went to walk, she recognised the face. Her first thought was to turn and flee, but had to force her way back through the surging crowd waiting to cross. At the edge of the crowd, she ran back the way she had come until she found an open shop door. She ran inside and stopped by the window.

What was her father doing here in San Francisco? What would he do now he had seen her?

Wanda let her heart rate return to normal whilst glancing at the morning paper. The limo drove past again, having circled the block. Wanda walked through the shop to the arcade behind it and used the morning crowd to hide her. She could take more than one route to work.

The need to stay undetected stirred her mind into action, dispelling some of the lethargy afflicting her. She moved a little faster, her eyes scanning everyone about her. When she finally reached the haven of the mail office she felt almost normal, but she had forgotten the special package in her bag.

Her actions were automatic, done from rote, not conscious thought. When she almost caused a serious accident, the Chief Sorter pulled her aside.

"You look like you shouldn't be here, Dean," he told her bluntly.

"I had to," Wanda told him, but she could not remember why.

"Not if you are a danger to everyone. Go home!"

"I don't think I can walk that far," Wanda admitted, beginning to shake.

"Take a cab," the Chief Sorter started to say, but Wanda was suddenly sprinting for the staff kitchen.

The Chief was about to follow, when he was called to the phone.

It was an urgent summons to the top floor. He frowned. They expected the same person to do that floor all the time. He went to see where Wanda was and saw that she was in no condition to do anything.

He sent the next available courier, the newest, Sheila, who was not yet seventeen, to answer the summons.

"Don't be put off by the security guards," he told her. "If they ask why Wanda isn't there, say she's been taken ill."

Sheila reached the Director's office, shaking as if she had narrowly escaped from danger.

She entered, seeing the Director's Personal Assistant, concentrating on something on his desk. After waiting for several minutes, she said timidly. "Excuse me; I've come for the urgent mail."

Joseph's head came up when he heard the unfamiliar voice. He had been preparing a barrage of scathing remarks for Wanda.

"Where's Miss Dean?" he asked more sharply than necessary.

"Sick, Sir. The Chief is going to send her home. She's throwing up in the staff room."

Sheila did not think she was being indiscrete and did not realise that the Big Boss had come out of his office.

"That doesn't sound too good," Richard said with genuine sounding concern. Sheila jumped and her face reddened.

"Thank you for coming up instead, Miss …?"

"Weeks, Sir. I'm Sheila Weeks."

"Miss Weeks, I'm expecting an important letter from one of our advertising companies. Do you know if it has come yet? It was promised for first thing today," Richard asked her.

"I'm not sure, Sir. The chief gave me a pile of letters. If it's not there, I will ask the Chief to check for you."

Sheila drew the letters from the bag and handed them to Joseph to look through. He glanced at Richard and shook his head.

"Please have the Chief check, Miss Weeks," Richard directed and he turned to return to his office.

Sheila was very glad to escape back down to the basement and hoped that someone else would have to come up next time.

Joseph took the opened letters into his boss's office.

"Find out about that parcel," Richard told Joseph abruptly. "Make it a priority. The Old Man has been on the phone asking if we had it."

Joseph merely nodded and went out. He took the lift down to the mailroom with a feeling of relief. The Boss was annoyed that Wanda had not sent the results of her night's work. However, in his opinion, annoyed was too mild a term. The Old Man, had wanted to know if the job had been done or postponed and the Boss did not know.

Joseph just missed Wanda in the mailroom; the cab had just departed. He scowled because now he would have to follow her all the way to her apartment. Well, at least he would be out of the office if the Old Man called again. Harrison Franklin must be a real ogre if even the Boss jumped at his orders.

Joseph parked his car in a loading zone outside Wanda's apartment block. He strode inside and cursed when it became obvious that the elevator was not working. He kept himself fit, but that did not mean he liked using stairs.

Wanda's door was ajar. Joseph pushed it open further and walked in without announcing himself. He glanced around the room as he pushed the door closed behind him. He found Wanda sprawled on her bed, still fully dressed and seemingly sound asleep. Rather than wake her up, he searched the bedroom and outer room for the parcel.

Having no luck, he returned to the bedroom, pulled Wanda upright, and shook her. When this had no effect, he slapped her hard across the face.

"Where's the data?" he demanded roughly when Wanda seemed to be waking.

After a second and third slap, Wanda's eyes focussed and recognition dawned. His question finally penetrated her foggy brain.

"Hand bag. I forgot."

Wanda had been lying on her bag. Now she fumbled with it until Joseph grabbed it and searched it.

"This it?" he asked finding the parcel.

Wanda nodded. Joseph pushed her back down on the bed before releasing her and stalked from the apartment.

Sometime later, Wanda woke with a gentle hand shaking her.

"Wan, hon, are you okay?"

"Jan?"

"Your door was open, hon," Janet told her.

"Oh."

"Did that man hurt you?"

Janet could see the red on Wanda's cheeks where she had been slapped.

"Man?" Wanda tried to remember.

"Shortish, lean, dark hair – balding on top, brown suit, lousy body odour." Janet described.

"Joseph." Wanda's mind was beginning to function again. She checked her handbag and found the parcel gone.

"I forgot to leave something at work. If he got sent to get it he'll be properly peeved." Wanda laughed. "The bastard doesn't like me, but he'll get his!'

"I liked the other one, hon."

"Which other one?"

"Came up last night, dark haired, been in a fight. He was polite."

"Jan, as a favour to me, forget you ever saw him."

"Why, hon?"

"Just forget." Wanda stood up unsteadily and walked out to her little kitchen. "Want coffee?"

"You sit; I'll get it, hon."

Wanda was happy to let Janet make them both a drink and for her to chatter on about her client of the previous night. Janet was a night relief nurse.

The first indication Wanda had of her next visitor was the arching of Janet's brows. Her expression was one of approval.

Wanda turned and saw Richard Franklin entering her apartment – without knocking.

"Thanks for the coffee, Jan," Wanda said by way of a dismissal.

Janet took the hint, put her cup in Wanda's sink and walked seductively to the door. Her broad wink suggested that this one was worth forgetting everyone else for.

Wanda forced herself to her feet.

"Can I get you anything?"

Richard waved the offer aside and sat in the chair Janet had vacated.

"I heard you had to go home. What's wrong with you?"

Wanda sat back on her chair gratefully.

"Some kind of bug," Wanda claimed. "Maybe the flu. Did you get the data? I'm really sorry. I totally forgot."

Richard accepted her apology. It was obvious that Wanda was not well and she had as usual done a superb job.

"Any trouble?"

"No, a breeze."

"Are you sure?" Richard was watching her intently.

"I told you no."

"Can you work tonight?"

"I won't be in top form," Wanda told him directly.

"Never mind. I'll get Joseph to do tonight. It isn't a difficult job. Take today off and tomorrow. I need you better by tomorrow night. You'll have to come out to the house tomorrow, after four. Bring a change of clothes. A group from the company are going to an official function. Lots of important and famous people. I will want you to mingle with the younger set, the children or protégés of the politicians and media people. Get to know them, find out about them, and listen to boasting about their elders. Remember what you can, the information may prove useful."

Wanda nodded her understanding.

Richard stood up and let himself out, leaving Wanda to wonder why he had made the personal visit.

Wanda made sure to lock her door before going to bed. Too many people had just walked into her place that day and she wanted no more.

Sleep was what she needed and when she woke again late in the evening she was feeling much better.

She lay in bed, able to consider the events of the previous night more calmly.

Mike Johnson was relegated to a distant part of her mind. He was going to bring down Sylvester Franklin – but Wanda dismissed the idea that Harrison or Richard Franklin would be affected. So if she was not threatened – why had she gone into such a mental fritz? It was not seeing her father that morning; the effect had begun before that. In fact, that had helped her. So what was it?

"Come with me." That is what had done it, those three little words. And maybe the other three, "I love you."

Mike's face seemed to hover before her. How could he love her? She worked for those he hated and did not want to stop – but he had kissed her.

She liked him, but she could not love anyone. If you loved someone – you had certain obligations. You did not do anything to endanger them; you had to keep them from harm. And you did not go out and endanger yourself either. But if you liked them, there were no strings. You could do what you could to help a friend. They did not have to know that the help came illegally.

Without any interconnecting sequence of thoughts, Wanda remembered thinking about copying the data from the camera cards. She had hardly wondered at the idea then but suddenly the idea intrigued her.

Thanks to her on going computer lessons, she now knew how to download the data from the cards and how to save the data. However, if she began to copy everything, how would she stop the casual uninvited callers from finding that she had done it?

It suddenly occurred to Wanda that she had decided to buy a computer of her own. She still was not sure why she wanted to copy stuff, except that if she found something on Sylvester she could ... what? When would she ever see Mike Johnson again?

"I'd like to know what they do with the photo's I take," Wanda whispered to herself. "And the only way I can find out is to look, really look, at the photos. I don't have time for that when I'm getting them."

The idea gave Wanda a sense of excitement. Richard had not said anything about not looking at the photos.

Her mind turned to how to protect any copies she made. From having a temporary hidey-hole in Janet's place to something more secure.

She would have to make sure that nothing incriminating was readily accessible – so when she got her computer, she have to save to CD or disc and erase the files from the main drive. The problems and possible solutions occupied her mind until she was ready to sleep again.

Wanda went to the electronics shop the following morning and told the staff member what she wanted, as opposed to what he was trying to sell her. It was amusing for her to realise that she now knew more than the salesperson did. Then she allowed him to advise her on what they had in the way of security devices and asked for what she had decided she wanted. Paying in cash impressed the staff member and an offer of delivery and help to set her system up was forthcoming – Wanda accepted the offer when she learnt the assistant was female.

The computer was to be delivered later that morning, so Wanda went back home to prepare the space for it. As usual, she examined the doorway before entering. The length of fawn thread, nearly invisible against the wood floor of the passage, was unbroken. No visitors had entered in her absence.

The woman bringing up the computer was lucky to find the elevator operating, and certainly knew her business organising the computer. Within an hour, the system was up and running, except for the modem. There was not a phone line in the apartment.

Chapter 16

Wanda played with her computer until she needed to get ready to go to Richard's mansion. She quickly packed an overnight bag with her evening clothes and a nightdress in case she stayed overnight there after the function. She also had her make-up case, as she decided that it would not be a good idea to look like her normal self. Then when she thought she had everything she needed she went out to the street and hailed a cab.

She paid the driver when she was a street away from her destination and walked the rest of the way.

The guard at the gate recognised her and allowed her to enter as well as announcing her arrival to the house. Wanda was shown to a small room by the butler, and told that a meal would be arranged for her before they left.

Wanda felt less than glamorous in her lilac silk gown; particularly when Richard Franklin was dressed in a perfectly fitted, exquisite quality dark blue satin evening suit. He looked at her studying her changed facial appearance and made no comment, except to say that when they arrived at the San Francisco Hyatt, she was not to be near him. In his limousine, he gave her more instructions and told her when she was to leave and come to the car at the end of the function.

In the first few minutes after arriving, Wanda observed other women and quickly picked up how she needed to act. Then with a faint smile of anticipation, walked boldly over to the drink server and asked for a mineral water with lemon. Her next action was to slowly circle the Hyatt ballroom, locate the little groups of the younger set, and decide which one to work her way into.

Since she was mainly to listen and chat, Wanda soon began to enjoy herself and the unusual extravagance of the food and setting. When asked whom she was with, she airily claimed 'a bunch of old business fogeys' – nothing more specific. They did not seem to notice that she was not wearing a nametag, but some of the other young adults were not either.

There was a large contingent from FCI at the function, Wanda recognised them, but thanks to her make-up, none of them knew her. Some of them she saw and spoke to nearly every day. The only eyes that seemed to be watching her were Richard's and he had seen her transformation before they left.

Wanda had not seen Harrison arrive, but he smoothly cut her out of the group she was in and shepherded her towards the main door of the ballroom.

"The man arriving with the blonde girl, see what you can learn about him."

"Who is he?" Wanda asked as the man was still too far away to see clearly and his head was turned away from her.

"A senator with dangerous ideas," Harrison moved away after speaking.

Wanda edged carefully between other guests and came within sight of the senator. She almost stopped, rigid, when the man turned.

Senator Charles Willard spoke to the girl with an arm through his. She was pointing to the refreshments. As they began walking that way, Wanda plotted an intercept course. She was feeling a tingle of excitement. Would he recognise her? What would he do if he did?

The smile on her face was genuine. She could see, from her father's expression that he was trying to place her.

Elisabeth's smile, while not broad, was also genuine. She knew! Wanda was relieved when she said nothing to their father.

A woman who wished to discuss business with him accosted the senator. He was torn between helping his daughter and the reason he was attending.

Wanda drew closer.

"Excuse me, Senator. I can assist your daughter and introduce her around," Wanda offered. She felt her father's eyes full on her and he still did not recognise her.

"That's very kind of you, Miss…?"

"Harris," Wanda said quickly. "I'm trying to escape from some old business fogeys."

The senator smiled, patted his daughter's arm and watched the two young women move off.

"Harris is it?" Elisabeth said softly.

"For tonight," Wanda admitted. She did not need to ask how her sister knew her – they were so close they would know each other anywhere.

"You look much better," Wanda continued.

"Are you?" Elisabeth asked, as they reached the refreshment table.

"I'm alright."

"What are you doing here?"

Wanda shrugged. "I moved to San Francisco because it was safer."

It was not quite what Elisabeth meant. She said nothing for a while.

"You're with Him," she accused.

Wanda knew she meant Harrison, but only shrugged again.

"Why did you run yesterday?"

"You don't need to be associated with me!"

Elisabeth sighed, knowing that Wanda would not say any more.

"Father is getting involved with the push against organised crime," Elisabeth commented quietly.

"Is he out to get at me or try to save me?"

"I can't say," Elisabeth admitted. "You know he never talks about you."

Wanda grunted. "I wish he wouldn't get too vocal about the crime angle."

"Is that why you are here? Fact finding for your criminal friends."

"Apt description," Wanda agreed, accepting the mild rebuke. "Do you want a drink?"

"Same as you," Elisabeth answered. "Who should I tell Dad to be wary of?"

"Look for the ones watching me," Wanda told her, sure that giving names would endanger her father. "How long have you been home?"

"Couple of weeks! I have to keep active, Rickard said. So I begged Dad to let me come to this when Vera couldn't. Maddie's got a temperature."

"Which one is Maddie?"

"The baby."

"Oh." Wanda felt just a moment of regret that she did not know all of her family.

"I suppose I had better start introducing you around. We've been chatting long enough."

Wanda saw Richard heading for her father and took an intersecting course, innocently slowing him for a moment and allowing her father to be shepherded away by one of the media contingent. She appeared not to notice Richard's slight frown.

"I'll re-join you in a moment," Elisabeth said. "I just need to speak to father."

Harrison came up behind Wanda again.

"Having trouble?" he suggested.

"I'm hardly important enough to interrupt his discussions," Wanda said, letting a trace of sourness tinge her voice. "I promised to introduce his daughter around, when she comes back."

"He couldn't keep his eyes off you," Harrison implied. "We could find a beau for his daughter."

"No!" Wanda tried to keep the disgust from her voice. She was not going to seduce her father.

"Why not?" Wanda felt Harrison squeeze her elbow.

"He's here with his daughter. She can't be older than me and she told me she's been very ill. I can't see her falling for a tumble or he leaving without her."

The pressure eased. "He'll keep then. See if you can make time with young Brandon Hurst."

"He's a dawk," Wanda protested. She had already met that young man.

"He'll be more grateful, more ardent," Harrison suggested.

"And he'll be spared the treatment for men who eye me?"

"For a time," Harrison answered not committing himself.

Wanda let Harrison see her smile. She guessed the man was going to be allowed some indiscretion and approached about it later. She did not care. He was obnoxiously arrogant in spite of his ordinary looks.

Elisabeth re-joined Wanda as Harrison moved off. She now knew two men to tell her father to avoid. The two of them went outside where the younger set had congregated and Wanda introduced the senator's daughter. Elisabeth was instantly at ease in the company and appeared not to notice Wanda making a play for one of the young men and later disappearing with him.

Wanda returned to the party half an hour later, showing no sign of the distaste and disgust she felt. Her paramour, Brandon Hurst, was undeniably smug. He liked to hurt his women, but Wanda gave him no sign that he had succeeded. He did not care when she did not stay around.

Wanda was feeling a vague sense of disquiet. She moved back into the main ballroom and scanned the crowd. Her father had a worried expression on his face and there was no sign of Elisabeth. She had not been outside with the younger set.

"Lishka?" Wanda thought. The sense of trouble intensified.

Wanda realised then that she could not see Harrison or Richard either.

Without volition, Wanda began to move purposefully to the stairs leading to the guest suites. She was in time to see Richard disappearing into a suite halfway along the passage. Wanda walked faster and slipped quietly into the same suite. Harrison and Richard were watching a monitor and did not hear Wanda approach from behind. She saw enough. Joseph - and her sister.

"Idiots!" she said without thinking of consequences. The looks that the two Franklins turned on her would have quarried stone.

"Sir," she gulped. "I told you, she's been very ill, she's only just out of hospital. No one will believe that she allowed herself to get drunk and do that. I tried to get her a drink – she can't have it. She's on medication. Her father will create hell. He won't believe she chose to do that."

Harrison stared at her, thoughtfully.

"I'll pull Joseph out," Richard began. Harrison stopped him.

"You go in there. You put a stop to it." Wanda was told.

Wanda stared back for a moment, trying to fathom Harrison's new plan. She had no idea. However, she did know how Joseph would react. Harrison moved a step forward; Wanda turned at once and walked into the next room.

Joseph had her sister pinned to the bed and was beginning to feel up her dress. From the other room, she heard Harrison calling hotel security.

Elisabeth had struggled, but now she lay exhausted, helpless. Tears were streaming from her eyes.

Cold anger blossomed in Wanda. Her sister did not deserve this.

"I didn't think you were a real man, Joseph."

Joseph recognised the voice but not the face.

"You! Get out bitch!"

"Make me," Wanda challenged recklessly.

"Do you know what you are interrupting?" he snarled at her.

"Candid camera," Wanda replied sugary sweet.

Joseph left the bed and came up to her. "The Boss will kill you!"

"He sent me in. Hotel security are on the way up. Her old man is on the rampage. You had better do yourself up and have a damn good story as to why you are in here with her. They'll be here any minute."

Joseph wasted no time fixing his clothes.

"Get out!" Wanda told him.

Joseph went over to the bed and hit Elisabeth hard enough to knock her out, then stalked from the room. A moment later, he returned. He deliberately pulled up Elisabeth's dress and pulled the top down off her shoulders.

He grabbed Wanda and shoved her against the wall.

"Play along, darling. Boss's orders."

They both heard a commotion in the adjoining room. Moments later two security men, guns drawn, rushed into the room.

They took in the scene and relaxed.

"What's happening here, Sir?"

"Mr Harrison and I returned to the suite for some papers and heard noises from in here. He sent me in and I found this woman holding the other down and well – licking her."

Joseph could not seem to think of what else to say. "The other girl was struggling, but I think she's fainted."

One security guard holstered his weapon.

"Are you trying to claim that this woman was going to rape the other?"

Joseph blushed. "I don't know. I didn't think a woman could…"

Senator Willard entered the room. "Elisabeth!" He went over to her, smoothed down her dress, and fixed up the top.

Wanda felt a second pair of hands holding her and putting handcuffs on her. She kicked out at the men behind her and was rewarded with a grunt of pain.

"I'm innocent you morons," Wanda yelled then. "I came in and found him pawing her! He grabbed me when I tried to stop him."

Harrison's smooth voice entered the conversation. "Mr Jones was with me. The young woman was already in the room with the other. I called you at once."

The second guard holstered his weapon and turned to the Senator.

"Sir, do you want us to call the police?"

Elisabeth was stirring, waking up. Charles Willard looked at his daughter and asked, "Are you alright?"

Elisabeth tried to move her arms and only then did everyone seem to realise that her arms were tied. The bindings turned out to be pantyhose. As they untied her, eyes went to Wanda who was not wearing any stockings.

"Yes, I'm okay, Dad, really. Nothing happened."

"You were attacked, tied up!" he reminded her.

Elisabeth spoke quietly to her father. Charles Willard turned back to the group.

"Thank you for preventing harm to my daughter," he said humbly to Harrison and Joseph. He stood up, went over to the defiant female, and held her face towards his.

"If you ever – come near my daughter again – I will put the police on you. Do you understand?"

Wanda said nothing.

"What is your first name, Miss Harris?"

"It's Kaylene," Elisabeth said.

"Kaylene Harris. I will remember that. We won't press charges this time."

Charles Willard dropped his hand in disgust. "My daughter and I will return to our hotel."

He shepherded her out of the room.

Wanda was forced to walk out into the reception area of the suite. Richard was noticeably absent and Joseph was scoffing a scotch. The monitor was not in evidence.

Harrison said, "Just hold her for a moment while I check the suite to see if anything is missing."

He made a point of searching the suite as the guards complied with his request.

"All seems to be in order. Have you any idea how she got into the reception? Is she part of a delegation?"

"We'll check, Sir. Either way, she will be asked to leave the hotel."

Harrison waved them out.

"Stupid bitch," Joseph said sourly, loud enough for Harrison to hear. His shin ached where Wanda had kicked him.

Joseph had no idea that Harrison was Harrison Franklin. He had only met the man that evening.

"She saved your skin, Joseph," Harrison reminded him. "You were told to leave that one alone."

"The boss said to try for any of the girls," Joseph tried to excuse himself.

"That was earlier. Miss Dean warned us about trying for that one and I know you were told. Fortunately, it worked in our favour. The girl didn't seem to remember who hit her and Senator is grateful to us."

Joseph visibly preened.

"Pack everything from here and take it to the car," Harrison ordered.

Joseph looked about to protest but decided to be prudent. He was not exactly sure who the grey haired man was, except that Richard treated him with deference.

Harrison watched him work, and when the phone rang, answered it.

"Good, we'll be down in five minutes."

Chapter 17

Wanda sat in one corner of the limousine and stared out the darkened glass of the window. Richard sat opposite her. He had "collected" her after she had been evicted from the hotel, and had said almost nothing to her since then. Sometime later, Harrison and Joseph entered and took the other seats.

Conversation was non-existent during the journey to the Franklin mansion. Joseph glowered at Wanda because she had caused him to be chewed out. He had begun to feel that he was not just PA to Richard but his second in command as well. And Wanda, well she was just a little bit thief that worked in the basement by day.

At the house, Richard took Joseph off for a 'meeting' and Harrison led Wanda to the room she had used before.

"You are looking pale, my dear," Harrison told her when they were in the room. "Get some rest."

Wanda nodded, heard Harrison leave and decided she needed a shower. It was a relief to find no visitors when she came out, dressed in a nightdress and more than ready to crawl into bed. She was not asleep when she heard the door open. She turned and saw a maid bringing a glass of water on a small tray.

"The Master says you are to take the tablet."

"What is it?" Wanda asked her.

The woman did not answer. Wanda stared at her.

"Put it by the bed," she said finally and watched until the woman left her room.

Wanda did not intend to take something if she did not know what it was. She left the tray alone. If it was a sleeping tablet, she did not want it. There were things she needed to think about – starting with how close her family had come to harm. Not from her, but from the people she chose to work for. It was not meant to be that way. Since leaving home and changing her name, she had never stopped to think about how her actions would affect other people. Deliberately, she allowed herself to recall all the types of jobs she had done for Harrison and Richard and what she had learned about the outcome of each. Sometimes, people had lost their jobs or companies had gone bust or been taken over. Some people had lost valuable, irreplaceable items. Others would be blackmailed…

The faint sound of the door opening alerted her. It was Harrison, she recognised him from his body scent. She did not jump when his hand touched her neck and began running down her back, uncovering her from the sheet. Already her body was beginning to rouse.

"You haven't taken the tablet."

"I didn't know what it was."

"Nothing harmful. I'm told it's called the 'morning after' pill," Harrison almost crooned.

Wanda was no wiser and still made no move to take it.

Harrison went on, "It will prevent unseemly accidents from your tumble this evening."

He made it seem as if it had been Wanda's choice.

Now Wanda sat up and took the tablet. If that was what it was for – she certainly did not want any 'consequences'.

"Good, good," Harrison patted her hand gently. "Now, you and I have some unfinished business."

"We do?" Wanda was thinking furiously.

"Lie down, turn over."

Harrison's voice was harsher. Wanda had long enough to wonder what he was going to do when the first of three stinging swats reached her back and buttocks.

"Now, I forgive you for calling me an idiot," Harrison said calmly.

Wanda's eyes watered, as she chewed on the corner of the pillow to stop herself making any sound. She had forgotten her unguarded comment in the greater concern for her sister. Harrison had let her off lightly. Oh, but her back hurt. She had better guard her tongue more carefully in future. Harrison expected absolute respect.

Harrison was doing something, but Wanda did not want to turn back yet. She had no choice when he sat beside her and gently rolled her over onto her painful back. Then he took the straps of her nightdress off her shoulders and put them down beside her breasts. Slowly he bared each breast and began to lick them. He had never done that before. Wanda dared to move a hand onto Harrison, working it down, slipping it into his trousers. The belt was not tight. Had that been what he had punished her with?

Harrison did not stop her, but when her hand found his manhood, it was limp, flaccid. He was rousing her to fever pitch, but it was having no effect on him.

"When you are finished, father, we need to talk. Something urgent has come up."

Richard acted as if he had not just walked in on his father in what could be considered a compromising position. In fact, he looked at Wanda as if she was not a half-naked woman but a cushion on the bed.

Harrison stopped what he was doing, leaving Wanda in an agony of lust. He extricated himself and went to talk to Richard.

When the pounding in Wanda's ears subsided, she heard, "The feds have him a safe house, spilling his guts. It's more than just a tape this time."

"We need to find where he is. Get on it. I'll be along in a moment."

Richard left without a further look at the bed. Wanda watched Harrison return.

"Beg me to finish," he whispered to Wanda, and to her shame, she did exactly that.

Where had her free will gone?

Wanda spent the rest of the night with thoughts that were not comfortable. It was well that she was undisturbed. The anger, that had filled her when she had seen Joseph with her sister, returned. It was directed partly at herself but mostly at Richard and Harrison. Particularly at the way they manipulated people for their own ends and disposed of them when they failed or were no more use.

So far, in their eyes, she was not a weak squeamish female. They were willing to correct her minor lapses. It was as well that they couldn't read her thoughts at the moment or even read her expression. She could not maintain the controlled façade that she usually showed them, the one that attracted them.

Wanda forced herself to see how Harrison had subtlety conditioned her. He was still doing it. In his presence, she only wanted to please him – be rewarded by him. And even accept his punishment for failing him. She would have to keep on letting him control her, to lull him with her obedience. But she had just upped the stakes.

Wanda Dean would be their perfect tool – cold, emotionless, efficient. And she would be doing things for herself. She would be finding out everything that she could about her bosses, everything about their "top advisors" – the ones that controlled sections of the "crime division" of FCI. Then she would find and follow their subordinates. She would make sure that the Franklins were shown for what they really were. Even if it meant incriminating herself. She was no better, she could not stop being a criminal – even if she wanted to – her past record would ensure she was given no mercy. She did not deserve any. So be it. Now – how to hide the records she intended to keep.

Initially, she would type all she remembered from Los Angeles and here onto her computer. She could remember clearly the dates, places, times and what she had done. Where she knew the results of her work, she would add that. At the end of each session, she would burn the files onto CD, and delete all traces of her work from her computer. The discs would be hidden in a place only she knew and which even a thorough search of her apartment would not reveal. She would copy any photographs she took onto the CD's along with where they were from and again any outcomes she discovered.

She was good at the sneak and peek raids. There was no mention in the press of her activities and if the police knew of them, Franklin's informant would have advised him. She reckoned she could beat Richards's security. Peters the nerd knew the systems backwards and forwards and he was using the security at Franklins as her training lessons. What would stop 999 people out of 1000 – was vulnerable to the one that knew how it worked and dared to try.

The thrill of danger tingled along her spine, spread to all her nerve pathways and made her forget her sore back. The decision felt right!

Wanda did not put her plans into action without considering all possibilities. In her mind was a mental checklist – beginning with checking to see if she was being watched. Richard had a watch on her at first, but not now. That situation could change at whim.

After that, she gave a great deal of attention to her identity. At work, during the day, she used little make up. When working for Richard at night, she had three standard faces – she needed to develop more. She would need to be able to switch from one to the other in minimum time. It would not be hard to remember each one.

Then she would need to gradually increase her frequency of going out at night. Until then, she had stayed home unless going to do jobs for Richard. She would need to be out some nights when she was not working.

She would also need to find more innocuous places to go where she could establish her presence and be able to go into the ladies toilets and change her appearance, then leave to visit the other places she intended to go. Though some, she could probably visit directly.

She already had a long list of places to visit – places sending or receiving correspondence from Richard Franklin's office. That would do for a start.

Then she would look through the offices of the senior managers and perhaps their homes. Some of them had to be part of the Crime division of FCI.

Her method would be systematic, but not noticeably so. An office, a nightclub, a house a shop – all seemingly unrelated and logic would not predict her next move.

It would all rely on her eidetic memory – she would be following several lines of investigation but only she would know where she was with each.

All the while, she would act exactly as Richard expected. She would make no spontaneous comments without thinking the consequences.

Her first victim, as she liked to think of him would be Joseph, poor ultra-polite, secretary Joseph.

It had not been hard to deduce that Richard, and perhaps Harrison, had warned him to expect trouble if he continued to act as if he was Richard's second in command.

Wanda knew he was seething about the reprimand and she had no doubt that if he caught her alone and thought he could get away with it - he would try something.

Joseph, however, was not as smart as he believed. He had no idea that Wanda was observing his apartment and had been for a week. When he went out one evening, Wanda slipped into his apartment and efficiently frisked it. It was neither spotless nor particularly dirty. It was a bachelor's flat, with no sign of feminine presence. The colour scheme was bland beige and cream, the furniture 'comfortable' and far from new. If he was doing jobs for Richard, he was either getting paid a lot less or putting his money into something else beside his living space.

Wanda found more than she expected. One item would have him arrested by the police; another would get him killed by Richard Franklin. The first item, she photographed next to a picture that was on Joseph's lounge room wall. The second, she pocketed and later put in an envelope with details of when and where she found it.

She also photographed some of Joseph's personal papers and his bank statement. Everything was returned to the exact place she found it. Joseph would never know she had been there.

Chapter 18

Wanda looked like a boy. The loose fitting and slightly ragged clothes hid any shape she had. Her hair was plaited and pushed up under a knitted cap, and she was wearing overshoes a size bigger than her normal size.

She sidled through the crowds that were walking around or dining out in the area of the Sausalito boat harbour. She had never been there before so the crowd of amblers provided cover for her covert survey. Her intended targets for the night were two of the vessels moored in the secure pens. The Franklin's owned – or controlled (it was a matter of interpretation) two large ocean going cruisers.

Wanda had descriptions, registration numbers and pen numbers. She intended to see what could find on board them. For now, she was memorising the area and planning escape routes. Later she would swim across, using the other boats for cover, and go on board the Franklins' motor yachts.

Under her old clothes, she wore a lightweight black body suit. It was made of a material that did not hold much water and dripped quickly. Around her waist was her tool kit, and in the pocket of her baggy denims was a folded dry sack, to hold her clothes when she was in the water.

The tourists she was following were looking at and discussing the boats. As they came to the gate leading to the secured pens they stopped, allowing Wanda to notice that the gates were locked electronically, and barbed wire was positioned to prevent people climbing around the fence to reach the walkway to the boats. The fence went around the whole area on the land ward edge, so she was going to have to approach from deep water and she was not a very strong swimmer.

Wanda kept walking even after the tourists had turned back. She was alert for trouble and for anyone who might be taking an interest in her actions. People grew fewer and the lights less frequent. Finally, Wanda found a dark lane leading down towards the water. There was enough moonlight there to see the rocks.

After checking to see that no one could observe her, Wanda slipped out of her baggy clothes and folded them into the dry sack. She sat on the sack to express excess air, before sealing it and putting its strap over her head and shoulder. With her cap pulled down over her face, Wanda checked the torch in the narrow pocket of the body suit and her tool kit. Then she scrambled carefully over the rocks and slipped into the cold water, ducking under quickly to get fully wet.

Wanda felt the pull of the current as she swam to get warm. It was taking her in the direction that she needed to go, so she let it take her, aiding her movement with gentle kicking. The shore was brightly visible and her destination easy to spot. She had to work harder to get inshore.

The rocks at the end of the breakwater were slippery, and Wanda turned to face them as she clung as best she could to them to keep out of the path of a returning trawler. It idled past her, heading for its berth and the wash from its engines bumped her against the rocks.

Wanda swam after it, and could see where it docked on the outermost arm of the marina. Lights came on around it and trucks pulled up next to it to be ready to take the unloaded catch. There was a low landing, seaward of the vessel and Wanda made for that. She clung to the end for a few minutes, listening to the activity on the dock. Feeling safe enough, she pulled herself onto the landing and climbed the steps to peek onto the dock and look for a hiding place. She needed to have a rest. At the end of the dock there seemed to be a stack of oil drums, they would be good enough to hide behind for a time.

The arc of a glowing cigarette butt, alerted her to the presence of someone on the dock on the far side of the drums. She had not heard the person approach, and before she could leave, she would have to be sure they had gone.

A second butt followed the first about five minutes later. About the same time, Wanda heard someone else approach.

"You are late, Petrov. You were meant to be back hours ago."

"Motor trouble, comrade." This voice had a thick accent.

"When will you be going out? We have the cargo ready to transfer. We can't do it in daylight."

"The captain wants the motor checked. Maybe tomorrow."

"It's too dangerous to wait! The deal's off."

"Your choice, comrade."

The second man walked way. Wanda waited a few minutes before peeking over the drums. A third glow arced into the water down near the trawler, locating the first man. The second was probably one of those standing near the trucks.

Wanda studied the scene and decided that she would not be noticed if she kept to the shadows and was quiet on her feet. She climbed around the drums and ran lightly along the dock, there was a man walking back along the dock beyond the boat, and Wanda followed him at a distance. After skirting behind the trucks waiting to be loaded she thought to turn her mask back into a hat. It would make her less suspicious looking if she were seen.

Wanda kept in the shadows, but each light he passed under briefly illuminated the man she followed.

At the end of the dock, the man turned left to where a limousine was parked. The interior light came on briefly as a door was opened and quickly closed. Wanda sneaked closer, using the other parked cars for cover. On impulse, she pulled her cap down again.

The man was speaking quietly to someone, reporting the conversation he'd had on the dock.

"It has to be done tonight," the man was told. Wanda recognised the voice – Richard Franklin. Wanda's curiosity flared. He was meant to be at a function for the company – so what was he doing here?

"Get the truck, back it down onto the dock."

Wanda backed away, she was in a dangerously open position. She needed to be back on the dock before the truck got there and she dare not be seen. Whatever Richard was doing here, could not be legal and if he saw her ... she would be feeding the fishes soon after.

The sound of a police siren did not worry Wanda, but it caused Richard to return to the limo, this time into the driver's seat, and drive it away from the dock. It made Wanda wonder if the man she had followed was Richard's chauffer. Maybe he was worth investigating.

Wanda retraced her steps to the dock and sprinted along it, again keeping to the shadows. When she heard the truck reversing back, she crossed away from the driver's side and crouched next to a bollard. After she was out of the arc of its headlights she moved again, guessing that nothing would happen until the other trucks had left. The one that backed down had an "ICE" sign on the sides and back. She crouched down twice more as trucks, full of fish drove past her. The drivers either did not see her or ignored her.

The remaining two trucks were still being loaded and she slipped past them without raising comment to reach the steps down to the landing. The tide had gone out further and her sack was now out of the water, though still hooked on a crack in the wood. She recovered the sack and moved to perch on a cross beam under the dock.

Any plans to visit Franklin's boats would have to wait, and that being the case, it was time to put her outer clothes back on. It was awkward, perching there and trying to get dressed, but Wanda had lots of practice changing in awkward places, but here, she was not able to avoid getting grassy muck on her clothes from the algae on the piles.

After the last two trucks drove off, the ICE truck reversed next to the trawler. The crew were starting to clean the decks. It was obvious that its driver was not used to the dock, because the other truck drivers had treated the dock like a road, not a stretch of unsealed terrain. Wanda saw the driver board the trawler and start to talk to the skipper.

The back of the truck was not visible to the driver, so Wanda snuck up the steps and went to the rear door. She quickly picked the lock, and as quietly as possible unclamped the door. It swung open soundlessly, and Wanda risked using her torch. She saw bags and bags of ice, and then a reddish stain, running with some water from under the bottom layer. She climbed in and looked behind the ice. A narrow way existed on one side. The torch shone on a man's body, she did not know if he was alive or dead, but she turned quickly to leave.

The lock snapping shut, made a noise, though the clamp did not. Wanda heard an exclamation so she dropped down beside the truck and rolled under it.

"What was that?"

Wanda saw two pairs of feet, one with gumboots and the other with polished shoes.

"Still locked, comrade. Sound travels near water. The noise could've come from anywhere."

"So when did you say the tide will turn?"

"Not for another hour. It would be best to wait until after that. Then anything dropped here will be dragged out into the bay. The ebb tide tends to bring stuff into this corner."

"I don't like the wait."

"My crew will be gone by then, better for you, no?"

"Very well!"

Wanda slipped out from under the front of the truck and once again slipped along the dock. She kept checking to be sure neither of the men saw her. There was a phone box at the end of the dock and she intended to call the police. If the unconscious man was still alive, perhaps they could save him. If not, that driver would have a lot of explaining to do. If she was lucky, Richard might go down to watch whatever was going to be done.

Wanda reached the phone box and immediately disconnected the light. She dialled the number for the operator by feel and asked for the police in a voice pitched lower than her normal.

"My name is John," Wanda claimed. "I just saw someone bashed and thrown in an ice truck. It went down onto the trawler dock at Sausalito. I think they might be going to throw him in the bay."

"Where are you calling from?"

"The phone box at the end of the pier."

"Wait there! A car is on its way."

Wanda was about to emerge when she saw the limousine drive up again and stop. She thought it was going to drive onto the dock, but a group of men were walking off the dock with bags and coats. They headed for some of the parked cars. Wanda used them as a distraction when she slipped out of the phone booth and headed again for the dock. She only got as far as the nearest low landing when she heard the whisper of the limo motor approaching, using only park lights to see by. Wanda ran down the steps, and waited for it to pass by.

Wanda heard another siren, and then a cell phone rang on the dock. The limo began to reverse. Wanda stood up, saw the Ice truck backing closer to the end of the dock, and guessed what was to happen. The men were not going to wait any longer.

She sprinted along the dock, past the trawler, now with only security lights lit, and down on to the seaward low landing. Without thought, she pulled off her shoes and waited. If the man was still alive, he might have seen who bashed him. He was worth trying to help, in case he could testify against the Franklins.

The men were fiddling with the lock, haste making them nervous. There were muffled curses before, "Got it!"

The siren was getting louder, but Wanda could not see flashing lights yet.

Wanda walked to the end of the landing and eased herself into the water, trying to make no sound. She floated along the dock, using the piles to pull herself along to the end. At the end, she used one arm to hold to a piling and the other to ease a sharp knife from her tool kit. Wanda heard the sounds of a struggle, grunting from one of the men and chain rattling. She saw a dark shape falling and a splash. Time was important. Wanda took a firm grip on the knife and a deep breath and dived.

Wanda kept her eyes closed. She would see nothing in the dark water anyway so used her arms to feel around for the man's body. She sensed a disturbance and felt the man's arm.

A hand gripped her, felt the knife in her hand and let go. Wanda felt ropes and a chain and searched for a gap to get her knife at the ropes. She sawed at the rope until she was forced to surface for another breath.

She took a quick but deep breath and dived again. The disturbance was getting more desperate. This time Wanda found the leg bindings and sawed at them. She felt the chain drop away as the man grabbed her, pushing her down in an effort to reach the surface. Wanda grabbed him and kicked for the surface. The man's kicking stopped, and he began to sink again. Wanda dragged him up with her. As her head broke the surface of the water, she took a deep breath and tried to blow air into the man's mouth.

The body floated away, she needed to get him somewhere solid. She grabbed it again, and swam towards the landing.

Tyres screeched on the wooden dock. Car doors slammed. Red and blue flashes touched the bollards on the dock above.

A bright light shone down into the water.

"Hold it right there!" a voice ordered.

"He's not breathing," Wanda called up as her free hand released her tool belt.

Footsteps thumped on the wooden stairs and hands were there to pull the man from the water. More hands helped Wanda from the water even as an officer was starting resuscitation on the man. In the light of the bright torches, she had her first really good look at the man she'd rescued. It was Mike Johnston, bashed, bloody and bruised.

A man in plain clothes brought a blanket to put around Wanda.

"Are you all right?" he asked her. Wanda nodded, her teeth were beginning to chatter and she was shivering.

"How long was he down?"

"N-N-Not long" Wanda forced out. She was feeling the knitted cap on her head beginning to slip and remembered it was the black mask. She pulled it off and allowed it to fall in the water. Her plaited hair fell down and it was obvious that she was not a boy.

"What happened," the plain clothed man asked.

Wanda sat mutely, thinking of a story and a way of getting out of being questioned. She wanted to know if Mike would be all right. The officer, joined by another, was still blowing air into him. It seemed to Wanda that they had found a pulse.

A siren heralded the arrival of the paramedics and their equipment. An ambulance was still coming.

The changeover was smoothly done and after a minute on the oxygen, Mike finally began to cough up the water he had swallowed.

The second paramedic turned to Wanda and asked her questions.

"We'll take you to the hospital and have a doctor look you over."

"I don't need a doctor, I'm fine," Wanda protested. She did not want to go to the hospital.

"Then you are well enough to come to headquarters and tell us what happened," the plain clothed officer suggested.

Wanda looked into the man's craggy face, and then looked away. She was tired now the need to act was over. She accepted the help of the paramedic, to stand up. Mike was being transferred to a stretcher. Wanda decided that she would have more chance of leaving the hospital unseen than a police station, so she followed Mike into the ambulance and obeyed the instruction to lie down on the other stretcher and be strapped in.

One paramedic remained in the ambulance and the other stepped outside and could be heard saying, "Captain, we'll be taking them to San Francisco General."

"Do you know the man's name?" Wanda was asked.

"No," she lied.

"How did you happen to be nearby?"

"I was just hanging around."

"Where do you live?"

"Here and there."

"What's your name?"

Wanda shut up.

"You saved his life, you know!"

Wanda stayed quiet and refused to talk. As the ambulance sped across the Golden Gate Bridge, Wanda pretended to doze.

At the hospital, Wanda discovered that the police had kept up with them. It was not the same man that she had seen at the pier. This one was younger. Mike was wheeled in first and the detective followed her. He sidled into the examination room and waited quietly as Wanda was asked questions and examined. She had stopped shivering by then, and told finally to go home and get out of the wet clothes.

"I'll get you a warm drink," the detective offered. "Then, I'll drive you home."

Wanda, still clutching the blanket, decided to accept the offer of the warm drink, but was considering ways to avoid the drive home.

"Okay, what's your name?"

The detective was feeding coins into a machine and not looking at her. Wanda was wondering if it was safe to talk to him. Richard had at least one police officer on his payroll. Her danger sense was niggling her, but only weakly.

"Call me Jane," Wanda said.

"Is that your real name?"

"It'll do," Wanda insisted. "Look I don't want to be involved anymore. I'll tell you what I saw and did. That's all you need."

"We'll start with that," the detective agreed.

"What's your name," Wanda asked.

The detective produced his identification and allowed her to read it.

"Brian Withers," Wanda read. He was a lieutenant.

Wanda made a decision.

"Could you not mention me, please? Could you just say you had an anonymous tip?"

"Were you the one that called in about the man?"

Wanda nodded.

"Go on," Withers encouraged.

"You need to get a guard on that bloke," Wanda surprised Withers by saying. "His name is Mike Johnson. Last I heard, he was going to the feds to tell about some crooks. He expected to be put in witness protection. That was, oh, about a week ago."

"Are you sure?" Withers snapped, suddenly alert. The name meant something to him.

"Yes."

"Do you know anything…?"

"No," Wanda interrupted.

"How did you happen to be around?"

"It was fluke. I didn't even know it was him till I saw him on the dock." Wanda spun a tale close enough to the truth that Withers did not doubt her. "There was a limo hanging around too. The driver of the truck spoke to someone in it. I wasn't close enough to see any of them."

Withers questioned her carefully and finally told her, "It was a courageous thing to do, going in after him. Wait here. I'll just make a call to get reinforcements here and then I will drive you home."

Wanda nodded, but as soon as he went out of the room, she took off the blanket and slipped out of the hospital. No one saw her go.

Chapter 19

Brian Withers was in a foul mood when he finally returned to headquarters. It was almost three o'clock in the morning, but his partner Captain Carter was still there.

"Found the girl yet?" Mike Carter asked.

"No!" Withers snapped irritably. "No one saw her leave. I had the hospital security alerted within minutes – no trace. I have a call out for her. And I have asked the cab companies to ask if any of their drivers picked her up. If she is on foot, she's good at hiding. I can't even be sure my description is good enough. You saw her – she had a lot of make up on. All I can be sure of is that she isn't black but apart from that I couldn't say if she was Caucasian, Italian, Hispanic or what."

"She identified Mike Johnson," Carter confirmed. "Could she have a record?"

"She was being evasive," Withers agreed. "But if she realised that she had dived into an attempted murder by a crime gang that may be why."

Withers told his partner what the woman had told him. "It could be that she knows more than she was saying ..."

"Johnson worked for Sylvester Franklin," Carter mused. "Do you think the girl works for him or his brother?"

"If she does, it would explain her evasiveness. She wouldn't want them finding out she'd saved him. I wish I'd thought of that earlier. I could have kept the cup she drank from to check for prints."

"Where is Johnson now?" Carter asked.

"Under guard by the local precinct at a nursing home. He's lucky to be alive; we should be able to question him in the morning."

"When are you going to call in the feds?" Carter asked.

"After we talk to him," Withers decided. "How was he found in the first place?"

"A leak?" Carter considered thoughtfully.

"Maybe," Withers conceded. "I have talked to the hospital administrator. If anyone calls about the man, they will get any details they can and let out that the man died."

"You expect another attempt on him?"

"If they know he's alive, probably. I'm actually hoping the girl will call. Anyone else will be a bonus. I thought to leak the news of the rescue to the press."

Whilst Withers had all police units looking for her, Wanda was on her way home.

She had no money or ID on her, so her only means of transport was walking or hitching and the latter did not appeal to her. She did not have shoes either; they were still on the dock as far as she knew. Her dishevelled state would attract attention, so Wanda kept away from the main road and at the first sense of danger, hid in a garden or somewhere. She had avoided at least four police cars that way. If she had her tools, she could have broken in somewhere and got some money and dry clothes, but her kit was in the mud of the bay. Still, there might be other ways. There were apartment blocks along the way – and possibly clothes left out to dry on lines – that would be worth checking.

The first place she snuck into had nothing out. The second place had some clothes roughly her size and she stole some jeans. In a dark corner of the garden, she changed into them. She rolled up her damp slacks and dumped them in a bin near the street entrance. Further along, she picked up a tartan shirt, too big for her, but clean and dry. Again, she changed out of her damp shirt and disposed of it. Finally, just as she was finding her feet were too sore to walk much further, she came to a gas station. In the ladies rest room, she discovered the mess her make-up was in. Using towel from the dispenser, she removed as much of it as possible. It would be one less way the police might recognise her.

As she was walking away, a couple of young men whistled at her. She turned and smiled over her shoulder, it was enough to send them both panting in her direction.

"Want to go for a ride?" one asked, his intentions obvious.

"Only one of me, but two of you," Wanda pointed out, continuing to walk off.

"Got a friend?" the other suggested.

Wanda stopped and turned to look at the young men. "As a matter of fact, I do. She wanted me to meet me at the Ko Ko Mo dance hall. Do you know it?"

"Yeah, I know it. Fancy joint."

"I can get you in," Wanda promised. "I know the owner."

"That right?"

"Come on, if you want to. You'll have to hurry. They close at three."

Wanda endured the pawing of the man who shared the back seat with her and his attempts at passionate kissing. It was worth the inconvenience to rest her aching feet.

At the club, Wanda went to the back door, near where the owner had his office. He knew her, and let her and her friends enter. She had done him a favour some time back and he felt he owed her one in return. He made no comment about her attire and accepted her request to see that both had a drink (she promised to pay him next visit) and the wink that told him she planned to lose both of them.

The men were both sure that the woman would return with her friend, but Wanda went to the ladies room, changed back into her disco gear and left via the front door. The shirt and jeans were left in the hidey-hole where her other clothes had been. Wanda was very pleased to get home and have a quick shower to wash from her hair, the oily scum from the water near the docks.

"Boss wants you in at work," Joseph swaggered into Wanda's apartment early on Sunday morning. Fortunately, she had recovered from her activities on Friday night by sleeping most of Saturday.

"Get out! Knock first and I will listen to you."

"Boss won't like it! He said this was urgent." Joseph insisted.

"Obviously it's something you are not smart enough to do!" Wanda was irritated by Joseph's habit of walking in on her whenever he chose.

Joseph snarled; the jibe annoyed him.

"I'll meet you down stairs, five minutes after you leave here!"

Wanda stared at Joseph and did not move. Joseph backed down first – he was no longer certain of his status with the boss.

When she emerged and had buckled herself in, Joseph drove as fast as he dared, cutting in and out of traffic but not exceeding the speed limit. If he thought he could terrify his passenger, he discovered he was wrong. Wanda looked very relaxed and his irritation increased. He had an important position in the company, but he was treated worse that a basement worker.

In her turn, Wanda knew Joseph was annoyed and did not care. In her opinion, he was a twit – even if he did have his own parking space in the sub-basement garage. It was more than she had, but she did not have a car anyway. If he had any sense, Joseph would feign cooperation when they reached Richard's office after taking the executive lift to the top floor.

Richard was behind his desk, leaning back on his chair, staring pensively out of the window. The Sunday paper was open on his desk. A second man was leaning against a filing cabinet.

Wanda had never seen Richard looking so uncertain. What was up?

"Joseph, wait outside," Richard directed.

His PA went with ill-grace and shut the door after him.

Richard sat up straighter and pointed to the paper. "Seen that?"

Wanda went around next to Richard so she could see the article. She gave no sign of recognising the face pictured.

"Do you recognise him?" Richard asked.

"I can't tell. He's been well worked over. Should I?"

"It's no matter," Richard told her. "The paper says he's alive. I've had word that he's dead. We need to know which it is."

"Do you know where I need to start looking?" Wanda asked.

The other man answered. "He was taken to San Francisco General by the ambulance."

Wanda nodded, mentally adding up pieces of information that she knew or had read in the paper. Two days ago, Sylvester Franklin had walked away from a second arrest on pornography charges. And the main witness, Mike Johnson had turned up bashed and almost drowned. It looked like Sylvester may have arranged to have him killed to prevent further evidence turning up. So, if he was alive, they'd want to try for him again. If he was dead they could bluff it out

"You think it might be a trap?"

"I told you she was smart," Richard told the other man. "The police are likely to be around in force. Don't get caught."

"Not on a Sunday!" Wanda said with a faint grin. "Have you tried ringing?"

"We don't want to make any inquiries that could be traced back here."

"I'll skulk around and let you know what I find out," Wanda promised.

"Get Joseph to drive you," Richard instructed.

Wanda's face hardened.

"He won't give you any trouble," Richard assured her.

"I can handle him," Wanda assured her boss in turn.

When Wanda told Joseph to drive her home, he wanted to know why.

"Use your brain, cretin," was her reply.

"Because you don't have to do anything?" he suggested.

"Brilliant suggestion!"

"But the boss said you had a job to do?"

"How did you ever get to be Richard's personal assistant?"

"He compliments me on my work. I do lots of important things for him," Joseph claimed arrogantly.

"Do you wipe his backside too?" Wanda asked sweetly.

Joseph's hands clenched the steering wheel. His face was set with controlled anger.

"When you get to my building, wait around the back. I'll be ten minutes at most."

He did not acknowledge that he had heard, but he let Wanda out and drove around to the service alley.

Wanda was tempted to let him cool his heels there, but she might need to get away quickly and Richard would want to know what she discovered as soon as possible.

Joseph thought his dreams had come true when the fresh faced and freckled girl entered his car. The red head looked innocent enough to want to kiss and more.

"What are you staring at?" Wanda's voice destroyed his daydream.

Joseph scowled and began to drive.

"San Francisco General Hospital," Wanda directed him.

They parked as close to the entrance as they could. Wanda became just another visitor – a sweet young thing with a worried frown who seemed to know where she was going.

The hospital had open visiting hours, between 10am and 8pm so no one paid much attention to her as she walked purposefully about each floor where there were wards. She saw police guarding a room down from the ICU, but that was the only thing that seemed out of the ordinary. It was not her intention to go to close to the guards, so she wandered down stairs to the emergency and outpatients section. She played with the idea of asking if a mythical relative had been brought in, and then spotted a locked office. As it was Sunday, most of the administrative staff would not be at work. After a quick look around, she forced the lock and entered the empty office.

As she hoped, the office had a computer and it was the work of moments to turn the monitor away from the door and boot up the system. She mentally thanked Peters the Nerd for teaching her more than the basics of using unfamiliar systems. It did not take her long to get into the basic patient records and admission data. There was nothing that matched Mike's case on Friday night, but he was mentioned on Saturday morning.

"John Doe, water ingestion and hypothermia, admitted 0100 Saturday, died 0300. Coroner to collect. There was also an entry about a Jane Christie, police officer, hypothermia, allowed to go home."

Wanda stared at the screen for a moment to be sure she read it right.

"Damn it, damn it, Damn it!"

She closed down the computer and took six deep breaths. She had her emotions under tight control when she carefully emerged from the office.

The man at the main hospital desk was familiar. When he turned, Wanda recognised Detective Withers. His eyes glanced at her then kept moving. Not surprisingly, because Wanda had made her face up to look nothing like the person Withers would be looking for. She didn't feel like smiling at her success at hiding in plain view. Instead she maintained a steady pace out the door and back to Joseph's car.

When she had closed the door, Joseph tossed a phone at her.

"The boss wants a report."

"What's the number?"

Joseph took the phone back from her, dialled the number and handed it back with a superior smile on his face.

"Yes," was Richard's brusque greeting.

Wanda reported what she had seen and discovered on the computer. Richard was silent for a while. "The room is probably a trap — I'll have someone else check it out. Good work."

Richard hung up.

"Drop me off somewhere," Wanda told Joseph. It was a silly comment, because Joseph began to drive off in a direction away from her apartment.

Wanda noticed, but said nothing for a while. Joseph was smirking.

"You like living dangerously, Joseph," she said in a relaxed tone. "You know, not only am I an important operative for Richard Franklin, Harrison f… me and that poor sod that was pulled out of the bay the night before last was your predecessor."

Her comment hit home. Joseph slowed the car and pulled over.

"Where do you want to go?"

"This will do. I'll get my own way home."

Joseph sat for a long time, watching Wanda walk into Golden Gate Park, before taking himself home.

Chapter 20

Wanda's determination to take down Harrison and Richard Franklin hardened. First, it had been Elisabeth, and then Mike.

Tears threatened to overcome her, but she refused to cry. Refused to release her anger or the sense of loss. Instead she kept all her feelings locked away to fuel the fires of revenge.

Well, there was one thing she could do for Mike. Go to his house; get the stuff he had there and put it somewhere safe. Then, when she was ready, she could take it to the police with her stuff.

Wanda walked back to the main road and hailed a cab and directed the driver to take her to the street she wanted. She walked from the corner, where the cab had dropped her along the road to 23A Worths Lane. The area was quiet and Wanda made no attempt to hide her actions. She went up to the door of the house and rang the bell, expecting no answer and getting none. Her body hid the actions of her hands and when she had unlocked the door she walked in and locked the door behind her.

The tiny house was simply furnished, neat and tidy but with no sense of being lived in. There was a thin layer of dust, noticeable on the shiny surfaces but not as much as she might have expected. Someone must come in periodically to dust.

Mike hadn't told her exactly where he had hidden the copies of his evidence against Franklin so he probably guessed that she would be able to find it easily, but others would not.

Wanda started by looking through all the rooms and then she began to search with systematic thoroughness and the utmost tidiness.

She found the key first, under a flap of carpet, under the armchair. This was quickly added to her own collection. The discs and papers and any videos or tapes remained elusive. Even when she had searched all rooms, she still had nothing to show. It was just beginning to occur to her that maybe Mike had already taken it to the police, when her danger sense flared and the doorbell rang.

Wanda heard the sound of voices outside the front door. She didn't make a dash for the back door, instead she recalled the manhole in the laundry and the step-stool in the kitchen. Working quickly and quietly, Wanda took the stool to the laundry, positioned it next to the wall but still close enough for her to stand on to reach the hole and climbed onto it.

It was the work of moments to push the hatch aside and pull herself up into the roof. She almost laughed. Even though she would have to wait to search up here, she could hide by sitting on the replaced manhole cover to stop the latest visitors looking up there.

From her position, Wanda could make out the tones of three voices, a gruff male voice, a younger sounding male voice and a woman's voice.

"I saw a girl go in, Detective Carter. She rang the bell and the door opened. I was sure Mr Deacon must be here."

Wanda heard that clearly. The people must be in the house.

"The back door is locked." That was the younger male voice.

"There's no one here now," said gruff voice. "You can leave things with us now, thank you Mrs Gordon. We'll lock up when we leave." That was gruff voice again.

The voices faded again and shortly after, and Wanda heard the sounds of the house being searched. Would they think to check the roof space? Wanda settled herself more firmly on the hatch, and when she felt the pressure on the hatch, she held her breath.

"Do you think they got here first?" young voice asked from directly below.

"Nothing looks disturbed. They wouldn't be neat," Gruff voice said. "I'll organise a watch on the place and get a crew in to search again. We have better things to do than stay here."

The voices moved away and shortly after, Wanda heard the front door close firmly. Even when she heard a car start up outside and move off, Wanda didn't move. Her danger sense hadn't abated. She continued to stay still and listen. Patience was one thing she had in plenty. It was an asset in her 'business'.

When the house had been quiet for about fifteen minutes, Wanda began to flex her muscles to loosen them up. After a while, she began to crawl along the beams searching up there for Mike's stuff. There was enough light coming in through the chinks in the tiles to see where she was going.

Some faint noises were inevitable, but there was no indication from below that the noise had been heard. The guard she still sensed must be outside.

In the furthest corner of the roof, pushed right into the corner of the eaves was a metal box. Wanda quietly pulled it out. It was dusty and locked – with no sign of a key.

Wanda eased her way back to the manhole.

The sudden glare of a powerful torch shone in her eyes, blinded her. She put up an arm to shield her eyes.

"Keep moving forward. Bring the box with you."

Wanda heard the click of a safety lock coming off a gun and her heart began to race. She recognised 'young voice'.

"Pass me the box, slowly."

"No!" Wanda argued.

"You are not in a position to argue, Miss," Lieutenant Withers warned. "Keep coming."

Withers took the box and stepped down off the stool. He kept his weapon on the girl as she swung down from the roof, awkwardly, and landed heavily on the floor.

"We'll talk in the front room," Withers said, taking Wanda's right arm in a gentle grip.

Wanda pretended not to hear and said nothing. Her mind had spun back to the first time she had been caught – before the training centre.

Withers took out a cell phone and pushed a button. He handled it with just his free hand. "We have a customer," was all he said.

A few minutes later, a second police officer entered the house. Wanda recognised him too.

"What are you going to do to me?" Wanda asked, trying to pull away.

"What were you doing here?" Withers challenged.

"Who are you?" Wanda asked.

Withers released her and drew out his badge to show her then introduced Captain Carter.

Wanda drew back further, licking her lips as if to moisten them. She was trying to make them think she was sweet, innocent and scared.

"I came to see a friend."

"Why did you break in?"

"I didn't, I had a key."

"Where is it?" Withers asked, controlling his scepticism.

Wanda slipped her hand into her pocket and felt around. "I had it before I went up into the roof. It must have slipped out up there. I can go and look."

"That won't be necessary," Carter told her, giving no indication as to whether he believed her. "We will have to take you back to headquarters."

Wanda kept her face controlled.

"What's your name?" Withers asked.

"What is your friend's name?" Carter tried when Wanda didn't answer the previous question. He wasn't expecting her to answer that either.

Wanda glanced around and decided to answer.

"Mike. Mike Johnson."

"Did he tell you to come here?" Carter asked.

"Sort of," Wanda said, moving her weight from foot to foot.

"When?"

"I last spoke to him months ago."

"So why come here today?"

"I promised him that I would mind some stuff if something happened to him. And I haven't heard from him for months," Wanda said quickly.

"Has something happened to him?" Carter asked her.

"He said he was going to testify against some big and important people and he wouldn't be able to see me again. I saw his picture in the paper." Wanda found it easy to produce tears.

Withers snapped his fingers.

"I remember now! I saw you at the hospital. How did you know he was there?"

Wanda shut up. The paper hadn't mentioned the hospital.

Carter took her face in his hand and looked closely.

"You rescued him!"

Wanda decided on a scene of hysterical tears, carefully calculated to reinforce young and naive. Withers helped her to a chair. They questioned her more gently.

"Why did you run that morning?" Withers asked.

"I was scared. I didn't want anyone to know what I'd done and it was a fluke I was even there."

"Why were you there?" Carter asked.

"I was just hanging around. It was something to do and I'd never been around there before. I was just sitting on the landing watching the boat unload and I was about to leave when I saw the body fall. I didn't even know who it was till you got him on the dock."

"Will you tell us your name or do we need to fingerprint you to see if you have a record?" Withers persisted.

Wanda widened her reddened, moist eyes.

"No, you don't have to. It's Gwenda Willard."

"If you come with us to Headquarters, we'll get your statement and we will keep this quiet. We will put the box in a safe place. Do you know what's in it?"

Wanda shook her head. "Not exactly. I think it's a copy of his evidence against the person."

Carter nodded.

"How do I know you'll keep me out of this? Someone must have found out where Mike was being kept, if they got at him," Wanda said reproachfully.

"We'll keep quiet about you. Did you get a good look at any of the people?"

"No, I told Mr Withers that already."

"Where do you live?" Withers asked.

"Richmond."

"With your parents?" Carter asked.

"No! I'm eighteen. I don't need them!"

"Do you have a job?"

"Odd jobs. Messenger, deliverer of advertising material and stuff."

"We can keep you in a safe house for a couple of days, in case anyone knows about you."

Carter offered. We have another friend of Mike Johnson there. He came and saw us earlier. You might know him."

Wanda sniffed and nodded, wiping her eyes carefully, with her sleeve.

Mike had mentioned 'friends' that worked for Sylvester Franklin. One of whom had spilt his guts to Rocky. She wanted to see this person. See if she knew him. Her disguise should hold.

Wanda travelled with the detectives to a nursing home. She decided that they had fallen for her innocent act. She only knew roughly where they were when they stopped in a quiet street, entered a building that looked like a large house and went through to a room at the back. The people she saw were the two police officers guarding a door. Withers instructed one of them to come in and take dictation.

Wanda didn't recognise the blond haired man who turned from looking in a mirror when he heard the door open.

"Miss Willard, this is Kevin Mason. You both know Mike Johnson," Carter said.

Mason stared at Wanda and his regard was disturbing.

"I suppose…" Mason began, "You know Mike died this morning."

Wanda nodded.

"Miss Willard almost saved him," Withers said, watching for a reaction from Mason.

"You went into the water?" Mason asked intently.

Wanda nodded.

"That took a lot of courage," Mason praised her. His voice was becoming huskier. "I told the police I would pay for the funeral expenses."

"I'd like to put something towards it too," Wanda said, making eye contact with the stranger. She was feeling decidedly odd.

"That's good of you, but they tell me it will be a while yet before they will release his body. I'm going to be travelling a bit so I'll give you the name of another friend of Mike's. David Martin – do you know him?"

Wanda's head shot up. She stared at Mason.

"I've heard of him," she said carefully hiding a sudden elation.

"He'll be handling things in my absence. Just tell him you want to help with the funeral. He'll know what to do."

Mason found a pen to write with and wrote a mobile number on a piece of paper Withers passed him.

"Would you like to tidy up, Miss Willard?" Withers asked then.

"Yeah," Wanda agreed, and she followed Withers to a small bathroom where she found a flannel, towel brush and comb.

She returned, feeling much better.

"Mr Mason has vouched for you," Carter told Wanda. "I think, this time, we won't charge you."

"Thank you," Wanda said humbly. She desperately wanted a moment alone with Mason, but she had first to make a statement.

Withers sent one of the guarding officers off to find a typewriter or someone who would let him use a computer. Withers then followed Carter out of the room for a private discussion.

"Mike?" Wanda asked in a tiny voice as soon as the door had closed.

Mason placed his hands on her cheeks and kissed her. The familiar electricity passed between them.

"Mike is dead and I don't intend to stay in protective custody for ever."

"What can I do?"

"Do you have the key?"

Wanda nodded.

"Make David Martin live. When I leave protection, I'll change with the double."

"You can't wear make-up all your life."

"I'll have to. They made a mess of my face."

"I've earned heaps from ... you know. I'll pay for you to have plastic surgery, please."

Mason's eyes betrayed his emotion at her offer. "How will you get me the money?"

"I'll make an account and tell my sister the details. Call her, I'll warn her first. What name?"

"Kevin Mason will do. That's my new identity."

Wanda nodded and told him the number of her sister's cell phone. They drew apart. She controlled her elation. She wasn't home free yet.

Wanda made her statement and waited while the officer typed it up for her to sign. Withers offered to let her stay at the house for a few days but Wanda wanted to go home.

The address she gave Withers was for a block of apartments a mile from her place.

He stopped outside and offered to walk her up, but she declined.

<h1 style="text-align:center">Chapter 21</h1>

Wanda checked her apartment. There appeared to have been no visitations in her absence as none of her passive sensors had been tripped. Once inside, she deadlocked her door. At this moment, she only wanted to be alone.

Her first action was to remove all of the make-up that made her look 'sweet Irish' and to remove the colour rinse from her hair. While she washed, she allowed herself to relive that exquisite moment when she realised that Mike Johnson, soon to be David Martin, still lived. It was the instant that she knew, beyond all doubt, what she wanted her future to be. Mike Johnson, never really had a chance. David Martin would.

As for herself, before she could be free she had to rid herself of the Franklins. It wouldn't be easy, but the result would be worth it.

A fleeting doubt assailed her. What would she do when she no longer had the danger, the risk, to sustain her? She told herself that day was a long way off.

Brian Withers went back to headquarters late in the evening and was surprised to find his partner still there.

"What have you got?" Carter asked him.

"Not a lot." Withers reported the results of his afternoon's investigations.

"Did you turn up anything on the girl?" he really wanted to know.

"Nothing from those watching the apartment," Carter reported. "I ran a check through missing persons – found a Gwenda Willard mentioned – seven years back. Wait for it – eldest daughter of Senator Charles Willard."

"Did you speak to him?" Withers was more than curious.

"He said his daughter had brown hair, not red, no freckles, and blue green eyes, not grey. Height was about the same, but she would be twenty-three, not eighteen and could never be described as a 'sweet young thing' or 'a nice kid'. The split was permanent he said, that his daughter had made it clear that she never wanted to see him again and he told her never to come back. He thinks she changed her name."

"So who is our shy young heroine?" Withers asked rhetorically.

"That's what I want to know. I also want to know why she was hanging around the boat harbour, disguised, and why there are no prints in the house except Johnson's and the housekeeper's. When you first saw her did she have gloves on?"

"Not that I noticed," Withers considered.

"We'll keep the watch on her. I don't want any accidents happening to her. I think she might know more than she's saying."

"Should we bring her in?"

"Not yet, let's see what happens in the next day or two."

Wanda did not see Richard for over a week. A very polite Joseph told her he was down in LA. Wanda relaxed, she did not object to a break from working for Richard. She could step up the pace of her own agenda.

If a watcher had been observing her over time, they would have noticed that she was spending less time in the dance clubs and more time at the theatre. If anyone had known and cared to quiz her, she had a dozen logical reasons ready. None of them related to an interest in a young actor, who was not too dissimilar to Kevin Mason, honest looking and in need of work.

Wanda talked to the man on a number of occasions, finally approaching him with her offer. He accepted readily, and listened to how he would have to act to be like David Martin. Payment and accommodation was arranged.

That done, Wanda arranged for money to be available to Kevin Mason. Then she called her sister on the mobile number she had memorised months ago and still remembered.

"Hello, Lishka" Wanda greeted her sister.

Elisabeth had the presence of mind to play down her reaction.

"Hello, how are you?"

"I'm great, but I need a favour?"

"Hang on, I'll just go and look."

Wanda guessed that her sister wasn't alone.

"What do you want? Dad won't let me protect you. I told him it was you who helped me that night and you'd risked yourself to do it. He told me that we weren't to do anything for you. He's stubborn…"

"I told him not to," Wanda said. "Anyway this isn't for me but for a friend of mine."

Wanda quickly explained what she had done and wanted her to do when Kevin Mason contacted her.

"That's easy, Wanda. You know I'll do it. This man – he's special?"

Wanda was silent for a long moment. "Yes."

"I'll take care of him," Elisabeth promised.

Richard walked in on her when she was having a session with Peters the Nerd. Since she was reassembling a complexly wired board, she let Peters greet him.

"Good morning, Sir." He stood up straighter.

"How is your student progressing? Does she know everything yet?" Richard asked, watching Wanda working.

Wanda answered before Peters could.

"Hell no! Every time I think I do he throws in a new twist. I didn't think it was possible for anyone to remember so much tech stuff."

Richard gave Peters a glance of approval. The latter smiled, appreciating Wanda's tact. He had mentioned at the start of that session that she almost knew all he did. However, Wanda did not want Richard to think Peters was of no further use.

"What are you doing?" Richard asked, interested.

"I told her to modify a security board to bypass one section," Peters explained.

Richard nodded with a faint smile. When Wanda put down her tools, he called a halt.

"I want you both, to collaborate on a project," Richard said as he took a seat in a vacant chair.

Wanda glanced at Peters the Nerd.

"Uh, Ok" Wanda agreed.

"Peters, I'll be taking you around to a number of important places. I want you to study the security and give me a report on how to improve it. Miss Dean. I want you to see if you can break it."

Wanda allowed a grin to spread to her face.

Richard went on, aware of Wanda's eagerness.

"Peters, you'll be getting a consultant fee for this. Miss Dean, You'll get a bonus for every system you get into and Peters will get it for every one that beats you."

Wanda turned back and pretended to study the boards she was working on.

"What's the criterion for proving that I've got in?" Wanda asked casually.

"I'll give you tokens to put in the safes," Richard said, and then added, "Put it in unobserved, leave undetected."

Wanda nodded. "Does this include your office?" She was still looking at the board as if the answer was not important.

Richard tensed a moment, then relaxed and smiled.

"Yes, yes I think it will. Same stakes as last challenge."

"Okay," Wanda accepted.

"You won't find it as easy as the other places," Richard warned her.

"I know more now!"

Richard smiled wider. "Peters, make sure you don't discuss your findings with Miss Dean. We don't want to give her too much help keeping your bonuses."

Wanda grinned wickedly.

"Tomorrow morning, Peters. 9 am," Richard said as he stood up to leave.

When he had gone, Peters looked at Wanda and shook his head.

"After hours, the guards have orders to shoot first. You won't do it."

"Well, it'll be an easy bonus for you," Wanda said. "But if he's worried about security on important places – what is more important that the security of the Director's safe?"

Peters gave her no argument, but he frowned slightly because she seemed so confident. He said nothing, but intended to install a minor modification in Mr Franklin's office before he left for the night.

Wanda walked openly into the IT section near lunchtime, collecting and delivering mail. Brad, who had once been in the mailroom, greeted her.

"Is Peters in," Wanda asked casually in return.

"No, he went upstairs," Brad said, turning back to his own work. His attention was for a program on the screen.

"I'll write a note and leave it on his desk. It's not important."

Brad just waved in acknowledgement. Wanda hoped he would forget she had even been there.

Wanda went openly to where Peters had his cubicle and found, laid out on his desk, exactly what she wanted. As she had expected, Peters had pulled out the security schematics for four of Franklin Industries' lesser buildings. Beside them was a neat list of parts of each building to concentrate on.

Wanda grinned – she would have a busy time the next two nights. These 'important places' were not ones that she knew of already. So, she would visit them quickly, find anything important, before Peters decided to change anything.

Wanda left the top floor round until slightly after her normal time. She did not miss the fact that the guards' weapons were more visible than normal. It was a sign that Richard had put them on high alert. She grinned at them as they checked her half-full mailbag more thoroughly than ever before. They had relaxed into only giving her a cursory search.

As she walked into the outer office, their attention was already turned back to the stairs and elevators. Wanda knew that Joseph had already left for the day. He wasn't one to willingly work back, especially when Richard was not due back until late.

The guards had no idea that she knew of the security override switch under Joseph's desk. That was something that Peters had talked about but he hadn't said there was one in the office here. She had deduced it and looked until she found it. That had been achieved when Joseph was away from his desk when she had come for the mail one day.

The switch only affected the security in Richard's office. It meant that when the main system came on line after hours, the alarms in there were neutralised.

Wanda walked into Richard's office without wasting time. Her danger sense was quiet as she worked on Richard's safe. He had changed the combination since the last time she had done this, but she still succeeded in opening the complicated lock in a very short time. From her pocket, she pulled a letter which she slipped into the safe. Just as she was about to close the safe again, she heard a faint click and a beeping began.

Wanda finished shutting the safe and began backing out of the office as the guards raced in with weapons drawn. At least the shoot first order did not come in until after p.m. One guard watched Wanda as his partner scanned the room.

The first guard quickly frisked her one his partner had assured himself the woman was alone.

"There's a card in my pocket," Wanda said calmly. "It will explain why I am here."

The guard found it and frowned at it. He must have at least recognised Richard's signature on it. What was so difficult to understand about it?

"He sent me in to test the security of his office," Wanda said into the face of the guard's confusion.

"You? The mail girl!" the second guard found that amusing.

"Yeah! He thought you might be so used to me as to be slack. Congratulations, you passed. Now you are meant to call him and brag."

The second guard went off to summon his superior, using Joseph's phone. Wanda waited with calm expectation. The first guard kept a firm grip on her arm and forced her to walk out into Joseph's office.

The guard leader arrived quickly and surveyed the situation for himself. He knew how to reach the director.

The silence in the room when the guard leader finished reporting to Richard Franklin enabled her to hear the reply being amplified into the receiver.

"Good work, Timms. Hold her there. I am on my way back. Make sure you maintain your other patrols."

"Yes, Sir. Of course."

Timms turned to Wanda and told her to sit on the spare chair in the corner of the room. It was away from any potential weapon, but Wanda wasn't going to try to escape. He then dismissed the other two guards.

"I don't know if I shut the safe again properly," Wanda commented.

Timms considered that and used his gun to indicate they would go in there to check.

Wanda was told to sit again, this time Timms used handcuffs to secure her to one leg of Richard's solid wood desk. He checked the safe and decided to sit at the director's desk. He would have a report when the boss was on his way back.

Wanda used the waiting time to scan the room with her eyes. Something had set off the alarm. She couldn't see parts of the desk, but there were no signs of anything about the safe. The walls were plain except for the few expensive art prints. The narrow frames looked unmodified and no part of the design could hide a sensor.

Timms had moved from Richard's seat as soon as his mobile phone had rung. The guard at the garage entrance to the executive lift had reported the boss's return.

Richard strode into his office within a couple of minutes of the report. He took in the scene in his office and went to sit behind his desk. He stared at Wanda for a long moment. Long enough for her to know she had lost out on this 'challenge'.

"You may release her Timms."

"Your evaluation, Miss Dean?" Richard asked as Wanda rubbed her wrists to get circulation back in them.

"I waited to come up so I was a little later than usual but not so late as to raise questions. It meant that Joseph was gone too. I used the switch on Joseph's desk to override the security on your office," Wanda said calmly. "I decided it was reasonable to assume that if I had noticed it, someone else might too. Of course, the main system doesn't come on until later. Your safe was not too hard to open but just as I was closing the safe, the alarm went off. The guards were in here within seconds."

Richard nodded. Timms looked pleased.

"What do you think betrayed you?"

Wanda remembered the click she had heard. That, she decided, must have been the alarm system resetting. She chose not to mention that.

"That damned fish eye lens," she said. "They must have seen me."

Richard went still. "What lens?"

Wanda pointed to a small dot in the corner of the office ceiling. That was something Wanda wanted to know more about.

"Timms, see if Mr Peters is still in the building." Richard ordered.

From his thoughtful posture, one hand massaging his chin, Wanda decided that Richard knew nothing of the lens. That was interesting.

Timms returned and said, "He's on his way up."

"Do you know anything about that lens in the roof?" Richard asked.

"No, Sir!" Timms said, craning his neck to look for the device.

"I'll call you if I need you again." Richard dismissed the man.

When the guard leader had gone, Richard opened his safe and checked the contents. He removed the envelope Wanda had placed in there; one of six that he had sent down to her earlier in the day.

"Almost, but not completely!" Richard smiled as he reminded her of the stakes of the game. "One unpaid task, as yet unspecified."

"Last time, it was – entertaining," Wanda said suggestively.

Richard's expression tightened. "I have no one needing entertaining at the moment. When I have a suitable job for you I will tell you."

Wanda subsided. Teasing Richard Franklin was like teasing a cobra. You couldn't be sure if he was going to strike. Right now, he had other things on his mind. Wanda hoped that if he thought she had enjoyed 'entertaining', that he wouldn't make her do that again.

Peters the Nerd entered Richard's office, slightly out of breath.

"You wanted me, Sir?"

"When did you last sweep this room for bugs?"

"Yesterday, Sir."

"Can you tell me what that is?" Richard pointed to the tiny lens.

Peters squinted trying to see it. He tried again without his glasses. Obviously, it was too small and too far away for him to see it. Instead, he took a small device from his pocket and aimed it in the indicated direction.

"It's not active, Sir," he said, studying the readout on the small screen. "I'll need to get closer to look at it. I know for a fact it isn't shown on the schematics, and I don't remember seeing it before."

"Tell Timms to organise the ladder," Richard said to Peters.

"No bonus for this job, Miss Dean," Richard said to Wanda. "Do you think Peters deserves it?"

"Well, if it wasn't that lens that gave me away, I don't know what did – yet," Wanda said, keeping the truth to herself. "So yeah, I think he does."

"But the system isn't foolproof. You still had time to get into the safe."

Wanda shrugged. He could decide for himself.

Richard sat back in his chair, deep in thought. As he had not dismissed her, she stood up, walked across to his window, and pretended to be interested in the view. In fact, she was considering the implications of the discovery. Her first concern was who had placed the lens and when, though not so much how. It led to her second concern of who was monitoring the office. Did the lens take film or pictures? Had that unknown person seen her in there before? And was there any chance of Richard finding out how many times she had been in and out of his office undetected before this time? On the same point, did the other offices on this floor have lenses in too?

Timms returned with a ladder and a few minutes later Peters returned with a bag of tools. He nimbly climbed the ladder and examined the lens.

"There must be a way to get to it from behind," Peters called down.

"Timms, take Miss Dean up to the roof and look around. Peters, you and I will see if there are any more of these things."

Wanda explored the roof, memorising every detail as she looked for a way the lens might have been inserted in Richard's office.

She was thoughtful as she walked back downstairs.

"Mr Timms," she asked politely. "When the electricians have to work on the lights and stuff for the top floor, where do they go?"

"There's a crawl space giving them access to the wiring. It goes in from the switch room."

Wanda had a mental picture of the switch room but she had never gone in.

Wanda reported her conclusions to Richard.

"Leave it with me for a while," Wanda was told. "Go and have a coffee downstairs. I may need you still."

A lot later, Peters joined her.

"The Boss, said you can go home."

"What were those things," Wanda asked.

"Micro digital cameras. Passive for all but a microsecond every so often. That is why my equipment never picked them up. It had a card to store the pictures and a modem connection. Every so often, someone dials into it and triggers a download and clears the disc," Peters explained.

"Not good," Wanda said. "Is the Boss furious?"

"I don't think he's mad at me, though it's hard to tell. Have you figured out what stopped you yet?"

"Not yet. But I will – eventually!"

Peters the nerd grinned. "See ya."

Chapter 22

The Starlight Casino was a popular attraction for tourists in San Francisco. Wanda knew that it was operated by what she privately called the Crime Division of Franklin Consolidated Industries. She had decided it was time she went there on a 'scouting mission'.

For the excursion, she prepared her disguise with even greater care because she had overheard Richard saying he would be meeting someone at the casino. Instead of just changing her hair and face, she also padded out her clothes to look less slender than she was and added cheek pads in her mouth.

Wanda had arrived by cab and wandered in through the front doors just as Richard and Harrison entered the foyer from a side room. The disguise had worked. Neither of the Franklins did more than let their eyes slide over her as she passed close to them.

Wanda felt the glee building inside herself and firmly controlled it. She was there to see if she could spot the people they were meeting and to learn the layout of the place.

Her first action was to get some chips and mingle with the crowd until she found a place where she could sit and watch the other patrons.

A blond head of hair belonging to one of the croupiers caught her attention. It almost distracted her from seeing Richard and Harrison shepherding three strangers upstairs. They were too far away for her to try to take photos. Wanda slipped over to the stairs and glanced up. The tuxedo-clad men on the stairs looked like muscle to her and the idea of trying to find the meeting became unwise. Instead, she decided to continue her look around – at the table with the blond croupier.

The man was concentrating on his job, taking bets on the spin of the roulette wheel. Wanda joined the group at the table, two people away from the croupier and studied what she could see of his face. It was tantalisingly familiar. She placed a bet and watched the wheel spin. She lost. The woman beside her moved away and Wanda moved into her space.

Wanda glanced at the croupier after she had placed a second bet and found him studying her. Their eyes met. The man's face wore a puzzled expression as if he had found something almost familiar about her. He went back to his task. Wanda continued to study him, finally becoming aware something strange about his face.

The man had a false skin of stretchy rubber, which would be held on by some special adhesive. This was enough to get Wanda thinking. That sort of disguise on an employee here was odd. It suggested that the man had something to hide from his employers.

A tingle of excitement travelled down Wanda's spine. It intensified when she glimpsed his name badge. David Martin.

Wanda almost jumped with excitement, all notions of further scouting completely forgotten.

The man, between her and David Martin, won that spin and decided to withdraw. Wanda moved into his space, and placed her third bet. She arranged for her hand to brush the croupier's hand. The electricity was still there.

As the wheel spun, she again met the croupier's eyes. He stared at her again, before a slow smile formed on his face. The smile remained even when his attention was on his work. The next spin, Wanda won giving her an excuse to smile broadly back at David.

Wanda kept placing small bets until another croupier came to relieve David. Then, she followed him to the bar and ordered a mineral water with lemon, for both of them.

David ushered Wanda into a more secluded corner.

"Kevin Mason didn't warn me you would be here," Wanda said deliberately. It was just in case David still wasn't sure who she was.

"I didn't tell him," David claimed with a grin. "I really have to thank you. That young woman you told me about, Elisabeth, is a really lovely person."

"Not like me, huh?" Wanda said.

David took her face in his hands and kissed her briefly. After that, neither of them doubted the identity of the other.

"Why the mask?" Wanda asked very quietly.

"It's just until the scars from the operations fade," David assured her. "They have done an excellent job. I owe you for this."

"No you don't. I did it because I …" Wanda couldn't say the words in her mind.

"Love you…" David finished. Wanda nodded and he took her hands and squeezed them gently. "I finish at eleven. Come and see me before you go. I have something to give you."

Wanda nodded, reluctant to leave David, now she had found him but recalling she was here for a purpose. "I will."

Shortly before eleven o'clock, Wanda cashed in her chips. She had come out of the evening slightly better off than when she started. She moved back past the roulette table and couldn't see David there.

He found her and whispered for her to follow him. She found herself walking through the staff portions of the casino and out to the trades and delivery entrance. David allowed himself to put an arm around Wanda as they walked to where he had a car parked.

Wanda slipped her arm around him too, enjoying the feel of his body next to hers. She did wonder what was in the flat parcel he was hiding under his jacket on the far side from her.

David drove away from the casino and asked where Wanda wanted to be dropped. She told him of a spot not too distant from her place. David stopped there and they talked for a while.

"I have a tape and some photos," David told Wanda. "The tape is of the meeting this evening and the photos show what was in the safe in the upstairs office. Think you can hide them?"

Wanda nodded, there was enough light coming into the car for David to see her grin.

"Good girl."

"Do I get a reward?"

David kissed her and they remained enjoying each other for a long time.

Wanda was still on a high when she reached the door of her flat. That did not mean she was neglecting precautions that were almost instinctive. As she searched for her key with one hand, her eyes scanned the doorframe. A tiny red light was just visible in the corner of the frame.

All other thoughts went out of her mind. The red light meant that someone had been in her apartment during her absence. She waited quietly. The red light remained steady. If the intruder was still in there it would flash as he moved. Wanda watched the light as she noisily unlocked her door. It still stayed steady. A good chance the intruder was long gone, but she would be ready.

Wanda turned on the light and closed the door, she didn't lock it yet. She slipped the parcel from David under the nearest armchair and threw her bag onto the coffee table across the room. Then she studied where everything was in the room and compared it with her memory of where things were before she left. The differences were slight, a small statue in the right place but at a slightly different angle, a picture she usually kept hanging at a slight angle, was now perfectly level, a fancy crocheted table mat was not at the same angle as she had placed it and the computer mouse was not on the same spot on its mat.

Her bedroom, bathroom and kitchen all revealed the same subtle signs of a thorough and careful search. The person responsible was not still in her apartment.

Wanda was thoughtful and more than a little concerned. Nothing incriminating would have been found. The only sensitive stuff around was what she had just brought in. She strode back to her lounge and locked the front door. Then she recovered the parcel and wrote the date on the paper David had wrapped it in. then she turned out her light and slipped out into the passage. Her senses told her she was alone. She knocked on the door of the apartment opposite, and heard no response. Janet would be out at work, as usual. Wanda forced the lock and entered. A quick check of the apartment assured her she was alone. She quickly hid the parcel in the hidey-hole with her spare make up and some emergency cash, then replaced the broken board, blew dust into the cracks and replaced the rug and chair over the hole.

With relief, she returned to her place and locked the door.

Just to be sure, she searched her place again. There was no clue to who the intruder had been and that unsettled her. Why had they searched? What had they hoped to find?

The problem occupied her mind as she removed her make-up and the padded outfit and slipped into her pyjamas.

It occurred to her to check her answering machine. The phone was a recent acquisition, insisted on by Richard. She didn't use it to call out on, except for perfectly harmless uses and she had not given the number out to anyone. She was wary of using the phone. They were too easy to bug.

She thought of it as the 'hot line' because the only one that called her on it was Richard. Two calls had been received, but no messages. Odd! Too bad this system didn't have the ability to store the caller's number. Maybe the calls had been wrong numbers. If Richard had instigated the calls, he usually left a terse message – call the office, call his mobile or call at home.

Wanda thought, as she lay in bed, that it might be wise to stop her private activities for a while. She needed to determine if someone was watching her. Her senses had not warned her tonight, but then tonight her senses had been enjoying the proximity of David Martin!

"If I am being watched," Wanda thought to herself three days later, "then they are very, very good."

All she had to go on was a 'funny feeling', nothing like as strong as her 'danger sense'. It felt like she had eyes watching her, all the way to work and all the way back. The feeling disappeared when she was at work in the Franklin building.

The first two days of it, she stayed home after work and tried to spot the watcher by wandering with apparent aimlessness around her apartment building. Whoever it was, they stayed well hidden. Too bad she didn't dare climb onto the roof of her building in daylight.

The third day, she went out in the evening to the local shops and wandered around doing her shopping. The sense of being followed persisted. She took her purchases home and decided to go out to one of her favourite haunts via the back way. All the time she was walking, quietly, she listened for footsteps behind her. In spite of the lack of footsteps and seeing no one, she was still convinced she was being followed.

Wanda ducked quickly into a side road, jumped over a low fence and hid where she could see if someone came after her. No one came. She waited half an hour. The funny feeling had eased, so she continued on to her intended destination.

Wanda stayed at the club for an hour and then decided to go onto an all-night drug store and then to a second club. The feeling of being followed had resumed.

Since her choice of destination could not have been predicted, it seemed to indicate that her follower had to know her regular habits and haunts. They had lost her near her apartment so they had come on to her places of entertainment. She had six favourite places – did that mean six people tailing her? Who considered her that important? The police? No, if they knew who she was they would pick her up right away. There were those outstanding warrants for her.

The next important question was – did these followers know when she changed her looks? She would test that out next time.

The following night, Wanda went to a dance club, stayed for a while then changed her clothes, make-up and hairstyle. She walked from there to the nearest picture theatre. She hadn't gone far when the funny feeling resumed. She bought a ticket for the movie due to start next and went into the theatre but left immediately via one of the side doors.

The funny feeling started again a short time later.

Damn, she had run out of ideas. Richard was not going to like this!

Chapter 23

Wanda made her usual morning round to the top floor. Joseph's desk was vacant, but Richard's door was open. He heard her come in and beckoned her into the office.

"Sit," He said as he walked around to his chair.

Wanda sat back in the guest's chair, but didn't relax.

"I have an important errand for you to do tonight," Richard began, stopping when he saw Wanda's frown.

"Is there a problem?"

"Yes, Sir. There is," Wanda spoke with careful politeness. "I think I am being followed. To work, from work and when I go out at night."

"Indeed," Richard seemed to go still and his voice became silkier. "Why do you think this?"

"It sounds silly, but I feel like I've got someone looking over my shoulder."

Wanda couldn't tell what Richard was thinking. "It feels a bit like it does when I am on a job and a guard comes up. I know to hide till he's gone."

"I remember Jack telling the Old Man about your uncanny sense of danger," Richard admitted, and Wanda relaxed a fraction.

"And someone searched my place four nights ago. They did a very tidy job of it but I have ways to tell someone was there. I've had this funny feeling since then."

Wanda related what she had done to try and shake her followers and how they always found her again.

"It's creepy, uncanny and I can't work if I feel I'm being watched. I intended to tell you today. This is way out of my league."

Wanda sat as still as Richard, betraying no outward sign of worry.

"You should have said something sooner," Richard said sharply.

"I wanted to give you something more concrete than a 'funny feeling'," Wanda said, meeting Richard's gaze. "I trust these feelings. If I didn't, I wouldn't be working for you now – I'd be in jail. But most people think I am making them up."

"I'll look into it," Richard promised. "Keep doing everything you normally do and don't try to be clever. I'll let you know when the problem is solved."

"Thank you, Sir." Wanda didn't have to pretend her relief.

Richard had not dismissed her. He leant sideways, took something from a drawer in his desk and threw it at her. He smiled faintly when she caught it instinctively.

"Keep that with you," Richard told her. "If I need to call you, I will use that. Check the phone at your apartment for bugs. If you are not sure, do not use it. Off you go!"

Wanda retreated quickly, waiting until she was in the stairway to release a huge sigh of relief. Richard was angry, yes, but not at her.

Wanda didn't learn until a week later, that six or seven other employees had also reported being followed.

Richard called a meeting of the people in his office, (though one was absent), and showed everyone a set of twelve photographs.

"Does anyone recognise these people?"

No one did.

"Are they Police?" The question came from a woman Wanda knew worked in the advertising section.

"No," Richard stated positively. "I am sure they are not the Police. I expect they are hired by a rival company to try to poach my up and coming experts. I intend to take the matter to the police. My employees should not have to tolerate stalking."

Wanda suddenly realised that all of the group, except for herself, were part of the 'special re-training program', and decided that the program was a euphemism for his special experts in non-legal activities.

Three of the men looked a bit strained – as if the idea of the police was unwelcome. These stayed back when the others left. Wanda doubted that Richard would draw police attention to her, so she left the office, smiled sweetly at Joseph and returned to work.

Two days later, Richard told Wanda that the problem had been taken care of. As there had been no mention in the press of a mass disappearance or mass murder, it was likely that people involved in following her had discovered 'urgent reasons' to go elsewhere.

However, Richard had an extra piece of advice for Wanda.

"I think that when the person searched your apartment, he planted something there."

"What?" Wanda was sure he was wrong.

"Come over here."

Richard took a small lamp from his desk drawer and plugged its lead into a power point.

The light was blue, Wanda recognised it as a UV lamp.

"Put your hand under the light."

Curious, Wanda obeyed and saw that her skin glowed faintly. Richard's did not.

"You also stand out to an infra-red scanner as being different to normal," he told her. "You need to replace whatever is in your bathroom."

"I'll do that," Wanda promised, intrigued by the way that someone had marked her. "Can I borrow that lamp to make sure I have all the muck off me?"

Wanda noted the absence of the 'being followed' sensation with relief. She did wonder though at the lack of "extra work" from Richard. It was like being on holiday. She had not resumed her own activities yet because she knew that Richard had increased the number or security guards at his 'sensitive' locations. Fortunately, she had already visited them, before Peters got at them and again after. The guards' weapons were still noticeable. It suggested that Richard was edgy about something.

The lack of activity gave Wanda the opportunity to visit the casino where David Martin was working. They acted as strangers, exchanging few words and those mostly impersonal. However, just being close to him was exciting. She did manage to tell him how to find her evidence against the Franklins and he had been able to warn her to be wary. He had heard rumours of a rival criminal syndicate trying to muscle in on the Franklin's operations. She had also told him the number for the mobile phone Richard had given her to use.

Her enjoyment was disturbed by the number of times that the phone in her apartment rang with no one speaking at the other end. She usually let it go to the answering machine after two rings.

As far as she knew, only Richard had the number but he had said he would call her on the mobile. (The charger had been delivered to her the day after she got the phone.)

She did not mention the phone behaviour to Richard or David. It seemed trivial.

More unsettling were the rumours going around the FCI building that some employees were 'missing'. Though three people amongst the thousand or so that worked there didn't seem significant. It was just that all three of those missing belonged to the special re-training group.

Therefore, she did not think it strange when Joseph knocked on her door, (an improvement over him just walking in), and told her that Richard had a job for her. He had found out where the three missing people were and the two of them were to get them away.

"Where are they?" Wanda asked.

"A house over in Alameda." Joseph sounded anxious to get away.

Wanda made him wait whilst she changed into dark slacks and jumper. The slacks had two long narrow pockets on each side where she could slip a couple of tools. A tiny torch went into her pocket.

Joseph jumped when she walked up behind him. He was examining the books on her bookshelf.

"Come on then," he urged.

Wanda followed Joseph to where he had parked his car.

"Why didn't you answer your phone?" he asked as they walked.

"When did you ring?"

"Twenty minutes ago."

That was another of the 'no-one' calls, but Wanda did not say so. "I was down in the laundry. You didn't leave a message."

Joseph concentrated on driving, not talking, as he took them across the Bay Bridge to a suburban area of Alameda.

It had grown dark by the time they crossed the bridge and when Joseph pulled into a parking spot near a park, the half-full moon was occluded by clouds.

"The house we want is in the next street. It's opposite the park, so we can cut through here to get to it. It's number 14, and it has a white picket fence," Joseph told her. He was speaking quickly as if reciting something memorised.

They walked quickly through the trees and slowed as the neared the other street. Wanda sank to a crouch behind some low bushes to examine their target. Joseph copied her, but seemed to be letting Wanda take charge.

Wanda watched the house for ten minutes. No light showed from the front windows. Beside her, Joseph fidgeted.

"I'll go down two houses and come up the back way," Joseph suggested.

Wanda nodded, pleased to be rid of him. He was making her nervous. She wondered if he expected her to make a frontal assault. That was not her intention. Something about the set up or setting did not feel right.

Wanda saw a man leave from the house at number 12. She heard the jingle of his keys as he put them in his pocket and watched him stride down the street towards the shops around the corner. It was as good a time as any to get closer to number 14 from the side.

When there were no cars coming, she walked across the street and into the unfenced front garden of number 12. Then she used the shadows beside the house to work her way to the back. She peeped over the wooden fence at the clear, open area of the back yard. In a brief moment of moonlight, she caught a glimpse of a dark shadow, limping slightly, dash from the bushes near the back fence to the back door of the house.

Wanda, her ears tuned for any slight sounds, heard the scrape of the door's lock being forced.

Wanda used the cross bracing of the paling fence to climb up the palings and rolled over the top, landing soundlessly. She dashed to the shadow at the side of the house and edged to the back door. She was about to enter when she heard stealthy movement on the other side of it.

Joseph re-emerged and jumped noticeably when he saw her just beside him.

"The whole place is empty! No furniture or anything."

Wanda accepted his statement calmly. It fitted with her feeling that something was wrong with the set-up.

"Let's get out of here," Wanda said quietly. "This feels like a trap."

"Trap?" Joseph echoed nervously.

"Yeah, perhaps whoever has people 1, 2 and 3, are trying for 4 and 5," Wanda explained in simple terms. She wondered how much scouting Joseph had done before charging into the house.

"There was a door in the house leading to the garage," Joseph told Wanda. "It seems to be jammed from the garage side. I think we should check it out."

Wanda considered the idea.

"I'll go in," she told Joseph, not impressed by his technique. "Wait near the back fence. If I am not back in five – go back across the road. If I don't get there in fifteen, get going and call the boss."

"Shouldn't I stay in case you need help?"

His help, Wanda though to herself, she would prefer to do without.

"If I'm not out in five, I've hit trouble. If I can't deal with it in ten minutes, it will take more than you or me."

Did Joseph agree too easily? Gutless wonder!

Wanda waited for Joseph to return to the back fence before forcing the lock on the garage. It was a simple padlock and the door opened outwards. With the door opened only a crack, Wanda listened for sounds with in – nothing. She pocketed the lock and entered silently, placing a stone to stop the door from closing fully behind her.

The garage was dark but it had an empty feel – like a dark, cool cavern. It smelt vaguely of petrol, dust, and something she couldn't identify.

She risked using her tiny torch and thus avoided falling down the two concrete steps.

From what she could see, the garage was also empty. Wanda decided on a quick look around and carefully walked down the two steps and stepped over the doormat. The door finished closing behind her but she did not worry about that.

The area was big enough for two cars and had some shelves along one wall but like the house, the garage was empty. The door leading into the house was bolted on the side she could see. That seemed a bit odd. The ones on the door she had entered through, yes having them in the garage made sense but …

A loud thunk caused Wanda to turn around. The bolts on the door leading outside had just moved into the locked position, seemingly by themselves. She was still alone in the garage, but her nerves were screaming 'danger' to her mind. Yes, she was trapped, but that should not evoke such an extreme reaction to her nerves. After all, she had her tools and could open the bolts.

Wanda walked back to the door and tried to pull the bolts up. They seemed stuck. The bolts on the door to the house were the same. She went over to the electronic door for the cars. There should be a manual switch inside somewhere.

Wanda swung her torch upward. A piece of rope dangled from a hole in a fine net that was strung from the corners of the roof. She ignored that and looked for a switch of some kind. There did not seem to be any, not even for lights. That was odd.

Before Wanda had time to ponder further, the net dropped onto her and the air became heavy with a sickly smell. She tried to struggle free, but only succeeded in becoming so tangled that she couldn't even block her nose.

Chapter 24

The room was dark. The floor on which she was lying seemed to be covered with carpet. So, she was not still in the garage. She was alone, but where?

Wanda did not need to hide her feelings in the dark. She was scared and helpless. Her muscles were aching and she could not move to ease them. Her arms were tied behind her and her legs were bound at ankles and knees. Someone wanted to be sure that she could not get away. What she could do, was the little flexing exercises that she used when she had to stay still on a job. That helped a little, but the ache was bone deep, terrifyingly familiar.

When her mind began to function, she wondered where Joseph was. Had he seen the person who had taken her from the garage? Had he followed them? Was he going to bring help? Her mind answered all the questions with – if you want to get out you will have to do it yourself. Just at the moment, she had no notion of how – all she could do was continue the little exercises.

After some time, Wanda could not judge how long, a faint light appeared, outlining a door. Her eyes went to the light and saw a dark outline enter. They had to be close when torchlight shone on her face.

"It's good to see you are back with us," the unfamiliar voice came from above her. "I'll just give you a chance to freshen up, and then we can talk."

The man left the room, but he left the door open. Wanda heard whispers. Two of them at least, she thought.

The man returned. Torchlight wavered as the man walked towards her.

"First a drink."

The torch shone away from her face but there was enough light to make out the straw sticking out of the top of a water bottle. The man directed the end to her mouth and Wanda drank greedily, her mouth was parched.

Next, Wanda felt the man's hand holding her face and a wet towel rubbing it. She tried to struggle free. It was as if she was a two year old again. The process continued in spite of her resistance. The light came on her face again.

"Welcome, Miss Dean."

"Go get stuffed!"

"You and I need to talk."

"I have nothing to say to you, bastard. Untie me!"

"Not yet. I need to check you for weapons and tools."

"You're an idiot if you only just thought of it."

"We didn't bring you here."

"Who did then? Gremlins?"

Wanda twisted as the man searched her and removed the few tools she had with her and her torch. Then to her surprise, he cut the ropes off her. Without warning, Wanda sprung into a low crouch and under the man's arms. In moments, she was through the door. From behind her, she heard a curse, and then felt herself slammed against a wall.

"Be an obedient little bitch and do as the man says."

"Joseph you slime crawling maggot…"

"I don't need to listen to you," Joseph snarled, slamming her again.

"Enough!" That was the other man, the stranger.

Joseph eased his grip.

"If you are smart, bitch, you'll at least hear the man out. If you don't, you will be very, very sorry."

"You had better go home, Joseph, before you are missed," the other said.

Wanda wondered who the stranger was if Joseph was obeying him.

"Yes, babykins, before Richard finds out what you are doing behind his back."

"I don't think you'll be the one to tell him," Joseph said in a whisper close to her ear. "I can prove I wasn't here. Can you?"

"Do you want to bet your life on it?" Wanda challenged.

"Back inside, Miss Dean." The stranger took her arm out of Joseph's grip, propelled her back into the dark room, and closed the door behind them.

"What is it you want?" Wanda asked belligerently

"Your cooperation."

"I don't cooperate with people who abduct me and assault me," Wanda stated.

"It would be in your better interest to do so," a new voice addressed her. This one was familiar.

"I don't deal with people I can't see, either."

"Ryan, educate her to the facts of the matter."

A dull light was switched on. Wanda saw the big man who held her. The other man was only a vague outline in the darkness in the far corner of the room.

"What I want, Wanda Dean, is to take you out of the picture. I don't want you available for Richard Franklin to use. He has no moral or ethical scruples and neither, it seems, do you. Joseph says you are Harrison Franklin's whore and from your activities at the trade convention – I believe him."

Wanda kicked the man in the shins, but he did not loosen his grip. He calmly kneed her in the back. That hurt, but Wanda kept her mouth closed and made no sound.

"However," the big man continued as if nothing had happened, "My friend is convinced you will help us."

"You have the wrong girl," Wanda insisted. "Nothing will convince me to betray the Boss. You couldn't pay me enough."

"We'll see," Ryan promised.

The second man came into the light. He carried a folder.

"You! You're just the nobody of an accountant." Wanda recognised John Hurley, Richard's accountant.

"Your first mistake!" Ryan snarled.

"And you, Miss Dean are a lucky amateur. That is why I need you to do something for me."

Wanda made a rude noise.

Hurley merely smiled. "You think that because the police don't know what you have been doing, that no one does. Have a look at what is in this folder."

Hurley put the folder on the table under the lamp and opened it. Wanda's photo was on the inside of the cover. On the next page were photos of her in various guises.

Wanda went still. Hurley continued to turn pages slowly. The next few were lists of dates places and activities and alongside were money figures – net value, commission.

Every job she had done since working for Richard Franklin.

"I see you understand," Hurley nodded approvingly. "Now, the next list may not be complete."

Again, the pages contained dates, places and activities. These were of jobs that Richard did not know about.

"I have photos and other things to substantiate these summaries. I am nothing if not thorough. I have been collecting data for five years now. I have dossiers on all of Richard's special operatives. You see, not only am I the accountant – I am also a director. I get to hear what goes on. I very nearly succeeded in getting Sylvester jailed – except that you, Miss Dean, stole the evidence. For now, he's out of reach, but he will go down with the rest."

"Do you know what we can do with this file?" Ryan asked her. He breathed the words in her ear.

"Show it to Richard and your friend will be lynched," Wanda bluffed.

"Closely followed by you!"

"Uh, uh," Wanda said with a smile. "You don't know everything I do." She pointed her finger at Hurley. "He's had me checking his security. How else do you think it was that I found your little spy cams?"

Ryan and Hurley exchanged a glance.

"Actually," Ryan said in a deliberate drawl. "My friend has promised me copies of all his dossiers. I'll be able to sell them to Antonio Diaz for a lot of money. He's just drooling to get his hands on you. Rocky Franklin's top agent. I can't promise you that he will be a genial host. He might be in too much of a hurry to learn all you know…"

Wanda felt the reaction in her gut. She had not even thought of that option. Ryan was right – someone like Diaz would only want her for the information she had. Then he would kill her. She would have no chance to finish Richard.

However, it was clear to Wanda that Hurley was trying to do just that.

"What's in it for me?" Wanda asked in an expressionless voice.

"If you do one job for me – I will, with great reluctance, withhold your dossier from the police and Ryan," Hurley promised.

"What would I have to do?"

Wanda had not decided if it was wise to help Hurley or not, but she needed to hear his answer. The threat of that file going to a gangster like Diaz, really scared her.

"I told you, Ryan, that Miss Dean would be reasonable," Hurley said approvingly. "I need you to get something for me from Richard Franklin's safe."

Wanda looked away from Hurley. She felt as if her whole world was caving in on her.

"No! I can't."

Ryan picked up the file with a wide grin. "Wrong answer. You're mine, now."

"No I'm not!" Wanda snapped, desperately trying to think a way out of her problem.

"Ryan, let me have a few minutes alone with Miss Dean."

"Is that wise?" Ryan questioned, looking Wanda up and down.

"She's not a violent person," Hurley insisted.

"What about the two murder warrants from LA?"

"Those are put up charges," Wanda said, controlling her voice. "I didn't kill anyone."

Ryan shrugged and left the room. Wanda massaged her arm where Ryan had held it.

"I know you are working against Richard Franklin," Hurley said gently. "And I appreciate why you don't want to say it. He probably has agents in Diaz's organisation too. What brought on the change? Was it Sam Elsworth? Jennie Cox? Mike Johnson?"

Hurley saw Wanda's eyes widen slightly, because he nodded.

"I thought so. I began to work for him in all innocence, as just one junior accountant amongst many. I was good though. Unfortunately, I tried a minor swindle. I needed some money urgently. Sylvester caught me out, but instead of calling the police, he offered me a promotion. I would be in charge of the books for an elite section of Franklins. I didn't understand the logic at first, but he soon spelt it out. My wife was ill and needed an expensive new drug – he offered to pay for it."

"And if you didn't behave – no drug for your wife," Wanda finished, disgusted.

Hurley continued. "My wife won't last much longer, even with the drug."

"What's the point of this?"

"Young Brad Longford succeeded in hacking into the computer that controls the spy cams. He downloaded some of the pictures and printed them out. I heard him say he would give them to Richard to put in his safe. However, Richard was at some meeting and Joseph put them in there. I know what pictures were on the system, but I don't know all the ones he downloaded. I want you to get them for me."

"Why should they matter to you?"

"There is a picture of me and Ryan in my office. Richard knows Ryan works for Diaz. If he sees that picture, I will have to run and I won't be able to get an important piece of evidence."

"I'm sorry but it's impossible!" Wanda told him.

"There are photos of you in his office with the safe open," Hurley revealed. "He may have them too. No doubt young Brad would know how to find the date of each shot?"

Wanda gripped her left arm with her right hand, and walked to the chair and flopped into it. She needed to think, but she could see no way out of her problem.

"Since he found the spy cams, he's increased his security," Wanda said looking up at Hurley. "It was my suggestion to check his office security. I failed!"

"Then you had better be prepared to die or to run," Hurley advised.

Wanda saw no pity in the accountant's eyes. He was facing the same dilemma as she was, and he had fewer skills to help him.

"He's going to be away two more days," Hurley told her. "Joseph will help you."

"Joseph hates my guts. Besides, why can't he get them if he put the photos in the safe?"

"Joseph was not aware of the significance of the photos at the time. When he put them in, the safe was unlocked. He told me of them later and then I found out what they were. Joseph is quite skilled, but he is not an expert, you are."

The idea of trying Richard's safe again did not ignite her sense of challenge. The timing was wrong. It felt like certain danger. Still, if there were photos of her, with dates, Richard would know she had been in his office when he hadn't authorised it. Damn.

"I'll try it. If I can. I can't make any guarantees," Wanda said slowly. She was considering how Richard would react if he saw the photos. "If I'm caught, I won't have a chance to get away. He won't trust me anymore, unless I tell him about Ryan's threats – then he might keep me alive. As for the photos, I think I can handle Richard, but if Harrison finds out…You won't be able to trust me to help you!"

"That will have to do," Hurley agreed. "Tell Ryan to drive you home."

Chapter 25

"You look like shit!" Joseph greeted Wanda with a smirk.

She wasn't amused. After trying to get to sleep for several hours, it had been time to get up. It had taken a thick layer of pale make up to hide the dark rings under her eyes.

"Is Richard in?" she asked, emphasising the name as a subtle slight to his status.

"No, he's due back tomorrow."

"Good," Wanda commented as she walked around to the side of Joseph's desk and leaned towards him. Her hand reached under the desk and flicked a switch. "Back me up, Joseph, or I will tell Richard why I'm doing this and who set the meeting up last night."

Joseph had leant back away from her.

"You wouldn't dare!"

"Try me. If the guards come in, tell them that I had permission," Wanda insisted.

"He'll still find out."

"Who is going to tell him? You? I don't think you have the stomach for it. If he finds out, he'll punish you. I think that scares you. I think the idea makes your guts knot up and makes you want to rush to the toilet." Wanda watched Joseph's face turn pale with red blotches on his cheeks.

"He'll punish you too," Joseph managed to say.

"Probably," Wanda said calmly. "But I've done hundreds of jobs for him, lots more than you. He appreciates my skills, and do you know what?"

"What?"

"The thought of him punishing me gives me a thrill!"

Joseph began to tremble. "You're warped!"

"Bingo." Wanda smiled maliciously as she turned and walked into Richard's office.

Wanda didn't rush to the safe. She wanted no surprises. The spy cam had gone and there seemed to be no other changes. Her movement towards the safe was halted by a vague sense of unease. She scanned the room again with her eyes. Then a shadow fell on the glass panel in the door. Her danger sense flared and she fled for the chair in front of Richard's desk.

The door opened but Wanda didn't look around, she was leaning back in the chair with her arms stretched along the chair arms and her legs stretched out and crossed at the ankles. She hoped Richard couldn't hear the thumping of her heart.

"Sir, she said you were expecting her," Joseph claimed in a voice pitched higher than normal.

"Indeed," Richard commented neutrally. "Get those files for me please."

Wanda sensed the movement behind her. When Richard walked into her view, he had removed his jacket and moved to hang it on the coat rack by his desk. So far, he acted as if Wanda was not there. He sat back in his chair, waiting for Wanda to speak.

He did not seem to be relaxed, he had one arm cross in front of him and the other was supporting his chin. The little muscles in the corner of his eyes were twitching.

Something had happened to make him angry. He couldn't have heard about her yet, so it had to be something else.

"Have you come to tell me why you weren't answering my calls last night," Richard finally asked her.

She was saved from having to answer immediately by a knock at the door. Wanda swivelled on her chair and saw Joseph at the door. She put a smile on her face.

"The files, Sir," he stammered, confused to see Wanda smiling and unscathed. He walked to the desk and placed them in front of Richard. Wanda followed his movement. He seemed to want to leave quickly.

"A moment, Joseph," Richard halted him. "Close the door will you."

Joseph obeyed, and turned slowly back around. "Sir?"

"Where were you last night, Joseph?" Richard asked, his voice steely cold. "Lie to me Joseph, and I will have Emmanuel train you today."

"Go ahead, Joseph, tell him. It's fine," Wanda invited still smiling.

"I was out, Sir. With Miss Dean, Sir."

"Really?" Richard raised his eyebrows and lowered his arm from his chin.

Joseph stammered out an account of an evening, an innocuous account of an evening at the movies as payment for a lost bet.

"That wasn't hard, was it, Joseph?" Richard leant forward and smiled.

Joseph relaxed, hearing approval in Richard's voice. Wanda was not fooled by the tone.

"Go and see if Mr Hurley is in, Joseph. If he is, tell him to come right up."

"You have something to tell me?" Richard asked leaning back again, his attention back on Wanda.

"Y…es," Wanda admitted, her gut feeling was that she needed to be bluntly honest and to act submissive. "I was considering breaking into your safe." Wanda kept her eyes down.

"For what purpose?"

"To remove some photos that Brad managed to get from the computer controlling the spy cam."

Richard leaned forward. "Why?"

"There may be some of me in there."

"There were plenty of you in there. Which ones did you mean? These ones?"

Richard took an envelope out of the folder and removed three photographs. He held them so that Wanda could see them when she looked up.

"Or these ones?"

The first three showed her in Richard's office, but only one had the safe open. The date was in white letters in one corner. The next five were taken in places Richard knew well and he hadn't told her to go there.

"Tell me why you were in my safe, two weeks before you received my permission to try?"

"I wanted to see if I could." Wanda admitted quietly. "It was the most protected safe I knew and being yours gave me an extra thrill."

"The others?"

"I was just looking. To make sure there was nothing in there that might be detrimental to you."

Richard considered her answer. "I'll accept that for now."

There was another knock at the door.

"Enter."

"Sir, Mr Hurley isn't in today," Joseph reported.

"Thank you, Joseph. Call down to Mr Brendan, ask him to come up in half an hour. Then call the mail room and tell them that Miss Dean has been taken ill and won't be returning to work today."

Joseph glanced at Wanda and a smile curled his lip. Brendan was Richard's personal trainer. Wanda, it seemed, was likely to be receiving his attention. He walked out jauntily.

"Did he tell you about the photos?"

"No."

"Did Mr Longford?"

"No."

"So, how did you find out?"

Wanda looked back down at her hands and told him about Joseph coming to her apartment with a story about helping the missing people and what had ensued. She didn't mention Hurley by name, only Ryan and a person who stayed in the dark.

Richard took out a photo of Hurley and Ryan.

"That was the man?"

Wanda nodded. Richard sat back, chin resting on his palm.

"So they wanted you to get this photo?"

"Yes."

"Why did you agree?"

Wanda looked up then. "I didn't have a choice. When he released the ropes on me, I tried to escape and didn't get far. They had someone guarding outside. Then they told me that they had a dossier on me, everything I had done for you. If I didn't cooperate, Ryan was going to get a copy of the file to sell to Boss Diaz. If I didn't say I'd agree, they were going to take me to him as well. I didn't want to be tortured into telling about you."

"So what do you think Hurley and Ryan are doing now?"

"Probably lying low until they hear if I got the photo or not."

"Then you will call him this evening and arrange a meeting," Richard decided, standing up. He walked around to her. "You will not warn him that I know about his scam."

Richard took Wanda's face in his hand and squeezed until he saw the muscles around Wanda's eyes twitch. "Will you?"

Wanda shook her head slightly. The pressure eased.

"Father will hear of this," Richard told her. "He won't be pleased. However, I need your skills – particularly now. I will trust you…"

"I won't disappoint you," Wanda promised.

Harrison Franklin flew in from LA, arriving at half past eleven. He strode passed a sullen Joseph without giving him a glance, and into Richard's office, closing the door behind him.

Joseph wished he could walk out, wished he could tell Richard Franklin to go to hell, but he did not dare. Security had orders to stop him leaving and even if he could, leaving now would be seen as breaking his promise to behave like a loyal employee and equal to a death sentence.

It was bad enough being treated like a child – one of Richard's personal trainers had been ordered to spank him. That had been Emmanuel, who hated him anyway. Then he had to defend himself in a boxing match with Brendan. And what the hell had they done to her? Nothing!

Half an hour later, as he leant forward to ease the pressure on his bottom, he heard sounds from within the office. He began to realise that she wasn't getting off unscathed.

Damn her though! She was only a slip of a thing (although she seemed taller when she taunted him) and he heard no sound from her. She must have laughed at him.

And damn it all, if she wasn't smiling as Harrison escorted her out of the boss's office. She had to be hurting, but even though she was white faced, there was no trace of tears.

"We'll be down in the gym if we are needed," the Old Man was telling Richard.

Again he walked past as if there was no one in the outer office.

He knew his name was slime right now, but she – must still smell of roses, damn her to hell.

Wanda forced a smile onto her face as she walked past Joseph. She did not want him to sneer at her or think she had received treatment like he had had. More importantly, she wanted Harrison to think she accepted his punishment as what she deserved.

In fact, she wished fervently that she was not in Harrison's company. Keeping her control was becoming very hard indeed. Losing control would label her as weak in Harrison's eyes and her position would become perilous.

She wanted time alone. She needed to will away the ominous shakiness she was feeling. For now the effect of the beating would mask it, but soon, Wanda knew, the illness she had fought off for six years would begin to win. She'd had no really good jobs for a while, none of the usual adrenalin rush to keep the illness at bay. At the moment, the stakes were too high, too complicated.

Wanda had never been in the gymnasium. It was for the use of the highest echelon of the company. Brendan and Emmanuel were both there. She had seen them on different occasions within the building, as well as in the staff cafeteria. The latter scared the nonsense out of Joseph who would never admit he felt threatened by gays but he was the one that Harrison told to tend to Wanda.

It was a very small part out of a personal concern. It was primarily to ensure that Wanda was fit to work that evening. Emmanuel led her to a warm froth filled bath, and left her with a large and luxurious towel to wrap herself in later.

Wanda felt her back sting as she lowered herself in the water, but she found it relaxing once the pain settled again. After about fifteen minutes, Emmanuel returned to tell her that he would be massaging her. Wanda obediently climbed from the bath and wrapped herself in the towel. Once she was on the massage table, she kept it over her like a blanket.

Emmanuel was very gentle, massaging soothing and numbing oils into her back. Wanda had her head turned to one side and could see Harrison training with Brendan.

"He keeps himself fit, that one," Emmanuel said quietly, noticing where Wanda was looking. "He has an excellent physique for a man his age."

"Not like me at the moment," Wanda muttered, feeling it was safe enough to release some tears of humiliation.

"I can appreciate perfection," Emmanuel qualified. "But I would not wish to be close to that one. He is like the cobra, perfectly poised, magnificently arrogant and deadly. If I may say this – if you play with snakes, you can expect to be bitten. You were lucky today."

Wanda was very aware of that. If her danger sense had failed her and she had been in the safe when Richard entered – her luck would have run out.

Emmanuel continued his gentle massage, and Wanda began to relax as the pain in her back receded. When he stopped, Wanda sensed a second presence. The touch of the hands on her back was different. Firmer, but still gentle. Harrison. Damn, he confused her.

"Is it still sore?" Harrison asked gently.

Wanda tensed. "Some," she admitted. "It reminds me of my disgrace. But it won't stop me working."

"Good. That's very good," Harrison crooned. "However, I think that Richard doesn't know all that you've been doing. I think there have been a lot more unauthorised excursions and if I find out the truth, I will punish you once for each occasion. However, little Ice Queen, Richard vouched for you today and we need your skills and absolute loyalty. Do you promise to be absolutely obedient to me?"

Wanda felt the familiar rousing, tried to fight the effect it had on her mind, but her body was not listening, it wanted to experience the ecstasy that Harrison aroused. Her mouth spoke the words of the promise.

Chapter 26

Joseph glanced at Wanda occasionally. She was sitting on the spare chair, in the corner of the office to the left of the door, reading the company publications left out on a low table for visitors. He didn't talk to her. Something about the way she was sitting with her ankles locked together and her hands gripping the magazine made him think she would explode at him if he tried.

She seemed to have recovered from her session with the Old Man. Certainly, she hadn't been moving more carefully than normal when she returned from the gym. She wasn't taunting him either. That might be a sign that she wasn't as confident of her position as she had been. The thought cheered Joseph slightly and he turned back to the view out the window.

Richard returned.

"Joseph, a word with you," Richard said as he passed his assistant's desk.

Joseph followed him into his office. Now was not a time to anger the Boss – even if he was still angry at how the he had treated him.

"Here is a list of phone numbers. Ring each and ask if Mr Hurley has been there today," Richard told Joseph.

Joseph nodded, rather than agreeing respectfully. Richard did not seem to notice the lapse.

"Tell Miss Dean to come in."

Joseph left the office as quickly as he could, glad Richard had not referred to the morning's discussions. He walked over to the corner.

"He wants you," Joseph said, looking down at Wanda. She stared back at him, her eyes seemed to be drilling a hole between his eyes.

As she stood, her whole manner changed. She straightened her shoulders; put her hands in her pockets with only the thumbs protruding and walked calmly into see the boss.

Within five minutes, she was out again.

"I am to ask you to call Gareth or Joe in Security. I need a ride home and back," Wanda said, standing close to the side of Joseph's desk.

Joseph wanted to keep her waiting, but since she wasn't moving back from his desk, he made the call.

"Someone will be up. Don't they trust you anymore?" Joseph asked with a scowl, when he had finished.

"Not lack of trust, creep. But since your little lark last night, I don't think it's a very smart move to even go back to my apartment. However, I have a special job to do and I need some of my stuff. It's you they don't trust. I hope you can swim."

Wanda's escort arrived at that moment and saved Joseph from having to reply. She smirked at him before leaving.

Wanda gave no sign as she entered her apartment that she knew someone had been in there in her absence. A quick glance around showed her that the outer room had not been disturbed.

"I won't be long, Joe," Wanda assured the guard as she went into her bedroom to change into something dark. That room seemed undisturbed also, so who had been here and why? Her tool kit was still in its hiding place, untouched. She shrugged. She had nothing here of value to her on an emotional level and the furniture was just furniture. No one would find anything incriminating there either – well except the tool kit but that place had not been disturbed. Time to go.

Joe drove her to a small building that Wanda knew was owned by the Franklins, through one of their subsidiary companies. She wasn't surprised to see that there were other people there. She recognised them all, but only knew Brad well enough to talk to. The others were the rest of Richard's re-training group.

Brad couldn't keep still and his eyes flicked everywhere as if looking for an escape. The hand that held a cigarette was shaking slightly

"I don't like the feel of this," Brad whispered to Wanda when she came over.

"Keep cool, Brad, just do as you're told," Wanda advised.

There was no time to say more. Richard and Harrison strode into the room. Each took a quick count of heads.

The instant Harrison began talking, every head in the room turned in his direction and all other conversations ceased.

"Franklin Industries is facing a grave threat to its existence," Harrison announced. "We need to act decisively to neutralise that threat. Each of you have a task to perform, based on your skills and training. You will be working in pairs to combine skills. We are firstly looking for our accountant John Hurley. We believe he has been taken by a rival company. Some of you will be looking for other things. We will tell each pair what they need to do and you will report back here when your task is done."

Richard eyed each of his group. "Tonight, company loyalty is paramount. Tell nobody what you are doing. If you remain loyal to the company, the company will take care of you."

Everybody in the room understood what he didn't say. No one doubted that the tasks they had to perform were illegal. All of the re-training group members had criminal records of some kind. All had particular reasons not to be caught. However, if they were, they would be safe as long as they didn't talk about their task.

Richard called out paired names and briefed each group. Brad and Wanda were called last.

"I need you two to go to Hurley's house. He hasn't been there all afternoon. Check his house thoroughly particularly his safe and his computer. Don't be seen. If he's there, bring him back with you. I don't expect it. I'm sure he has already done a flit."

Brad frowned slightly. The last comment contradicted the earlier one.

"Good work on the photo's Mr. Longford," Harrison praised. "Very good work. It helped us to discover this threat early. Do you agree Miss Dean?"

"Yeah. It was brilliant. Do you know where the computer was that you got into?"

Brad's frown changed to a grin. "No but it was local, from its IP address."

Harrison had a faint smile on his face as Wanda met his eyes. Wanda's back began to ache, but she didn't change her expression. Now was not the time to show any weakness.

Brad's car was parked near the building. He would be using it to drive them both to Hurley's house.

"I still don't like this," Brad said. "I haven't done an illegal entry for ages, not since I left the mailroom. I thought I had put all that behind me."

"Yeah, well I don't think they miss much. Anyway, you can leave the entry to me if you want," Wanda assured him. "I've done plenty. You concentrate on the computer. But if I say drop everything and run, do it, OK?"

Brad stared at his companion. "And what are we going to do if he's there?"

"Leave him to me," Wanda said with assurance. "We'll be in trouble if he has that hulking brute Ryan with him. That's the man you got in a photo with him."

"What's going on?"

"Hurley's turned on the Boss and the Old Man. I had a run in with him and Ryan last night. He has a file a half-inch thick on me. I think he'll have one on you too. I want that file – real bad. He threatened to sell my file to Diaz, the mobster."

Brad shuddered. "I'd rather the police."

"So would I," Wanda agreed. "But I'd rather destroy that file. I not only have priors, but there are some outstanding warrants on me from LA."

"Wouldn't all that put you in the shit with the boss?"

"Do you think he doesn't know?"

Brad paused as if thinking. "Good point."

"Look, Brad, all we have to do is the job we've been given. We go back, report honestly and truthfully, the good or the bad, and he'll respect us. If we make mistakes, we just have to take the reprimand without grovelling."

"You probably have the right of it. Everyone knows you're Richard's pet."

"Hardly. Can't you drive any faster?"

Hurley's house was in one of the higher-class residential districts. He must have been well paid by Richard or rather Sylvester, as the one that Brad pointed out to Wanda was large and set back from the street. They drove on for three more houses.

Their arrival was expected, because no sooner than Brad had parked in an area of shadow, than a man approached Brad's window.

"He's still out. No one has been here. I'm parked a street over."

The man pointed and was gone. Brad and Wanda got out of the car, leaving it unlocked for a quick getaway.

The two of them walked across the road, arms around each other. If there had been an observer, they would seem totally engrossed in each other. They went into the front garden of the house nearest them and into the shadows of the trees screening the house.

Once there, they broke apart and used the next two houses to screen their approach to Hurley's. When they dropped over the last fence, Brad chose to enter from the front. Wanda took the back. She scanned the two-storey house. It was modern, the doors and windows would most likely have security locks. Perhaps not on the second floor.

Wanda moved back out of the shadow of the house and looked up. One of the upstairs windows was open about an inch. She smiled. Her luck was in. She had no trouble finding handholds to climb up onto the roof. A quick feel around what she could reach of the frame, after slitting the fly wire, confirmed a lack of window alarm. After a quick glance over the back yard, she climbed in. Her senses told her the garden was empty.

Wanda paused inside and listened. Quiet sounds from downstairs told her that Brad was also inside. She closed the window to hide her means of entrance.

Wanda searched upstairs, thoroughly. One room was a bedroom, still full of women's clothes and accessories. Another room was a sewing room. The rest were empty. She went downstairs and gave a quiet whistle. Brad appeared from the kitchen.

"Clothes are gone from the downstairs bedroom, and the fridge is empty. There's a safe in the office, but all the drawers in the desk are empty. I found another safe in the library room, behind some shelves. I'm booting up his computer," Brad reported.

"Right, I'll look at the safes." Wanda turned to head to the room that looked like a library.

The shelves were pulled back from the wall, so the safe was revealed. Wanda opened it quickly, but it was empty. She followed the sound of Brad cursing softly and saw where he had pulled back a mat to reveal the second safe, set into concrete. This one was more complex. She set to work. It took time, too much time, to open it. It too, was empty.

Brad came up behind her.

"I've taken any discs I could find, but the main drives on the computer have been wiped or removed. I can't access them. Let's get out of here."

Wanda agreed and followed Brad to the front door, but as he reached out to open the door, Wanda pulled him back and pushed past him. The door was opened a crack and when Wanda peeped through it, she saw two men approaching.

"Back way! Police."

Wanda pushed the door shut and locked it. They both sprinted for the rear of the house. There was no movement at all in the back yard.

"Split up," Wanda told Brad. They ran to opposite sides of the garden and scaled the side fences.

Wanda was sensing the presence of danger, but she wrongly assumed that it was from the two police at the front. She was unprepared for the figure that dropped from the tree that straddled the fence. He dropped lightly and grabbed her in a tight grip before she could avoid him. She struggled but to no avail. He quickly handcuffed her, still maintaining his grip. Wanda heard a faint whisper of sound. Her captor was talking into a microphone headpiece, reporting her capture. He had no idea who she was, and Wanda decided to mislead him.

"Let me go! I'm no crook. Paul and I were just kissing and stuff."

Her comments made no impression on her captor. He hurried her through to the front of the house and put her into the custody of a younger officer. Six police cars blocked the road, and Brad's car was trapped.

Wanda chose not to struggle further. It was making her back hurt and she didn't want to draw more attention to herself, especially not that of the two police that had just entered the house. Instead she acted small and docile. The young officer helped her gently into the back of a patrol car. "Stay there," he directed.

"But I haven't done anything. Paul and I just went there for a bit of privacy. Dad'll kill me if he gets called by you guys."

"Sort it out with Captain Carter, Miss. Just keep quiet for now. You are safer here."

Wanda saw the man who had captured her standing in the light from the street light. He looked to be wearing a bulletproof vest. What were they expecting?

The lights went on in the house and even the young officer turned to look. It was the chance that Wanda was waiting for. The police hadn't searched her. She still had her tool kit. All she needed to do was get her hands from behind her to the front and that was simple. It was no harder than changing her clothes in the back of the late Harry's car. Opening the handcuffs took seconds, once she could reach her tools.

Wanda glanced around at the activities of the police. No one, not even the young officer, was paying her any attention. Next time voices came over the police radio, Wanda opened the door and began running. She didn't even pause to see if she was being followed.

Brian Withers, talking to the leader of the SWAT team, saw the dark figure cross the road and took off in pursuit. The young officer belatedly realised that his prisoner had escaped and joined the chase.

Wanda dodged obstacles and scaled fences for six houses before changing direction to get into the next street. She kept running. A car was revving up and approaching her from behind. She risked a glance, she couldn't tell if it was an unmarked police car. It stopped next to her with a squealing of brakes, hands grabbed her and dragged her inside and the door was slammed shut. As the car accelerated down the road, Wanda struggled upright.

"Brad! Thank God," Wanda was relieved to see him. She recognised the driver then as the man who had spoken to Brad earlier. They reached the main road without incident and slowed to blend into the traffic flow.

As they returned to report, Wanda savoured the adrenalin rush and the renewed feeling of wellbeing. For the moment, even her stiff back was forgotten.

Wanda was smiling as she walked into the room where Harrison was talking on the phone. Richard was talking to another pair of operatives. When they went out into an adjoining room, Richard came over to her and Brad.

Wanda let Brad give the report of their lack of success and how the police had arrived, forcing them to leave his car behind and escape on foot. She took over and gave the details of the presence of the SWAT team and her tangle with the police.

"I didn't expect the police to move in on him," Richard said thoughtfully. "That changes things. We'll have to move faster. Mr Longford, go and bring Tom and Frank over here. You've got more work to do."

Brad moved off.

"Did they get a good look at you?" Richard asked. Wanda was expecting that question.

"It was dark out the back and the bastard who caught me was more interested in the rest of the raid. I was pretending to be a silly teenager caught kissing with her boyfriend. They put me in a car, but I got out of there in no time. The officer watching me didn't even see me go."

The contempt in Wanda's tone and her direct gaze satisfied Richard and seemed to please him. No need to tell him she was chased. They hadn't seen the car she escaped in.

"There's food and drink in the other room. Stick around. We will need you again."

Wanda went into the other room but she wasn't hungry for pizza. The smell made her stomach cramp. She did want a drink so she poured out some lemonade and went to curl up in an armchair. As she sipped her drink, she thought over the events at Hurley's house. She was sure she had not been recognised. It had been a risk though, working without her normal disguising make-up.

Wanda had a sense of time running out. Hurley would expect a call by tomorrow morning if she had got the pictures. Surely, he hadn't given her file to Ryan yet. So what caused the police to raid his house? Had Hurley gone to the police already?

There was not enough data to make decisions on or even good guesses. The adrenaline rush from her escape had gone and she was feeling trembly again. That was another worry. How long could she continue to hide her illness? How long would she be capable of working? She could not leave yet.

The lack of sleep the previous night and the events of the day took their toll. Wanda fell into a deep sleep.

Chapter 27

The man talking angrily to Mike Carter and Brian Withers in Carter's office, was worried. He was calling himself Ted Ryan and pretending to be a member of the crime syndicate run by Antonio Diaz, but in fact, he was an undercover cop from the east coast brought in by Carter to investigate the Franklin organisation. He had discovered that Hurley was a mole in the highest echelons of the organisation and carefully nurtured and supported him.

That was until he had taken the woman home. When he had returned, Hurley was gone and there had been no message for him.

Ryan had spent the rest of the night and all day searching for Hurley. He had not been at any of his usual haunts and even his phone was off. In the course of his search, he had noticed the watchers at his club and city apartment. He had called Carter and Withers then and they had arranged the raid on his house in the hope that he would be forced into police custody and his data would be there. The raid was sprung when a watcher in the house opposite had seen a man at the front door. But Hurley wasn't there and the house had been searched before they got there.

"We are looking for him," Carter told Ryan. "We are doing everything we can."

"You had better find him before Rocky Franklin does," Ryan insisted. "Franklin is onto him. That girl you let get away – that's Rocky's top operative. I didn't get a look at the other one, but two went in."

Carter glanced grimly at Withers.

"That girl is trouble. Hurley has a thick file on her and he was using it to make her get some photos from Rocky's safe. He was convinced that he could trust her. He was going to lie low until he heard if she had them. I think I can safely say that she never intended to get them and sold him out."

"These photos you mentioned, what is so important about them?" Withers asked.

"They are from those spy cams I had put in some of the offices at the Franklin Consolidated building and some of their other buildings. We have files and files of photos taken by the cameras. We only keep the ones that show visitors to the offices. We accidentally had one showing me with Hurley. It should have been deleted, but the person we had monitoring the system didn't recognise me and didn't delete it. Before we traced the file and fixed the mistake, someone hacked into the system. Hurley heard that some photos were downloaded – we didn't know which."

"You have no idea where he is keeping his files," Carter asked Ryan.

Ryan shook his head in frustration.

"None. I've seen the files on all the operatives. They were at his house and I have them on the films I gave you. They are dynamite. In some files there is enough evidence to put the person away for thirty years."

"Why didn't he bring the data to us?" Withers asked.

"He wanted the evidence air tight. Rocky Franklin and the Old Man have that staff of high priced lawyers – you know the problems. I think he believed the girl would get the photos and he could keep working. Besides, he thinks I'm working for Antonio Diaz. He is probably right in thinking that Rocky has agents in Diaz's organisation."

Ryan stalked around the room rubbing his hair.

"Franklin hasn't got him yet," Withers said. "We've had reports of break-ins at all of the places you told us about. He hasn't been seen at any of them and we weren't the only people asking."

"Tell us about the girl," Carter suggested. "The one at the house. I didn't see her but Brian said she was short."

Ryan described her. "Short, about five foot two. Brown hair, blue green eyes. I made sure by rubbing off all of the make-up. Her name is Wanda Dean. She is working in the mail department of the Franklin Consolidated building, but she spends a fair bit of time in Rocky's office."

"Girlfriend?" Withers suggested.

Ryan snorted.

"Richard Franklin is a confirmed misogynist," Ryan told them. "That's what caused Hurley to get onto her. He must brief her on the jobs while she is in there. His nickname for her is Ice Queen. It's appropriate. Nerves of ice, she has. Hurley has a record of what she earns on the jobs she does. Five thousand a job or five percent of the value of goods taken. She did the diamond heist at Albert and Baxby's – earned herself fifty thousand for that one. Though I believe, what she does most of is corporate espionage. I would guarantee that most of the places she has been in, never knew they'd been visited."

"The name rings a bell," Carter mused.

"I found out yesterday, that there are two outstanding murder warrants for her. They are about six months old. That would be about when she started up here. Rocky's PA, that spineless twit Joseph, claims she's Harrison Franklin's whore, and I agree. He says she will do whatever Harrison orders, including seducing someone for blackmail."

"Where is Joseph now?" Carter asked.

"I haven't heard from him today," Ryan admitted, but I haven't been around the phone. "The girl probably told on him too."

Carter said. "We'll put a call out for him."

"Back to the girl," Withers said.

"Rude mouthed bitch," Ryan said. "She refused to betray her boss, and she seemed unconcerned with the thought of Rocky seeing the photos of her or Hurley's file. I think that was bluff because some of the places we have her on film – I am sure he never sent her but she claims he sent her into those places to check the security. Anyway, she didn't like the idea of the file getting into the hands of Diaz. That's when she agreed to do what Hurley wanted. We know she'd been into Rocky's safe before. We have pictures of her, and Rocky can't have known. That's why Hurley thinks she is playing a double game but I don't trust her. Do you have those photos I took of the FCI employees? I'll point her out."

Carter leant down beside his desk and picked up a briefcase. He opened it on the desk and took out a folder containing photos, twenty-five to a page. Ryan scanned the images until he found the one he wanted.

"That's her."

Ryan let the two detectives examine the picture.

"I had Radkovic following her, but he's been missing since then. It took six people to keep up with her. She uses make-up to change her appearance, dodges in and out of disco's and cinemas and clubs – often even changing her clothes in the process. She doesn't miss a trick, that one. Spotted us following her right off. She's uncanny like that. It is almost as if she can sense danger."

"Where does she live?" Withers asked thoughtfully.

Ryan gave him an address in Richmond.

Withers used the phone to arrange for a squad to go and pick her up if she was at home.

"Wanda! Wake up! The Boss wants you."

Wanda groaned and opened her eyes. Brad stopped shaking her.

"The Boss wants you now," he repeated.

"Ok, Ok" Wanda said sleepily. She tried to stand up but fell back into the chair. Brad pulled her to her feet.

"Are you all right?" he asked with concern.

Wanda felt sick but said, "Yeah, I just need to wake up. Where is the Boss?"

"Other room." Brad preceded her in the direction she had to go.

Wanda checked her watch. She had only slept an hour and still felt tired.

Richard took note of her appearance as she returned to the room and flopped into another chair.

"How were you meant to contact Hurley?" he asked her at once.

"Phone. He told me a cell number." Wanda yawned.

"Very good. I want you to ring him and arrange to meet him. Make it somewhere public, not private."

Wanda nodded and reached for the phone. Brad fetched it the last few inches for her.

Wanda dialled the number and waited a long time for Hurley to answer.

"Are you still on about those photos?" she asked without introducing herself.

"Yes! Where are you?" Hurley responded.

"Where can I meet you? Name a place."

"How about Lucky Sam's in Richmond?"

"No go. That's too close to my place, which is probably being watched."

"The Pancake Parlour, in Murray St?"

"Are you daft? That's right next door to the precinct house."

"Tante Laurie's then. Skipton Street?"

Wanda pictured the place. "That will do. I'll be there in half an hour. You get a table near the back and have a vacant chair backing to the crowd."

Wanda hung up and told Richard where Hurley would be. He beckoned to two big men slouching against the far wall.

Wanda listened whilst Richard briefed the people who would go with her. All she had to do was identify the target, distracting Hurley so the others could get him. Richard's driver, Jesse was to have the getaway car standing by. Ted and Frank were to subdue Hurley and get him outside. Brad would be the catalyst to get him moving.

It wouldn't take two men to handle Hurley, but if Ryan was there one would deal with him. Wanda and Brad were to escape on foot, not in the car. They were to meet at the Franklin mansion this time.

Wanda saw the muscles around Brad's eyes twitching, but his face was impassive. If he didn't like what he had to do, well Wanda liked it even less. She had seen what Rocky and Harrison had done to Mike Johnson. What they would do to Hurley would be worse. He would be made to tell them where the files were. She hoped to be the one sent to get them. In spite of what she told Ryan and Hurley, she didn't want Harrison or Richard to see the file on her. And she didn't want them to see and destroy their own.

Damn! Hurley deserved her help. If she went for the files, she'd grab them and run. That's all she could do. She couldn't rescue him on her own.

Jesse drove Brad and Wanda to a point just down from the restaurant before driving around the block to the rear. Ted and Frank parked a second car out the front. Wanda went in first, and looked around. The clientele at the restaurant appeared to be dressed in a much classier fashion than the clothes she wore. Wanda hadn't considered that point. She glanced around and spotted a small coat room. As there was no one around, she slipped in, grabbed a dressy vinyl coat, and returned to the foyer.

The usher arrived, finally and asked for her name.

"It's Jenny Wright"

"Do you have a booking Miss?"

"I'm meeting my boyfriend here. We're eating with a couple of Paul's friends. They will probably be here soon. Is there somewhere I can wait?"

"You may wait at the bar, Miss."

"Thanks."

The usher showed her the way and departed. Wanda took a seat and studied the seated diners. The barman asked if she wanted a drink and Wanda realised that she had no money on her so just shook her head.

Wanda spotted a big man walking across the eating area to a table in the far corner.

That's when she spotted Hurley as the big man sat down.

Wanda wasn't ready to move towards them. She was waiting for Ted and Frank to be ready. The appearance of Brad, would be the signal.

The barman was watching her, so Wanda decided to move away from the bar. She spotted a public phone and went over to it. She had no money for it, but she rang David Martin's number and asked to reverse the charges. If she had to run tonight, he'd be ready to help her. Using the phone caused the barman to forget her and she had an excuse to watch the activity around her. As soon as she saw Brad at the bar, she hung up the phone. David would understand.

Wanda wove her way between the tables with the grace of an experienced table server. Ryan spotted her when she was three tables away and glared at her. Wanda merely smiled at him and sat down in the spare chair.

"Did you get them?" Ryan demanded.

Wanda gave him a silent glance and ignored his question.

Hurley repeated the question.

"I went in to try in the morning. Richard wasn't due back until the next day, but he walked in before I even got to the safe. I had to do some quick talking to explain why I was in his office and why I didn't answer his calls the evening before. Now, before the incredible hulk here explodes. Richard had already seen the photos and they hadn't been in his safe at all. He recognised Mr Incredible here and your name is mud, Mr Accountant. Now, I did what I could, I want that file!"

"Where's Joseph?" Ryan snarled.

"I have no idea. And I care even less."

Ryan grabbed her wrist. "What did you tell Rocky Franklin?"

"I simply corrected Joseph's version of my evening," Wanda said deliberately.

"Joseph rang me this evening, gibbering," Ryan accused. "I couldn't understand him."

"Gibbering! How appropriate. He's no great loss."

Ryan gripped more firmly.

"Very well then, Richard wasn't pleased with him for helping to get me abducted. He's very strict about behaviour standards. Joseph was treated like the naughty little boy he was and given a lesson on how to be a man. When he tried to run off like a sulky child, he found out that security had orders to stop him. That's all I know."

"And you are the fair haired girl," Ryan sneered. "Rocky's pet! No punishment for being in his office…"

Wanda shrugged.

"…or for being in places where you shouldn't?"

"I told you cretin, he knows I was in those places," Wanda insisted. "Now where is that file?"

Brad touched Wanda on the shoulder and whispered in her ear. "It's time."

"Time I was going," Wanda suddenly announced as she stood up. Her movement drew their attention to the two men approaching. Hurley turned pale and Ryan cursed and pulled him to his feet.

"Out the back way," Ryan pushed Hurley to get him moving, then pulled a mobile phone from his pocket a pushed a button to speed dial a number. "Move in now," was all he said into it.

Ted, who looked very much like Richard Franklin, moved faster. Brad stepped back out of the way as Ted drew a gun and held it to Ryan's, side.

Wanda and Brad were to return to the car out the front, but Wanda changed their plan.

"Back way, Brad."

Carter and Withers were forcing their way through the gaps between tables.

Wanda was aware of two things the instant she emerged from the back door of the restaurant. First, was Jesse and Frank bundling an unconscious Hurley into the back of the car, and the second was Ted fighting with Ryan.

Jesse dived into the driver's seat and began accelerating away even before the door was fully shut. A police car pulled up at the restaurant, saw the car leaving and took off after it. Brad took off on foot to the left. Wanda ran after the police car, thinking it was safer following a speeding police car than running in the direction it had come from. She looked out for an alley to duck into or a fence she could climb over. Someone was chasing her. She could hear their boots pounding the concrete behind her. There was an opening ahead. Too late, it was a dead end. Wanda glanced up and saw the lower step of a fire escape just above her head. She jumped and caught the rung.

Rough hands grabbed her feet and yanked. Her arms were suddenly weak and she fell heavily to the ground. Before she could catch her breath, her wrists were grabbed behind her and handcuffs were fastened tightly.

Wanda made her body go limp and closed her eyes. She gave no reaction when her captor turned her over and examined her grazed and bleeding face, nor when he frisked her for weapons. He removed the tool kit from her waist, but didn't find the two narrow tools in the special pocket of her trousers.

"Well, well, well, a not so little fish," Wanda recognised the voice of Brian Withers. "Good work, Drummond. Help me get her back to the car. Hold tight, I think she's faking."

Wanda dangled between them, all the way back along the alley.

A third pair of hands grabbed the front of her jacket and slammed her against the police car.

Wanda groaned involuntarily.

"Where - are – they – taking – him?"

Wanda opened her eyes, and spat at Ryan. "I'll have you for assault you son of a bitch."

There was no sign of Ted or Brad.

"I haven't started yet! Where are they taking him?"

"How the hell would I know? I thought they were after me," Wanda said belligerently.

"After you? What for?"

"Associating with filth like you," Wanda countered. "Does Diaz know you are a slimy bastard of a cop?"

He slammed her against the car again, causing her back to flare into agony. She took a deep breath and held it until the worst of the pain subsided. She counted to ten slowly.

"That's enough, Ryan," Withers said firmly.

"Why were you here?" Withers asked Wanda. He waited for her face to clear of the signs of pain.

"I came to tell Hurley that I couldn't get the pictures and that Richard had seen them already. That's all. I was trying to do him a favour."

"And the others…?" Withers prompted.

"I don't know!"

"You were at his house earlier." Withers challenged.

Wanda kept silent. She wasn't going to incriminate herself.

"Put her in the van, Ryan, and make sure she knows her rights."

Wanda stumbled and tripped as Ryan dragged her down to the van parked away from the restaurant. She was doing it deliberately to annoy him as he quoted the rote formula about her rights. He ignored her tactics and stopped outside what looked like a prison van.

"All for me," Wanda said sweetly. "How kind of you."

Ryan opened the door and pushed her up the step. He was not expecting the attack when it came. As soon as Wanda had her hands at the height of Ryan's chest, she surprised him by punching him in the face with both closed fists. The first punch was followed by a second when Wanda swung around.

He had time to see Wanda had her hands free, before something hit him from behind.

"Quickly," Ted hissed.

Wanda jumped over the unconscious Ryan and ran after Ted.

They were well away by the time the escape was noticed and in a stolen car, being driven by Brad, before a search was started. Once again, Wanda had to free herself from handcuffs.

David Martin listened to the police scanner he had plugged into the cigarette lighter socket. He had responded to Wanda's call for back up. She had felt uneasy. It was enough to send him racing to his car.

The police were responding in force to surround the restaurant. He wouldn't be able to get close, so he waited. Wanda wasn't an amateur, she would probably get away. He pulled in down the road and waited.

News of her escape came in the form of an instruction to all units to watch for her and a warning that she could be violent. David knew better, Wanda hadn't been alone. David drove slowly past the restaurant and around the corner to where the alley opened out. He saw no sign of any running figures. As time passed with no reports about her he began to relax. The reports of the chase of the car containing the abducted man continued. David drove in the general direction that car was headed.

Chapter 28

Brad dumped the car, half a mile from Franklin's Mansion and they ran the rest of the way. The guards stopped them at the gate, but finally recognised Wanda. They claimed to have no orders to let them in, but that they would call up to the house. In the meantime, the guards took them into the guardroom and opened a door. They were pushed into a dark but not airless room. It was unfurnished, and the floor was wood. Wanda found a corner to sit in and slumped to the floor to let her breathing return to normal. After a while, Brad sat beside her.

"He's going to go right off," Brad groaned. "First the house, now this."

"The Old Man's mood will depend on whether the others got Hurley away," Wanda predicted. "You did what you had to do and you got me away. I am grateful."

"I heard what he did to Joseph."

"That was different. Look Brad, like I said before, look him in the eye and tell it like it was. You weren't caught again. I was."

"How can you be so calm?"

"I'm used to them. I know how to bluff and how to hide my thoughts."

"And you have the Old Man on your side," Brad said with disgust.

"The down side of that," Wanda decided to admit. "Is that he expects perfection of me and absolute obedience. He will be angry with me."

They waited in the cold darkness for an hour before the door was opened and they were told they could come out. The guard walked them up to the house and into Richard's office. Harrison was sitting in Richard's chair.

"Tell me what happened," Harrison demanded in an icy, venomous voice. He was looking at Wanda, forcing her to speak.

Wanda felt herself to be curiously distant as she reported fully and without emotion. She left nothing out, not even the fact that the man, Ryan, who was actually a cop, recognised her.

Brad took his cue from Wanda. He confirmed her report and added what he had seen and done. Ted gave his report in short terse sentences.

Harrison stood and prowled around the room. His movements were like those of a leashed panther – ready to spring at the least provocation.

Wanda stayed very still. She knew him best and sensed the violence in him, having tasted its virulence only that morning. She didn't want to have it directed at her again.

Harrison wasn't angry at them, but at the lack of information about Hurley's whereabouts. The matter was out of his control and it could turn on him – he obviously didn't like the situation. Hurley threatened the empire that

Franklin had built, the power he craved and his pleasures. Franklin had to find the information Hurley had gathered and destroy it.

Right now, Harrison Franklin needed to know how things stood. If the police had Hurley, his empire was finished. Sylvester was a disgrace, Richard would be brought to his knees and he would have his life destroyed. The police might even be on their way already.

Wanda knew with certitude that Hurley would not survive the night. The knowledge chilled her soul. Her hand would not be the hand that killed him, but she felt as if she would be responsible. His murder would be on her conscience.

"Mr Harrison," Wanda ventured to interrupt his prowling. "I don't think the police have the information Hurley had. They seemed desperate to find out."

"That's right Boss," Ted agreed. "The cop that was with Hurley was really roughing the kid up."

Ted probably didn't know what the whole matter was about, he was mainly muscle.

"They wanted to know where Hurley was being taken, but I said I didn't know. I said I'd only come to tell him I hadn't got the photos."

Harrison stopped in front of her. "You should have kept your mouth shut," he raged, giving her a slap across the mouth that caused her to bite her tongue and her lip to bleed. Wanda kept her head high, accepting the rebuke, even as her lips grew swollen and blood dripped onto her clothes.

Harrison walked away, turning his back on them.

"It seems that you weren't followed here," Harrison said in a calmer tone. "However…"

The phone rang, Harrison reached it in two strides. He spoke in monosyllables, then said, "Bring him here. Be sure you aren't followed."

Harrison turned and stared at his three subordinates. A stare that would make the guilty shudder. Wanda didn't flinch. The two men stared back.

Harrison took two envelopes from his pocket, gave one each to Ted and Brad.

"New identities. Enough money for you to get far away. Be very sure, I can still find you. If you even think of discussing confidential matters, I will find you. Go!"

Wanda didn't turn to watch the two men leave. She kept her eyes on Harrison.

"What can I do, Sir?" Wanda asked calmly.

"Go and clean yourself up and come back here. I have preparations to make."

Wanda returned to the office ten minutes later.

"We'll be leaving as soon as we have what we want from Hurley. You'll be coming with us. You are too valuable to leave behind, especially now that the police have found you."

"I'll stick with you, Mr Harrison. No matter what," Wanda promised.

Harrison allowed himself a faint smile.

"Go and find a room to rest in, my dear. You've had a long day. I'll wake you when we need you."

Wanda nodded and left the office, relieved to be out of Harrison's presence, but too stressed to sleep. Harrison believed he owned her soul, but he didn't. She had fooled him, again. She must continue to fool him for at least a little longer.

After a time, Harrison came into the bedroom. Richard followed, looking less than composed. She pushed herself into a sitting position.

Harrison smiled at Wanda; the smile was full of malice.

"I have found a use for your new notoriety," Harrison said, drawing a mobile phone from his pocket. "I want you to call police headquarters. Did you hear the name of any policeman tonight?"

Wanda nodded warily.

"Very well, ask for that one. Then tell him you have information about the kidnapping. Say the man is in the basement of the Berringham Building. Talk fast and low."

Wanda took the phone and a deep breath.

She dialled the number and was put through to the office of Captain Carter.

"Carter."

"I have some info. About that kidnapping. I don't want no part of murder. He's in the basement, of that old building on Sixteenth, the berry something building."

"Where are you? What's your name?" Carter almost shouted.

"I snuck upstairs....oh shit!" Wanda faked a scream and broke the connection.

Harrison smiled approval. "Wait here."

Wanda waited, sitting in the chair with nothing to do but think. She needed to leave – before Harrison sealed his hold on her soul. But she had to help Hurley, if she could. She had not seen him being taken upstairs to the room in the attic – but he would be there. Her mind was supplying pictures of what they were doing. Her body was throbbing with his pain.

Harrison entered the room, found her curled up in the chair, staring across the room. He stood there for a minute before slapping her face. He did it a second time before Wanda came out of her trance state.

"I'm sorry, I..." Wanda realised she hadn't a clue what had just happened, except that now her face hurt again.

"You are needed upstairs. Richard is waiting. The second door at the top of the stairs."

Harrison's expression was pure evil. Wanda felt cold and remote. She felt like a puppet as she walked along the passage and up the stairs.

Richard was smoking a cigarette, watching the man slumped on the couch. He turned, hearing Wanda enter. She did no more than walk a step into the room.

His eyes were bright, pupils dilated. The aura in the room sent shivers down Wanda's spine. She wanted to turn and run, but you did not do that in the presence of feral animals. They would sense your fear and turn on you.

Richard walked towards Wanda, his eyes on her in an intent fashion. Wanda knew that type of look. He touched her face as he pushed the door shut.

The temperature in the room seemed to drop ten degrees.

Wanda found her voice. She looked past the covered figure of Hurley, not at him.

"Did he tell you what you wanted?"

"He had no choice."

Richard smiled, moving his left hand over Wanda's face and neck. Wanda hid her feeling of revulsion. Richard was aroused by what had been done to Hurley. Did Harrison hope he would take her, while he was in that state?

Wanda knew how to change that. With blatant purpose, she moved closer to him. She forced her body closer to his, rolling her hips into his groin. Then deliberately, raised her jumper and shirt. Richard placed his left hand up her front and felt around. The other undid her tool kit.

As if an off switch had been activated, Richard's attitude switched back to Ice Mode.

"He's drugged at the moment. That should wear off in an hour. I'll be back before then. Let me know if he says anything."

"Ok, Boss," Wanda agreed, calmly tucking herself in again. "What if the police come?"

"Kill him," Richard told her, watching her face.

"With what?"

By pretending that this wasn't real, she managed to speak calmly, but her heart was pounding and her head felt light.

Richard took a small automatic pistol from his pocket, and gave it to her. His right hand, which had a glove on it, lingered on hers for longer than necessary. Wanda pulled her hand free and slipped the gun into her pocket.

"We'll lock the door," Richard watched her face as he spoke. "You'll be safe in here. The police will need hours to get in. We'll be back when we have the information."

Wanda nodded. "You'd better go then."

She dropped her face to avoid his gaze. He forced her to look at him and his smile turned feral. "Yes, I'll be back to get you."

He released her with a swift movement, and strode from the room. The lock clicking shut seemed very loud.

Wanda froze in position – her danger sense blossomed. Harrison and Richard wanted her to be a prisoner. So she couldn't run? He knew he couldn't risk her talking to the police, which was why he'd slapped her before. She was his most successful lock artist. They needed her …

She was not aware of the tears leaking down her face.

"Don't go to pieces now."

The voice startled her. It was low and strained. Wanda spun around. Hurley was conscious.

"Can you get me out of here?"

Wanda calmed her nerves by making a thorough study of the room. Escape was impossible, even if she had her tools.

"No. There's no way out. I've seen this room from the outside too."

Wanda studied the battered face.

"Did you tell him about me?"

"He didn't ask."

Hurley coughed. Wanda moved closer, aware of a burnt smell about the man.

"Stay away!"

Wanda didn't obey him. She moved beside him and gently turned back the cloth that covered his almost naked body.

Burn marks, scratches, deep cuts, bruises, contusions – the worst of the wounds were covered with a clear film that slowed the bleeding.

Wanda replaced the cover gently and dropped to her knees beside him.

"I'm sorry," Wanda buried her head on his arm. "I knew he'd do this but…"

"You could have done nothing," Hurley said trying to be forceful. "You still can help me. Will you?"

Wanda nodded, still with her face buried.

"Look at me."

Wanda lifted her head. Tears she hadn't permitted herself for years, were streaming down her face.

"Don't break now," Hurley tried to lift his arm and failed. "If you can carry on, not all is lost. Will You?"

Wanda nodded again.

"I told them about the house. Where we met. It's a false trail. They will be there a while, checking." Hurley had to stop and catch his breath.

"They'll kill me. I can't take much more."

Wanda buried her head again.

"I'm ready to die. My wife went two days ago. I buried her today. Tell Ryan that."

Wanda nodded, lifting her head again. "Where is the stuff they want?"

"I left a letter and a key, in your apartment. Give them to Ryan."

"A gangster?" Wanda asked, even though she knew better.

"No, he's police."

"Ok, I'll do it. Somehow. But, I don't think they'll let me go."

"Get yourself under control. You will get your chance."

Wanda took a deep breath.

"I can end this for you," Wanda offered, pulling the gun from her pocket.

"No, dear child. You aren't a murderer."

Wanda nodded and took more long deep breaths. Finally, she felt the calm she sought, descend over her.

She knew what she had to live to do. She could not die until it was done. So be it.

Chapter 29

"I told you not to trust her," Ryan snarled as he held a pad of material on the wound on the back of his head. "If John dies, I'm holding her personally responsible."

"Sit down," Withers told Ryan. "You aren't fit to do anything. If you keep prowling around you are going to pass out again."

Ryan agreed with ill grace, and accompanied Carter and Withers when they returned to headquarters.

Carter pushed Ryan into a seat and then went to check for messages.

"The girl hasn't been back to her apartment," Carter commented.

"Well, she wouldn't would she?" Ryan snarled. "She isn't stupid."

The telephone rang.

Carter listened intently. "Where are you? What's your name?"

The others in the room heard a shrill scream coming through the phone receiver.

Carter dialled the switchboard and requested a playback of the last call. He indicated that Withers should listen.

"That sounds like the girl," Withers agreed. "In trouble…"

Carter wasn't wasting time, he mobilised more units to go to the Berringham Building.

"Coming?" Carter asked Ryan.

"No, I reckon it's a trick. If you can get me a driver, I'll go out to the house. If John talks, he'll reveal that place first."

"If you see anything, call it in. Don't be a hero."

As soon as Captain Carter received Ryan's report, that he had spotted Rocky Franklin at the house, he knew the Berringham building was a diversion. He called the SWAT leader and withdrew the extra units to go to the house. He was too late. Ryan and the car were missing and the driver was unconscious on the ground. Ryan answered the radio and said he was following Franklin who was heading for his mansion.

David Martin had driven towards the Berringham Building, but it didn't seem right. Rocky, like Sylvester would put the man in their 'safe'. The room he had been kept in once, before he became David Martin. He heard Ryan report seeing Rocky but he had not mentioned Wanda. His gut told him that the Franklins would have her. They would not want her caught and talking. He drove as fast as he dared to the mansion.

The door burst open, Richard Franklin burst in. His clothes were subtly disarrayed. Harrison followed. His attention was focussed on the man on the table.

Wanda scrambled up from where she was sitting on the floor.

Hurley had begun to hallucinate, his skin had turned cold, clammy and pale. In the time after they had talked, Wanda had loosened some of the clear patches on the deepest wounds. Hurley had been losing blood steadily since then. He was fading quickly. She hoped they wouldn't see where she had wiped her bloodied hands.

"He's conscious, Boss, but raving."

Richard simply stared at Hurley.

Harrison said curtly, "Wait in the office."

Wanda scurried to the door. Harrison put out his arm to stop her. His timing was instinctive, for his attention was also on Hurley.

"The gun!"

Wanda pushed the gun into his hand and kept going.

"Wait."

Wanda halted. Harrison turned her to face him.

"The police are all out looking for you. Very dangerous is what they are saying. It means that if they see you and you show any sign of resistance, they'll shoot."

Wanda felt the pull of his personality, his conditioning of her.

"I don't want to go out there," Wanda said in a small voice. "I want to stay with you."

Harrison nodded, turning his attention back to Hurley.

Wanda heard the door close, as she walked with pounding heart to the ground floor. She went, puppet like to the office, unnerved by the silence.

The office door was open, the furniture was there, but the shelves were empty. She knew the Franklins were going to run.

Run.

Her chance.

Go!

Go!

Wanda's feet took on a life of their own. Her mind filled with the need to flee.

It was dark outside. Wanda had lost track of time, but her senses were full out.

All of Richard's staff might have gone, but there were still guards around, watching the edges of the property.

Wanda simply ran. She sensed a gap in the guard's cordon and instinctively went that way. She jumped and caught the top of her fence and pulled herself up. She saw nothing below, and jumped down, landing heavily. Scrambling up, she began to run. Something grabbed her, almost dislocating her arms. She struggled, kicked behind her, connecting twice. One of her arms was released, but an arm wrapped around her neck.

"Struggle, and I will break your neck."

"Let me go, Ryan. When he finds me gone, he'll kill me."

"No more than you deserve," Ryan growled. He was pushing her towards a car parked a short way along the street.

In the night's stillness, they both heard a single shot.

Wanda slumped in Ryan's grip as if she had been hit. Ryan dragged her.

A hissing noise passed Wanda's ear. Ryan grunted and released her. She landed on the path, not immediately comprehending her freedom. She pushed herself to her feet, as her sense of self-preservation re-surfaced. She began to run, stumbling with fatigue. Her heart pounding, the pulse in hear ears deafening her to the sound of pursuit. It was harder and harder to breathe. It hurt to breathe.

As darkness gripped her mind, she cried out in her mind. "David! David!"

Harrison strode into the office, expecting to find Wanda waiting. For the first time in many years, he was lost for both words and action. Then his anger surfaced. She was dead! When he found her, she would die. Slowly, painfully, by his own hands. He imagined the process.

The faint sound of a siren returned him to sanity. He ran out to the back where the helicopter was waiting, its engines idling. Richard was already inside; Harrison climbed in and gave the pilot the signal to lift.

"Scan the area," Harrison ordered. He didn't have to say for what. Richard drew out a sniper's rifle from a side pocket of the copter.

They lifted rapidly, the spotlight lighting the grounds and then the road outside. Richard spotted and aimed at the small running figure; fired just as the guard reached for her.

The small figure fell and the guard on top of her. The helicopter lifted and flew away. Police cars were already converging on the area.

David approached on foot; saw the big man scouting outside. He matched the quick description of Ryan that Wanda had given him when she called. He saw Wanda drop over the fence and Ryan catch her. He heard the shot from inside the grounds. Then, moments later, Ryan dropped and Wanda struggled to run. She wasn't running fast.

A guard briefly checked Ryan, then ran back into the grounds. David recognised him, Firth. He hated Rocky Franklin, and he was keeping a promise he had made to Mike Johnson, to help Wanda. His mate decided to chase.

David heard the helicopter start up and knew instantly that was the Franklins. He dived into shadow as the spotlight illuminated Wanda. His gorge rose as he heard the shot and saw Wanda fall almost simultaneously. When the brilliant light was doused and the helicopter moved off, he ran to her.

The guard had taken the bullet. A high powered charge for maximum damage. It had struck him from the front and passed out his back. David dragged the dead guard off Wanda. His blood and gore were all over her.

"Wanda?"

David Martin shook her gently. He felt for a pulse. It was strong, but her breathing was slow. He lifted her and carried her to his car. He put her down gently while he opened the rear door, then lifted her in and covered her with a blanket. The sirens were even closer. Ryan was still back there on the ground, but he had to get Wanda away.

He made a decision. Ryan was tough, and the police were almost there. Wanda needed his care. He jumped into his driver's seat and took off.

Chapter 30

For the third time that night, Captain Carter ordered a major callout. The first units to arrive found Ryan, still alive and the dead guard. The signs on the ground indicated that the guard had been moved, so someone else had been around. The ambulance arrived quickly and took Ryan to hospital.

The police moved onto the Franklin estate, cautiously. Six guards instantly threw down their weapons and allowed the police to proceed.

The house was deserted, no obvious signs of a hurried departure, but the normal occupants had moved out. There were no personal effects.

Certain 'hidden' rooms were located and carefully searched and photographed. Carter went up to the highest level and found the rooms with the steel doors that had been described to him. It took two hours for four technicians to burn through the two doors. The first room was empty, the second room contained the body of John Hurley. Carter took in the signs of torture and the bullet wound. The wound hadn't bled much. It seemed that Hurley had died first. He turned and saw the gun by the door.

It seemed he wasn't destined to get to bed that night.

David Martin looked down at the sleeping Wanda, he sat down next to her on the bed and touched her face gently. He wondered if she had concussion and if so could he risk bringing a doctor to see her. She had done no more than moan during the drive back to his apartment. She had groaned as he touched the swollen lip and the scratches on her face. He'd cleaned her face of blood and dirt and seen the state of it. Then he had checked her for other wounds, removing the fouled clothes. He was relieved to discover that the bullet that killed the guard had missed her. He grew angry when he saw the whip-like marks on her back – still vividly red. He found some soothing cream to rub on them.

With extreme gentleness, he dressed her again in some of his clothes. About then she had woken…

Wanda woke, struggling and fighting him. She was weak, too weak to overcome him. He held her down, talking gently. Her mind wasn't in the here and now and he was worried about her. When she quietened, he held her face gently and kissed her.

Sanity returned to her face, she grabbed onto him and wept. She was too depleted to keep it up for long, but he held her for as long as she needed him.

"I have to get to my apartment. Hurley left a letter there for Ryan, and a key."

"The police are all around your apartment," David told her gently.

"I don't know if Hurley talked before he died."

Wanda buried her head on David's chest. He could feel her shaking. "They tortured him…" She told him in detail, what had been done to Hurley, and how she had been forced to stay with him. Then she admitted to helping Hurley to bleed to death.

"I said I would carry on. I promised."

"Of course you will," David agreed. "But right now, you need to rest. Trust me to help you now. I'll get into your apartment and find the key and letter, and I will get your stuff from the other place. Did Hurley tell you where he put everything?"

Wanda shook her head. "I think he put it in the letter."

"Did he say anything else?"

"He was ready to die. His wife died two days ago. He buried her yesterday. I had to tell Ryan that."

"Sweetheart, sleep until I get back. You will be safe here."

Wanda lay back, and feeling safe, was asleep in a moment.

David stood and watched Wanda for a moment, marvelling at her strength. The worst was over now, but the danger wasn't. He had to make sure her efforts were not in vain.

Rocky Franklin and the Old Man might think her dead, but they would check and discover that her body was not found. They would be after her in earnest. For the Old Man, it would not be business, it would be personal.

Turning suddenly, David tore his thoughts from what 'might be'. He made sure his apartment door was locked when he went out to his car to drive to Police Headquarters.

David spoke to the reception officer. "I need to speak to Captain Carter or Lieutenant Withers."

"They are out on a case," the man told him. "Can anyone else help you?"

"No. I have some information for them about the case they are on. It's urgent and I won't talk to anyone else."

"How do you know what case they are on?" the officer asked suspiciously.

"I have a scanner," David admitted, seeing the officer frown. He may not like people listening in on the police frequency but it was legal.

"Give me your message. I will pass it on," the officer suggested.

"I'll wait. Just tell them someone needs to speak to them about the case."

David sat on a hard wooden chair and watched the officer talking on the phone. He returned to the counter a short time later.

"What's your name, bud?"

David walked back to the desk; he didn't want the two men just being dragged in to hear him. "Who wants to know?"

"Captain Carter," the officer said impatiently.

"Tell him I am a friend of Kevin Mason."

The officer went back to the phone and returned quickly. "He wants to talk to you, this way."

David followed the man to the phone.

"Captain, this is David Martin. I am a friend of Kevin Mason. He's heard that Hurley left a letter and a key in Wanda Dean's apartment, for Ryan."

David heard Carter giving orders in the background.

"Does Kevin Mason know where Wanda Dean is?" Carter asked sternly.

"He didn't say," David hedged.

"You tell him, that if he's hiding her, he could be charged with accessory to murder," Carter insisted. "I suppose they met while working for Franklin?"

"You tell me," David skipped the question.

"Will you wait there for me?"

"If you won't be too long."

Carter arrived within half an hour. He must have come directly from the Franklin Mansion.

"We'll talk in my office," Carter instructed and he led the way upstairs and through the detective office to his smaller office and shut the door.

"We should have a report from the officers at Dean's apartment soon. How long have you had that message?"

"I came here as soon as I heard. Then I had to wait. An hour, about."

"Why didn't you ring it in," Carter accused.

"Kevin had reason to suspect the security of the information," David said delicately. "He said he trusts you and your partner."

Carter accepted the remark without further comment.

Instead, he asked, "How is Kevin Mason? He promised to keep in touch."

David shrugged. "I guess he just did. How is Ryan?"

"What do you know of him?"

"What I heard on the scanner," David said at once.

"Nothing was said on the radio. Ryan was undercover."

David realised his mistake.

"All right!" David gave in and told Carter all he had heard and seen near the Franklin estate. However, he claimed that Kevin Mason had taken Wanda away to some place unknown.

"The shot you heard first, how long after it did you see Wanda Dean?"

"It was the other way around. Ryan had grabbed her, and then I heard the shot."

Carter leant back in his chair, deep in thought.

"You are saying, that Dean ran off, rather than escape with her boss? Did he drop her because we are on to her?"

"No, she could have gone with them," David said, his voice odd.

"She wants to do a deal, is that it?" Carter asked cynically. He seemed to be weighing the benefits. "Where is she? There's no deal if she doesn't give herself up."

David eased himself up from the chair.

"I'll pass on the message and try to find out where she is," David said. "But she may not want to come yet."

"Why is that Mr Martin?"

"You'll figure it out by morning," David sighed. "The Franklins are on the hop. If they find and destroy Hurley's information, they will be back, full of alibis. If not, every little crook that knows anything about them and has ever spoken out against them will mysteriously vanish. And if they find her – you'll be finding pieces of her all over the state."

"You seem to have a lot of sympathy for an accused murderer and major criminal."

Carter sounded suspicious.

"I've met her and spoken to her a few times. She's..."

"A criminal!" Carter repeated.

David sat again.

"Yes, I know, but ... Kevin introduced us, not long after she saved his life. I won't try to say she regrets her life style, but she has been working against Rocky Franklin, even if she couldn't break free of him and the Old Man. Let's say, she accepts that when they go down, she will too. Mike Johnson was in love with her."

"That was her?" Carter kept his voice low, but it was intense. His ideas suddenly veered in a new direction. "She called herself Gwenda Willard. I asked Senator Willard if she was related."

David tensed. "Please, don't even think of that. Not now, not ever. She doesn't know that I know."

"She is related?"

"The name she gave that day is, was, her real name. When she left home she changed it."

"Does the senator know?"

"I think he suspects, but she distanced herself from him."

Carter made a decision.

"Tell Kevin Mason to keep her safe." Carter looked directly at David. "Tell him to keep me informed of where she is. I won't move in on her unless there is danger to her or the Franklin's are in custody and I won't rescind the arrest warrant. If she is found, she will be brought in and charged. If she decides to plea bargain, it will be considered."

David nodded.

"I suggest too, as a sign of good faith, that she begins to make a notarised statement – telling all she knows about the Franklins. I want to receive a copy and she should keep one safe."

David nodded again, and stood up.

"I just remembered something else. Hurley wanted her to tell Ryan something." David gave him the cryptic message about Hurley's wife.

Wanda slept until the following afternoon. David was getting very concerned.

"I wasn't dreaming," Wanda said as soon as she woke and saw David's worried face.

"How do you feel?" David asked her.

Wanda considered the aches and pains and decided, "Functional."

"You need to eat," David insisted. "Soup?"

Wanda nodded.

"I'll put some in a saucepan."

"Come back."

David nodded. She looked dreadfully pale.

He sat next to her when he returned, and she pulled his face to hers and kissed him. He returned the gesture with a hug. That was all he intended. Wanda had other ideas and all thoughts of caution flew out the window.

Wanda hugged him tightly afterwards.

"I wanted that," she said. When I feel the pull of Harrison, I will think of that. He rouses my body. You make me soar."

David hugged her again and went to salvage the soup. She needed food and to get ready to leave.

Wanda managed to smile as she was changing into more of David's clothes. She even joked as he cut her hair very short. Then she concentrated on making up her face to look as boyish as possible.

David watched her, noting her deliberate movements. He guessed that it hurt for her to move and she hadn't been able to eat much soup. She wasn't well, and she was deliberately hiding it from him. He had to pretend not to see it. She was doing what she had to do. As he must. They had prepared for this day, weeks ago.

The make-up hid the pallor and the finished job was remarkable.

He passed her the overnight bag he had packed and the wallet containing money, a false ID and an open ticket for bus and train. They had no set destination in mind. Wanda would travel, changing buses at random, until she found a place to stay.

"I'll drive you out of town," David decided. "Far enough that Franklin's agents won't be watching for you and I'll wait until you get a bus."

Wanda hugged him, betraying with her fierceness a trace of desperation. Then she pulled free and took a deep breath.

"I'll be OK, Dav. I just have to keep moving. When I go to ground, I'll call you."

David told her the gist of what Carter had told him. Wanda accepted the information.

"I'll do that," Wanda promised. "And I'll call you when I can, on the way. Let's go."

David took her to a borrowed car that he had parked down the street. He was taking no chances. He drove towards the southeast, stopping just on dusk in a tiny town away from everywhere. They waited at the bus stop for an hour before the bus arrived. In all that time, no other vehicle had driven past. The bus showed "Florida" as its destination, but it would have many stops between here and there and at one of them, Wanda would transfer somewhere else.

He stood and watched the lights of the bus disappear in the distance before walking back to his car. As Wanda had done, he took a deep breath and moved on. He had things to do too.

Chapter 31

Wanda travelled for three days, zigzagging generally southeast and alternating buses and trains. She ate little, for the fast food outlets didn't appeal to her. She existed mainly on water. At Bakersfield, she saw a sign for "Miracle Hot Springs" and decided that was where she would go. She needed to stop travelling and she needed sleep - desperately. The naps between stops had not refreshed her and she had forced herself to get out at the stops to walk around and loosen up. She had no doubt that the illness she had fought for seven years was taking hold of her.

There was no temptation to let it have her. Even without a reason to keep going, she wasn't going to let it win. It had taken her mother, almost taken her sister, and she was too stubborn to let it get her. She had to be.

Every chance she got, she rang David. She left cryptic messages for him of route numbers and directions. Once she had caught him at home and heard news of Frisco. It wasn't a healthy place to be right now, and other major towns would be the same.

She was a city brat. If Harrison was looking for her, he would expect her to lose herself in a city, not in a two-horse town out near the Arizona border.

When the bus pulled into the town with the hot springs it was almost midday and the temperature was already high. Wanda stepped from the air-conditioned bus and instantly felt like wilting. She waited for her bag to be unpacked then walked to a building that showed the information sign.

Inside was a lot cooler than outside, but she couldn't stay there. She looked at an accommodation board and chose a bed and breakfast place at random. After asking for directions to get there, she set off on foot.

The heat was giving her a headache and the sun reflecting of the footpath was hurting her eyes, but Wanda pressed on. She hardly realised that her pace was growing progressively slower until she stumbled into a parked car.

"Are you alright there?"

A man spoke and Wanda could barely focus her eyes on him but she sensed no threat.

"I haven't got far to go," Wanda told him, having no idea if that was true.

"If you're after somewhere to stay," the man said thoughtfully, "I have a couple of rooms that I let out occasionally. That's if you intend to stay a while. Be cheaper than a motel or those fancy BB places."

To Wanda's mind, it sounded much better, more private.

"I am hoping to stay a while," Wanda admitted. "I hadn't booked anywhere, I saw the name of a place down this way. Are you sure it's no trouble?"

"No trouble and it is just at the next street."

Wanda followed him.

"If you pardon me saying, you don't seem too well."

"I should be better after having some sleep," Wanda said carefully.

"I think you need a hat on too," the man added. "You're from the city?"

"Yeah."

"Come for the hot springs?"

"Thought I'd give them a try," Wanda agreed, though cold springs sounded better right then. With an effort, she managed to keep walking straight.

"On your own, then?"

"Yeah."

"My place is the next house."

"Great."

"I'm Tom Davis. What's your name?"

Wanda almost told him her real name, but remembered her alias. "Lee Martin."

She followed her benefactor into a house, blessedly cool after outside, and without thinking wiped the sweat from her face and much of her make-up.

Tom Davis went to fetch his wife and returned with a glass of cold water. He handed it to his guest without asking if she wanted it. Wanda took it gratefully.

He noticed his guest's change of appearance, but made no comment. He decided that his guest was a woman after all, in spite of the clothes, and ill too. She was pale where the make-up had been removed.

He let his wife take over and show their guest to the little unit they kept for when their children visited. She would find out what she could. Perhaps he would need to call a doctor.

David expected another call from Wanda, but five days passed and he had heard nothing. He was getting very worried. Finally, he received a call on his mobile. The man had a slow drawling voice. It finally dawned on him that he was talking about Wanda and his stomach flopped.

"Mr Davis, thank you for calling. I've been worried about her."

Davis went on to talk about how sick she was, giving David time to think about what to do. He needed to get someone there to be with her, but who? If only he could go. But he was needed in Frisco to monitor what was happening on the streets.

"I'll arrange for someone to come," David promised. "Can I get your address and phone number?"

Tom Davis obliged, and David told him to call if his guest got any worse.

David rubbed his head and ran through his options. He'd have to ring Carter and tell him where Wanda was. The police officer was starting to give him a hard time. If he couldn't find someone else to go to Wanda, it might have to be the police. Damn!

There was her family, her sister, the one that had been in hospital. No, this was too dangerous for her and Wanda had made it all too clear she wanted no contact with the rest of her family. Yet, she had entrusted him with her sister's phone number. To call her if. Just if.

If! David reached for his mobile phone and found the number in his wallet. It rang for a long time after he dialled and he was about to hang up when a woman answered.

"Elisabeth Willard."

David pictured the petite blonde daughter of the LA senator.

"Um, I was given this number by … a friend. I'm David."

"Hello David. How can I help you?" Elisabeth said gaily.

"My friend said to call you if…"

"If what, David?"

"She didn't say, but I think, If - is now."

There was no sound at the other end of the connection for a long moment.

"Yes. Yes I think you are right," Elisabeth said soberly. "Where are you? Is she with you?"

"No, she's not. I had a call…"

"She's sick, isn't she?" Elisabeth listed the symptoms.

"Yes, how did you … no, I know. You were in the hospital. You almost died, didn't you?"

"David, don't go to pieces. I got better. Where are you? We need to talk."

"I can't take her to a hospital," David said desperately.

"David! Where are you?"

"Frisco. I shouldn't have let her go."

"Can you get to the Penrith Hotel on the Avenue?"

"Yes, but what…"

"Go there and ask for the Senator's suite. I'll call ahead and ask them to let you in."

"Okay. I'll do that."

"What is your last name, David?"

"Martin. I'm David Martin."

"Ok, now how long has she been sick?"

"I don't know. She never said anything. Never complained."

"No, I suppose not. She refuses to admit when she's sick. She controls it by, well, by what she does."

"You know? She's … she can't go to hospital. She's wanted…"

David heard a sigh. "I know," Elisabeth admitted. "I'm going to have to talk to Dad. He'll have to pull some strings. We'll come as soon as possible, I promise, but convincing Dad won't be easy."

"She's going to testify," David blurted. "I'm keeping a police captain advised of where she is. I feel so helpless."

"David, she's stubborn. She won't give an inch. Is she planning to testify to save her own skin or is there another reason?"

"There's another reason. A very good reason and she made a promise."

"Keep reminding her of it."

"I can't call her. She's hiding. We don't want to trust the cops or the feds."

Elisabeth was silent, thinking.

"Find a way, David. It's important. The man with grey hair has an awfully strong hold on her. She allowed it to happen and it won't be easy to break. If she gets too weak, she might want to go back to him. You know what that will mean."

"Yes." David knew only too well.

"Go to the hotel, David. We'll talk there."

"What the hell do you mean by pulling rank and ordering me here?" Sandy Willard raged at his father. His uniform still looked very new.

"I'm the newest rookie in the precinct," he continued loudly, "Yet you get heavy with the Captain, I'm pulled off my patrol, bundled into a car and driven here, assigned to you, I'm told. Everyone will be screaming favouritism."

"It's family business, Son," Charles Willard said calmly. "Get in the plane."

The conversation was continued in the hired executive jet.

"Where are we going?" Sandy asked, his tone less belligerent.

"San Francisco."

"Why? Has this got something to do with Gwen?"

"She's sick, Sandy," Elisabeth interrupted.

"So what? She's told us often enough that she doesn't want us or need us."

"We owe it to her to help her," Elisabeth pleaded.

"You can't be saying that you are going to help hide her?" Sandy was astounded.

"All the police in the state are hunting for her," Sandy continued. "She's in the top ten most wanted. I even saw her face on my milk carton this morning. Do you know how hard it is to say nothing when she's mentioned? Do you know what would be said if they knew she was my SISTER? And now that she is up to her eyeballs in shit, she calls for help!"

"Settle down, Stuart," Charles Willard said sternly. "You don't know all the details. I do not intend to pervert the course of justice and no, she did not ring. A friend of hers, by the name of David, called Elisabeth."

"Who is this David? Some crim like her? Did he tell you to use your influence?"

"He sounded nice," Elisabeth said firmly.

"How can you tell that? I bet that friend of hers that tried to rape you was nice too, at first."

Elisabeth's eyes sparked angrily. "That had nothing to do with Wanda, and she stopped it. Anyway, David sounded frantic."

"He probably wants the reward for turning her in," Sandy jeered.

"No, he wants someone to be with her."

"Oh no. Not me! If I get near her, so help me, if I don't strangle her, I'll take her in, sick or not," Sandy promised.

"She has promised to testify against the Franklins," Charles Willard said when he had the chance.

Sandy's jaw dropped open.

"Nah!" Sandy argued. "She's saying that to save her miserable skin."

"Let's say no more for now and wait until we've spoken to David," Charles Willard mediated.

Sandy stood back, arms crossed and glared at David Martin. The man greeted his father and sister as if he was the image of respectability. However, if he knew Gwen, he had to be crooked.

David glanced his way without cringing.

"Stuart, come and sit down," Charles Willard directed. "My son, Stuart Willard," Charles explained.

David held out his hand, Sandy ignored the gesture.

As he dropped his hand, David thanked them for coming.

"Elisabeth insisted and I couldn't refuse her on this. I will stress one thing – I will not interfere with the law," the senator said.

"I'm not asking you to," David acknowledged. "I need to get someone to where she is to help her."

"She can rot!" Sandy said deliberately. "She's rotten, rude, crude, a whore and a criminal and cares for no one but herself and those lowlifes."

"That's not true, Sandy. She saved my life."

Sandy dismissed his sister's objection with a flick of his hand.

"The last vestiges of filial concern. Who else has she ever helped?"

David stood and walked to stand in front of Sandy.

"There was a young man named Mike," David began.

"Who rode on a three wheeled trike," Sandy interrupted rudely and was glared at by his father. David smiled faintly, appreciating the quick repartee. He continued calmly.

"He worked for Sylvester Franklin. For reasons of his own, he tried to put that scum in jail. Through a combination of shrewd defence and evidence theft, Sylvester Franklin got off. Mike continued trying to get evidence against him, but one day someone talked and the Franklins discovered what he had done. They beat him, tortured him and when he was unconscious, dumped him off the end of a pier. That should have been the end of him, but for some reason, Wanda had been close by. She saw someone tipped into the water and went down after them. She had to release him from the chains and bring him up. In short, she saved his life. She didn't have to get involved and she risked a lot doing it. "Unfortunately, Mike Johnson died later, but she saved MY life."

Sandy looked more closely at David.

"I don't see any scars." Sandy had guessed what David hadn't admitted.

"She also paid for plastic surgery and never once betrayed me to her bosses."

"Probably protecting her own hide. What's this about testifying against the Franklins?"

"Just that." David confirmed

"Nah! Like I told Dad, she's just saying that so that she won't be charged and jailed."

David took a deep breath.

"What do you see as your duty in this situation?" David asked.

"She's wanted for murder. If I saw her, I'd take her in."

Sandy was adamant. There was a look of pain on Elisabeth's face, but the Senator had his under control.

"Murder, accessory to murder, countless robberies, corporate espionage – that's quite a record for someone who is only twenty four. If, as you claim, she only wanted to save her skin, why did she run away from Harrison Franklin? She could have gone with him. He hasn't been found yet."

Sandy shrugged. "I don't know."

"I do know," David admitted, waiting for Sandy to react.

"Go on," Sandy urged.

David explained how Wanda had been working against Richard and discovered Hurley. Then he told them what he knew of events leading up to the present.

"So, it's thanks to her that the powers have a chance to get the evidence Hurley collected on the Franklins as well as his special agents. That is in spite of the fact that she knew there was also a thick file on her with it. Look at this."

David took a folded sheet of paper from his pocket. It was a sample of the data the police had on Wanda.

Sandy took the paper and studied it. He handed it back wordlessly, less sure of himself.

"Let the cops mind her, or the feds."

"You are a cop," Elisabeth reminded him.

"Do you agree that the Franklins must be stopped?" David insisted.

"Yes, of course. Oh, all right!" Sandy gave in. "But it makes me sick that she will get away with everything."

"She isn't asking for immunity in return for testifying," David surprised him by saying. "She could have given herself up at once – there are two cops up here that she would trust. This way, however, the Franklins are kept guessing. They may know she isn't dead, but they won't know her intentions. She told me to tell the police that she is ready to accept punishment for her crimes."

"Even if it's the electric chair?" Sandy asked bluntly.

David ducked his head, trying to control the intense emotion that question had raised.

"Well?" Sandy insisted.

David looked up, no longer trying to hide his tears. "Even that."

"She's sick! No one would willingly..." Sandy began, his thoughts considering possibilities.

"All right! I'll go and baby sit her. I will make sure she doesn't kill herself, if that's what she intends. I'll keep her alive to testify and to incriminate herself so thoroughly... Where is she?"

Charles Willard rose and helped his daughter up. They left the room without a word, though Elisabeth gave David a final glance.

"Why aren't you with her?" Sandy asked in a gentler tone.

"I have to be here. I have a network of informers – all out looking for those slime crawlers. I want them found, more than you can guess. Now is not a time for what I want to interfere with what needs to be done."

"She is only saying that she will accept punishment because she thinks she is going to die," Sandy said bluntly. "She knows that Elisabeth can't help her get better and she'll fight it as long as she can – then give up."

"Whatever her rationalisation," David thought aloud. "Can you see how much more effective her testimony would be if she was free to say exactly what she did for them and why?"

Sandy had no answer for that.

"She's in a little town..." David told Sandy how to find Wanda.

Unexpectedly, Sandy reached out for David's hand and shook it. A wordless approval passed between them.

"I'll take you to meet the officer's I'm liaising with," David offered. "They'll be pleased she has a police guard. You don't have to tell them who you are or pretend you like her."

"Get them to come here," Sandy suggested. "I need to contact the specialist that treated Elisabeth and ask for advice."

"I'll arrange it," David nodded.

Chapter 32

Tom Davis, retired Justice, was no fool. He could see the girl was ill. That was why he'd offered his two spare rooms for her use. His wife had been a nurse and could help her, but the girl was getting progressively worse. He was seriously considering taking her to hospital when he heard the knock at the door.

The tall young man standing on his door step was visibly agitated.

"Good day, I'm Sandy Willard. Are you Mr Davis?"

Tom Davis nodded. "How can I help you?"

"I was sent to help with your guest, Lee Martin."

A great weight lifted from the old man's mind.

"She is using the little apartment at the end of the house. My wife is with her at the moment, she used to be a nurse. This way."

Sandy Willard still hadn't settled in is mind what his feelings were for his eldest sister. He still felt a lot of anger…

When they entered the small apartment, the woman by the bed stood up.

"Jean Davis," she said

"Sandy Willard. Your husband said you were a nurse?"

Jean nodded.

"That's no end of a relief." Sandy admitted, dumping his pack on the floor. He took his jacket off and noticed the look of concern on the faces of the old couple. They were looking at his gun.

Sandy blushed, feeling self-conscious. He drew out his identification and the laminated card confirming his temporary attachment to the San Francisco detective division.

"Are you here on official business?" Davis asked directly.

"Partly," Sandy told them. "There are some matters that I need to discuss with you and Mrs Davis. However, my main reason for being here is to help your guest."

"Am I right in thinking that her name is not Lee Martin?" Davis asked.

Sandy smiled wryly. "As I said, there are matters we need to discuss."

Tom Davis was prepared to wait for the details. "I'll be in my den when you need me."

Sandy went over to Wanda and lifted one wrist. The arm was limp, the bones prominent but the pulse was still strong.

"What is wrong with her?" Jean asked.

"There is a long winded name for it," Sandy told her. "I have some medical notes in my bag. They may make more sense to you. Basically it is a genetic problem."

Sandy described the symptoms and then what the doctor had suggested to treat them.

"You seem quite familiar with the problem," Jean commented.

"My sister has it too," Sandy admitted carefully. "As a result, your guest and I are acquainted, though not on the most cordial of terms. That however, is actually an advantage. We need to get her to react. To get up and moving around. So, I am going to have to get rough with her. And you will need to be prepared for some less than polite language."

Jean Davis smiled. "I've heard plenty of that in my time. What is her real name?"

"She calls herself Wanda."

Sandy bent down to get the notes from his bag. Jean Davis went and spoke gently to her patient.

"Wanda, dear, you need to get up and move around."

Sandy left the notes on the table, took a deep breath and strode over to Wanda. It was one thing to be angry with her when she was being a smart mouthed bitch, swearing at him -but to pick a fight with someone who was looking deceptively innocent?

Jean moved away from the bed and hid her expression when Sandy slapped the girl hard on the face.

"Get up you bitch. You made a promise, remember. I am not going to let you wriggle out of it. Now get up!"

There was a slight reaction from Wanda.

"I know you can hear me. There is no use pretending you can't. Get up now, or I am going to drag your carcass to hospital."

There was a more definite movement now. Sandy allowed Jean to place a straw to Wanda's lips so she could drink. Then he continued his harangue, working off some of his anger at her, at what she was, what she'd done and the grief she'd caused his family.

Jean continued to maintain silence at this unorthodox treatment. She could see the results.

"You bastard, Sandy. Leave me alone." Wanda's voice was weak.

"Is that the best you can do?" Sandy jeered. "Nah! It looks like I'll have to take you back to Frisco."

Wanda cursed and swore at him, using language that caused Tom Davis to raise his brows when he came in with a message. It caused Sandy to blush more than once, but all the time, Wanda was forcing herself to sit up and then to stand. She had tears in her eyes from the pain of every movement.

Sandy's anger at her suddenly evaporated, but he hid his sympathy. She had to do this herself.

"Now you are up," Sandy said harshly, "We can give you something for the pain. But you have to keep active, walking at least. With short rests at intervals."

"I know," Wanda said subsiding. "I was just so tired."

"That's the danger," Sandy said more gently. "That's the mistake we made with Elisabeth – we thought she needed more rest."

Jean Davis took the vial containing the drug recommended for this purpose and administered it expertly. She helped to support Wanda as she determinedly circled the room at a painfully slow pace.

Tom drew Sandy aside and passed him the paper with the message he had taken.

"Your friend, David, rang and asked me to tell you that."

Sandy read, "Ryan died without regaining consciousness. Urgent you question Wanda about the location of the data."

Sandy ran his hands over his face.

"Can we talk privately," he asked the older man.

"So that is the situation," Sandy finished. "I will understand if you want her taken elsewhere."

Tom Davis leant back in his chair and considered what he had been told.

"Is that why you are here? To see she doesn't run?"

"Only in part," Sandy said. "I've dealt with this illness before, with my sister. And yes, I can keep an official eye on her. I'm not here to arrest her yet."

"So, the police know she's here?"

"Two senior police officers know. The special team of investigators know there is a witness somewhere. Her name is not being mentioned. If Harrison Franklin hears she's alive, he'll go all out to get her. That's why she's here until the Franklins are in custody."

"Shouldn't she be making statements – in case?" Tom suggested tactfully.

"That is one of my instructions," Sandy said. "And one reason to get her functional."

"She doesn't like you. Will she cooperate with you?"

Sandy laughed wryly. "I think she will cooperate, in spite of the history between us. I don't like her either."

"Personal or official?"

"Personal."

"She hardly looks capable of all you've told me," Tom Davis admitted. "Though her language is colourful."

"That is mild, Sir." Sandy grimaced. "And being slight, waif-like and calculating is a potent weapon in her arsenal."

"What did that message mean?"

"It means that Wanda isn't going to be left in peace, like she probably hoped. She is the best chance there is to help figure out where Hurley put his evidence against the Franklins. She was possibly the last to speak to him. The investigators have the data on Rocky Franklin's elite agents and they are checking that but we need the rest. With Ryan's death, she is the only witness they have that can testify against the Franklins. No one has been able to find any of the other elite agents."

"I see," Davis said, thoughtfully. "I believe in seeing justice done. I've heard things about the Franklins for a long time. The stink behind the public image. She can stay. I'll help watch her."

Sandy nodded.

"I want to talk to her too. I want to know who thrashed her. Jean says she has five marks like whip lashes on her back."

Sandy managed to keep his thoughts to himself. "My guess is Harrison Franklin."

Davis nodded.

Wanda returned from the hot springs, moving with greater ease than before she had left. The pain had diminished to a bearable level. Jean Davis had a meal ready for her and Sandy on their return.

"I didn't expect you to go to so much trouble," Wanda thanked her.

"It's no trouble and you can repay me by helping with other jobs," Jean assured her.

"And Officer Willard can help with any tall jobs," Wanda suggested, with a trace of humour.

Sandy gave no reaction. He didn't trust his sister in this docile mood.

Jean Davis had gone off to some "Ladies do" when Tom Davis decided to broach his questions.

"What Sandy told you is true. All of it. And more," Wanda finally admitted. "But I am on my best behaviour right now."

Sandy snorted at her understatement.

"I am not a nice person, Mr Davis. I chose to do what I did. I like the thrill I get from the danger, from the robberies and from working for dangerous men. You don't need to feel sorry for me."

"Why are you testifying against them? Because they turned on you and thrashed you?"

Davis asked, watching Wanda's reaction.

Wanda went tense. "That was – a miscalculation."

"So…"

"Harrison and Richard murdered someone important to me and conspired to try to rape another. I realised that others had suffered more humiliation at their hands than I had."

Wanda stared across the room. "And I promised Hurley that I would finish what he had started."

"What do you expect to get out of this?" Davis asked.

"Justice," Wanda said simply.

"What does justice mean?" Davis probed further.

"Harrison, Richard and Sylvester Franklin will be shown for what they are and what they've done and be punished for it," Wanda said.

"And you?"

"I don't expect to be treated any different," Wanda said, turning away. "I'm a criminal too. I chose to be one. I am no better than those I worked for. I chose to work for them."

"And if you didn't choose?" Tom prompted.

"That's irrelevant," Wanda snapped. "I did." She didn't want to think about Harrison and how he had trained her.

"David thinks that Harrison conditioned you," Sandy interrupted.

"If he did, I was happy to let him."

"I don't think you are really a bad person," Davis told her. "If you can recognise that what you have done is wrong and are prepared to take the consequences, there is hope for you."

"No there's not," Wanda said flatly.

"There is another option. Counselling."

"No! It won't work on me. Do you think counselling would cure Harrison or Richard?" Wanda said. "Do you think that just because they give thousands of dollars to charity each year that they are trying to atone for their actions?"

"They aren't coming forward to own up, are they?" Davis replied.

Sandy decided it was time to mention the message about Ryan.

"Hurley didn't tell me. I told David about the letter and the key Hurley left in my apartment for Ryan. He told Carter. I assume they got them."

Sandy didn't know if they had, but he would mention it in case. "What else?"

"He told me to tell Ryan about his wife."

"What about her?"

"She'd died, two days before and he'd buried her."

Sandy couldn't see any significance in that information. He questioned her further, this time about Hurley's death. He knew the police thought she had killed him.

Wanda enjoyed the look of horror on Sandy's face when she described Hurley's injuries.

"Richard gave me a gun. I offered to shoot him to stop them hurting him further," Wanda said bluntly. "I would have if he wanted me to."

"Did he?" Sandy didn't hide his disgust.

Wanda shook her head. "Harrison took it off me when he got back. I was outside struggling with Ryan when they shot him."

"Your prints were on the gun, not theirs," Sandy told her.

"I didn't shoot him," Wanda said. "Is that how he died?"

"How else would he have died?" Sandy asked.

"They had put plastic stuff on the worst of his wounds to stop them bleeding," Wanda said. "I loosened them so that he would bleed more. He was still alive when I left, delirious though. I hoped he'd die before they got back. I didn't want him able to talk. That's when I ran."

Sandy stared at his sister, speechless. Tom Davis however, wasn't shocked.

"Young woman, do you have a lawyer?" Davis asked.

"I don't want one. I can't corroborate Hurley's evidence by being gagged by a defence counsel. I'll tell the truth as I know it and I don't care if it incriminates me."

"Would you object to me acting as your counsel," Davis offered. Wanda turned in surprise.

"Why?"

"You still need a counsel to tell you when not to make admissions, and to stop you being tied up in knots by their lawyers."

"Thanks, I will accept your offer. Just as long as you understand what I intend to do. Now if there's nothing more, I need to rest."

Wanda woke covered in sweat and with her heart pounding. The remnants of the dream – explained the sensation. For once, she was grateful for having a nightmare. The flood of chemicals through her system had banished the encroaching stiffness. She found she could easily get out of her bed and walk to the low bed where Sandy was sleeping.

She kicked him, gently. He woke instantly.

"Twitchy, aren't we," she teased mildly.

"What is it," he snapped.

"I'm about to run away. Somewhere you can't find me. What are you going to do?" "Strangle you," Sandy promised.

"Good to know you haven't gone soft in the head," Wanda went on. "Tell whoever you report to, to exhume Mrs Hurley's body. I think the stuff might be there."

Sandy sat up, less surly. "What gave you that morbid idea?"

"I had a nightmare about being buried alive. I think it might be symbolic."

Wanda turned and walked back to her bed. Sandy drew on some pants and went to wake up Tom Davis.

David Martin called Carter, waking him from a sound and well deserved sleep, to tell him he had an important report. Carter drove to meet him at an all-night drug store and suggested they talked in his car.

This report was too important to wait for their normal meeting.

"Sorry to drag you out," David began, "But I have a line on two of those missing FCI employees, a possible sighting of Sylvester Franklin and one of the company directors that you want to talk to. It's all written down. And one more thing, Sandy Willard called me – he suggested that you should exhume Mrs Hurley's body."

Carter betrayed his interest. "Why didn't we think of that? It makes sense."

"Too much," David agreed.

"I'll look into it. Meanwhile, listen out for any suggestion of a cop on Franklin's payroll. The copy of Ryan's films that we had in the police evidence locker has vanished. Fortunately we made multiple copies."

"I'll do that. How is the investigation coming?"

"They have enough evidence to issue warrants if we ever find the people. Would your friend know where they might be?"

David shrugged. He would get Sandy to ask.

Chapter 33

Tom Davis watched Wanda as she walked in the door. She was relaxed and moving easily after her session at the hot springs. In fact, she was more relaxed than he had seen her. It seemed that she and young Sandy Willard had buried their differences.

The faint smile on her face disappeared as soon as she became aware of the two men seated in the chairs. Her face became, not rigid, but controlled. Tom likened it to a shutter coming down over a window. It happened when she did not want anyone to know her thoughts or feelings. It was a defence mechanism, but he was not sure what it was defending against.

It was there most times when she spoke to try to shock Officer Willard with admissions of her criminal activities and her rewards. He had noticed that she never spoke of her failures, or her miscalculations.

One of the men, dressed in a suit, stood up. Davis stayed back. He had asked this man here, to evaluate his guest.

"Miss Dean, Officer Willard, I'm Graham Cooper. I'm part of the team investigating the Franklin family."

Wanda had stopped two steps inside the door with her hands formed into fists at her side. Sandy shoved her forward, so he could come in and close the door.

"My colleague is a psychologist," Cooper did not mention the other man's name.

Tom Davis sensed that Wanda distrusted Cooper.

"I invited him here," Tom interrupted. "He is adept at questioning witnesses and extracting important information."

Wanda relaxed her hands and put them in her pockets, but her shoulders were hunched. She was still wary; the distancing trick was still active.

"I didn't think I was so important," Wanda said casually. "I suppose you have ID of some kind?"

Cooper drew out his wallet and pulled out a card. Wanda made no move to take it, she watched as Sandy did. His eyebrows rose in amazement. "State Department – and its genuine. I know what to look for."

Wanda's danger sense was not warning her of anything, but she had the sense of things being not as they seemed.

"My ID is genuine too, but I'm not Lee Martin," Wanda said to Sandy, but her eyes were on Cooper. "So what's your angle, Cooper?"

Cooper answered readily. "The State Department is taking an interest in the investigation because important men are involved and some of them are in public office. We are simply watching the situation to make sure everything is done properly. I am also here to debrief you."

"And your pet shrink. Do you expect me to claim insanity?"

"It is part of the process," Cooper said, telling her nothing with that statement.

"Process be damned," Wanda stated looking at Cooper. "Who will you be reporting to?"

Cooper held out his hand and suggested that Wanda be seated. She ignored the gesture, bringing her hands from her pockets and folding her arms.

"I will be asking you questions and taping the answers. Later, I will make transcripts of each session. These tapes will be kept in a secure place until you are needed to testify – the transcripts will be given to the prosecutor. If you are able to provide details relevant to the ongoing investigations – these will be passed to the investigating officers through Captain Carter in San Francisco."

Cooper's hands were open and empty. Wanda let her arms drop to her sides.

"Whenever you are ready, then," Wanda agreed. "But I'd rather stay standing, if you don't mind."

Tom Davis nodded slightly when Cooper glanced his way.

Cooper set up his recorder on the table.

"You will need to stay close to the table Miss Dean," Cooper said calmly. "And direct your answers in the direction of the microphone."

Wanda had a smile on her face as she walked closer to the table, as if the whole business was a joke. Cooper frowned slightly, but caught Tom Davis shaking his head slightly. He still saw the closed expression in Wanda's eyes, and knew she was hiding her true emotions.

"This is serious, Wanda. Quit clowning. It's time to come clean, like you promised," Sandy told her as she passed him.

"Shut up!" she hissed in return.

Cooper spoke into the microphone, recording details of the time of the interview and the people present. Then he turned to Wanda. He had declined to return to his seat, and being taller than Wanda, maintained his control of the interview.

"We have had information to suggest that Franklin has informants in the Police Department and the Prosecutor's office. What can you tell us about that?" Cooper started with the question Sandy wanted the answer to.

Wanda instantly recalled her first job in San Francisco. She told Cooper everything she remembered about going to retrieve the tape about Sylvester Franklin. Dates, times, actions, descriptions of the people with her, what they wore, what names she had for them and how she had spirited the tape out from under the Prosecutor's nose and the payment for services. She gave precise details.

Cooper was impressed and did not try to hide it. He nodded at several points of her narration as if he had correlated them with other information.

"That is impressive," he commended Wanda. "Your report tallies with the report made by the prosecutor. You will make an excellent witness. I can't understand why you haven't asked for amnesty in exchange for your testimony."

"I told him why," Wanda indicated Davis with her thumb. "And it's not relevant to the matter in hand. Next question."

Wanda endured two hours of questioning before Sandy halted the proceedings. Cooper didn't ask for a reason, just nodded and packed up his equipment.

"We'll start again this evening," he told Wanda. The so far nameless psychologist, closed up his note book and quietly followed Cooper.

The next two days followed the same pattern, but on the third day, Cooper arrived early in the morning just as Wanda was leaving to go for a session in the hot springs.

"I'm not going to be around for an hour or more," Wanda told him. She forced herself to try to move normally, but Cooper's expression told her she'd failed. "I'm not my best in the morning."

"I understand," Cooper said with genuine sympathy. "I thought I might join you this morning. We could talk, off the record."

"No one is stopping you. You might even be better company than Sandy," Wanda shot her brother a glance. Sandy merely scowled.

Cooper politely ignored the exchange.

"Yeah, Okay, who's driving?" Sandy asked.

Cooper drove and kept his conversation to checking the directions to the springs.

"There's a dirt road to the left, after the bridge. It leads to a rocky area on the far side. Fewer people go there," Wanda told him. She had no inclination to annoy Cooper, not the way she did with her brother.

Wanda settled in the hot water pool and leant back with her eyes closed, waiting for the heat to seep through her aching body. She was aware of Cooper joining her in the water, a polite distance away. He was an unobtrusive presence. He let her relax and didn't seem to need to talk just for the sake of talking.

"Why did you come here, Cooper?" Wanda said once she felt the aches leaving her.

"Just to talk." Cooper said.

"Try to find out what makes me tick, do you mean?"

"Perhaps."

"Good luck," Wanda said wryly. "You won't be the first to try that, and fail."

"Did you decide to come here because of the springs?" Cooper asked her.

"Only by chance," Wanda admitted. "I was running away. The place sounded interesting."

"It's good for what ails you."

"Yeah, it's been a real help."

"Tell me about your illness."

"I'm not sick," Wanda told him, opening her eyes to watch him. "It's nothing more than an inconvenience, like arthritis or something."

Cooper's face didn't change its expression. "Tell me about Harrison Franklin."

Wanda looked away.

"Off the record, just between you and me," Cooper said gently. "How did you meet him? Take your time."

"When I met him, I didn't know who and what he was. I did something that really pissed him off."

"What happened?"

"Nothing then. I got away and kept out of his way."

Cooper waited for her to continue, not pushing her for details.

"A while later, I started seeing some of the men I knew worked for him. So, I was going to do one big job and run."

"That was when you were caught." It was a statement, as if Cooper already knew that.

"Yeah. I learnt later that the bastard had set me up."

"I see…." Cooper murmured. "How did he get onto you after your release?"

Even though these events were over five years old, just thinking of them bought them back into crystal clear focus. Now, with the benefit of hindsight, she considered various events in her past. She had ignored her sister's advice, and the invitation of that man who had helped her when she was sick. She had thought she could do things her way.

Now, knowing Harrison better, she recalled various events.

"I was trying to leave the city, but I kept seeing his men – people I knew from earlier. Thinking on it now, it was like they were herding me."

"Why do you say that?" Cooper asked.

"Because one of his beasts mugged me and took what little money I had. He must have known I was coming because he stepped out – right in front of me and grabbed me."

"Then what?"

Wanda glossed over details of the attack, "Oh, I got away, Harrison's people found me again and abducted me to Harrison's mansion."

"Is that where he conditioned you?"

"Must have been. He had me beaten when I arrived – punishing me for wrecking some scheme he'd had in motion. After that, he kept punishing me until I stopped saying what I thought."

"You never tried to escape?"

"I…no…" That was something that she had never considered back then. "I think he had me drugged for a while. It was sort of like I knew I couldn't get away, and if I did what he said, he would treat me well, and if I didn't, he'd hurt me worse."

"Sleep conditioning?"

"Maybe…my head was certainly screwed. I craved his rewards, and it makes me feel sick, thinking of it now, but I wanted to please him so much that he would make love to me. He never did though, but he could rouse my body to mindlessness, and I craved that. I was never, ever, good enough for anything more intimate with him. He kept me wanting to please him, and to be punished if I failed him."

"So when you were suitably obedient?"

"He got someone to teach me to open every kind of safe – I was in heaven."

"You don't seem the type to take orders," Cooper suggested.

"You've been talking to Sandy," Wanda accused.

"Why would he know?"

"Never mind. He just knows me, that's all. But you're right, I wasn't. Harrison started me working with a guy I called Harry. I think his real name was Jack something. Harrison gave Harry permission to whack me if I didn't obey instructions. When you got right down to it, it didn't matter to me where I was breaking into or why. I got the thrill, he paid well and I had a certain amount of protection."

Wanda found it easy to talk to Cooper. He wasn't shocked by anything she said and he was an uncritical listener. He encouraged her to continue when the memories were the ones she tried hardest to forget.

"Why did you stay with him?"

Cooper asked into one of Wanda's silences.

"It wasn't an option to leave," Wanda told him. "I had him figured early on. What he decided was his – he would get and keep. Like me. He treated me well when I did as I was told and didn't think too much out loud. Like I said, it didn't matter, it suited me. If I showed too many signs of initiative or nosiness, like I said, he had Harry knock it out of me. He wouldn't let me work on my own."

"I would say you learnt to manipulate him," Cooper suggested.

"Yeah," Wanda agreed with a sense of satisfaction. "I figured him out and Richard too."

"You were fortunate that your relationship never went further than it did," Cooper said. "Did you know that Harrison was married twice?"

"No."

"Both of his wives committed suicide. A number of his 'lady friends' are psychologically scarred by his treatment of them. Two are missing and another is physically and mentally damaged. You must be a truly remarkable woman, Miss Dean."

"I'm a criminal with no scruples," Wanda claimed. "That's all."

Cooper didn't argue her statement. "We can discuss that another day. It's time we headed back."

"There was a message for you, Mr Cooper," Sandy said when Cooper escorted Wanda back into the small apartment. "Tom Davis has the details."

When Sandy was alone with Wanda, he handed her a folded newspaper.

"So they found the crooked cop and the paid off prosecutor," Wanda said. "A sign of my good intentions."

"Read the article on the next page," Sandy said without humour.

Wanda opened the paper so she could read the second page.

The main article was about the death of a woman in the remand cells. Wanda stared at the photograph.

"She was one of Rocky's agents wasn't she?" Sandy asked.

Wanda nodded. "Her real name is Flora Bonnay, not Bonnie Siffer. She was one of the graphic designers in the advertising section. She was probably into forgery of some kind. How much did she tell the police?"

"Not enough. If they had known she worked for Rocky they would have guarded her better."

"Tell Cooper to get his stuff," Wanda said. "I think I can handle three sessions a day."

"I heard from David that they found Hurley's stuff, right where you suggested. They thought they might have to open the coffin but he'd buried his stuff under it."

"When did he ring?"

"When you were out."

Wanda didn't sigh aloud, but simply wished she could have at least heard his voice.

Chapter 34

Wanda had just emerged from the hot springs and was pulling on her tracksuit when she heard the scream. Her head swivelled to look in the direction of the rock face where a trickle of a waterfall brought cooler water to mix with the hot springs.

Sandy sprung to his feet from the rocks where he had been lounging. He was staring at a point half way down the face.

"Hurry up!" he ordered. "The kid has landed on the ledge. If he moves, he will go over. We need to get to the top."

Wanda finished dressing as she ran towards Sandy's car. She was barely belted into her seat when Sandy revved the car into a tight gravel crunching turn and sped back along the dirt track to the top of the bluff.

He knew exactly where to stop, and they only had to follow the sound of a woman screaming "John, John."

Two small children clung to the woman and all three were much to close to the section of bluff that had collapsed. Wanda glanced down the rock face but couldn't see the boy below. Her attention went to the hysterical woman and she dragged her back from the edge and shook her gently.

"He's on a ledge half way down," Wanda said loudly. "We'll do what we can. You need to think of your other children, and keep them back from the edge."

Sandy was bringing a long towrope and a first aid kit from his car. Wanda grabbed the end of the rope and began to tie it around her. Sandy grabbed her arm.

"You aren't going down!"

"I can do this!" Wanda challenged him. "I'm not afraid of heights and I've done plenty of climbing."

"You haven't the strength for this," Sandy argued with the blue green eyes that were alight with challenge.

"I'm well enough to support my weight," Wanda told him. "You could pull me and the boy up if you have to, but I couldn't pull you up."

Sandy wanted to argue the logic, but time was important.

"Go down, see what you can do. I'll call for help."

Sandy tied the other end of the rope to his car while Wanda finished tying a makeshift harness.

"I can see you've done that before," Sandy said with a touch of accusation.

"A few times, yeah. More fun when you're twelve storeys up though."

Wanda grinned briefly at the shocked look on her brother's face. "Keep the rope off the edge."

Sandy had to admire her nerve, well in this instance at least. She eased herself over the edge and walked down the rock face with a slow and easy motion. This wasn't something she couldn't have done before the soak in the springs.

In less time than he expected he heard, "I'm down, give me a minute, then pull up the rope and send down the kit."

Sandy pulled out his mobile phone and called Tom Davis. The old man would know who to call. When he finished, he handed the phone to the woman who was looking pale.

"If it rings, could you answer it?"

She nodded.

Sandy pulled up the rope and tied the end to the first aid box. He carefully lowered it down.

Wanda reached for the kit to stop it landing on the boy. He was breathing, but unconscious and had a number of bleeding gashes and a definite broken leg.

The kit had an inflatable splint and neck brace, but she kept them aside for the moment. The gashes needed attention first so the boy would not bleed to death. When they were covered with pressure bandages, Wanda carefully eased the flat plastic collar into position and blew into the valve to inflate it.

"He's alive, broken leg, some gashes," Wanda called up.

"Help's coming," she heard Sandy call down.

The boy groaned.

"Don't move. You've had a fall. You need to keep still. Help is on the way."

Wanda crouched between the boy and the rest of the drop. The kid was lucky. The ledge wasn't much longer than six foot long and four wide.

The dangling rope disappeared upwards again, so Wanda knew that the promised help had arrived. She moved to one edge of the ledge to give the figure in the orange overalls room to descend. He was dislodging small rocks that were fortunately not landing on the ledge.

The paramedic obeyed Wanda's directions as he neared the ledge and avoided landing on his patient.

"There is a litter coming down," the man said as he unclipped the rope from his belt.

"I'll deal with it," Wanda assured him.

"You did well here," the paramedic commented. "Why didn't you put the leg splint on?"

"Wasn't sure what to do about the bone," Wanda admitted.

"We can use the inflating splint," he told her and she watched what he did.

"I'll need your help lifting him. I'll support his head and neck. You help with his legs. On three. One, two, three."

Wanda watched as the medic climbed back up with the litter, to prevent it from bumping into the rock face. When the rope came down again, she climbed up with deliberate slowness, savouring every second of the thrill she felt.

There was even a bounce in her movements as she climbed into Sandy's car for the drive back to town.

The presence of a hire car outside the Davis's house did not register as Wanda stepped out of the car. For the first time in weeks, she felt well. The relief from the constant ache was almost euphoric.

She walked through the door and pulled up short recognising Captain Carter and his partner, Lieutenant Withers. Sandy closed the door behind her.

"Good day, Captain, Lieutenant," Sandy greeted, giving Wanda a shove forward.

Carter nodded. Withers stared intently at the woman in front of him. He was poised to move if she tried to run.

Wanda gave her brother a sour look before turning her back on him and walking toward the officers. Her heart was pounding. This was the moment when her decision became irrevocable.

She stood before them, not trying to control her fear. The thought of losing her freedom was one she tried not to think about.

"Captain, David Martin told me that before you would do any deals, I had to give myself up voluntarily. I am prepared to do that. I am only asking for protection until the Franklins are in jail."

"You'll have protection," Carter promised.

"Better that what was given to Bonnie Siffer?" Wanda added.

She had scored a hit. Carter's face hardened. He was reminded that the woman was a criminal, and her redeeming moments were fewer than her crimes. He nodded to Withers.

"Wanda Dean, you are under arrest for the murder of John Hurley, assault on a police officer, two counts of accessory to murder. More charges will be laid against you when you return to San Francisco. You have a right to remain silent ..."

Sandy Willard listened with an odd mixture of satisfaction and sadness. He had arrived in this little town, anticipating this moment and expecting to feel vindicated, his sister was finally going to face the consequences of her chosen life style. Instead, he felt sadness because over the past few weeks he had stopped hating her and come, grudgingly to respect her. He had to admire her determination to do what was right, to testify against her bosses and her refusal to give in to the illness that was draining more life from her day by day. Even her annoying habit of needling him and picking fights with him no longer angered him. Not when she would so readily risk herself to save a kid's life.

Wanda kept her head down, until she felt she had some control of her emotions. Then she nodded. "I'll just go and pack a bag," she said in a subdued voice.

Carter nodded for Sandy to escort her into the other room.

Wanda had very little to pack but took each article of clothing, and packed it separately. It was a delaying tactic and she knew it. She was aware that Sandy knew it too because he was tapping the fingers of his right hand against the back of his left. Wanda finally drew the bag closed and walked past him, going back to the front room.

"I appreciate the position of my colleague, Houston De La Court, but I don't believe that taking Miss Dean back to San Francisco at this time is advisable."

Cooper had arrived while Wanda was packing.

"I'll go if they want me to," Wanda said quietly.

Cooper turned to her; his gaze was uncompromising. "Miss Dean, you will go and sit down and say nothing. You have no voice in this conversation. Officer Willard, will you please bring Mr and Mrs Davis in here."

Sandy moved to obey, but Wanda still stood a few steps into the room. Cooper returned his attention to her. He said nothing. Wanda stared back at him, equally mute. It seemed like a battle of wills. Then Wanda held herself rigidly and walked the short distance to the chair with a deliberate step. It seemed that her change in status had hit home.

Sandy did feel a moment of glee. Wanda had never taken orders well when she was still living at home. Since meeting her again, he had the feeling that if she seemed to be obeying an order it was for her own reasons. Now she had given up the freedom to do that.

As he walked to the main house, Sandy had to wonder why Wanda had kept doing what Harrison and Rocky Franklin had directed. Perhaps she had learnt then that obedience was a survival trait as important as competence. Perhaps she had indeed been conditioned, like Pavlov's dogs. What would happen if she saw Harrison? Would her resolve hold?

He still pondered the idea as he returned with the Davis couple.

Sandy chose to stay out of the official conversation between the detectives and Cooper. Instead, he perched on the arm of the chair where Wanda sat.

"What is David Martin to you?" he asked Wanda

"None of your business," Wanda snapped quietly, betraying her tenseness.

"He's a decent bloke. He seems to care a lot for you. I wondered…"

"You've never approved my friends before, Sandy, don't bother starting now. You know what I'm like. I'm a frigid hearted bitch, remember."

"Yeah. I remember."

Cooper came over when the discussion concluded.

"Miss Dean, You will be remaining here a while longer. I will arrange for your doctor to come here and examine you to make sure you will be fit to testify. I will take a copy of your deposition to the prosecutor and if he has any questions about it we will arrange for him to talk to you via a secure video link. As of now, you are to stay within this apartment. Two officers from the local station will be coming to assist Officer Willard. Any attempt on your part to leave this apartment without authority will be considered trying to escape and you will be transferred to the local station lock up. We will notify you when you are required to testify."

Wanda slumped back into the chair and simply nodded. She stared at the opposite wall and ignored everyone until all of them except Jean Davis had left. The older woman came and gave Wanda's shoulder a gentle squeeze of encouragement.

"I know this won't be easy, but you are doing the right thing. You are doing it for the right reasons too. For all the victims who can't defend themselves from the powerful bullies."

Wanda didn't respond, even though she appreciated the gesture of support.

"There's one more thing I thought you might like to know. John Stilton will be fine, they've set his leg and he's resting comfortably in the hospital. His mother is full of praise for the angel that rescued him."

"Tell her she needs her eyes tested. I'm no angel and I don't have wings."

Jean squeezed Wanda's shoulder again.

Sandy waited until he was outside before quizzing Cooper.

"Are you expecting an attempt to be made on Wanda if she went back now?"

"I think there is a good chance. The presence of an important witness had to be revealed when the warrant was taken out against the three Franklins. For as long as possible, we intend to keep the identity of the witness secret. I will use a decoy to see if we can lure any more of Franklins' agents out – maybe even the Old Man himself. Miss Dean is probably correct in saying Harrison will be angry at her for running off instead of leaving with him. He may suspect she is still alive. She thinks if he suspects the witness might be her, he'll try to get her back so he can punish her for her disobedience. Then kill her in some slow and painful way."

Sandy felt sick.

"She couldn't take much, not now." Sandy told Cooper. "He might kill her without intending to."

"I am aware of that danger," Cooper assured Sandy. "Your concern does you credit. I intend to see that Miss Dean is alive and fit to testify at the trial."

"It's after the trial I'm worried about," Sandy admitted. "I can see that she's getting worse. She wouldn't last long in prison even if Franklin's agents let her live but she isn't considering that because I really think that she doesn't expect to live much after the trial. She may feel she doesn't deserve to."

Cooper laid a gentle hand on Sandy's shoulder.

"I know she isn't asking for amnesty, and the charges against her are serious, but I intend to have those charges dropped. The three warrants for murder or accessory to murder, won't stand up in court. They are simply an excuse to hunt her out so we could get her to inform against her bosses. David Martin has given us proof that she was already working against them. Her other crimes are not capital offences and I agree that sending her to jail would be a death sentence that she doesn't deserve."

"At the same time, I feel thwarted, because she will get away with all those crimes. It doesn't seem right probably because I don't like her," Sandy admitted.

"Liking is irrelevant," Cooper told him bluntly. "She doesn't want you close because that would make you a target."

"She stood by and let those sods beat me up!"

"She stood by and let you walk off alive!" Cooper corrected. "I have a great deal of respect for your sister. Yes, I know she's that. She is highly skilled at what she does and instinctively knows how to survive. She knows how Harrison thinks and how he will react in different situations. And she knows that even though we have Johnson's and Hurley's evidence – we are hampered by the fact that both of them are dead. We have investigators working to get corroboration of the information but most of the witnesses are dead, missing or scared witless. All we have is Miss Dean – she's willing to talk, but she can't corroborate the evidence without incriminating herself. I don't want any chance of Harrison getting close enough to influence her. She is afraid she won't be able to get free of him. Our case would be very weak without her."

Sandy sighed.

"Let me handle things," Cooper advised. "You need to monitor her condition. This illness is something that she won't discuss with me, and it's an important factor in any plans I make."

Sandy thought of something Elisabeth had said.

"Then you had better convince her that there is a purpose in life after the trial."

Cooper looked thoughtful, then nodded. "I'll be in touch."

Chapter 35

The hunt for the Franklins was continuing. Sandy heard nothing from Cooper about the success or failure of his decoy. He had several calls from David Martin, apparently passing on snippets of information, but in reality wanting to know how Wanda was. He had not been able to be encouraging.

Dr Rickard had arrived with two colleagues and equipment provided by Cooper. He examined Wanda thoroughly and spoken privately with her.

"I'd prefer to have her in hospital," Rickard confided in Sandy as he was leaving. "Call me at once if anything changes. Make sure she eats and drinks and if you can keep up with the massaging, morning and evening, that will help."

"What about the tablets? What are they?"

Rickard seemed reluctant to answer.

"We've synthesised a compound that is very close to the antibody that we isolated from her last year. It has no adverse effect on mice, and that is all we could try. Normally we would never be able to use it on humans with so little testing. This is an exceptional case. I have permission to use it as a last ditch attempt to head off this illness. The level in each tablet is extremely low and it may not even work. It may have side effects, we just don't know."

"She may not confide in me," Sandy admitted. "But Jean will be watching her too. If either of us have any concerns, we'll call you."

For the two weeks since then, Wanda had stopped annoying her brother and was religiously following the regimen that Rickard prescribed. She seemed to get no worse, but neither was she showing improvement.

Sandy woke in the middle of the night and heard retching. He followed the sound and saw Wanda leaning over the washbasin. He wordlessly fetched a beaker of water and a washcloth.

"How long have you been throwing up?" he asked as he helped her back to bed.

"Last couple of nights," Wanda admitted, breathing carefully. "If it kept up much longer I would have mentioned it."

"Any other problems?"

"Not really. Just the headache and general nausea. But I've been feeling that way for ages."

"You told Rickard?"

"Yeah, Yeah."

Sandy decided to mention that and the throwing up to the doctor in the morning.

The result was that Wanda's diet was changed to one that would make most doctors wince. Fibre foods were eaten in the morning and the rest of the day the foods were high energy, high calorie, and fast digesting substances. It was working and with an increase in the number of tablets, Wanda actually seemed to be better.

Sandy was in the Davis's front garden, weeding it for them, when his cell phone rang.

He answered it and recognised Elisabeth's voice.

"Lizbeth, how are you?"

Sandy heard her, "Going okay," and then silence.

"What's up?" he prompted.

"Well it's … possibly nothing, but … When you come back to San Francisco, be careful, huh? I think they'll be waiting to have a go at Wanda."

"We're not going anywhere yet!"

"You will be. I'm sure of it," Elisabeth insisted. "Take care of her will you?"

"Of course I will," Sandy assured her before she rang off.

He was still scratching his head and wondering at the strange call when two cars drew up. Cooper and two men emerged from one, Withers and Carter from the other.

Sandy stood up. Their presence could mean only one thing. They had come to move Wanda back to the city. How had Elisabeth known?

Cooper hung back, and waited for Sandy to come to him. He had a grim smile on his face.

"The Franklins are in custody – protesting their collective innocence. They have a dozen lawyers raising hell about them being kept separated and in maximum security. So they are being allowed certain luxuries."

Sandy scowled.

"Innocent until proven guilty," Cooper shrugged. "The trial will start on Monday. How is Miss Dean?"

"A bit stronger than at your last visit. Where were those creeps hiding?"

"Florida. They own a resort there. The rest of the millionaire guests were not impressed when the place was raided."

"Was it your decoy that drew them out?"

"One of them. Richard Franklin went with the team sent to get her, but stayed back out of the action. He never saw us coming. Very stupidly, he had a box of matches from the resort in his pocket. Is Miss Dean well enough to fly?"

"You'd better ask the doctor."

Rickard gave Wanda the okay to fly, but he insisted that a doctor accompany her and warned that she might need oxygen.

Cooper was prepared. One of the men with him was a doctor. The other man turned out to be the pilot of the executive jet that was to take them back to San Francisco.

Within an hour, Wanda was seated comfortably, with oxygen mask ready and the rest of the group was strapped in waiting for the plane to take off. The doctor was next to Wanda, and every five minutes he made her take a breath of the oxygen. Sandy watched her too, wondering if he should mention Elisabeth's incredible premonition.

Finally, he stood up and leant over to speak to Cooper.

Cooper didn't dismiss the idea.

"We told no one that we were coming to get Wanda. However, the Franklins will know that we have a witness and no doubt their people are trying to find who it is. An attempt is a real possibility."

"I can't believe that Elisabeth could know," Sandy protested.

"If nothing else, it is a spur to take extra care," Cooper said calmly. "We have vests to put on before we leave the plane and I will call ahead to have a security sweep done of the area and the court building."

"One will be in the crowd," Wanda said suddenly, removing the oxygen mask to speak. "Another will be on a roof."

"What!" Sandy exclaimed.

"I saw them, like I was seeing a picture in my head. And I know something bad will happen."

"Hallucination and paranoia," Sandy decided, speaking aloud.

Cooper passed no judgement on the truth of the claim.

The area around the court building was thick with police. Cooper received a report when one sniper was arrested. He told them to keep looking.

Wanda felt the full impact of her danger sense and wanted to pull back and stay in the car. However, she was now no more than a playing piece, to be moved around at will and she was expected in the office of the prosecutor.

Police formed a wall around her. All of them were head and shoulders taller than she was and wore thick bulletproof vests. She began to walk in step with them, from the car to the steps of the building.

A shot whined past her ear and struck the officer in front of her. He stumbled from the impact, but was uninjured. A second shot, struck one of the rear guards in the leg and he dropped. Before the cordon could close ranks to fill the gap, a third shot hit Wanda in the leg.

Wanda stumbled, the pain worse than anything she had experienced. She grabbed the nearest officer in an attempt to stay upright. She fought to stay conscious as one of the officers picked her up like a child and raced her into the building.

Someone was ordering everyone out of somewhere, an office, Wanda saw blurrily. She felt herself being laid gently on the carpeted floor and firm hands pushing down on her leg. A voice that sounded like Cooper's was giving orders, to have the prosecutor come down and to have an ambulance called. Wanda wanted to close her eyes and let the blackness take the pain from her but Sandy was swearing at her and making her angry. She concentrated on her anger and hung onto awareness.

After an eternity, she saw the normally dignified prosecutor, kneel down beside her. He spoke gently, asking her to confirm her intention to testify. Wanda forced the words out and repeated her intention to waive her right to be silent.

The Prosecutor had forms that he had intended the witness to sign, but that was impossible at that time. The officers standing guard were witness to the intention.

As soon as the paramedics arrived, the prosecutor moved aside and let them work. Cooper walked over to the prosecutor and handed him a thick envelope.

"Miss Dean's deposition. There will be more following."

Brian Withers drove Sandy Willard to the hospital as soon as he could get clear of the court building. By then, two snipers had been caught and a third had escaped. Wanda's condition was unknown, except that the doctors were operating to remove the bullet. The shot officer had gone to a different hospital.

Sometime later, Carter arrived with an edgy David Martin. He sent Withers off to fetch coffee for them all.

Sandy went over to the window where David had drifted. His agitation was betrayed by the fidgeting of his hands.

"She's a stubborn bitch," Sandy said with sympathy.

"I know that," David agreed. "But why did this have to happen. She's gone through so much..."

"You know why," Sandy said more harshly than he intended. "Her knowledge is dynamite. The bastards know it. However, some good has come of it. The two snipers are from that special group of Rocky's. Both were involved in the abduction of Hurley and both can't talk fast enough. They are insisting on protection."

Elisabeth sat patiently at Wanda's side, staring at her face and mentally telling her to get better. She had forgotten the bars on the window and the bars outside the door of the security ward.

Being shot, and Elisabeth shuddered at the thought, had upset the precarious balance that Wanda had achieved. The illness that Wanda had fought stubbornly had taken hold of her. Rickard was personally treating her, and his face looked haggard. He knew how important it was for Wanda to testify. He checked on her frequently, monitoring the drip in her arm, the flow of oxygen and the readouts of the monitors.

As he left, he would gently pat Elisabeth on the shoulder, glad of her presence and aware of her concern for her sister.

When the door opened yet again, Elisabeth didn't even look up. A soft cough, caused her to turn around and see two strangers.

"Hello, I'm Brian Withers," the man introduced himself.

"I'm Judge Morton," the dark skinned woman spoke immediately after. "Are you Elisabeth Willard?"

"Yes."

Withers was struck by the resemblance between the blond girl and the patient in the bed. When he and Carter had first investigated the identity of Wanda Dean, they had dismissed the notion of a relationship between Wanda and Senator Willard. However, seeing the Senator's daughter next to her, there was no doubt. Both faces had the bones well defined, both were pale and tired looking.

"I've come to talk about Wanda," Judge Morton continued. "We have a room nearby which will be more comfortable."

Elisabeth nodded and stood up. Withers opened the door and allowed the two women to precede him. He nodded to the guards as he passed.

Judge Morton was evaluating the deliberate movements of the woman she was to talk to. She knew that Wanda Dean's sister was recently recovered from illness herself so she made certain Elisabeth was comfortable before she began her questions.

"Tell me about Wanda?" Morton asked.

Elisabeth didn't answer immediately.

"Wanda and I have always been close," Elisabeth began. "Even at her worst, she was never horrid to me…"

Elisabeth told how Wanda used to be before she changed into a malicious and smart mouthed brat. She admitted that even when Wanda had cut herself off from her family, she still sent the occasional unsigned letter to say she was still okay.

"She was stubborn, even before she turned horrid, and it took me a while to realise that this was her way of fighting the illness that killed our mother. I convinced her to leave home – she was having real shouting matches with dad and upsetting the whole family. I don't think her actions were deliberate at first, it was more reacting to fear. Later, they were and I think she changed her name when she was arrested so that we wouldn't suffer because of her."

With prompting from Judge Morton, Elisabeth told what she knew of Wanda's life since she left home; her early forays into crime, her time in the training centre, the time when she might have changed before she fell into Harrison's clutches.

"Quite frankly, I think she enjoyed being a thief and revelled in the thrill of getting away with her crimes. Even though she resisted Harrison at first, he gave her protection and paid her to steal for him. She didn't care what she stole, it was fun to her. It stopped being fun when the man she partnered in LA killed the guards. But she couldn't run away then. In fact, she took a very great risk in coming to help me when I was sick. It was right after that incident. Anyway, she saved my life and ignored the very real risk that she'd get sick again too."

The conversation continued for almost an hour. Judge Morton had no doubts about the honesty of Elisabeth Willard, she told what she knew whether it flattered her sister or not. In fact, it agreed closely with what Wanda had revealed to Cooper.

"Thank you, Miss Willard," Morton said finally. "You have been a great help."

"She expects to go to jail," Elisabeth blurted out suddenly; the words were spoken roughly. "I know she says she doesn't want amnesty, but if she goes to jail, they'll get her. I know they will. I don't want her to die. I know she's a criminal, but I need her…"

"I can't make any promises," Judge Morton said gently, laying a hand on Elisabeth's shoulder.

Elisabeth nodded mutely, fighting tears. She made no move to get up when the others left. Only when she had control of herself again, did she return to the security ward. The officers knew she was allowed to come and go freely.

David Martin was seated in the chair she had vacated. He jumped up when he heard the door open.

Elisabeth smiled at him; she liked him. "You don't like hospitals, do you?"

"Uh – no."

"I don't either. But Wanda helped me and I want to help her."

"So do I," David said in a soft voice, edging towards the door.

"Please don't go," Elisabeth begged. "I know you love her. Perhaps if we both send psychic messages to her, she'll wake up and realise she still has a job to do."

David stopped moving and turned back. He went and perched on the far side of the bed. He took Wanda's left hand in his. It was the one with the drip in the wrist. He noticed that Elisabeth had taken Wanda's other hand.

David began to speak softly to the unconscious form in the bed. He had been keeping track of the progress of the trial and knew things that had not been reported in the press. He was aware of Elisabeth's interest.

"They've finally settled on a jury," David said. "It's only taken them a week. The Franklin lawyers have been obstructing procedures wherever possible. They start presenting evidence today, mostly based on Hurley's data. Those three bastards just sit in the court and smile in that faintly superior way. They are so damn sure they will get off and don't look worried at all. I reckon that will change when they see you! And I bet they don't know that the two snipers are talking up a storm. The prosecutor is keeping them in reserve. I think he wants the jury to get the big picture first."

Both David and Elisabeth felt a faint pressure from the hands they held but Wanda's eyes stayed shut.

"Wanda, come on, open your eyes," Elisabeth breathed.

David damped a tissue and gently washed Wanda's eyelids. The eyes flickered open and stared up at David. Elisabeth felt a greater pressure.

David made a sound like he was in agony, but he lifted the hand he held and kissed it. Elisabeth pretended she didn't see the tears in David's eyes.

"Don't you dare scare me like that!" David said, staring at Wanda. "You have to finish the job you started."

He felt the pressure on his hand increase again and once more he kissed the hand.

"Then you and I can run off together, like I wanted to do the first time I saw you."

Elisabeth saw Wanda smile faintly. She was suddenly a lot more hopeful. David was good for her sister.

Chapter 36

Wanda continued to slip in and out of consciousness for several days. She wasn't able to move much and talking took too much energy, but she forced a smile for Elisabeth and David when they came in.

Dr Rickard, working against time to get Wanda fit to testify, devised a new treatment that he thought might help. The synthetised antibody was added to the saline drip and the flow increased. He had urine and blood samples tested at regular intervals. He was relieved when the levels of the protein in Wanda's blood began to drop.

Wanda was taking short shaky steps when Graeme Cooper and Tom Davis entered the ward. The nurse supporting her on the left glanced at them and returned her attention to her task. David, supporting her on the right went tense. He knew that if these two were here now, the trial of the Franklins was going badly.

"Help me to the chair," Wanda said softly.

The nurse left when Wanda was settled with a rug over her legs. Cooper indicated that David could stay. He went and carried two chairs closer to Wanda.

"Crunch time," Wanda said, and she saw Cooper nod.

Tom Davis settled into one of the chairs before speaking. "I've been following the trial. As things stand now, the decision could go either way."

"So you will need me to testify soon," Wanda deduced aloud. She reached out for David's hand.

"We have a two day adjournment," Cooper told her. "Then we will put one of the snipers on the stand. It's a risk though."

"Then you want me. Have you spoken to my doctor? Does he think I am up to it?"

Tom Davis answered that. "He fears you are not strong enough for the ordeal of testifying. What do you think?"

Wanda considered for a moment. "I'll be sitting down, and all of my testimony is on tape."

She glanced at Cooper and he nodded.

"So if they played that, part by part, and only asked questions on each section – I might manage that."

"The judge is aware of your condition," Davis told her. "I can request that you be permitted to rest between sessions. You need to tell me if it is too much for you.'

Wanda nodded. "Do they know it's me that will be testifying?"

"The defence knows we have a witness that we haven't presented yet and have been trying to find out who it is. Why do you ask?"

Wanda didn't want to verbalise her sudden dread, so she simply shook her head.

"What is it?" David asked.

"I guess I am getting nervous. Stupid way to be."

"You'll be well protected," Cooper promised.

Wanda gave a wry laugh as her leg twinged. "Yeah!"

"Weren't you ever scared on any of your little excursions?" Cooper asked.

"That was different. I was in control of my actions then. Being scared – heightened my perceptions, revved my mind, heated my blood…" Wanda tried to explain. "I'm not in control here. It's different to consider danger in cold blood."

Only David Martin truly understood what she was trying to say.

"You've got nowhere to run," he said.

"Not even in my mind," Wanda agreed. "That's not all. I am really afraid, that when I am in that witness box and Harrison looks at me, that I will want to crawl away and say nothing."

Wanda hunched into her chair and refused to meet anyone's gaze. Neither Cooper nor Davis belittled the idea, but they had no solution to offer.

David simply said, "Remember Mike Johnson."

Wanda squeezed his hand.

The following day, Davis visited her. She was sitting in the chair again, but this time she was alone.

"You will be having visitors soon," he warned her. "The judge, prosecutor and the chief defence attorney. I put your suggestion to the prosecutor and he spoke to the judge. Both of them are agreeable. However, the defence want to be sure that you are not faking this illness. And I am sure they are wanting to see who you are too."

"No doubt!" Wanda agreed.

"You will have two doctors in court, monitoring you," Davis went on.

"Two?" Wanda asked in surprise. "Rickard?"

"Uh, no," Davis said with a slight smile. "You have met one of them before. He was with Cooper at my place."

"Oh him," Wanda hadn't paid that man much attention. He was only a psychologist.

"When you get too tired, you need to tell the judge or signal one of the doctors.

"Any other advice?" Wanda asked.

"Later," Davis promised. "When the others have gone, we'll be having a session with the prosecutor."

The expected guests arrived then. Wanda was aware of the intense scrutiny of the defence attorney and the more neutral gaze of the judge, identified by the brief nod Davis gave him.

The judge questioned Wanda about how she felt, and considered the factual answers that Wanda gave her.

The defence attorney inserted a question when the judge finished.

"Why are you not demanding amnesty from prosecution in exchange for your testimony?"

Wanda stared at him and answered slowly. "Who told you I'm not?"

The man returned her stare. Wanda moved her gaze from him and decided how to answer.

"I may be testifying against your clients, pal, so they get their just deserves. I'm just as guilty, I'll get mine later."

The defence attorney smiled faintly, arriving at some interesting conclusions from her answer.

"You don't look at death's door," he challenged then.

"Heaven doesn't want me and it seems the devil doesn't either," Wanda said. "I think the powers in both places want me to suffer here. It's hellish just trying to cross between here and the bed. Perhaps you would like to help me back?"

The man looked about to refuse, but changed his mind.

Wanda knew she had lost a lot of weight and she was feeling trembly. She hoped he'd sense both and be convinced of her illness.

Davis was smiling faintly, aware of her intention and approving it. The judge merely observed.

Wanda was relieved when only Davis and the prosecutor remained. Even so, she was tired and not wanting to discuss her debut appearance in court – scheduled for the following afternoon. Cooper came in after a while and told her his plans for getting her into the court unnoticed.

Wanda was wheeled into the courtroom by a white haired man, wearing glasses like Cooper's, a suit identical to the one she had always seen Cooper in and a voice identical to Cooper's. He wore a small nametag identifying him as Dr Rupert Cross.

He had collected her from the hospital in a delivery van belonging to a stationery firm, and she had only needed to walk the short distance from the van to the back door of the court. Just inside the door, the wheel chair was waiting for her. There was a collection of medical equipment attached to the back of the chair – oxygen bottle for instance. They went first to a small room to wait until summoned.

Wanda was not interested in talking, and once Cross had told her how to signal him if she needed to stop, he remained quiet too. Wanda was tempted to challenge the man but letting her mind conjure reasons why Cooper would be in disguise, helped pass the time.

The low buzz of conversation in the courtroom hushed as Wanda was wheeled in. From the corner of her eye, Wanda saw the fleeting expression of anger on Harrison's face, the look of distaste on Richard's and a sullen expression on Sylvester's. The three of them were wearing expensive suits and appeared well groomed.

By the time Wanda had been helped into the witness chair, Harrison and Richard had masked their expressions. They were leaning back in their chairs, with one hand on the table in front of them in identical poses of almost boredom.

Wanda did no more than glance their way, but she knew them both well enough to realise they were watching her intently, in spite of their pose. Even without looking, she sensed their regard.

The judge explained to the court that Wanda's deposition would played to the court in sections and that questions would be permitted.

Wanda stared at her hands resting in her lap as the tape of her voice was played. During the questioning, she kept her eyes on the person addressing her. The prosecutor's questions related to the points he wanted to introduce from her testimony. She clarified points, expanded on others and neither justified or rationalised her own actions. She kept to the facts of what she was told to do.

During the cross examination, the defence attorney attacked her testimony and tried to throw doubt on her memory of events. He kept to the limit of what he thought the judge would tolerate. He couldn't shake her testimony.

The judge called a halt to the questioning after three hours and recessed the court at that time. Wanda stayed in the witness box until after the Franklin's and their retinue of lawyers had left and only a few observers remained. She waited for Cross and his colleague to help her, because she knew even the short walk to the chair was beyond her strength.

"You are as white as a sheet of paper," Cross admonished her. "You should have indicated earlier."

"I want to get this over with," Wanda said trembling now from reaction and weariness. "I cannot stand Harrison's unwavering regard."

"Still, you did well," Cross praised her. "Your testimony must be devastating to the defence."

"What the hell do you know – you're only a doctor!" Wanda snapped. "Get me back to that damn hospital so I can collapse!"

Cross acted on her request, and wheeled her from the almost deserted courtroom. Two reporters, holding back from rushing to the phones, observed her weak condition. One took the opportunity to take a picture with a palm-sized camera.

"Vultures!" Wanda muttered.

"All to the good," Cross told her cryptically.

David Martin merely smiled as he listened to Wanda cursing and swearing. Since returning from court, she had rested and eaten and had regained some colour in her face.

Davis took his cue from David and suggested to the nonplussed prosecutor that some coffee would be an idea and they left the ward.

As soon as they had gone, David applied his own method of quietening Wanda.

"You were great. Better than great," he told her when they had finished kissing.

"I felt like an animal in a cage having sticks poked at me," Wanda said. "I could feel Harrison staring at me. I know what he wants to do to me and I would deserve it."

Wanda shivered. David took her face in his hands.

"No you don't deserve it!" he said forcefully.

"But I promised to obey him!" Wanda tried to struggle free.

"He – does – not – deserve – your – loyalty," David said carefully enunciating each word.

"But…"

"He has tried to kill you three times," David told her. "Loyalty as far as he is concerned is all one way. Think about your old partner, Harry. And then there's Joe, he was one of the snipers that shot you. Someone got to him too. And there was a rash of underworld killings, as soon as the Franklins were arrested. No – they only care for themselves."

"I didn't know all that. When did they try to get me the third time?"

"When you were out to it. Cooper's crowd foiled it. They never got close to you."

"Cooper's crowd?" Wanda asked to distract herself. "What do you mean, Dav? And why is that doctor a white haired copy of him?"

David shook his head. "Just forget about it for now. Things are afoot."

"What?"

"I can't tell you," David told her. "But do you really want to go to jail? When you could be somewhere else, with me?"

"I don't deserve…"

David put a finger on Wanda's lips.

"Everything you've done, is a drop in the ocean compared to what those scumbags are responsible for. They will be lucky to escape a death penalty – you have never deserved that."

"But…"

David heard the door open and moved away.

The prosecutor congratulated Wanda on her effort that day, making no reference to her childish behaviour a short time ago.

"How many more sessions like that," Wanda asked.

"Three or four," he estimated. "How did you feel you went?"

"You tell me," Wanda countered. "By the end, I was having trouble remembering my name. And you haven't mentioned what will happen when the other side begins their defence."

"We are hoping you will be stronger by then," De La Court said reluctantly.

"And if I'm not? If I collapse in the middle – how will that affect your case?"

"Your Doctor says you are recovering," Tom Davis commented. "Though he is concerned by how tired you were. I think, though, that the challenge of outwitting Harrison and Richard Franklin is – shall I say – amusing you."

"Those two were mentally throwing daggers at me," Wanda protested.

"Imaginary weapons do no harm," David said snidely. "Think how frustrated they must be. How impotent they are, now that their obedient puppy has changed into a ravening wolf!"

"Yeah!" Wanda agreed, suddenly feeling more alive. "Yeah, this is the most dangerous thing I've done yet. Yeah!"

"Can we go over tomorrow's testimony?" De La Court interrupted.

Wanda endured four more days of testifying through sheer dogged stubbornness. On the second day, Harrison's glare got to her and she began to lose track of her thoughts. It wasn't until David walked to a position behind the defence table, giving her something else to focus on, that she got back on track.

Each day she was wheeled into the courtroom and managed to walk into the witness box. At the end of every session she had to be helped out. Not one of the juror's doubted the effort it was costing her to be there. In the back of all their minds was the little detail, struck from the record, that she was testifying, incriminating herself, without being granted immunity from prosecution. Every one of the jurors would have deemed her guilty had she been the one on trial. How much more so were the ones who had controlled her? However, the defence case hadn't started yet.

The final day of her testimony, when she had to answer questions about Hurley's death, was the worst. She had returned to the hospital in tears and Rickard had no hesitation in prescribing a sedative for her. Then when she was asleep, he organised for a series of tests to be done. He had the laboratory rush the results back to him.

Chapter 37

"Considering her state of general exhaustion," Rickard commented in answer to questions from Cooper. "Her condition is encouraging. She has been off the antibody treatment for five days and the levels are still dropping. I think, once she gets back to an active lifestyle, she will recover fully."

Rickard was aware that an active lifestyle was unlikely for Wanda Dean, particularly if the court decided to put her in prison.

"That's excellent!" Cooper agreed. "Now, I have a medical question for you. How do you think Miss Dean will be affected by…?"

Cooper mentioned a certain drug. Rickard's eyebrows went up in amazement.

"Are you joking?" was Rickard's initial reaction.

Cooper was serious and quickly sketched his reasons.

"Is it legal?" Rickard insisted, battling with his sense of ethics.

Cooper glanced around, to be certain no one was in earshot.

"Miss Dean has come to the attention of a higher authority," Cooper began. "Once the trial is over, she will be offered a complete pardon – providing certain conditions are met. It has been concluded that simply putting her into witness protection will be insufficient. As you pointed out, she needs an active lifestyle and I will add, stimulating mental challenges – to stay well. To ensure that the people who wish her ill won't find her…"

"You kill her off," Rickard finished, still unsure.

"To all appearances," Cooper confirmed.

"I will have to consider this carefully." Rickard said. "It would be dangerous for a normally fit person. Miss Dean is still very weak. When do you expect to perform your charade?"

"Not until the defence has concluded their case," Cooper told him. "That could be up to a fortnight."

"And during that time, she will be recalled by the defence," Rickard asked.

Cooper nodded.

"Give me a week to try and build up her strength," Rickard decided. "If there is any sign that the protein level is increasing again, I won't allow it. If all goes well, you will need to make her aware of the risks involved and your reason for doing it. If that reason is compelling enough, the odds will be in your favour. Miss Dean's stubbornness is my most potent ally in treating her."

Cooper smiled. "We'll go with your decision, Doctor."

"I assume that those who know the truth will be limited?"

"Of course," Cooper said.

"You will need to talk to her sister. Elisabeth Willard will know - whatever you do. And you had better make sure young David Martin knows …"

"I am aware of the situation there," Cooper assured the other man.

Rickard nodded, satisfied for the moment, and went off to his other affairs.

He looked like Cooper this time, but Wanda felt sure the dark hair was a wig.

"Hello, Mister Cooper – Cross," she greeted pointedly, after the door had closed behind the man. She was sitting by the window, reading the newspaper.

"I wasn't intending to fool you. We need to talk."

"Do we? Why don't you start by telling me who and what you really are?"

Wanda was feeling strong enough for a decent argument.

"Who I am is unimportant" Cooper evaded. "What I can do for you, is what we need to discuss."

"What can you do?" Wanda was curious, in spite of herself.

"I have the authority to offer you a full pardon. There are, however, conditions. Firstly, we will have to convince the Franklin family that you are no longer a threat. Then, if that is achieved, you will have to undergo a comprehensive psychological examination and if you pass that – you will have to use your talents in the service of your country and not for personal gain."

"Join the army?" Wanda made a guess.

Cooper shook his head.

"Spying?" Wanda guessed again, this time with a contemplative smile.

"In a manner of speaking," Cooper admitted. "If you agree to the conditions, you will leave here a free person. You will be directly answerable to my superiors and if you wilfully abuse the conditions of the pardon, it may be revoked."

"A free person with strings attached," Wanda corrected.

"At first," Cooper amended. "If you don't wish to accept the conditions, the alternative will be, as you have chosen, to be tried and convicted for your crimes."

"You have put a lot of time and effort into me and I'm grateful, but why?"

"Because I can make good use of someone with your capabilities, your addiction to surviving dangerous situations and luck."

"I'd work for you," Wanda considered, glancing at Cooper for confirmation.

"I believe, what you offer – is suitable," Wanda agreed. "But how can you be sure that I won't fail you? And I don't mean that threat of revoking the pardon."

"I have decided that you have a strong, underlying moral code," Cooper said carefully. "This business of not asking for amnesty – any other criminally minded person would have demanded it to escape going to jail."

"It wasn't just that," Wanda corrected.

"No, and I am not sure I see it correctly, but let me try. After the trial – when your skills and face are well known – you won't be able to keep doing what you were to stop being sick and supplying your habit of getting high on danger. Somehow, you see being in jail as some sort of challenge and deep down, you didn't expect to survive both the illness and Franklin's hit squad."

"Close enough," Wanda agreed. "But there is still the hit squad, and I am not so sure about being cured."

"Your medical prognosis is good and I believe I have a way to neutralise the hit squad."

Wanda tossed the newspaper aside. Her attention was fully on Cooper.

"So you are saying that I can be a legal thief?"

"I wouldn't put it that way," Cooper qualified. "It will be for a worthwhile cause, but – with the sort of work we would be doing, there are no safeguards. We are on our own if we are caught – the government won't admit knowing about us… We almost lost a good man during the Haushka affair."

That name, mentioned so casually, dislodged a memory in Wanda's mind. The name of the eastern European violinist had made headlines when he had arrived in America, after escaping from his country. He had claimed a small group of people had done the impossible. The American government had denied any involvement, but the musician was undoubtedly a free man.

"I'll work for you, Cooper, if that really is your name," Wanda said. The thrill of the challenge was exciting her already. With that sort of incentive, facing down the Franklin's defence lawyers would be a breeze.

Cooper saw the gleam of the challenge in the eyes of the woman.

"Good girl!" he smiled. He was satisfied that his instinct to enlist her was worthwhile. Now to rid her of those who wished her dead.

"I have had word that you are to be available tomorrow," Cooper told Wanda and he knew she was listening intently. "Now, nobody is aware of your marked improvement over the past week…"

"All I've done is sleep!" Wanda complained.

"For a good reason. Any one that enquired about you was given the impression that you were fading away."

Wanda began to grin. "So, I am to pretend to still be sick. Isn't that unethical, Dr Cross? What else are you planning?"

Cooper grinned with amusement. The woman was quick witted. "Just that, for now. You have to stay to the end. Here's what I want you to do…"

Cooper didn't say what this was leading to, but Wanda guessed. The only way to stop Harrison trying to kill her was to convince him she was dead. How he was going to do that would become clear in time.

The man that slipped quietly into the ward with Cooper was not introduced, but his skilful hands applied cosmetics to make her look paler that she had looked a week ago.

"Put dark shadows around my eyes," Wanda suggested when the mirror showed her the effect.

The nameless man considered the suggestion and complied. When he was finished, the effect was exactly as Elisabeth had looked at her worst.

Cooper nodded his approval and the make-up artist sprayed a fine layer of lacquer over the top. Even close up, no one could tell it was make-up and the lacquer would prevent it from rubbing off at the wrong time.

"The spray will make your face sweat a bit," Cooper warned. "But that is part of the effect. Now all you have to do is sit as if you are very weak and to talk slowly and deliberately. Think you can do it?"

The head nod was vigorous and the grin contradicted the effect, before Wanda slumped back into the seat.

Cooper ran through a series of subtle signals for her to watch for – and what to do when she saw them, and others for her to give messages back to him. Only then, did Cooper tell Wanda to hop in the wheelchair ready to go to court.

The onlookers saw an obviously ill woman wheeled into court and helped into the witness chair. The murmur of voices discussed how much worse she looked.

Wanda caught the smirk on Richard's face and hoped it was because he thought she was dying not that his lawyers were going to shred her. She had to hide her amusement at the concern shown by the judge. He asked if she was fit enough to answer questions. The presence of the doctor, standing as close to her as he could without being in the box with her, was a dramatic touch.

In clear sight was David, grinning slightly. She hadn't seen him for some days and his presence was her lifeline.

The defence desperately wanted to discredit her testimony. The questions were fired at her rapidly, two or three at a time. If they thought to confuse her, they failed utterly. Wanda slowed down the proceedings by answering the first question, slowly, then asking for a repeat of the second question.

The prosecutor was enjoying the situation. His witness might be ill, but her wits were still sufficient. He had to keep reminding the defence that the witness was not the one on trial.

After half an hour, Wanda caught a signal from David. She was to pretend to be out of breath. Cooper, in his guise as the doctor, spoke softly to the judge. A five-minute break was called and Cross passed her an oxygen mask and held it on her until the end of the break. This happened at intervals during the proceedings. After three hours, the judge insisted that the defence call a different witness and recall Wanda later. The suggestion was not well accepted but was obeyed.

Wanda was lifted out of the witness box and settled in the wheelchair. Cross made a show of clipping on restraints to stop her slumping forward and covering her legs with a light rug before taking her out of sight.

The same charade was acted out on the following two days, until the defence decided that their case could not be helped by further cross examination of the witness.

Wanda had a week's break before Cooper visited her again. This time, he had David and her sister with him.

Elisabeth came and hugged Wanda.

"You feel so much better," she marvelled. "I saw the news and you looked dreadful."

Wanda glanced at Cooper before answering. "I am better, but there is a reason for appearing otherwise"

Elisabeth looked first at David, as he had been keeping her informed of the progress of the trial, and then at Cooper.

"Tomorrow, the defence will finish its summing up," Cooper told Elisabeth. "They insist that Miss Dean be present in the courtroom that day. The prosecutor argued strongly against it, but at my suggestion, the judge ruled in favour of the defence. I am sure that something is going to happen. And I want to emphasise, Miss Willard that I will be taking very good care of Miss Dean."

Elisabeth frowned, not quite understanding what he meant.

"I am not going to die, Lishka," Wanda said very softly. "I'm too darn contrary for that. But you have to go back home. I don't want any chance of harm to you. I might not be able to see you again, but I will find a way to keep in touch."

This time, Elisabeth understood, or thought she did. She gave Wanda a long wordless hug and then allowed David to lead her from the ward.

David walked in silence as he escorted her back down to the ground floor. She looked like she had just lost her best friend. He saw several men hanging around. Two he recognised as being reporters and a third was one of Cooper's men. No doubt the reporters knew that he and Elisabeth visited the security ward. It was part of the reason why they had been told to keep away for the last two weeks.

"Look, you did your best Miss Willard," David said unexpectedly. "Some people just refuse to be helped. It would probably be for the best if she dies. I doubt that one would ever change her ways. Some people are just bad, through and through. Save your pity for someone that deserves it."

Elisabeth was startled, but soon became aware of the man following close behind them.

"I still don't wish her dead."

"To your credit, of course," David went on. "You will just have to accept that if she pulls through, which doesn't seem likely, she will be going to jail. It's the best place for her."

Elisabeth did not reply and David lapsed into silence, pleased with the scene just played. He saw Elisabeth to her chauffeured car and walked on to his own.

The summing up by both the defence and the prosecution was over and the jury was being instructed by the judge when the muffled shot was heard. Heads swivelled to see where the danger was and the security guards began to walk purposely towards the non-descript man edging out of the courtroom.

The furore would erupt later about how a weapon passed the security screen, but first there was the tableau of the prosecutor's prime witness, slumped in the wheel chair, bleeding from an apparent chest wound and being tended to by her frantic physician.

In the confusion, Wanda felt a prick in her arm and in moments, lost consciousness.

The doctor unstrapped his patient from the chair and laid her gently on the floor. He checked for a pulse and for breathing and began going through the motions of trying to revive his patient.

The oxygen mask was slipped into place as CPR was commenced. In the back ground, the jury was being shepherded out and an ambulance was being sent for.

The defendants were in no hurry to leave. One of the lawyers was also a qualified doctor. He opted to go and assist. When he could feel neither pulse nor respiration after five minutes of effort, he insisted to Cross, that no more could be done. His voice was deliberately sympathetic as he eased Cross away, removed the oxygen mask and covered the woman with her rug. When the stretcher arrived, he walked back to the defendants table and the group left the court.

The instant the group moved off, Cross, injected a second substance into the 'dead' woman. He breathed a quiet but heartfelt sigh of relief when he felt Wanda spontaneously draw a breath. His questing fingers felt the slowly increasing pulse.

Wanda was transferred to the stretcher, still covered, but the oxygen mask was replaced on her face.

Police were converging on the scene by then, but the 'body' was removed in spite of their insistence of not disturbing the crime scene. However, the killer had been caught and he was loudly bragging of his deed and several quick-witted journalists had snapped pictures of the scene. They had to accept the inevitable.

Cooper had left nothing to chance. The ambulance waiting outside contained a comprehensive array of intensive care equipment and Doctor Rickard was waiting to examine Wanda. As soon as she was inside, with the door closed, he went to work. He was aware of the ambulance moving, but not how quickly it was dodging in and out of traffic. He gave his encouraging findings to the driver, and instead of making for the nearest hospital, they continued to the City Morgue.

There, the ambulance backed up to the double doors and a stretcher identical to that which left the courtroom was taken inside on a trolley. As soon as the empty stretcher returned, the ambulance doors were closed and the vehicle moved off at an unhurried pace towards its depot. If anyone was following it, they would have seen it back into its garage and that would be all. The instant the doors closed to hide it, new signs were pasted onto its sides. It then backed out into the rear compound, and was driven out from the rear entrance – still as an ambulance, but to all concerned, a completely different vehicle.

The second ambulance travelled in a leisurely fashion to an exclusive private hospital well out of the city. Wanda was beginning to revive by then, though not enough to feel like sitting up. Rickard kept the monitors on her, even though he was satisfied that all was well.

Chapter 38

Wanda slept, sedated, for the best part of the following day. She was kept under observation, to ensure that she had fully recovered.

Cooper had her guarded, unobtrusively, and allowed no one near her but a select few people.

On the second day after her arrival at the hospital, Wanda was up and pacing the small room. If she had been allowed, she would have been climbing all over the roof for something to do. David Martin's arrival was a welcome distraction. He had added a reddish tinge to his normally blond hair and brushed it forward instead of sideways, but his grin was as familiar as ever. He tossed a rolled up newspaper at her and it was a sign of her recovery that she caught it without thinking.

"What has been happening?" she asked him. None of her carers had told her anything.

"You were a media sensation, my love."

He came up close and caught her in an embrace. "That's yesterday's paper, read it later – if you have the stomach for it. It's so treacly. They make you sound like a valiant avenging angel, cut down by the dreadful scum you fought so hard against. Bleh! It's full of nauseating details of your illness, the scandal of how a gun came to be in the courtroom and a rather colourful description of the gunman who was caught before he left the courtroom and started screaming obscenities about you. All of that."

"He was one of Cooper's men, wasn't he?" Wanda was wondering how he would get out of jail.

"Yes, Love, but don't worry. It's all taken care of," David assured her. "Oh and you are being cremated today."

"Can't get rid of me fast enough," Wanda said straight faced but real humour was bubbling up inside her. "Isn't that a bit fast for a murder victim?"

"It was a straight forward case," David kept a straight face but he betrayed it by the twinkle in his eyes. "It will be a private cremation."

"What if the Franklin lawyers want proof?"

"What? More than seeing you die and having their man prove it?" David asked her. "Don't worry. Cooper is on top of everything. That man is positively Machiavellian. It's probably why I like him."

Wanda just shook her head and changed the subject.

"When do they expect a verdict?"

"Possibly early next week. They have many charges to consider. You'll be told as soon as it's known. Cooper thinks they will get off on some minor charges, but he is pretty certain the major ones will stick."

"I hope they get the death penalty," Wanda said, staring across the room.

"So do I," David agreed. "But they will appeal, you know that."

"Yeah," Wanda hugged herself to stop a shudder. David put his arms around her.

"You are rid of them," David said firmly. "I know that you still fear the effect Harrison has on you, but as soon as I can organise it, Mrs David Martin will be too busy to think about other men."

"If that is a proposal, you lout, I accept." Wanda turned and hugged David. "One thing, Cooper."

"Oh, him," David dismissed lightly. "He told me he had recruited you and he shanghaied me as well – to keep you in line." David's grin was malicious. "The guy doesn't miss a trick."

Cooper led Wanda into a room where four people waited. David moved in after her and took a spot by the window, out of the way. He watched as Elisabeth Willard went immediately to her sister and hugged her. Wanda returned it, sharing in those few moments, what thousands of words couldn't express. They parted without a word. Elisabeth joined David by the window and both watched the reunion between father and daughter.

Wanda found it hard to speak to her father. In spite of the understanding they had reached when she had gone home to help her sister, there was still a lot of history between them. They simply stared at each other for a long time, before Charles Willard placed a gentle hand on the shoulder of his eldest daughter.

"The slate is clean, Gwen. I'm proud of you."

Wanda swallowed before speaking, her hands moved to cover his.

"I am sorry, Dad. For everything horrid I said and did to you and the others."

Charles Willard drew his daughter into an embrace that she, for the first time in ten years, didn't pull away from. "God be with you," he whispered.

Cooper escorted Senator and Elisabeth Willard out, whilst Wanda faced away from everyone, trying to control some unfamiliar and deep emotions.

The other two men waited patiently, unsure of exactly why they were there - in the presence of a pale but very obviously alive 'ghost'.

Lieutenant Brian Withers attempted some humour to lighten the mood.

"I'm glad to see you looking so well, Miss Dean. Though, I thought that you had to have a shot in the arm to have such improved health."

Wanda wiped her eyes on her sleeve and turned around.

"Glad, Lieutenant? I thought I would be your worst nightmare come back to haunt you."

"Not quite that," Captain Carter added his opinion. "If it wasn't for you, the Franklin family wouldn't be facing life in prison. If they were still free, that would be worse. We were surprised at being summoned here."

"I insisted," Wanda explained. "I thought I should apologise for doing you out of the pleasure of locking me up and tossing away the key."

Both detectives smiled, the jest had been close to the truth, but not any longer.

"I guess that thanks to Hurley and my big mouth in court, you can write solved on a lot of unsolved crimes."

"And some we didn't know about," Withers agreed with a wider grin.

"Yeah, I was good, wasn't I?" Wanda boasted. She went on quickly, "The other thing I wanted to do was thank you for trusting me and letting me stay with Tom Davis instead of dragging me back. And for helping me get back safely. I know you took a big risk, doing it. Therefore, I consider that I owe you one and if you ever get a case where by talents would be useful, call me in. Cooper, give them your card."

Withers shrugged and Carter just shook his head.

"I'm glad you have got over your grief about Mike Johnson," Withers said unexpectedly.

Wanda moved her gaze to a point over Withers' right shoulder.

"So you figured that was me," Wanda said quietly. "Yes, I did. Once I realised that he wasn't dead at all. Did you know that I used some of the money Franklin paid me to allow him to have plastic surgery to change his face and hide the scars?"

Wanda saw the dawning comprehension on the faces of the two detectives as they glanced at David. He came up and put a possessive arm around Wanda.

"All the best," Withers said formally. He shook David's hand and Wanda's too.

When the door closed on the departing detectives, Wanda and David turned to Cooper. He merely gestured for them to precede him from the room and to take the first steps in their new life.

They were driving south east, on the freeway, when Wanda remembered something from a long time before.

"I had a feeling your name wasn't Cooper. And I should have known... "

"What do you mean?" David asked her.

"Him," Wanda pointed at Cooper who was driving. "He's got one of those fake faces on – like you used after your operations."

Since Wanda seemed amused rather than worried, David waited for her to make her point.

"One day...." Wanda recalled what Jim had said to her years ago.

Cooper grinned and used his indicator to pull to the side of the road. He seemed to scratch his forehead, but he pulled off the layer of fake flesh.

"Jim," Wanda said, "If you had told me seven years ago the type of thing you did..."

"I couldn't," Jim Phillips apologised. "And that failure has haunted me ever since."

Wanda thought of all the things between herself when she had first met Jim and now. "You not only put one over the Franklins, and the police – you put one over me."

"Are you angry?"

"No," Wanda admitted. "You knew then I had a lot of growing to do – hard lessons to learn. Neither you nor my father had a hope back then. And – I'm glad I didn't listen to you back then."

"Oh?" Jim asked softly.

"I wouldn't have met David."

David squeezed her hand.

The End

NOVELS
WANDA: FROM BAD TO WORSE

If she was going to die young, like her mother, Gwen Willard was determined to die rich and she had very few years to do it. Her first step was to leave home. She met Hooch, who taught her some exciting and illegal skills. She was the Dracos lucky mascot until she came to the attention of the police. Then her uncanny knack for predicting trouble, warned her to flee to the city and change her name. Life wasn't easy. She was 15, had little money and no regular job, but her new skills came in handy. Then she crossed the path of an evil and unscrupulous man and she didn't want him to have his way.

WANDA: CHOOSING CRIME

Wanda was free. She was never going back to jail. But she was homeless, almost penniless and Harrison Franklin had a long and vengeful memory.

Jim Phillips had a long memory too, and Wanda had saved his life. Could he save her from Franklin?

KORVU: THE BEGINNING
The prequel to The Wild One

Jai Ansuni was the first female Atapi sorcerer for thousands of years, but she dare not reveal it. However, when tribal sorcerer, Stacion Ansuni escalates the enmity between Atapi and Kumatan to an ominous level. Jai and her womb mate, Con, try to mitigate his atrocities but can two young Atapi, not even a score of years old, win against the powerful sorcerer?

THE WILD ONE

Sixteen year old Jai Cassidy thought she was finally free of her family until she is discovered by her other relatives…the ones that aren't human. Jai uses her natural perversity and cunning to escape their control, but catapults herself into the middle of a deadly feud between two alien races.

ATAPI SORCERESS
The sequel to The Wild One

Jai Cassidy is beginning her mission of reversing the decline of the non-humanoid Atapi. As a sorceress and an Atapi-Human hybrid, she is vehemently disliked by the male Atapi sorcerers and the humanoid rulers of Korvu. Her task is complicated by the treachery of a group of alien engineers, who are inciting insurrection and harsh reprisals.

THE TYMOREAN TRUST BOOK 1 - POWER RISING

The Tymorean Trust - When peace rules Tymorea - Peace reigns in the universe.

Chosen to be the Advocates of the mystical and incorporeal Guardians of Peace, twins Tymos and Kryslie must first learn to control and use the power rising in them - or it will destroy them.

On Tymorea, only the ruling Triumvirate Governors are powerful enough to guide the strong-willed alien-bred twins until they have mastered their power.

THE TYMOREAN TRUST BOOK 2 - GREAT ONES

The peace of the Guardian Planet, Tymorea, is in deadly peril. War there will create ripples of unrest and destruction throughout the settled universe.

Tymos and Kryslie, still adolescents, have barely mastered their power and Llaimos is still less than a year old, but they are the three chosen to be Advocates of the mystical Guardians of Peace, to safeguard the Tymorean Trust.

THE TYMOREAN TRUST BOOK 3 - RETURN TO EARTH

Even before the war on Tymorea, the Elders foresaw that Great Ones Tymos and Kryslie would have an imperative mission on Earth.

But as the Tymoreans prepare to build an Earthbase to support them, they discover that specifications for two vital protective shields are missing.

Now, nearly a century later, Tymos and Kryslie must find his work and build the generator before the base is found.

THE TYMOREAN TRUST BOOK 4 - EARTH MISSION

Just before their graduation from the prestigious WSRA Washington University, Tymos and Kryslie Ward deliberately disappear.

The Great Ones have foreseen the capture and death of the new Tymorean missionaries and discovered that the leader of the Eastern Imperium plans to undermine the United World Nations.

Tymos and Kryslie must protect their kin and prevent a potentially devastating world war.

THE TYMOREAN TRUST BOOK 5 – ALIEN CONTACT

Tymos and Kryslie Ward, hide their Tymorean intelligence and abilities while working as low ranked technicians at the WSRA's lunar base. When an alien ship arrives at Lunar One, pursued by a powerful enemy who will stop at nothing to get what he wants, only the two Tymorean Great Ones have the knowledge and abilities to overcome him, but to do so they must risk their sanity, and their souls.

THE TYMOREAN TRUST BOOK 6 – INVASION

Great Ones Tymos and Kryslie go to rescue the crew of Earth's first deep space mission – and discover that Ciriot space pirates have discovered Earth's location. When the Ciriot invade in force, the Great Ones reveal themselves so that Earth can gain vital help. However, Kryslie becomes the victim of Ciriot, who want to control her mind and make her betray the people of Earth.

TRICKS

Tom and Jo Dwyer had a reputation for playing tricks – and getting detention. They didn't seem to care about that, so long as they made their class laugh. That was until someone began to turn their tricks against them, and it was no longer funny.

Connect to Margaret Gregory

Friend me on Facebook:
http://www.facebook.com/margaret.gregory.399